BLACK SCIENCE

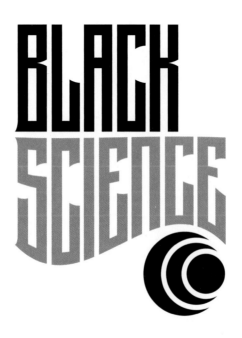

IMAGE COMICS, INC.

Robert Kirkman — Chief Operating Officer
Erik Larsen — Chief Financial Officer
Todd McFarlane — President
Marc Silvestri — Chief Executive Officer
Jim Valentino — Vice President

Eric Stephenson — Publisher/Chief Creative Officer
Jeff Boison — Director of Publishing Planning & Book Trade Sales
Chris Ross — Director of Digital Sales
Jeff Stang — Director of Direct Market Sales
Kat Salazar — Director of PR & Marketing
Drew Gill — Cover Editor
Heather Doornink — Production Director
Nicole Lapalme — Controller

IMAGECOMICS.COM

PRODUCTION DESIGN: ERIKA SCHNATZ

BLACK SCIENCE VOLUME 9: NO AUTHORITY BUT YOURSELF. First printing. October 2019. Published by Image Comics, Inc. Office of publication: 2701 NW Vaughn Street, Suite 780, Portland, Oregon 97210. Copyright © 2019 Rick Remender and Matteo Scalera. All rights reserved. Originally published in single magazine form as BLACK SCIENCE #39-43. BLACK SCIENCE™ (including all prominent characters featured herein), its logo and all character likenesses are trademarks of Rick Remender and Matteo Scalera, unless otherwise noted. Image Comics® and its logos are registered trademarks of Image Comics, Inc. No part of this publication may be reproduced or transmitted, in any form or by any means (except for short excerpts for review purposes) without the express written permission of Image Comics, Inc. All names, characters, events, and locales in this publication are entirely fictional. Any resemblance to actual persons (living or dead), events or places, without satiric intent, is coincidental. For information regarding the CPSIA on this printed material call: 203-595-3636. PRINTED IN THE U.S.A. For international rights inquiries, contact: foreignlicensing@imagecomics.com.

ISBN 978-1-5343-1213-5

GIANT GENERATOR

RICK REMENDER
WRITER

MATTEO SCALERA
ARTIST

MORENO DINISIO
COLORS

RUS WOOTON
LETTERING + LOGO DESIGN

SEBASTIAN GIRNER &
BRIAH SKELLY
EDITORS

BLACK SCIENCE CREATED BY
RICK REMENDER & MATTEO SCALERA

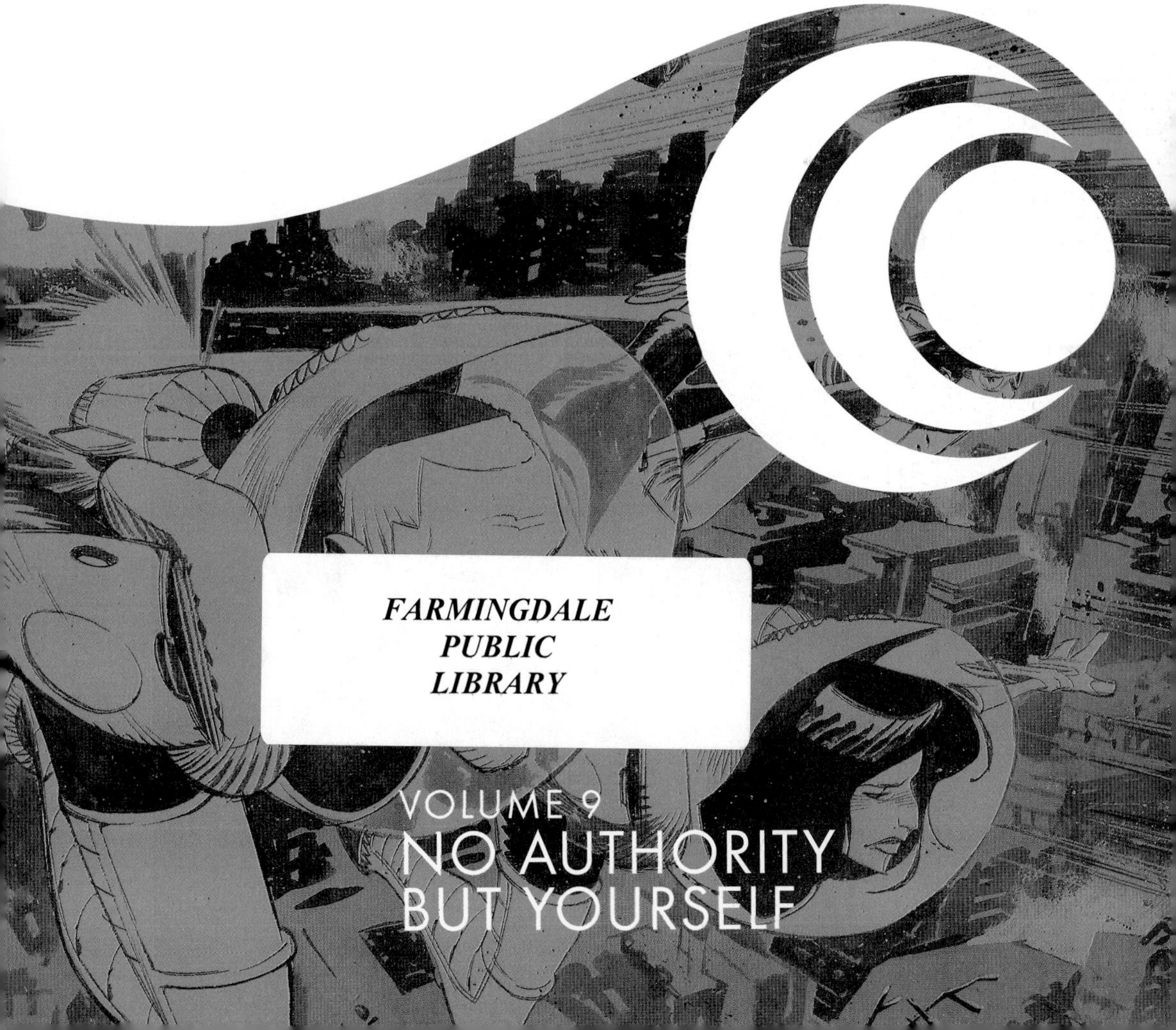

VOLUME 9

NO AUTHORITY BUT YOURSELF

39

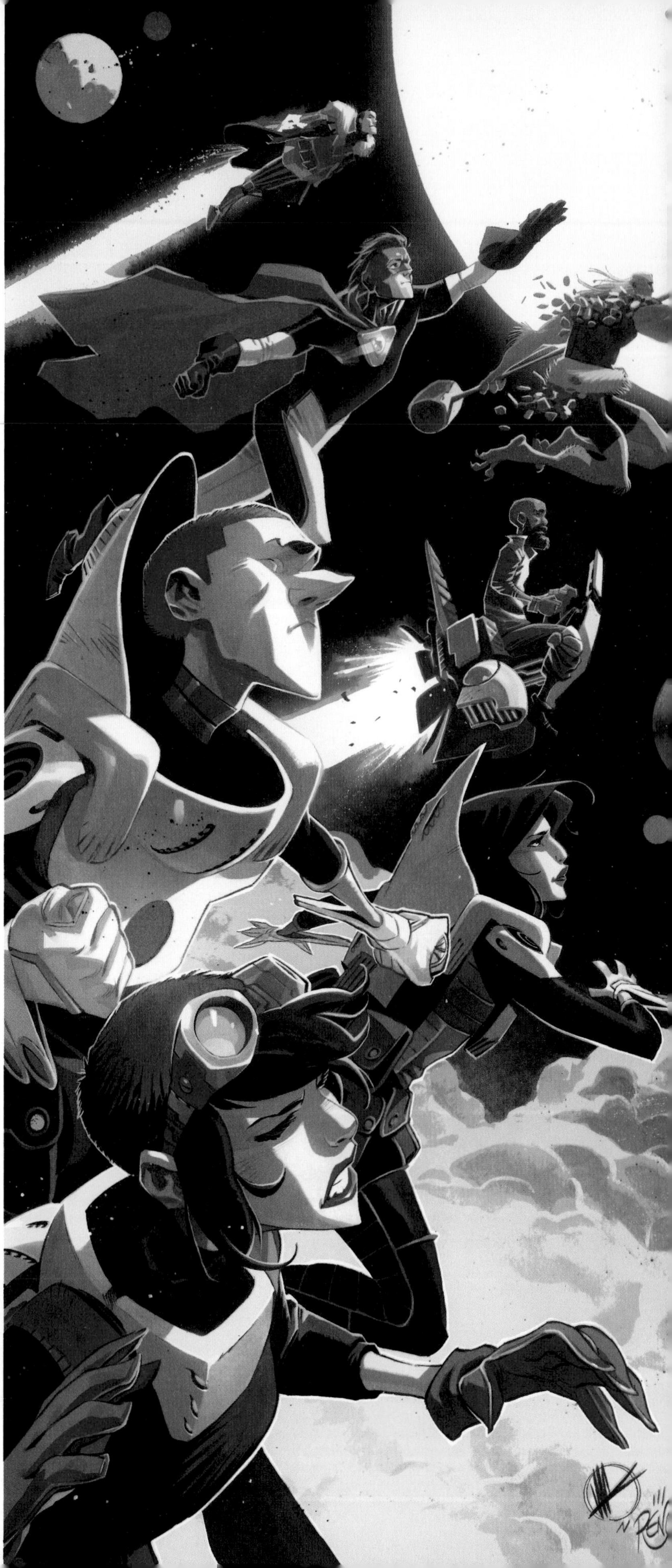

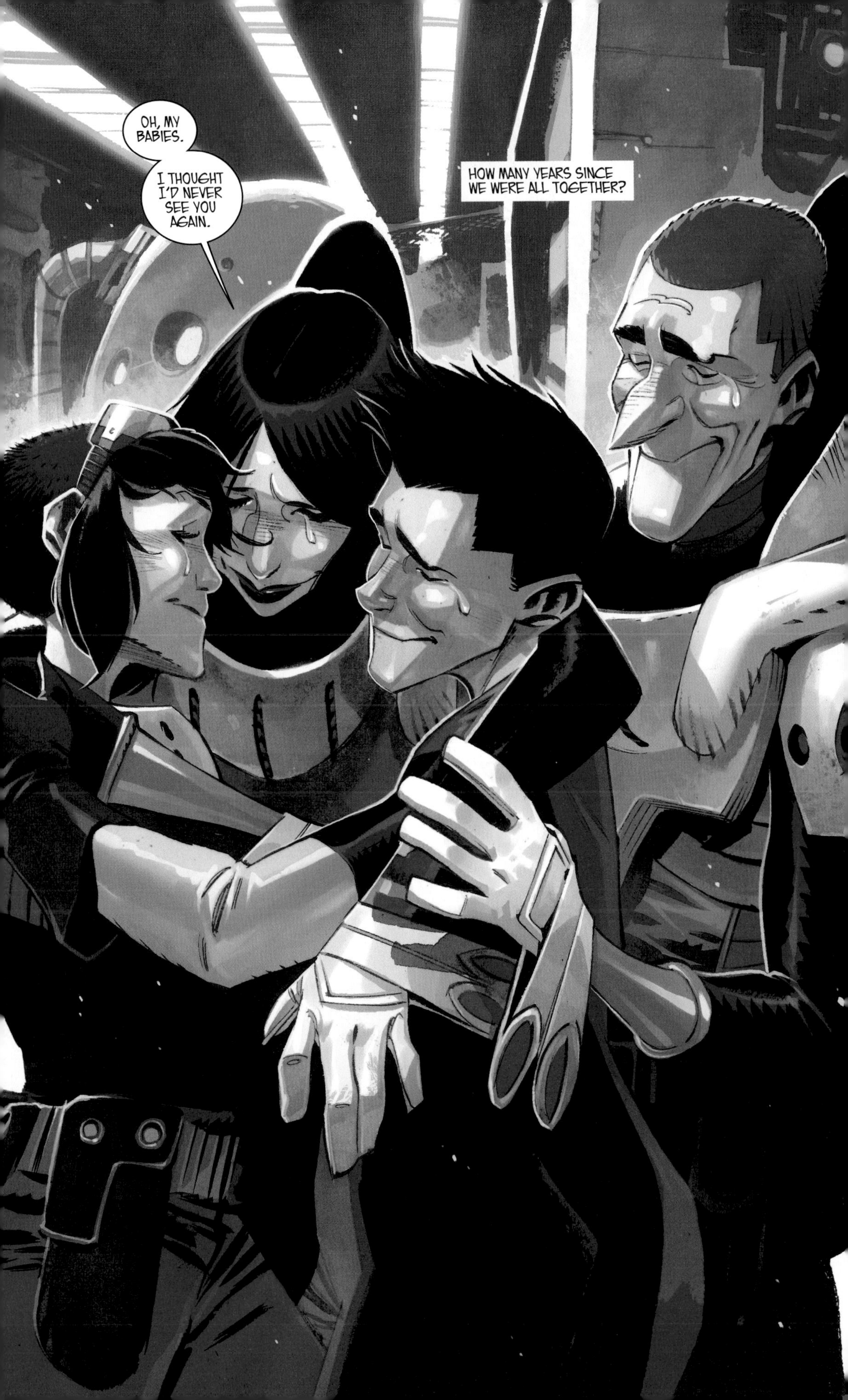
OH, MY BABIES.
I THOUGHT I'D NEVER SEE YOU AGAIN.
HOW MANY YEARS SINCE WE WERE ALL TOGETHER?

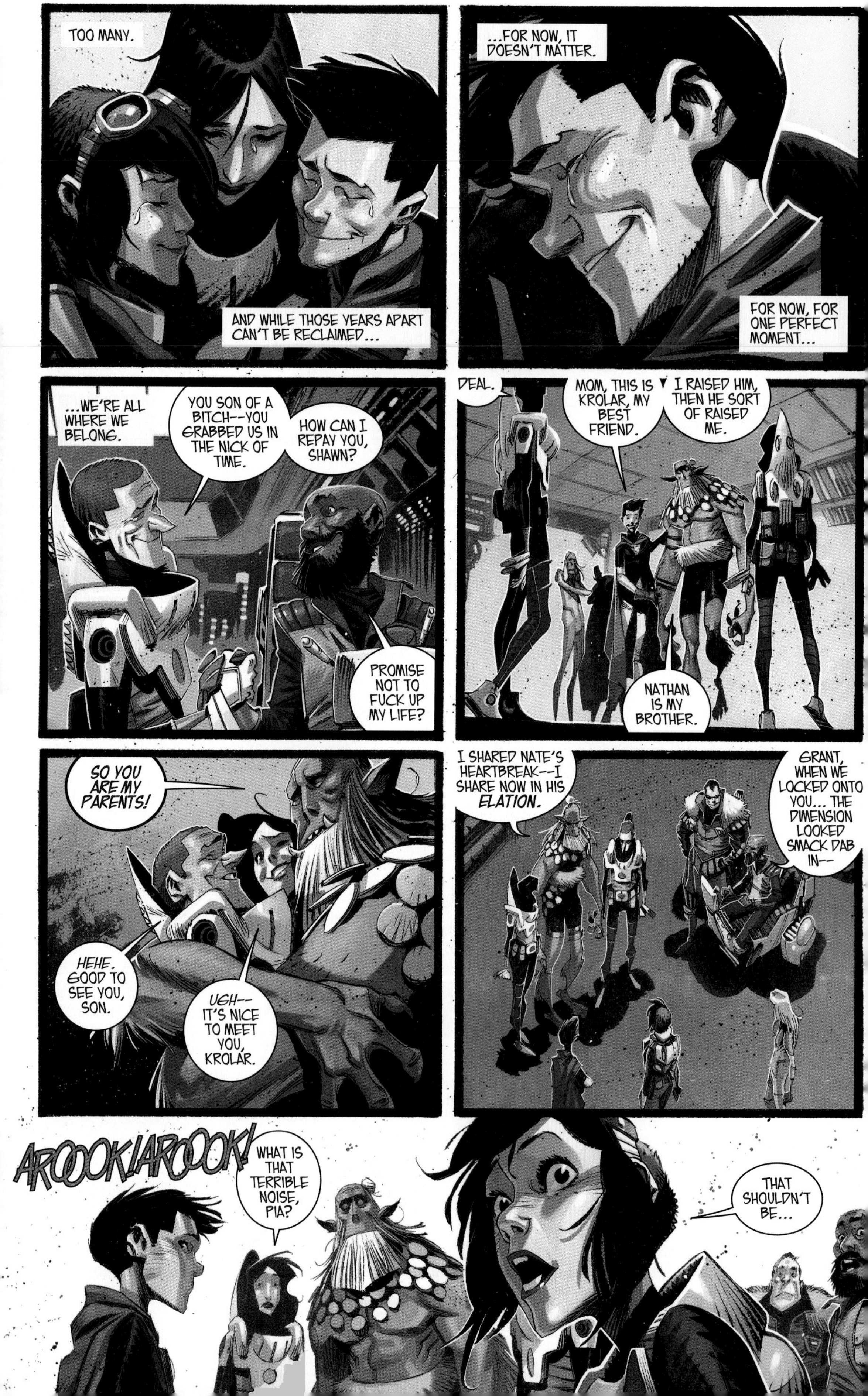

TOO MANY.
AND WHILE THOSE YEARS APART CAN'T BE RECLAIMED...
...FOR NOW, IT DOESN'T MATTER.
FOR NOW, FOR ONE PERFECT MOMENT...
...WE'RE ALL WHERE WE BELONG.
YOU SON OF A BITCH--YOU GRABBED US IN THE NICK OF TIME.
HOW CAN I REPAY YOU, SHAWN?
PROMISE NOT TO FUCK UP MY LIFE?
DEAL.
MOM, THIS IS KROLAR, MY BEST FRIEND.
I RAISED HIM, THEN HE SORT OF RAISED ME.
NATHAN IS MY BROTHER.
SO YOU ARE MY PARENTS!
HEHE. GOOD TO SEE YOU, SON.
UGH--IT'S NICE TO MEET YOU, KROLAR.
I SHARED NATE'S HEARTBREAK--I SHARE NOW IN HIS ELATION.
GRANT, WHEN WE LOCKED ONTO YOU... THE DIMENSION LOOKED SMACK DAB IN--
AROOOK! AROOOK!
WHAT IS THAT TERRIBLE NOISE, PIA?
THAT SHOULDN'T BE...

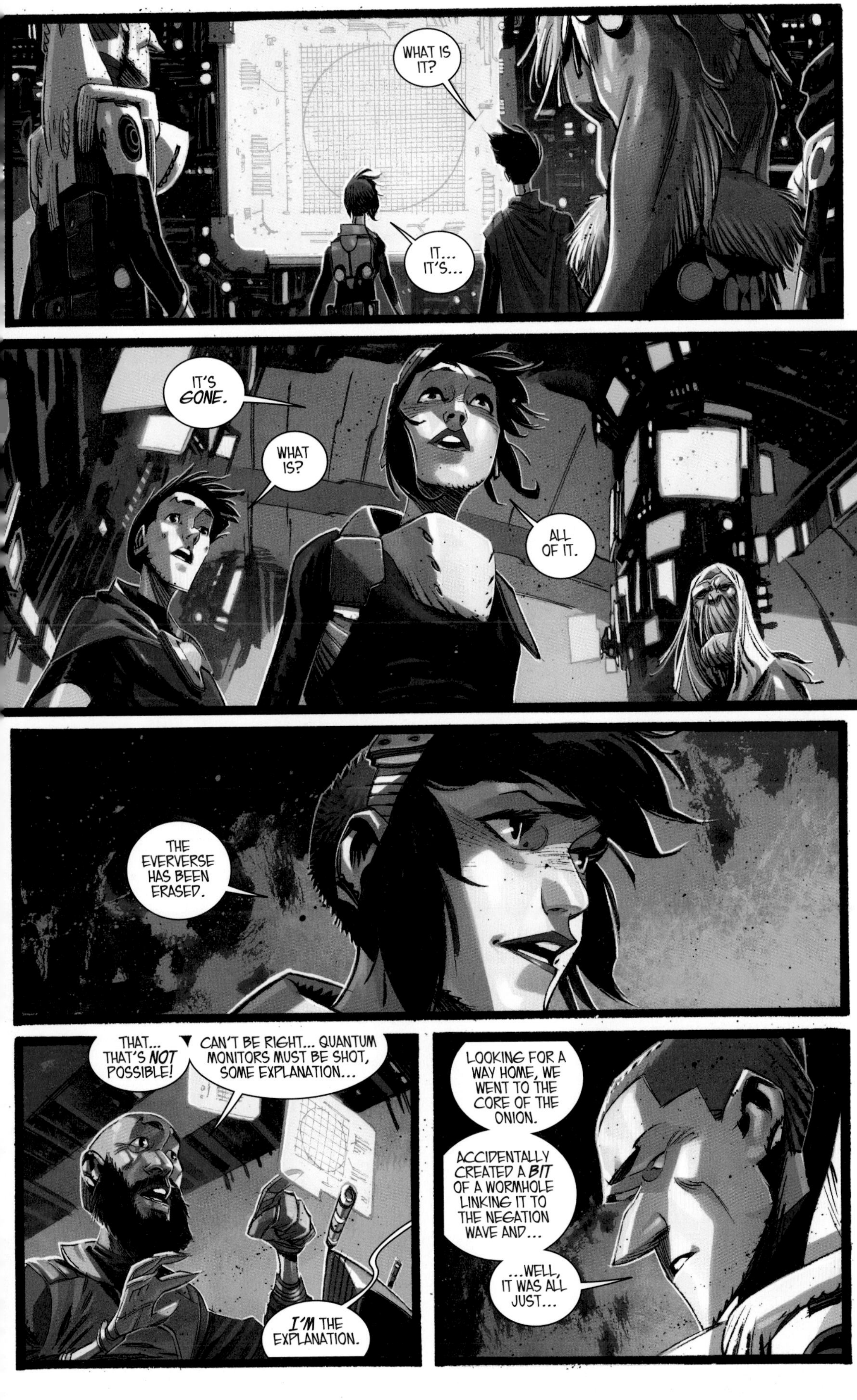
WHAT IS IT?
IT... IT'S...
IT'S GONE.
WHAT IS?
ALL OF IT.
THE EVERVERSE HAS BEEN ERASED.
THAT... THAT'S NOT POSSIBLE!
CAN'T BE RIGHT... QUANTUM MONITORS MUST BE SHOT, SOME EXPLANATION...
I'M THE EXPLANATION.
LOOKING FOR A WAY HOME, WE WENT TO THE CORE OF THE ONION.
ACCIDENTALLY CREATED A BIT OF A WORMHOLE LINKING IT TO THE NEGATION WAVE AND...
...WELL, IT WAS ALL JUST...

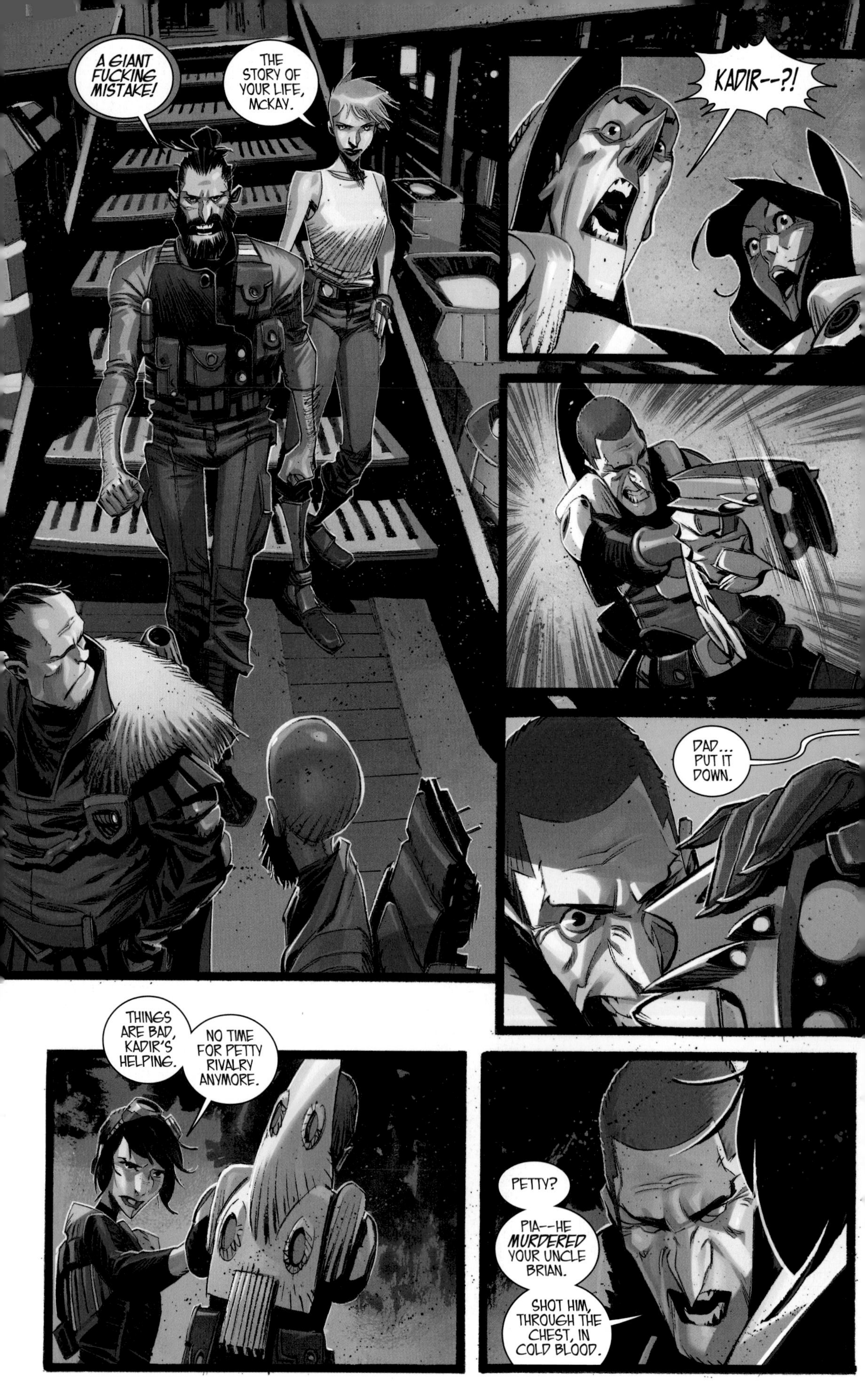
A GIANT FUCKING MISTAKE!
THE STORY OF YOUR LIFE, MCKAY.
KADIR--?!
DAD... PUT IT DOWN.
THINGS ARE BAD, KADIR'S HELPING.
NO TIME FOR PETTY RIVALRY ANYMORE.
PETTY?
PIA--HE MURDERED YOUR UNCLE BRIAN.
SHOT HIM, THROUGH THE CHEST, IN COLD BLOOD.

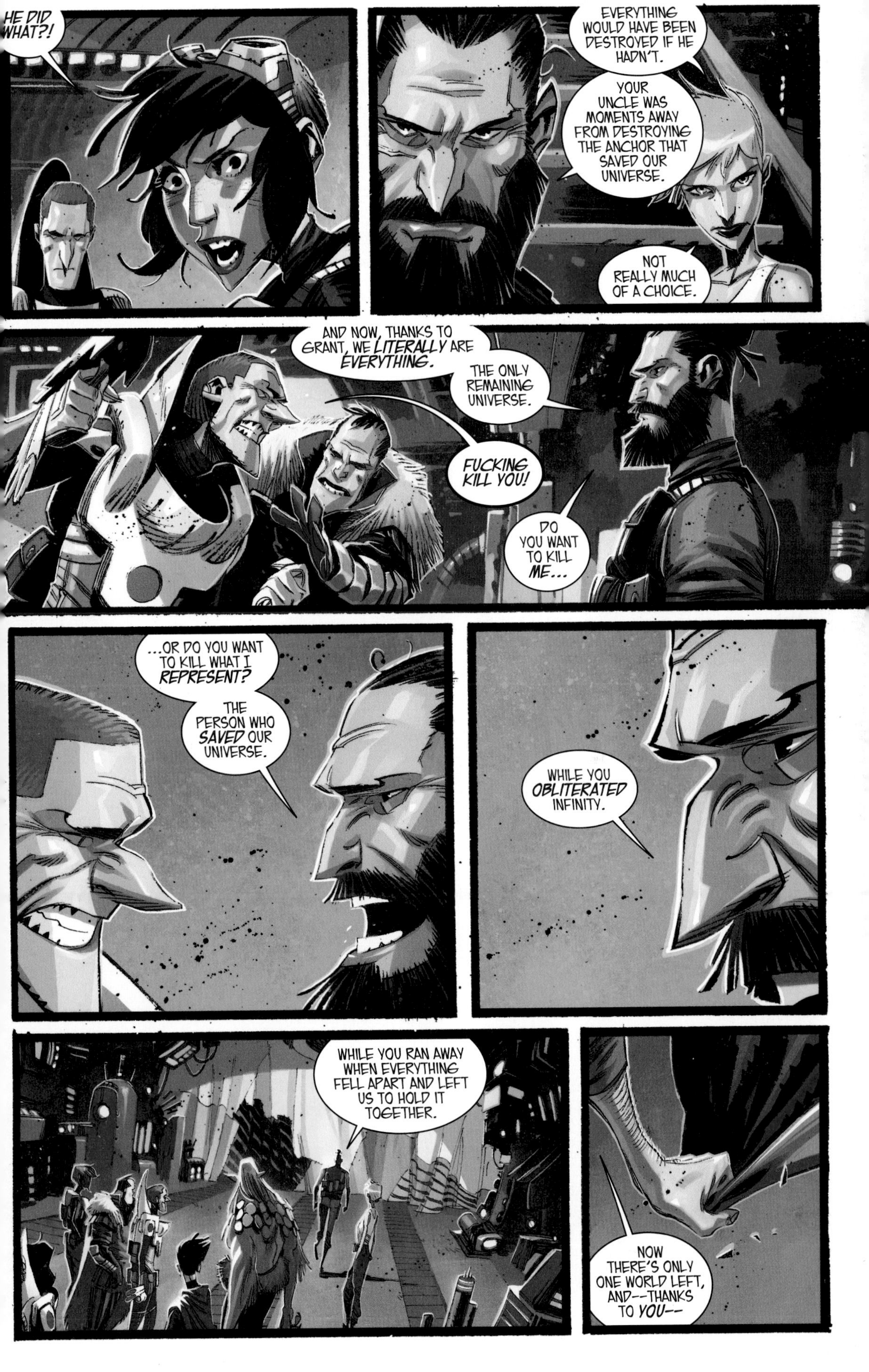
HE DID WHAT?!
EVERYTHING WOULD HAVE BEEN DESTROYED IF HE HADN'T.
YOUR UNCLE WAS MOMENTS AWAY FROM DESTROYING THE ANCHOR THAT SAVED OUR UNIVERSE.
NOT REALLY MUCH OF A CHOICE.
AND NOW, THANKS TO GRANT, WE LITERALLY ARE EVERYTHING.
THE ONLY REMAINING UNIVERSE.
FUCKING KILL YOU!
DO YOU WANT TO KILL ME...
...OR DO YOU WANT TO KILL WHAT I REPRESENT?
THE PERSON WHO SAVED OUR UNIVERSE.
WHILE YOU OBLITERATED INFINITY.
WHILE YOU RAN AWAY WHEN EVERYTHING FELL APART AND LEFT US TO HOLD IT TOGETHER.
NOW THERE'S ONLY ONE WORLD LEFT, AND--THANKS TO YOU--

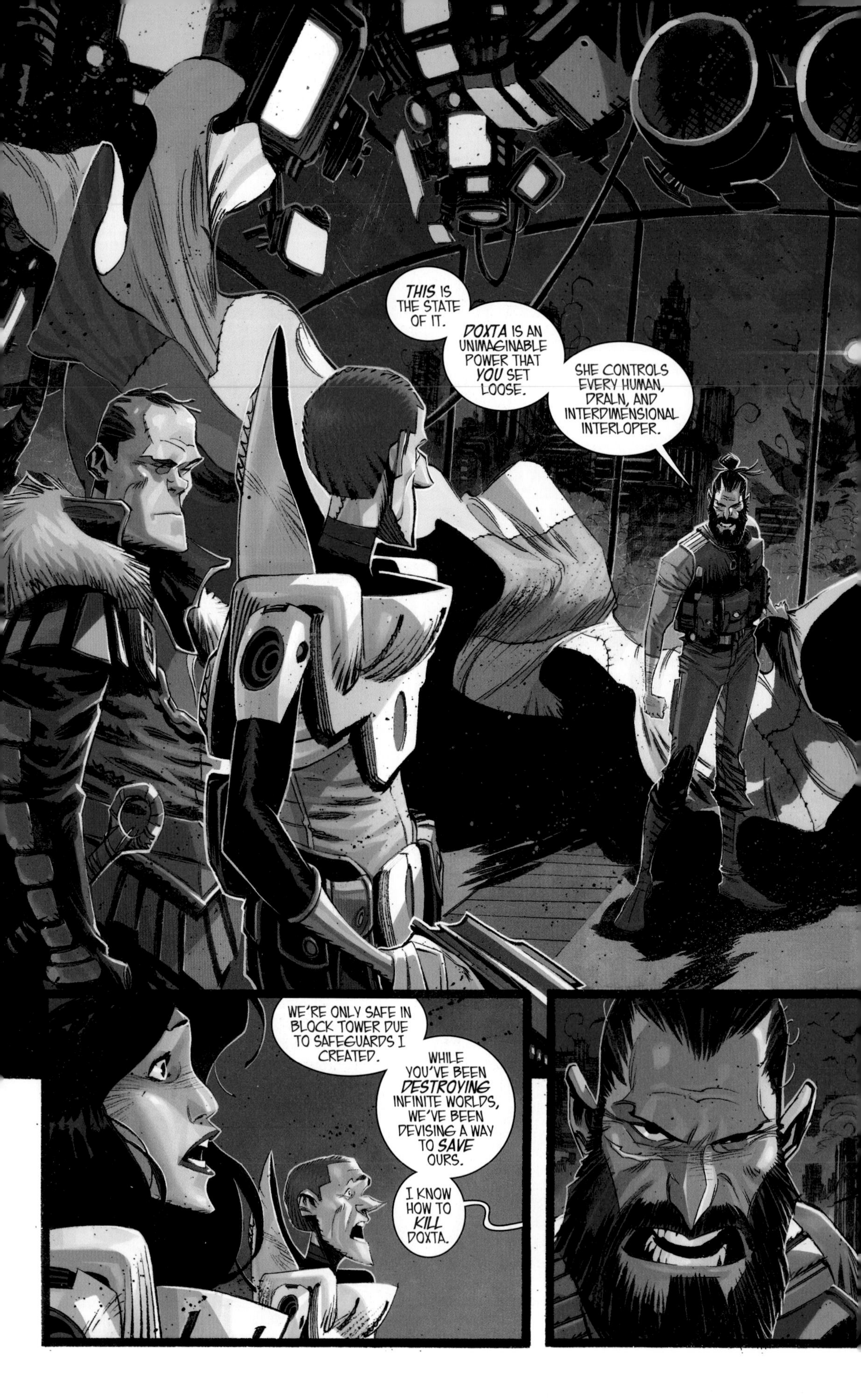
THIS IS THE STATE OF IT.
DOXTA IS AN UNIMAGINABLE POWER THAT YOU SET LOOSE.
SHE CONTROLS EVERY HUMAN, DRALN, AND INTERDIMENSIONAL INTERLOPER.
WE'RE ONLY SAFE IN BLOCK TOWER DUE TO SAFEGUARDS I CREATED.
WHILE YOU'VE BEEN DESTROYING INFINITE WORLDS, WE'VE BEEN DEVISING A WAY TO SAVE OURS.
I KNOW HOW TO KILL DOXTA.

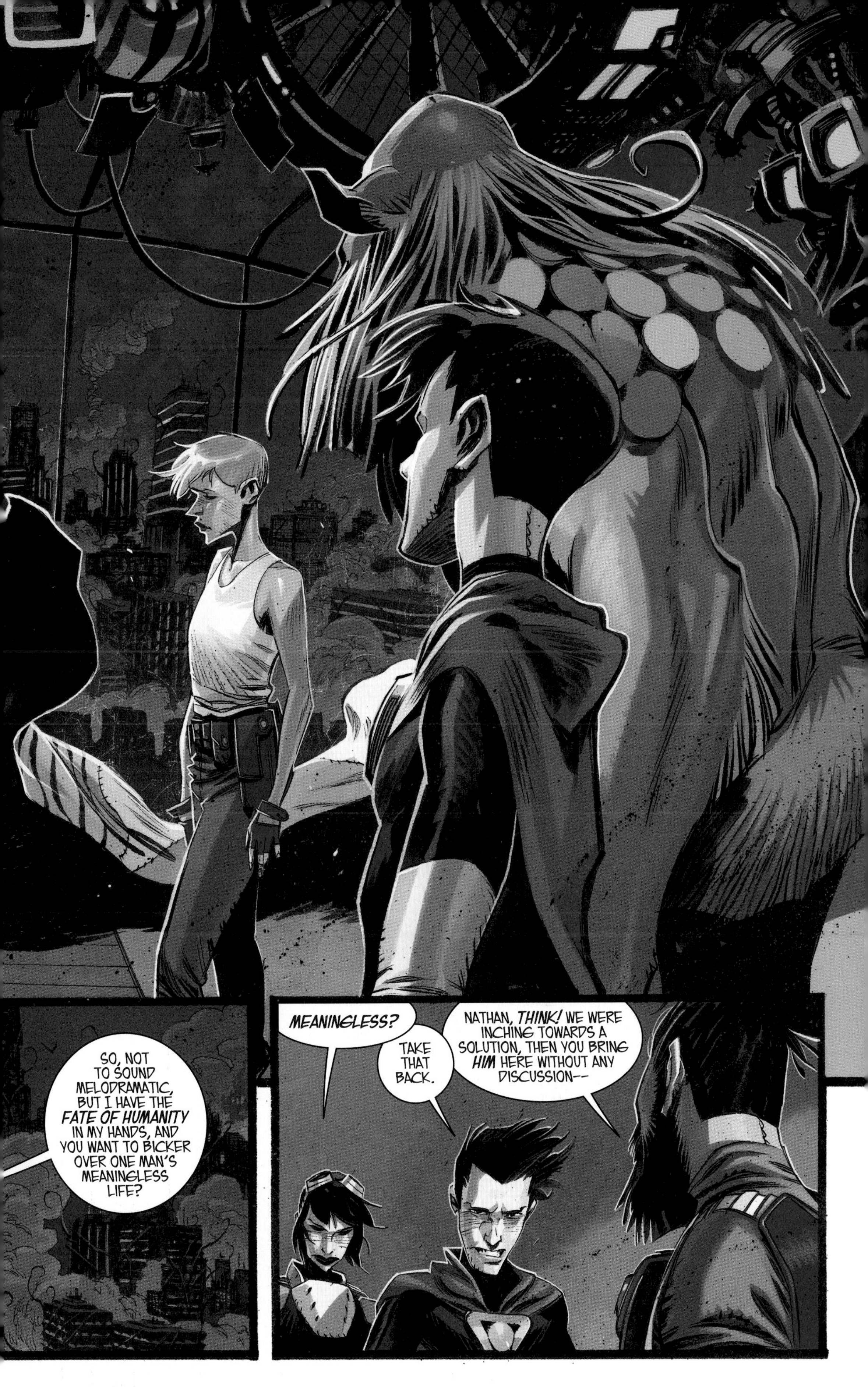
SO, NOT TO SOUND MELODRAMATIC, BUT I HAVE THE FATE OF HUMANITY IN MY HANDS, AND YOU WANT TO BICKER OVER ONE MAN'S MEANINGLESS LIFE?
MEANINGLESS?
TAKE THAT BACK.
NATHAN, THINK! WE WERE INCHING TOWARDS A SOLUTION, THEN YOU BRING HIM HERE WITHOUT ANY DISCUSSION--

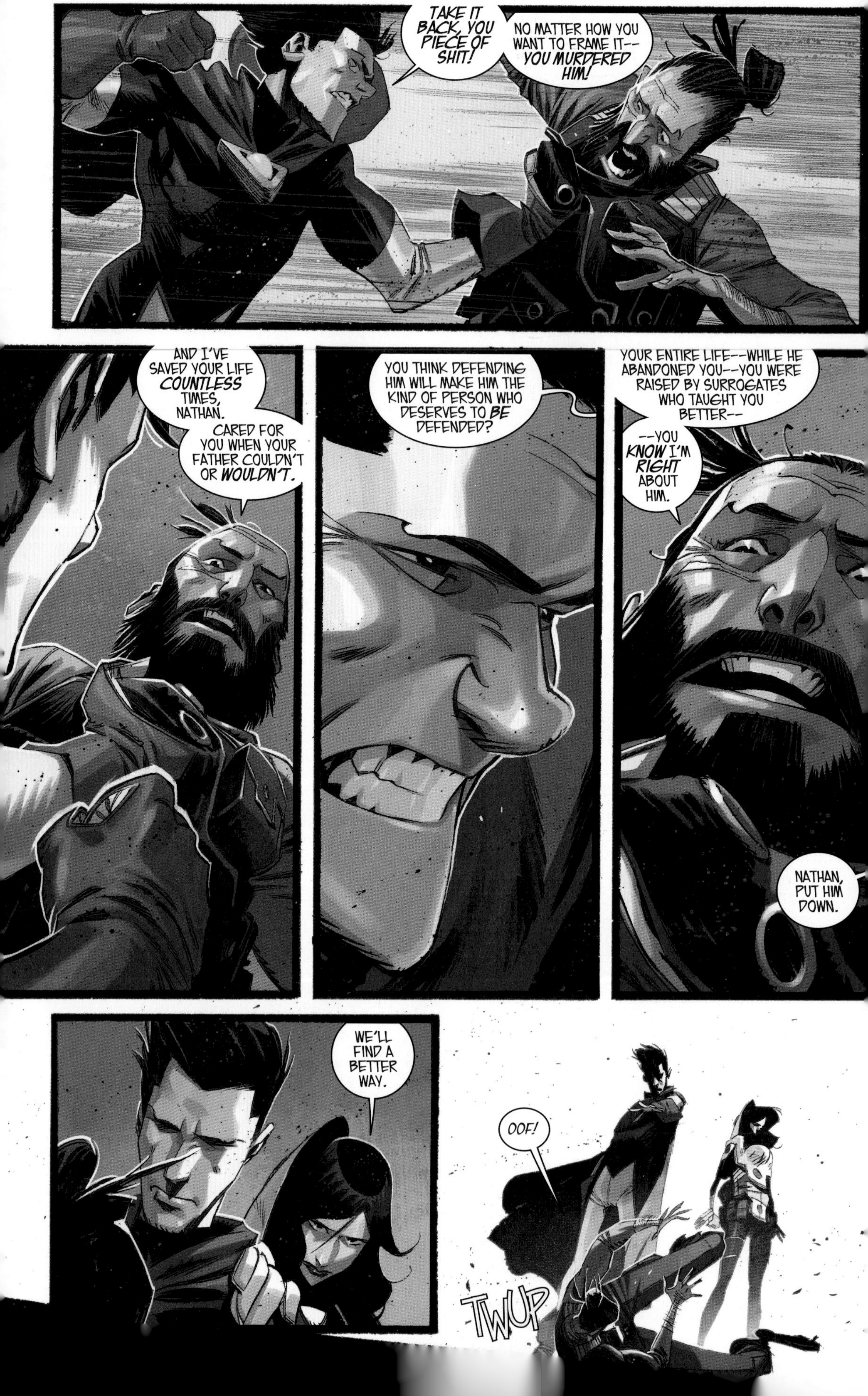
TAKE IT BACK, YOU PIECE OF SHIT!
NO MATTER HOW YOU WANT TO FRAME IT-- YOU MURDERED HIM!
AND I'VE SAVED YOUR LIFE COUNTLESS TIMES, NATHAN.
CARED FOR YOU WHEN YOUR FATHER COULDN'T OR WOULDN'T.
YOU THINK DEFENDING HIM WILL MAKE HIM THE KIND OF PERSON WHO DESERVES TO BE DEFENDED?
YOUR ENTIRE LIFE--WHILE HE ABANDONED YOU--YOU WERE RAISED BY SURROGATES WHO TAUGHT YOU BETTER--
--YOU KNOW I'M RIGHT ABOUT HIM.
NATHAN, PUT HIM DOWN.
WE'LL FIND A BETTER WAY.
OOF!
TWUP

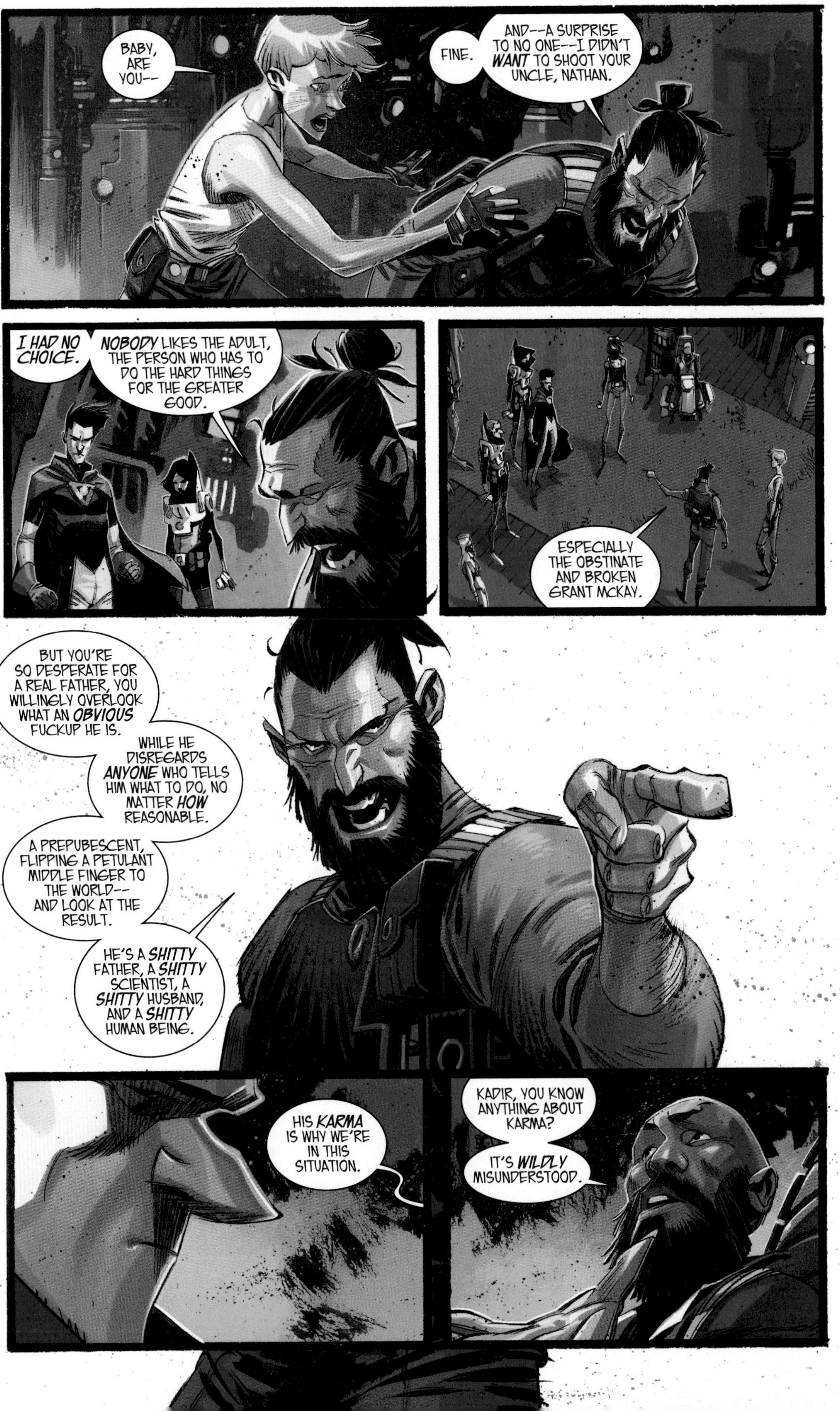
BABY, ARE YOU--
FINE.
AND--A SURPRISE TO NO ONE--I DIDN'T WANT TO SHOOT YOUR UNCLE, NATHAN.
I HAD NO CHOICE.
NOBODY LIKES THE ADULT, THE PERSON WHO HAS TO DO THE HARD THINGS FOR THE GREATER GOOD.
ESPECIALLY THE OBSTINATE AND BROKEN GRANT McKAY.
BUT YOU'RE SO DESPERATE FOR A REAL FATHER, YOU WILLINGLY OVERLOOK WHAT AN OBVIOUS FUCKUP HE IS.
WHILE HE DISREGARDS ANYONE WHO TELLS HIM WHAT TO DO, NO MATTER HOW REASONABLE.
A PREPUBESCENT, FLIPPING A PETULANT MIDDLE FINGER TO THE WORLD-- AND LOOK AT THE RESULT.
HE'S A SHITTY FATHER, A SHITTY SCIENTIST, A SHITTY HUSBAND, AND A SHITTY HUMAN BEING.
HIS KARMA IS WHY WE'RE IN THIS SITUATION.
KADIR, YOU KNOW ANYTHING ABOUT KARMA?
IT'S WILDLY MISUNDERSTOOD.

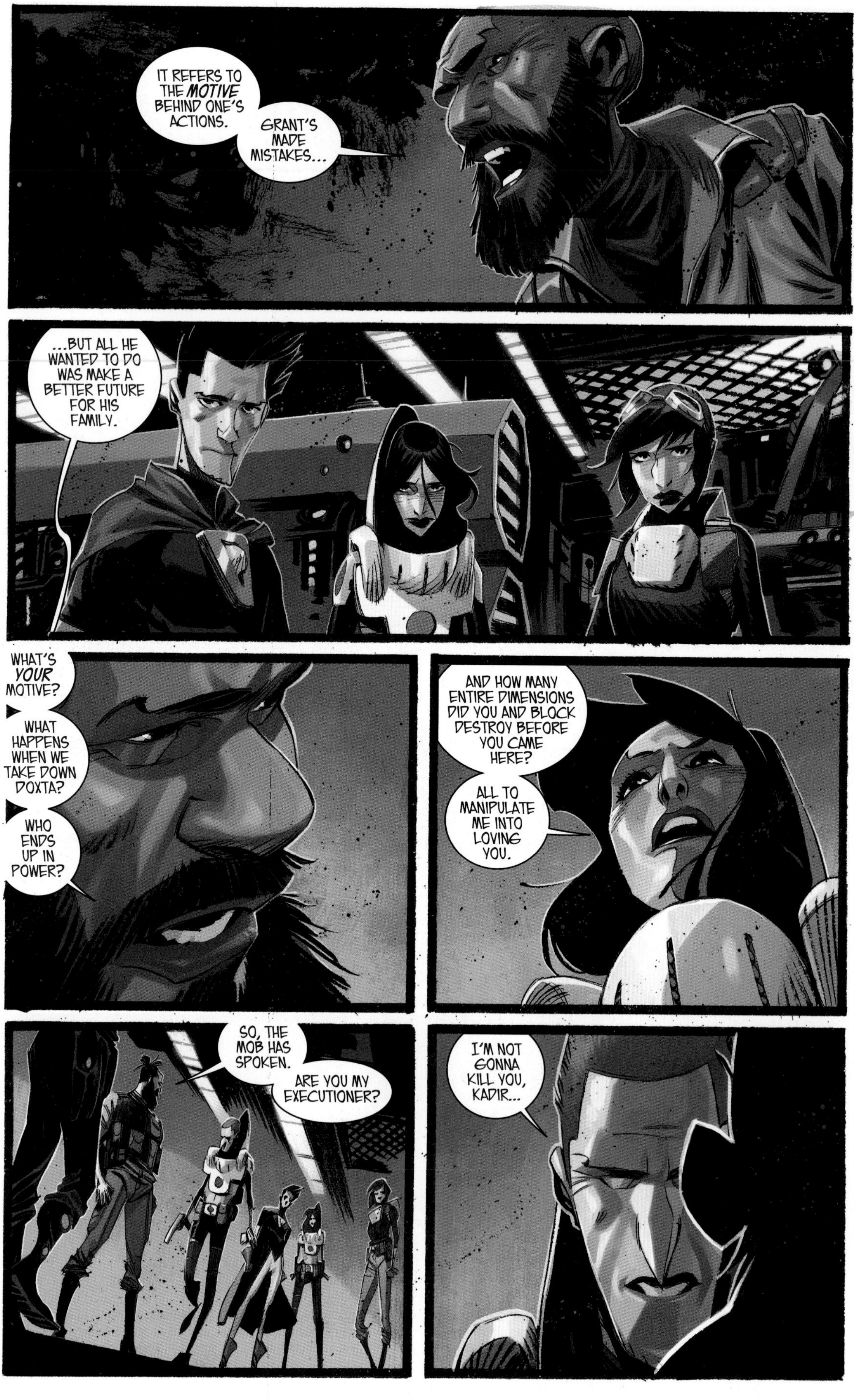
IT REFERS TO THE *MOTIVE* BEHIND ONE'S ACTIONS.
GRANT'S MADE MISTAKES...
...BUT ALL HE WANTED TO DO WAS MAKE A BETTER FUTURE FOR HIS FAMILY.
WHAT'S *YOUR* MOTIVE?
WHAT HAPPENS WHEN WE TAKE DOWN DOXTA?
WHO ENDS UP IN POWER?
AND HOW MANY ENTIRE DIMENSIONS DID YOU AND BLOCK DESTROY BEFORE YOU CAME HERE?
ALL TO MANIPULATE ME INTO LOVING YOU.
SO, THE MOB HAS SPOKEN.
ARE YOU MY EXECUTIONER?
I'M NOT GONNA KILL YOU, KADIR...

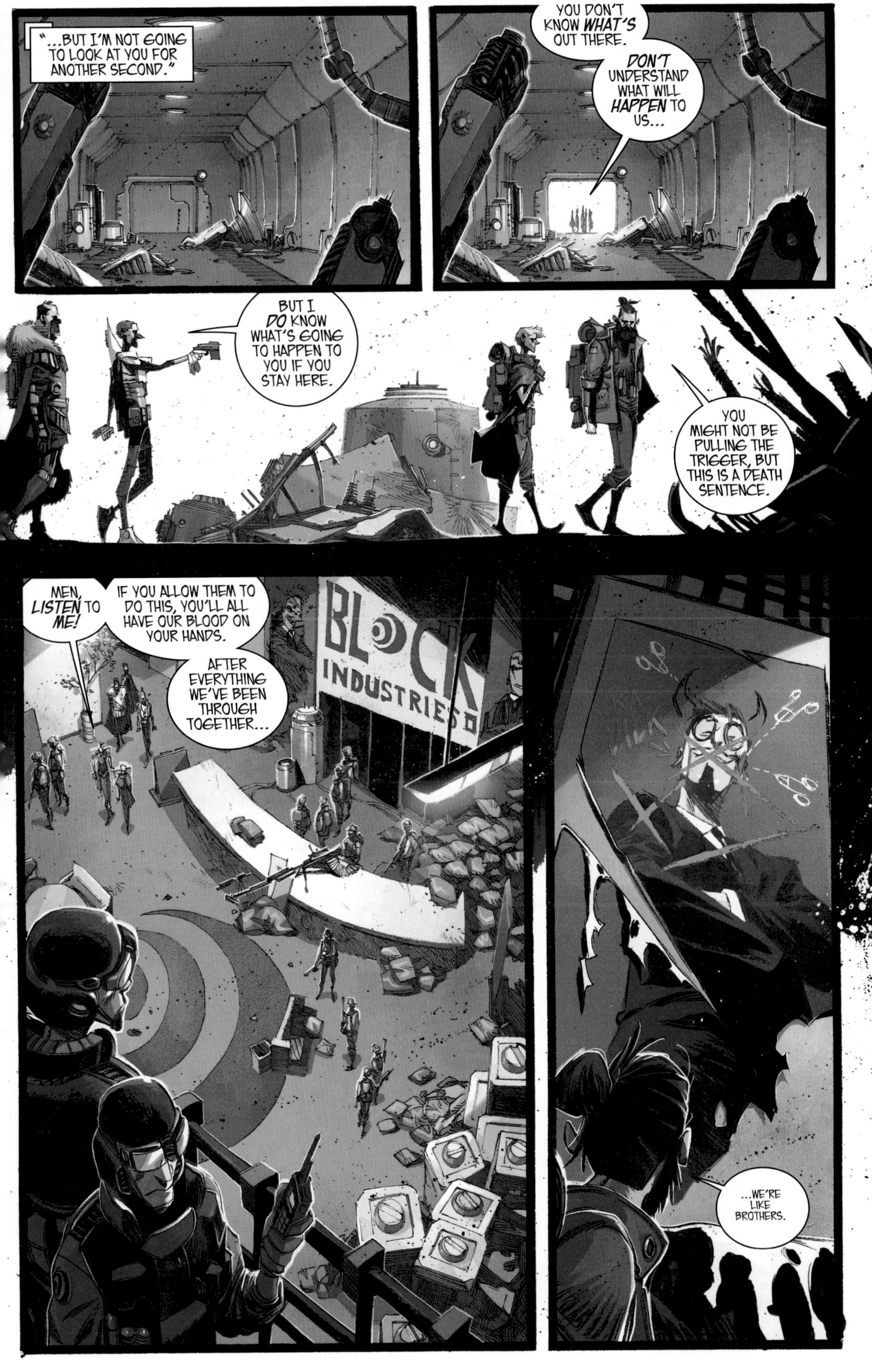
"...BUT I'M NOT GOING TO LOOK AT YOU FOR ANOTHER SECOND."
YOU DON'T KNOW WHAT'S OUT THERE.
DON'T UNDERSTAND WHAT WILL HAPPEN TO US...
BUT I DO KNOW WHAT'S GOING TO HAPPEN TO YOU IF YOU STAY HERE.
YOU MIGHT NOT BE PULLING THE TRIGGER, BUT THIS IS A DEATH SENTENCE.
MEN, LISTEN TO ME!
IF YOU ALLOW THEM TO DO THIS, YOU'LL ALL HAVE OUR BLOOD ON YOUR HANDS.
AFTER EVERYTHING WE'VE BEEN THROUGH TOGETHER...
BL CK INDUSTRIES
...WE'RE LIKE BROTHERS.

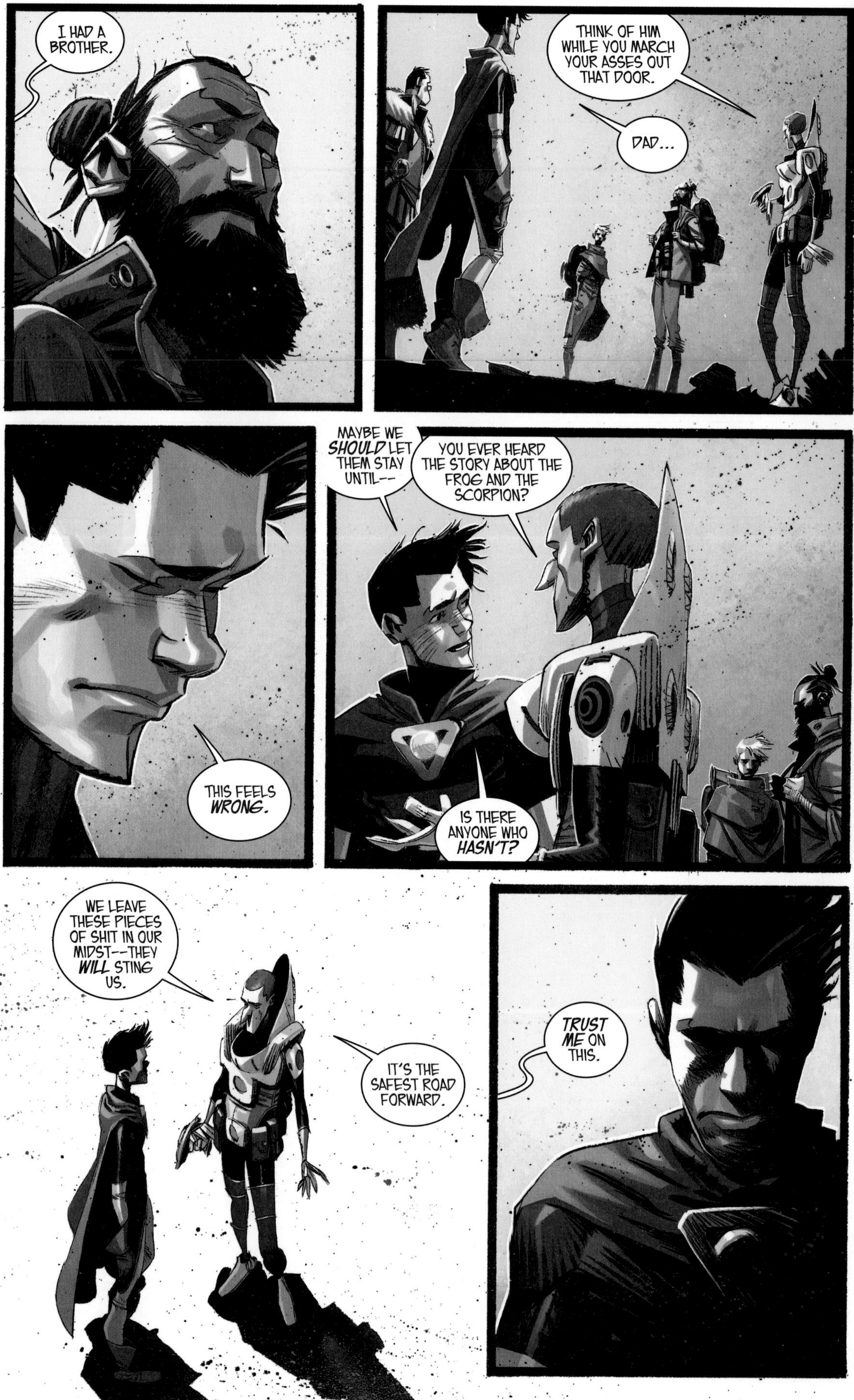
I HAD A BROTHER.
THINK OF HIM WHILE YOU MARCH YOUR ASSES OUT THAT DOOR.
DAD...
THIS FEELS *WRONG.*
MAYBE WE *SHOULD* LET THEM STAY UNTIL--
YOU EVER HEARD THE STORY ABOUT THE FROG AND THE SCORPION?
IS THERE ANYONE WHO *HASN'T?*
WE LEAVE THESE PIECES OF SHIT IN OUR MIDST--THEY *WILL* STING US.
IT'S THE SAFEST ROAD FORWARD.
TRUST ME ON THIS.

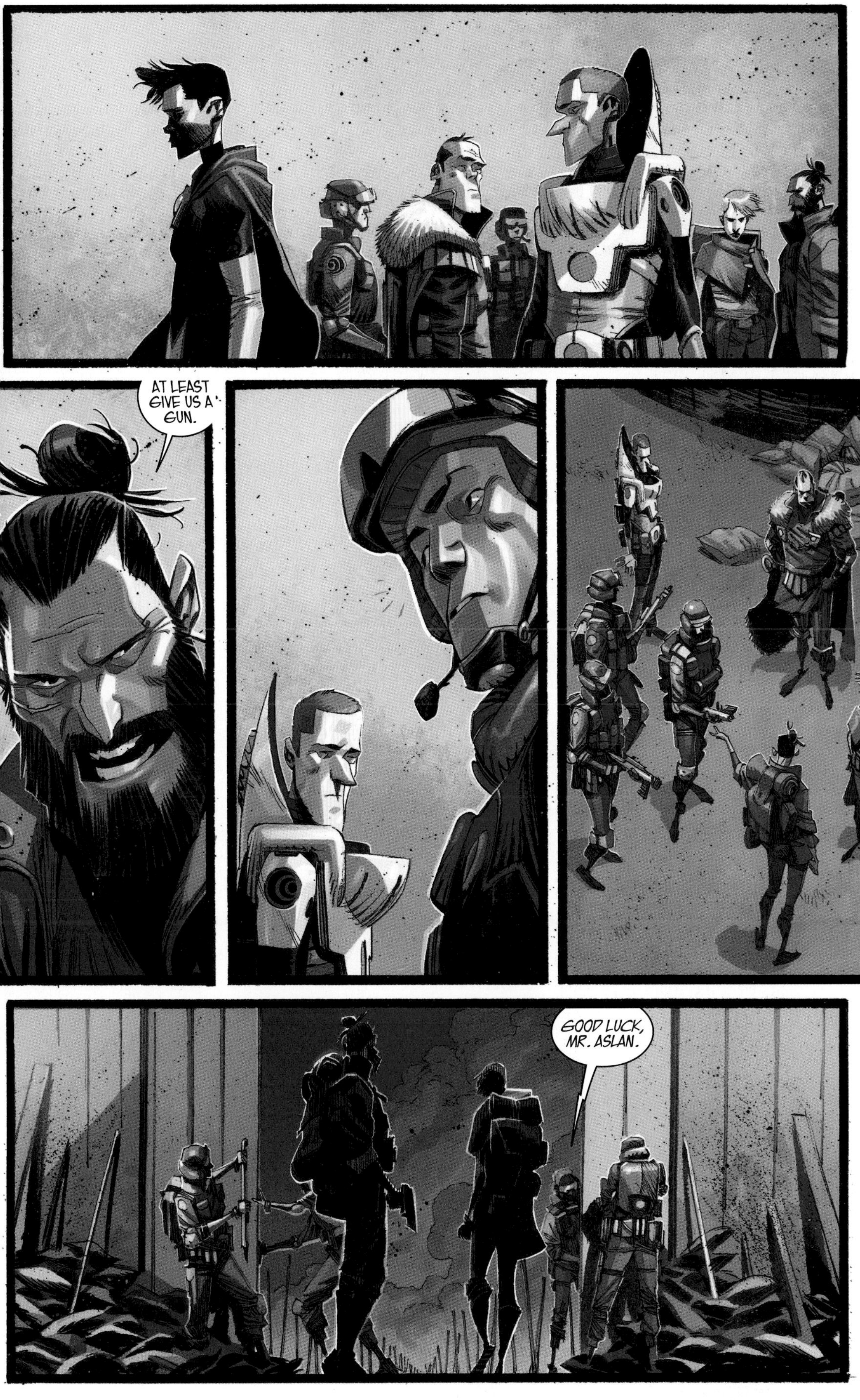
AT LEAST GIVE US A GUN.
GOOD LUCK, MR. ASLAN.

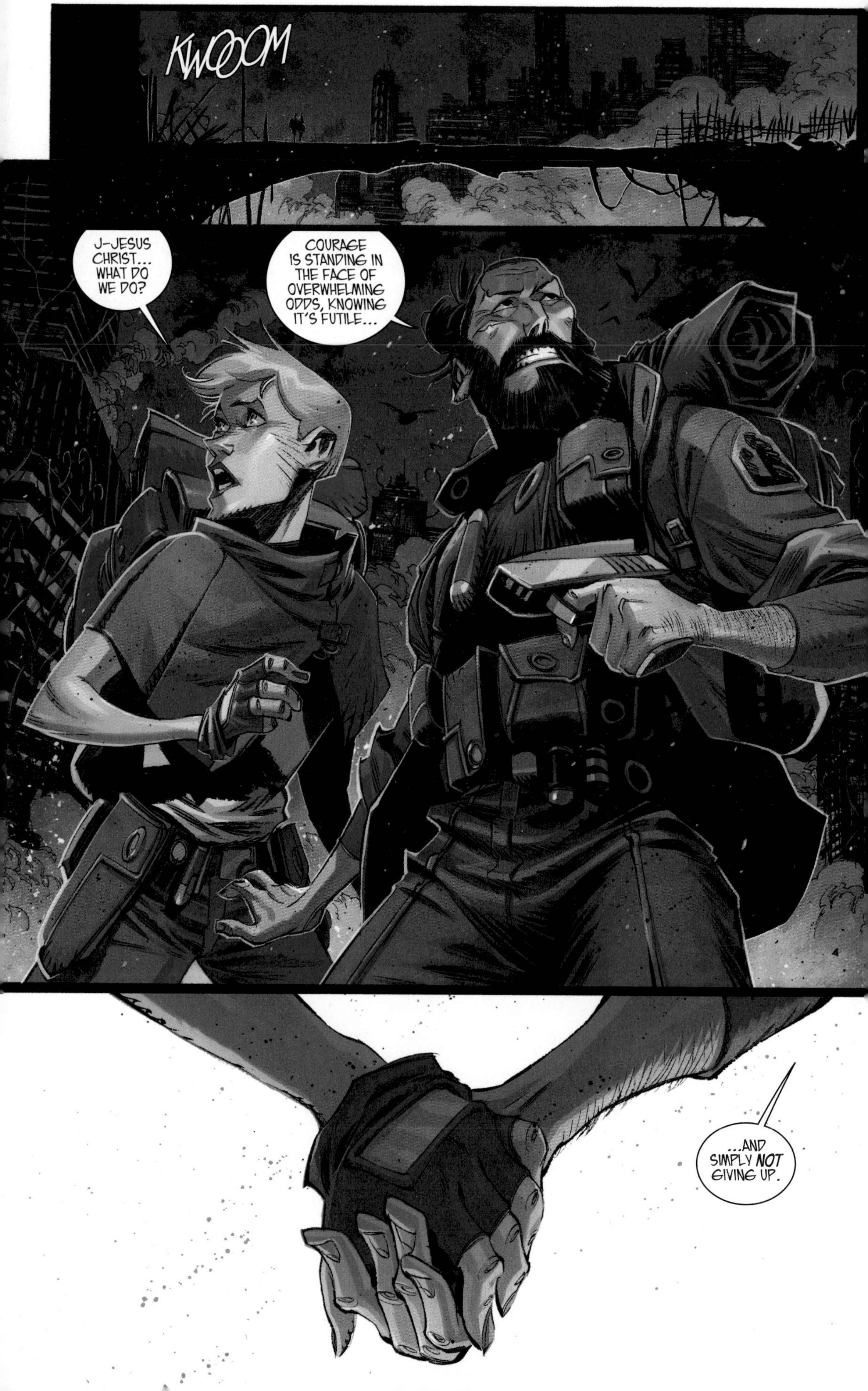
KWOOOM
J-JESUS CHRIST... WHAT DO WE DO?
COURAGE IS STANDING IN THE FACE OF OVERWHELMING ODDS, KNOWING IT'S FUTILE...
...AND SIMPLY **NOT** GIVING UP.

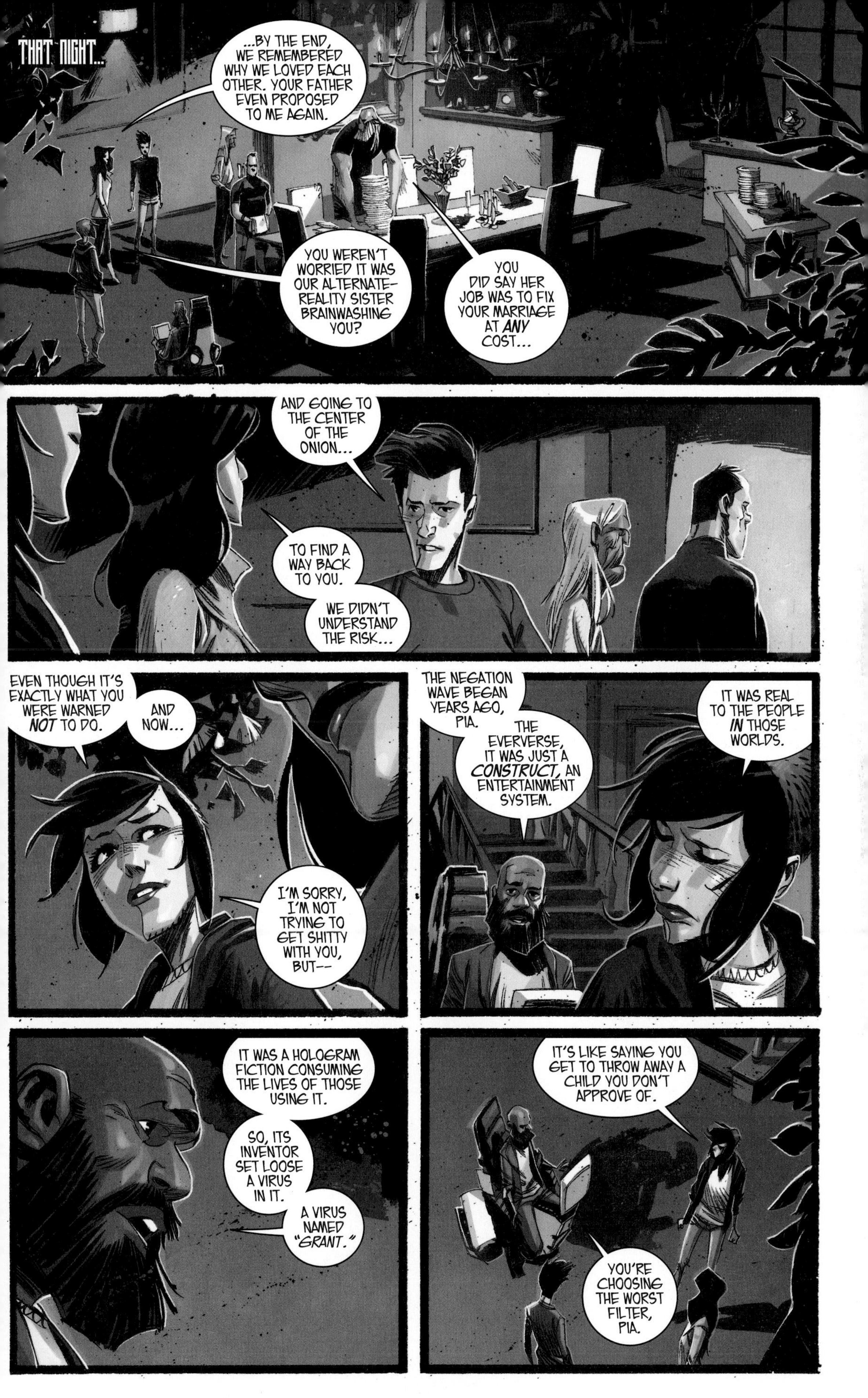
THAT NIGHT...
...BY THE END, WE REMEMBERED WHY WE LOVED EACH OTHER. YOUR FATHER EVEN PROPOSED TO ME AGAIN.
YOU WEREN'T WORRIED IT WAS OUR ALTERNATE-REALITY SISTER BRAINWASHING YOU?
YOU DID SAY HER JOB WAS TO FIX YOUR MARRIAGE AT ANY COST...
AND GOING TO THE CENTER OF THE ONION...
TO FIND A WAY BACK TO YOU.
WE DIDN'T UNDERSTAND THE RISK...
EVEN THOUGH IT'S EXACTLY WHAT YOU WERE WARNED NOT TO DO.
AND NOW...
I'M SORRY, I'M NOT TRYING TO GET SHITTY WITH YOU, BUT--
THE NEGATION WAVE BEGAN YEARS AGO, PIA.
THE EVERVERSE, IT WAS JUST A CONSTRUCT, AN ENTERTAINMENT SYSTEM.
IT WAS REAL TO THE PEOPLE IN THOSE WORLDS.
IT WAS A HOLOGRAM FICTION CONSUMING THE LIVES OF THOSE USING IT.
SO, ITS INVENTOR SET LOOSE A VIRUS IN IT.
A VIRUS NAMED "GRANT."
IT'S LIKE SAYING YOU GET TO THROW AWAY A CHILD YOU DON'T APPROVE OF.
YOU'RE CHOOSING THE WORST FILTER, PIA.

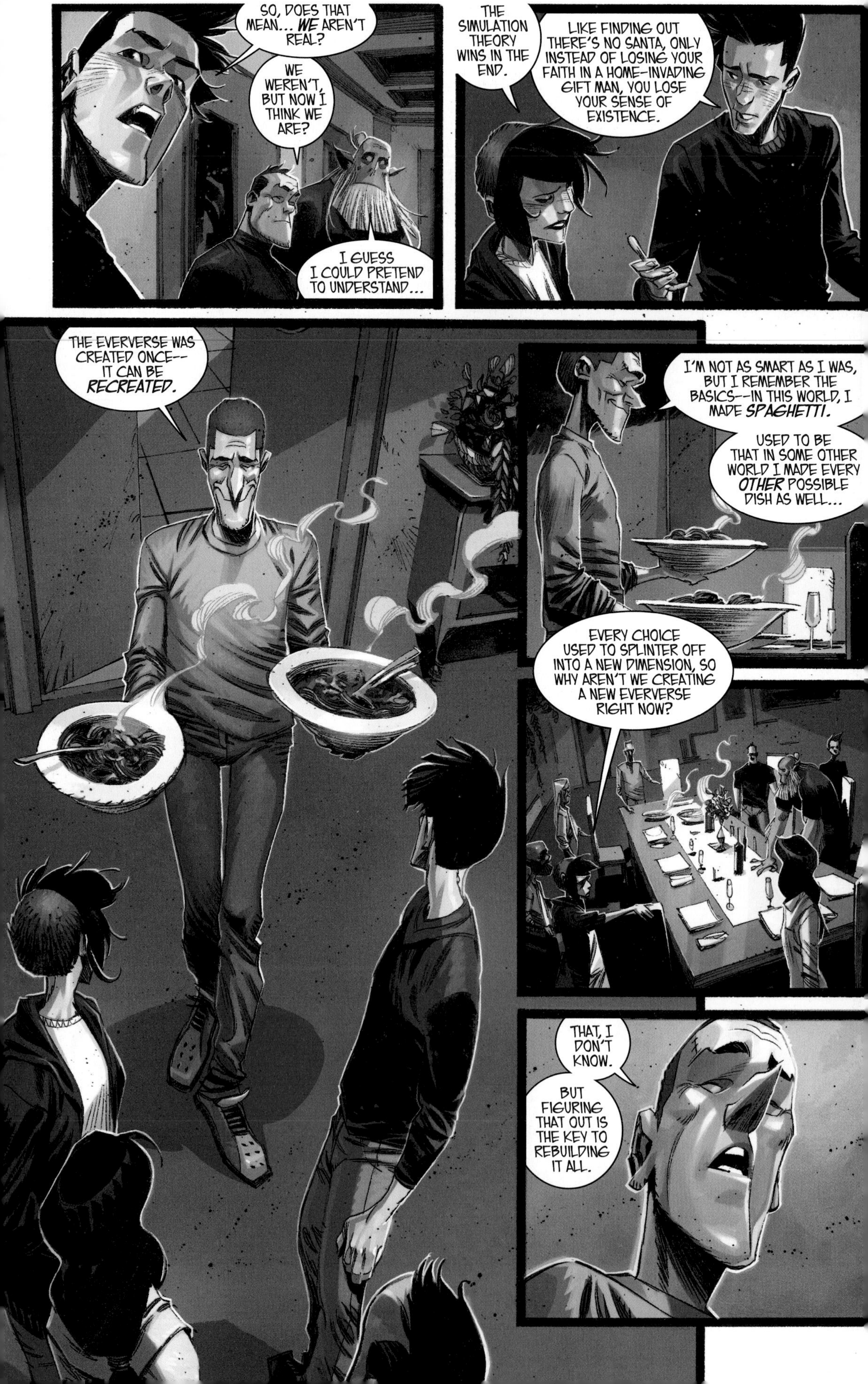
SO, DOES THAT MEAN... WE AREN'T REAL?
WE WEREN'T, BUT NOW I THINK WE ARE?
I GUESS I COULD PRETEND TO UNDERSTAND...
THE SIMULATION THEORY WINS IN THE END.
LIKE FINDING OUT THERE'S NO SANTA, ONLY INSTEAD OF LOSING YOUR FAITH IN A HOME-INVADING GIFT MAN, YOU LOSE YOUR SENSE OF EXISTENCE.
THE EVERVERSE WAS CREATED ONCE-- IT CAN BE RECREATED.
I'M NOT AS SMART AS I WAS, BUT I REMEMBER THE BASICS--IN THIS WORLD, I MADE SPAGHETTI.
USED TO BE THAT IN SOME OTHER WORLD I MADE EVERY OTHER POSSIBLE DISH AS WELL...
EVERY CHOICE USED TO SPLINTER OFF INTO A NEW DIMENSION, SO WHY AREN'T WE CREATING A NEW EVERVERSE RIGHT NOW?
THAT, I DON'T KNOW.
BUT FIGURING THAT OUT IS THE KEY TO REBUILDING IT ALL.

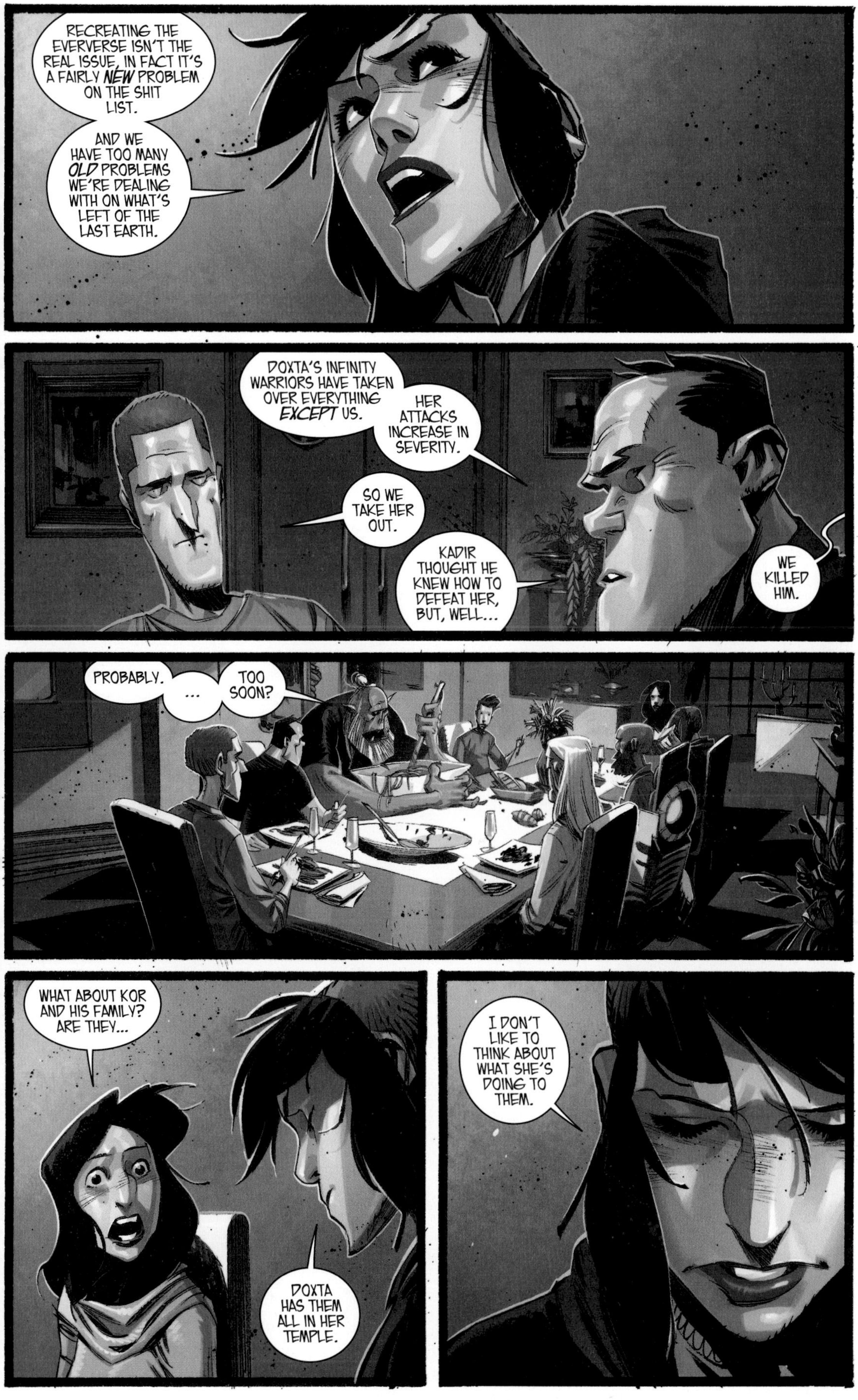
RECREATING THE EVERVERSE ISN'T THE REAL ISSUE, IN FACT IT'S A FAIRLY *NEW* PROBLEM ON THE SHIT LIST.
AND WE HAVE TOO MANY *OLD* PROBLEMS WE'RE DEALING WITH ON WHAT'S LEFT OF THE LAST EARTH.
DOXTA'S INFINITY WARRIORS HAVE TAKEN OVER EVERYTHING *EXCEPT* US.
HER ATTACKS INCREASE IN SEVERITY.
SO WE TAKE HER OUT.
KADIR THOUGHT HE KNEW HOW TO DEFEAT HER, BUT, WELL...
WE KILLED HIM.
PROBABLY.
...
TOO SOON?
WHAT ABOUT KOR AND HIS FAMILY? ARE THEY...
DOXTA HAS THEM ALL IN HER TEMPLE.
I DON'T LIKE TO THINK ABOUT WHAT SHE'S DOING TO THEM.

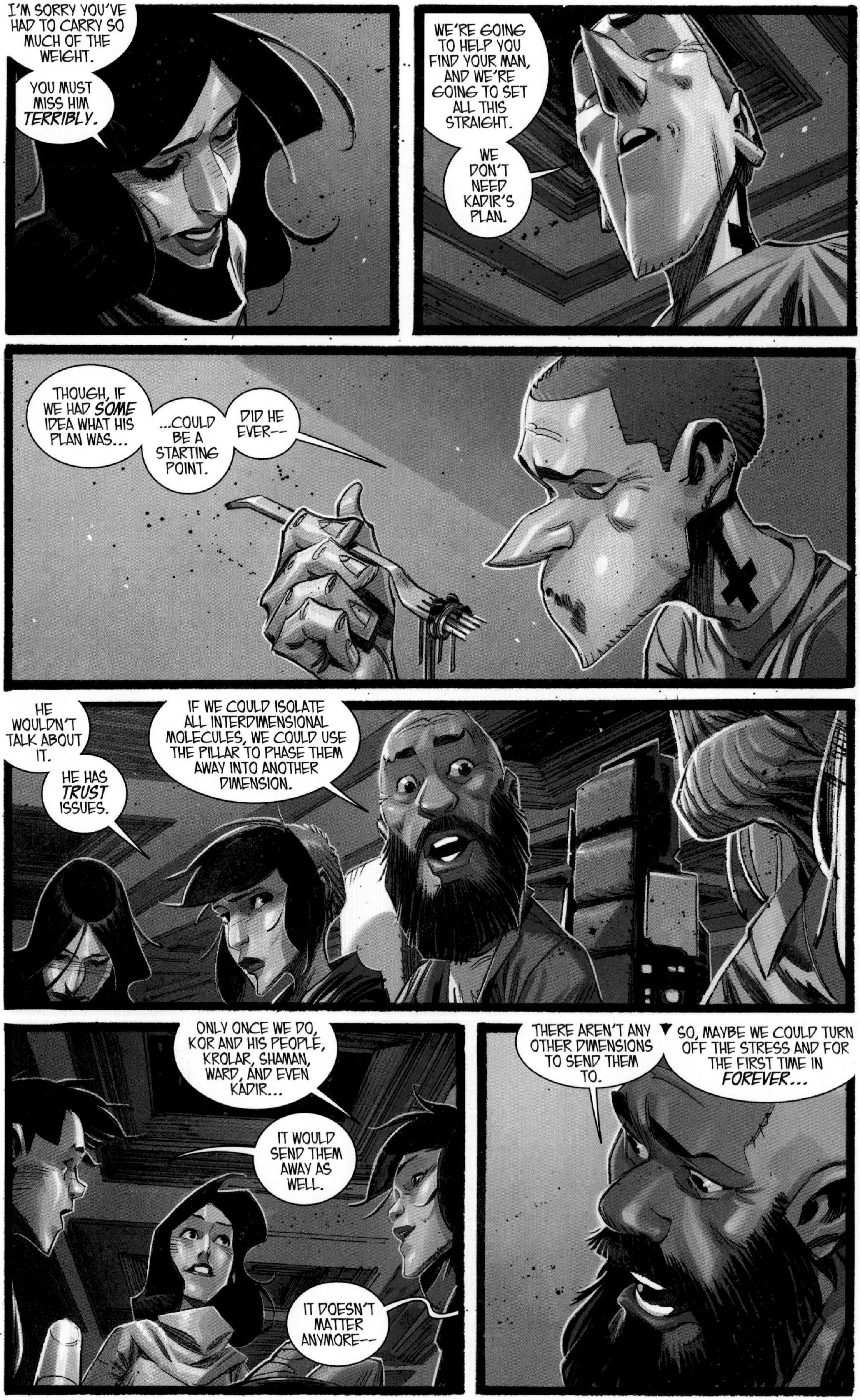
I'M SORRY YOU'VE HAD TO CARRY SO MUCH OF THE WEIGHT.
YOU MUST MISS HIM TERRIBLY.
WE'RE GOING TO HELP YOU FIND YOUR MAN, AND WE'RE GOING TO SET ALL THIS STRAIGHT.
WE DON'T NEED KADIR'S PLAN.
THOUGH, IF WE HAD SOME IDEA WHAT HIS PLAN WAS...
...COULD BE A STARTING POINT.
DID HE EVER--
HE WOULDN'T TALK ABOUT IT.
HE HAS TRUST ISSUES.
IF WE COULD ISOLATE ALL INTERDIMENSIONAL MOLECULES, WE COULD USE THE PILLAR TO PHASE THEM AWAY INTO ANOTHER DIMENSION.
ONLY ONCE WE DO, KOR AND HIS PEOPLE, KROLAR, SHAMAN, WARD, AND EVEN KADIR...
IT WOULD SEND THEM AWAY AS WELL.
IT DOESN'T MATTER ANYMORE--
THERE AREN'T ANY OTHER DIMENSIONS TO SEND THEM TO.
SO, MAYBE WE COULD TURN OFF THE STRESS AND FOR THE FIRST TIME IN FOREVER...

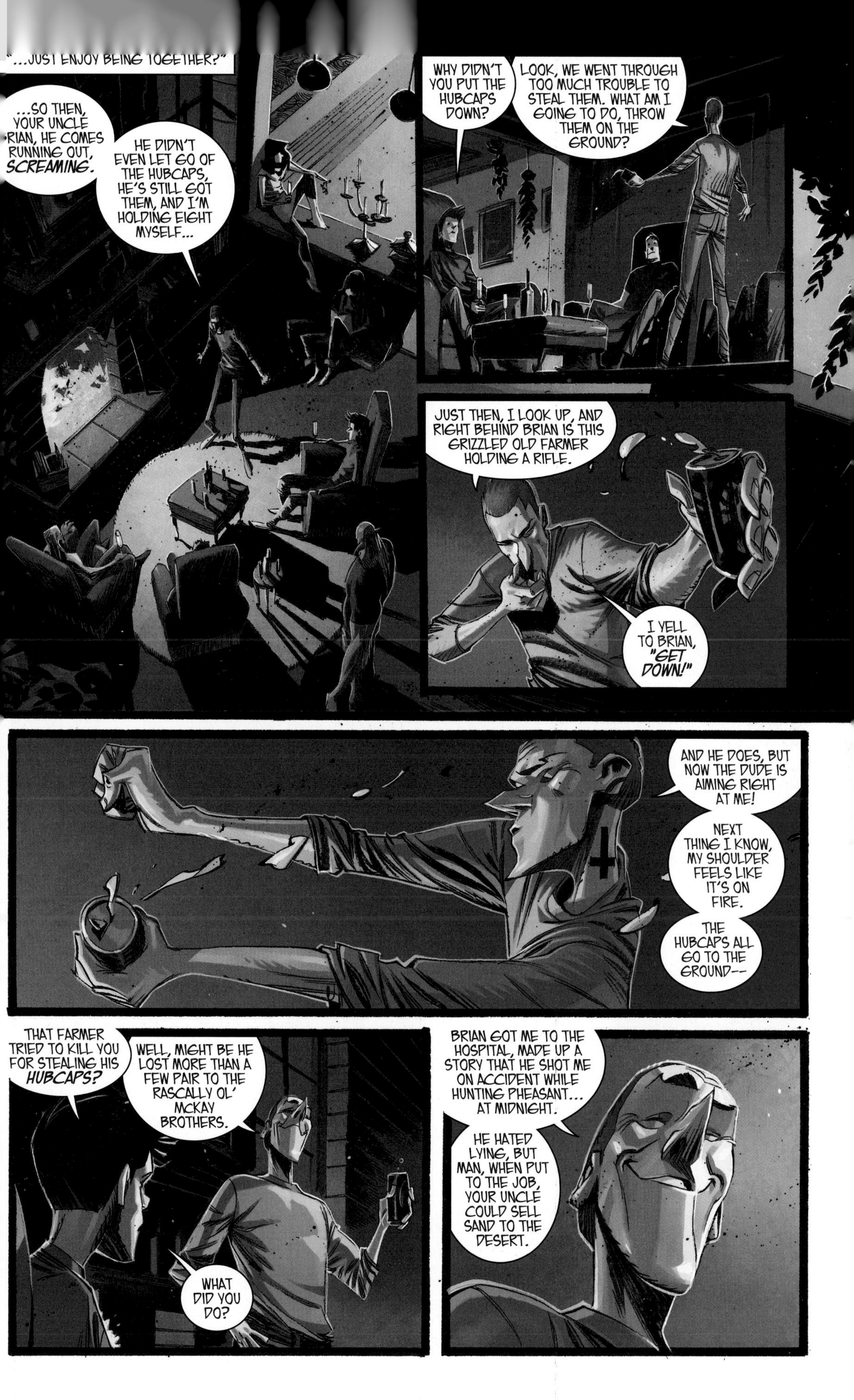
"...JUST ENJOY BEING TOGETHER?"
...SO THEN, YOUR UNCLE BRIAN, HE COMES RUNNING OUT, SCREAMING.
HE DIDN'T EVEN LET GO OF THE HUBCAPS, HE'S STILL GOT THEM, AND I'M HOLDING EIGHT MYSELF...
WHY DIDN'T YOU PUT THE HUBCAPS DOWN?
LOOK, WE WENT THROUGH TOO MUCH TROUBLE TO STEAL THEM. WHAT AM I GOING TO DO, THROW THEM ON THE GROUND?
JUST THEN, I LOOK UP, AND RIGHT BEHIND BRIAN IS THIS GRIZZLED OLD FARMER HOLDING A RIFLE.
I YELL TO BRIAN, "GET DOWN!"
AND HE DOES, BUT NOW THE DUDE IS AIMING RIGHT AT ME!
NEXT THING I KNOW, MY SHOULDER FEELS LIKE IT'S ON FIRE.
THE HUBCAPS ALL GO TO THE GROUND--
THAT FARMER TRIED TO KILL YOU FOR STEALING HIS HUBCAPS?
WELL, MIGHT BE HE LOST MORE THAN A FEW PAIR TO THE RASCALLY OL' MCKAY BROTHERS.
WHAT DID YOU DO?
BRIAN GOT ME TO THE HOSPITAL, MADE UP A STORY THAT HE SHOT ME ON ACCIDENT WHILE HUNTING PHEASANT... AT MIDNIGHT.
HE HATED LYING, BUT MAN, WHEN PUT TO THE JOB, YOUR UNCLE COULD SELL SAND TO THE DESERT.

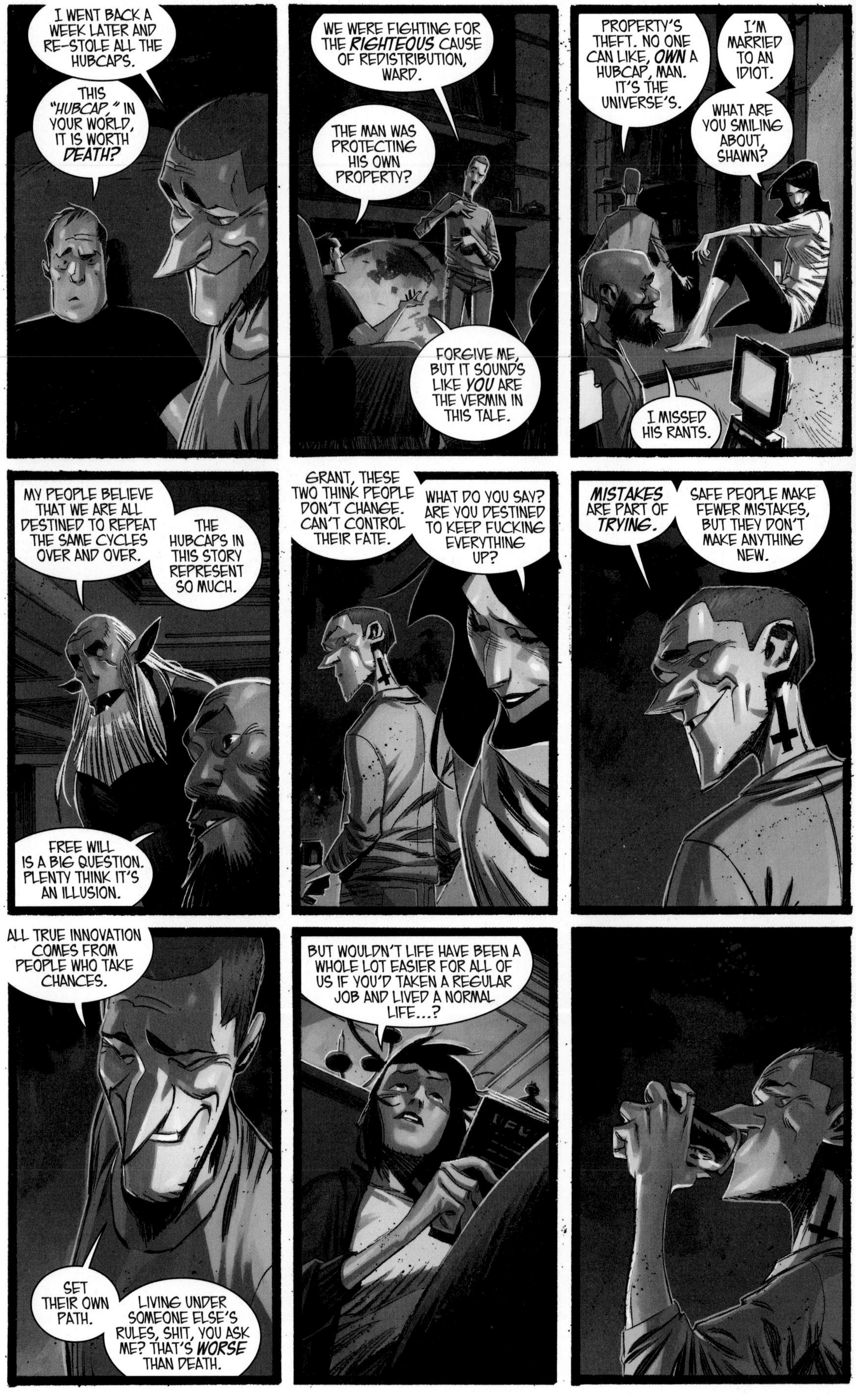
I WENT BACK A WEEK LATER AND RE-STOLE ALL THE HUBCAPS.
THIS "HUBCAP," IN YOUR WORLD, IT IS WORTH *DEATH?*
WE WERE FIGHTING FOR THE *RIGHTEOUS* CAUSE OF REDISTRIBUTION, WARD.
THE MAN WAS PROTECTING HIS OWN PROPERTY?
FORGIVE ME, BUT IT SOUNDS LIKE *YOU* ARE THE VERMIN IN THIS TALE.
PROPERTY'S THEFT. NO ONE CAN LIKE, *OWN* A HUBCAP, MAN. IT'S THE UNIVERSE'S.
I'M MARRIED TO AN IDIOT.
WHAT ARE YOU SMILING ABOUT, SHAWN?
I MISSED HIS RANTS.
MY PEOPLE BELIEVE THAT WE ARE ALL DESTINED TO REPEAT THE SAME CYCLES OVER AND OVER.
THE HUBCAPS IN THIS STORY REPRESENT SO MUCH.
FREE WILL IS A BIG QUESTION. PLENTY THINK IT'S AN ILLUSION.
GRANT, THESE TWO THINK PEOPLE DON'T CHANGE. CAN'T CONTROL THEIR FATE.
WHAT DO YOU SAY? ARE YOU DESTINED TO KEEP FUCKING EVERYTHING UP?
MISTAKES ARE PART OF *TRYING.*
SAFE PEOPLE MAKE FEWER MISTAKES, BUT THEY DON'T MAKE ANYTHING NEW.
ALL TRUE INNOVATION COMES FROM PEOPLE WHO TAKE CHANCES.
SET THEIR OWN PATH.
LIVING UNDER SOMEONE ELSE'S RULES, SHIT, YOU ASK ME? THAT'S *WORSE* THAN DEATH.
BUT WOULDN'T LIFE HAVE BEEN A WHOLE LOT EASIER FOR ALL OF US IF YOU'D TAKEN A REGULAR JOB AND LIVED A NORMAL LIFE...?

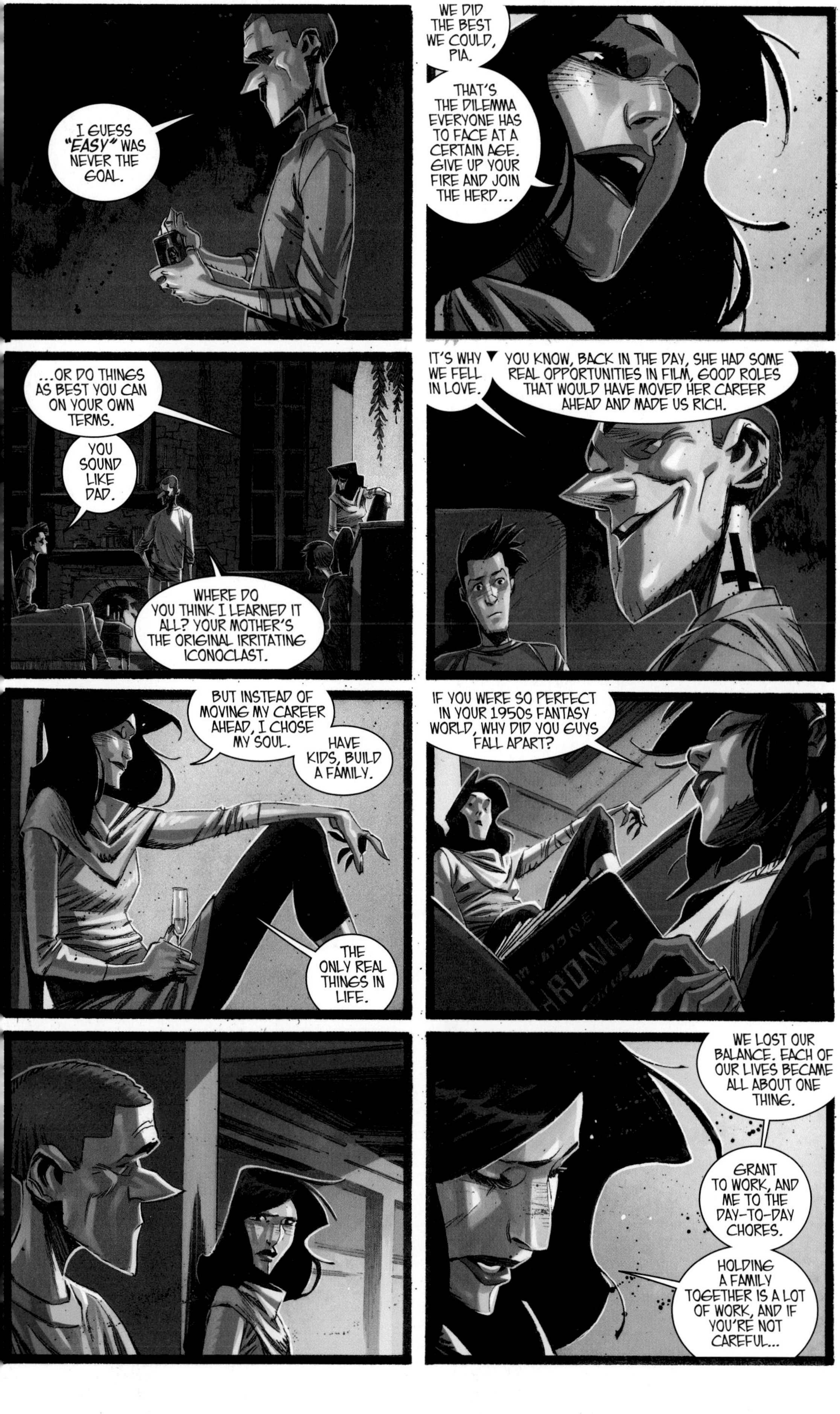
I GUESS "EASY" WAS NEVER THE GOAL.
WE DID THE BEST WE COULD, PIA.
THAT'S THE DILEMMA EVERYONE HAS TO FACE AT A CERTAIN AGE. GIVE UP YOUR FIRE AND JOIN THE HERD...
...OR DO THINGS AS BEST YOU CAN ON YOUR OWN TERMS.
YOU SOUND LIKE DAD.
WHERE DO YOU THINK I LEARNED IT ALL? YOUR MOTHER'S THE ORIGINAL IRRITATING ICONOCLAST.
IT'S WHY WE FELL IN LOVE.
YOU KNOW, BACK IN THE DAY, SHE HAD SOME REAL OPPORTUNITIES IN FILM, GOOD ROLES THAT WOULD HAVE MOVED HER CAREER AHEAD AND MADE US RICH.
BUT INSTEAD OF MOVING MY CAREER AHEAD, I CHOSE MY SOUL.
HAVE KIDS, BUILD A FAMILY.
THE ONLY REAL THINGS IN LIFE.
IF YOU WERE SO PERFECT IN YOUR 1950s FANTASY WORLD, WHY DID YOU GUYS FALL APART?
WE LOST OUR BALANCE. EACH OF OUR LIVES BECAME ALL ABOUT ONE THING.
GRANT TO WORK, AND ME TO THE DAY-TO-DAY CHORES.
HOLDING A FAMILY TOGETHER IS A LOT OF WORK, AND IF YOU'RE NOT CAREFUL...

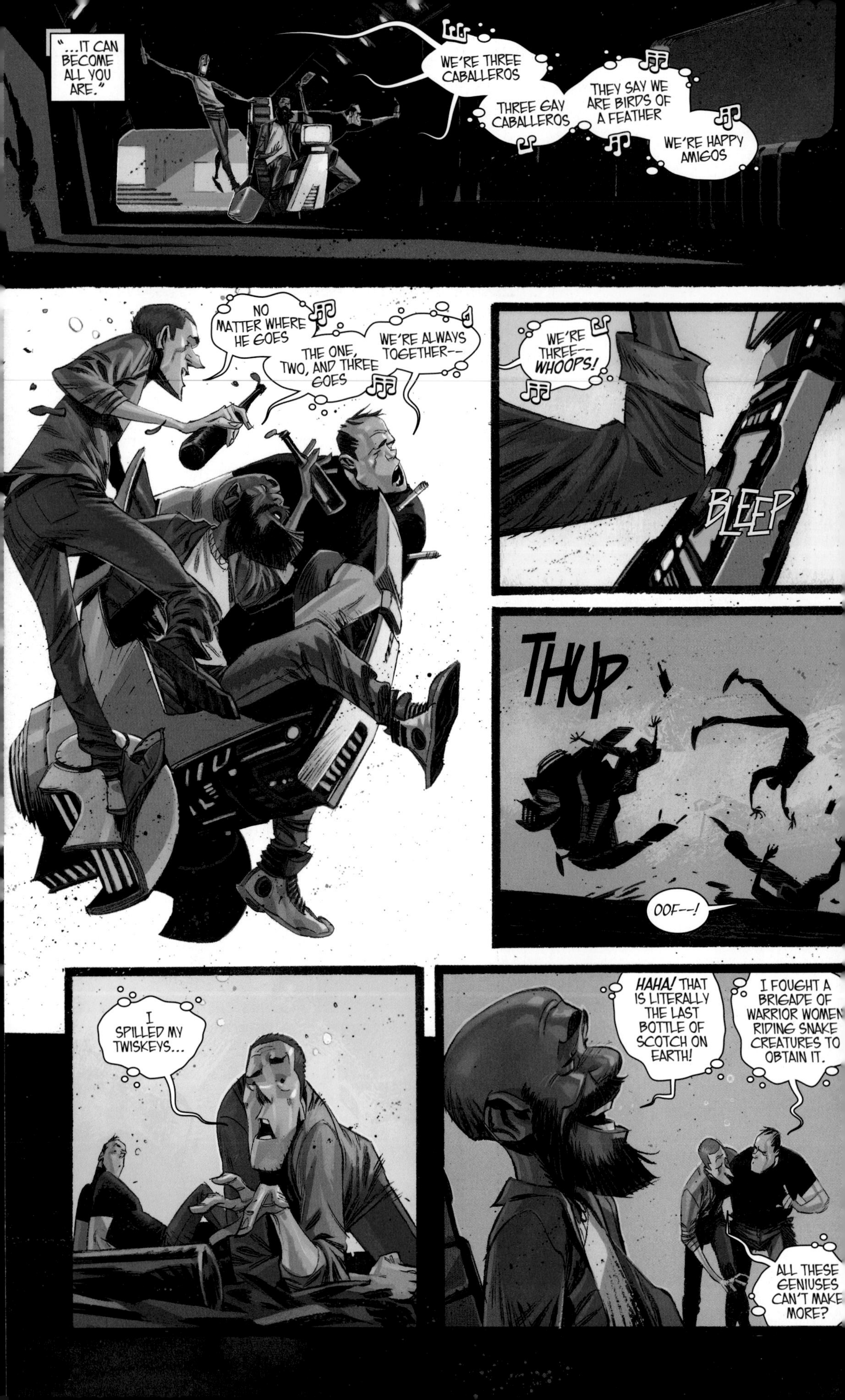

"...IT CAN BECOME ALL YOU ARE."
WE'RE THREE CABALLEROS
THREE GAY CABALLEROS
THEY SAY WE ARE BIRDS OF A FEATHER
WE'RE HAPPY AMIGOS
NO MATTER WHERE HE GOES
THE ONE, TWO, AND THREE GOES
WE'RE ALWAYS TOGETHER--
WE'RE THREE-- WHOOPS!
BLEEP
THUP
OOF--!
I SPILLED MY TWISKEYS...
HAHA! THAT IS LITERALLY THE LAST BOTTLE OF SCOTCH ON EARTH!
I FOUGHT A BRIGADE OF WARRIOR WOMEN RIDING SNAKE CREATURES TO OBTAIN IT.
ALL THESE GENIUSES CAN'T MAKE MORE?

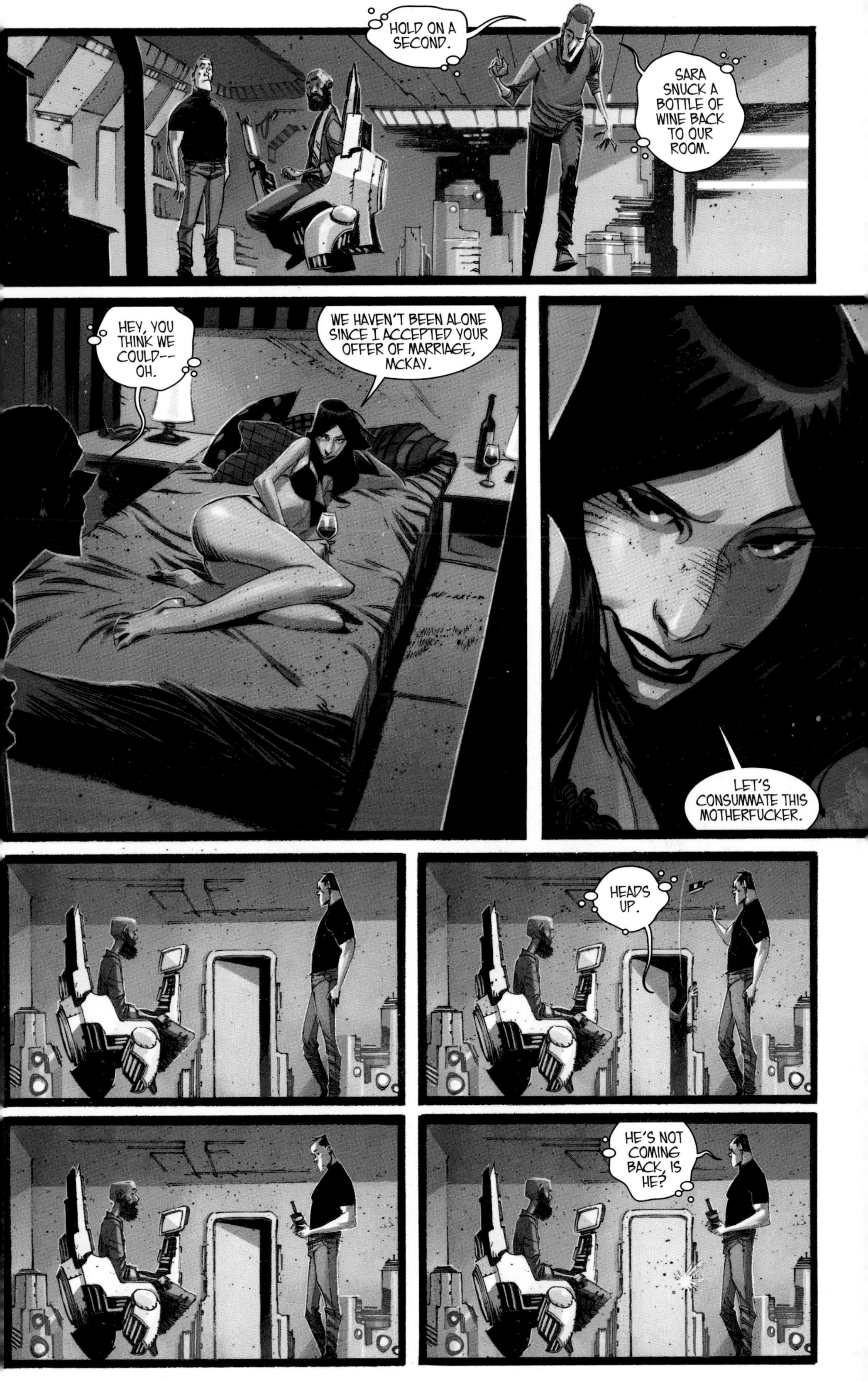

HOLD ON A SECOND.
SARA SNUCK A BOTTLE OF WINE BACK TO OUR ROOM.
HEY, YOU THINK WE COULD-- OH.
WE HAVEN'T BEEN ALONE SINCE I ACCEPTED YOUR OFFER OF MARRIAGE, MCKAY.
LET'S CONSUMMATE THIS MOTHERFUCKER.
HEADS UP.
HE'S NOT COMING BACK, IS HE?

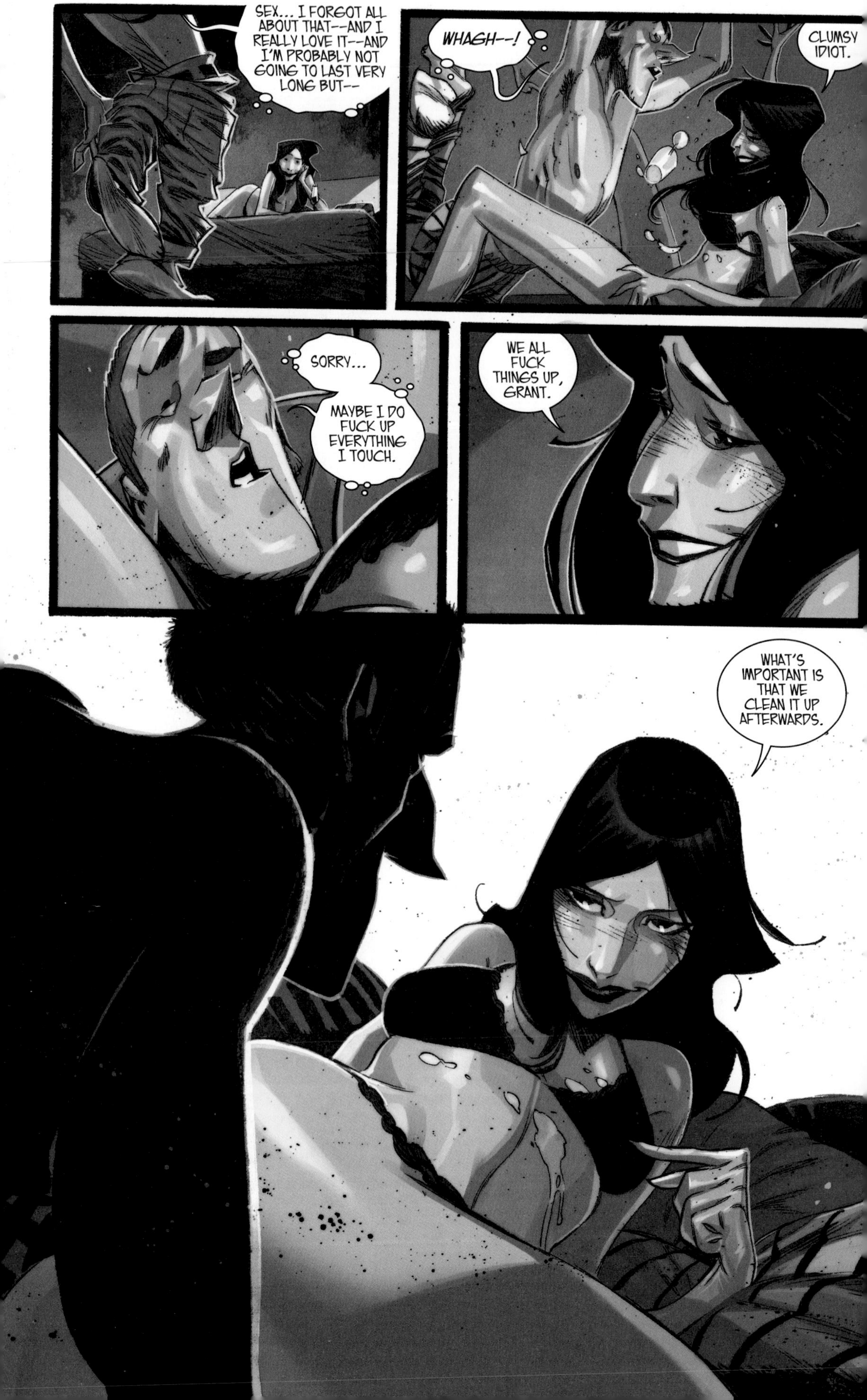
SEX... I FORGOT ALL ABOUT THAT--AND I REALLY LOVE IT--AND I'M PROBABLY NOT GOING TO LAST VERY LONG BUT--
WHAGH--!
CLUMSY IDIOT.
SORRY...
MAYBE I DO FUCK UP EVERYTHING I TOUCH.
WE ALL FUCK THINGS UP, GRANT.
WHAT'S IMPORTANT IS THAT WE CLEAN IT UP AFTERWARDS.

40

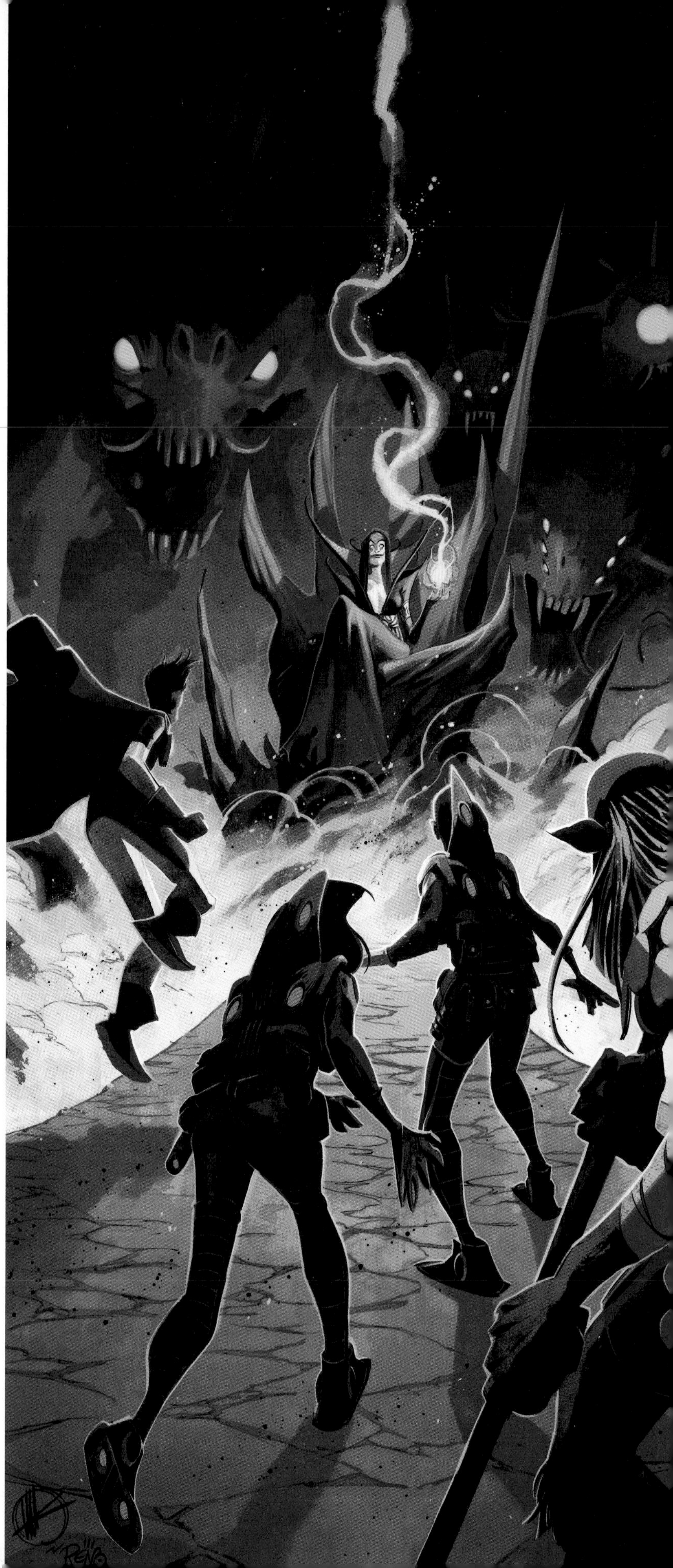

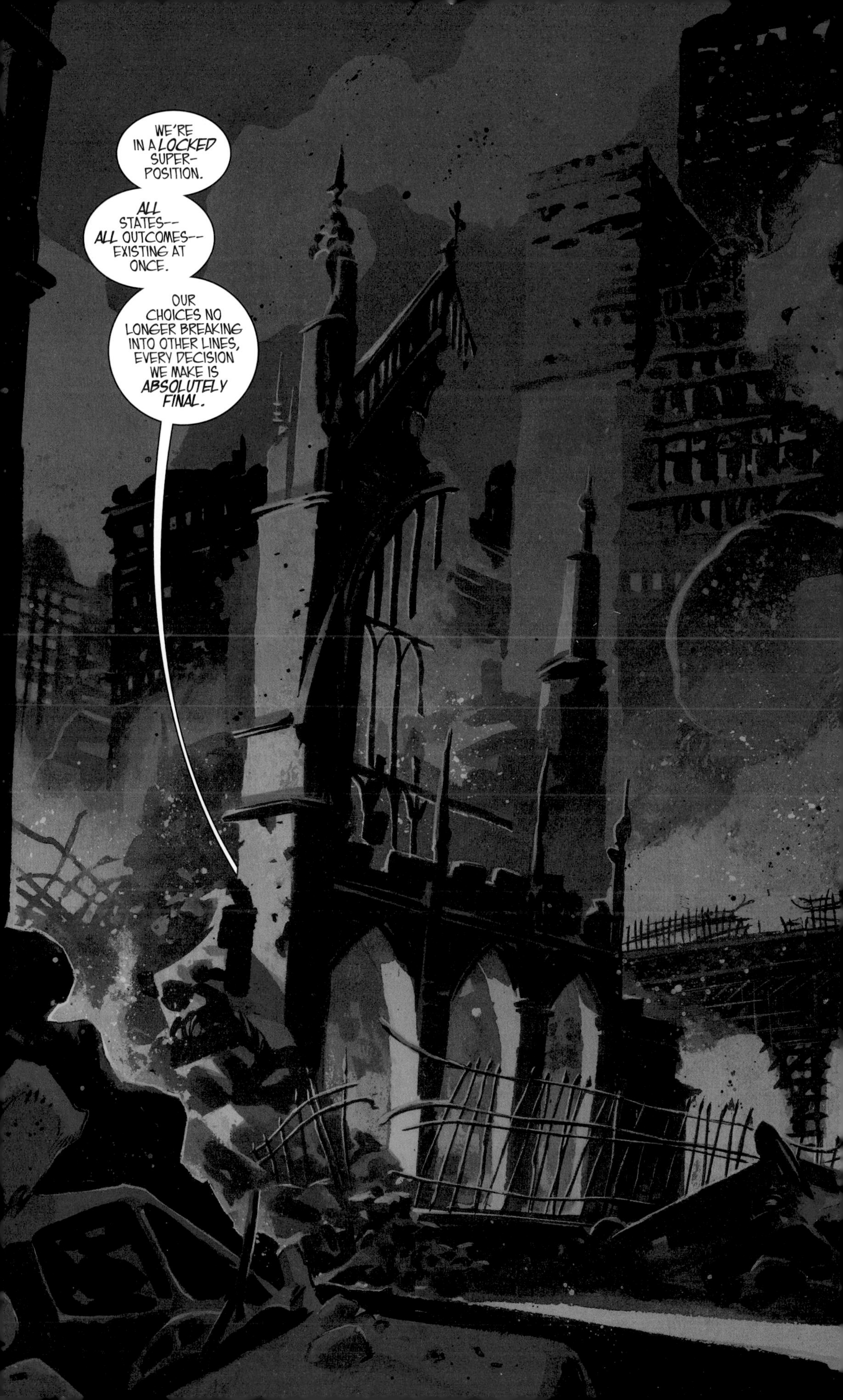
WE'RE IN A LOCKED SUPER-POSITION.
ALL STATES-- ALL OUTCOMES-- EXISTING AT ONCE.
OUR CHOICES NO LONGER BREAKING INTO OTHER LINES, EVERY DECISION WE MAKE IS ABSOLUTELY FINAL.

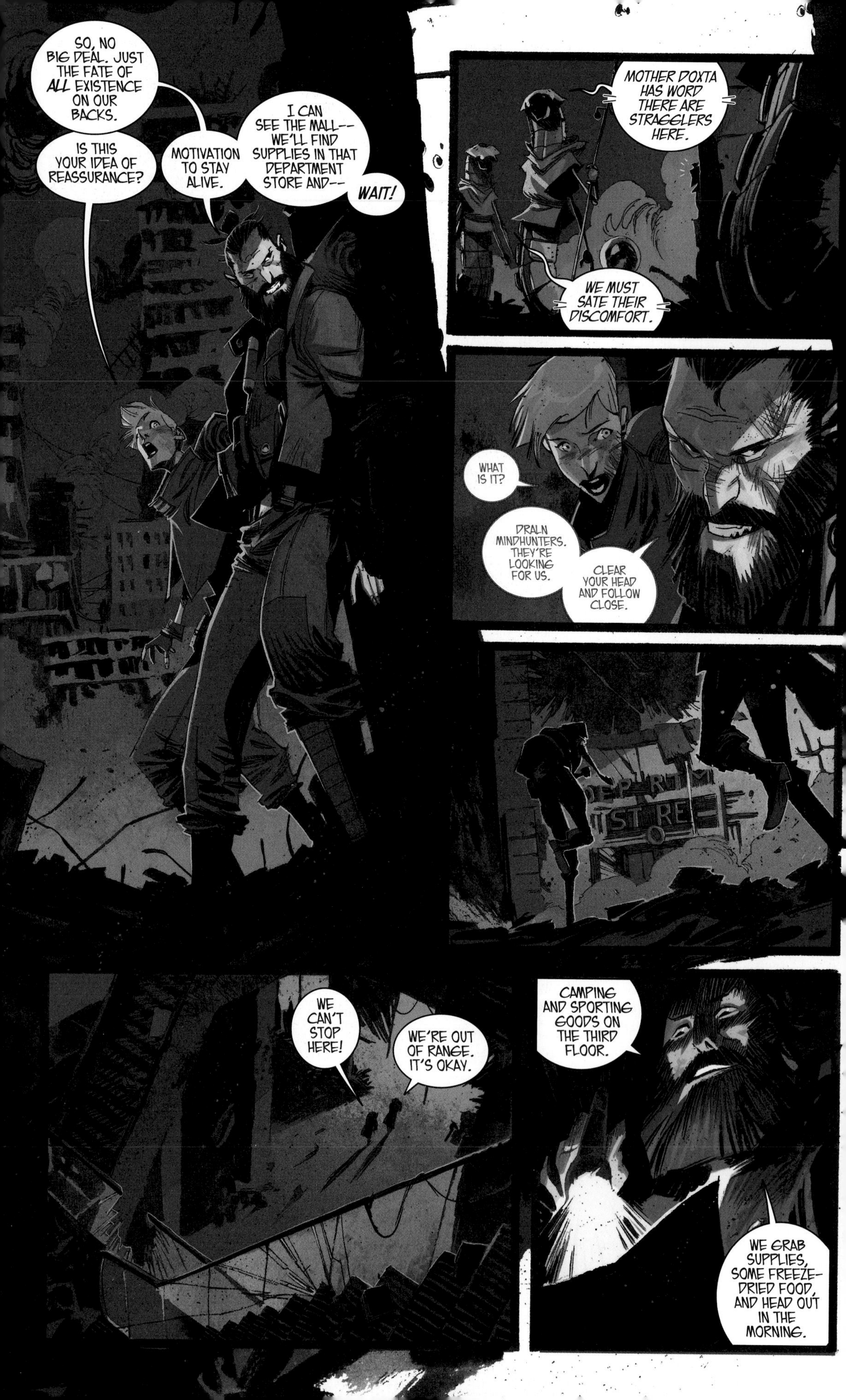
SO, NO BIG DEAL. JUST THE FATE OF ALL EXISTENCE ON OUR BACKS.
IS THIS YOUR IDEA OF REASSURANCE?
MOTIVATION TO STAY ALIVE.
I CAN SEE THE MALL-- WE'LL FIND SUPPLIES IN THAT DEPARTMENT STORE AND--
WAIT!
MOTHER DOXTA HAS WORD THERE ARE STRAGGLERS HERE.
WE MUST SATE THEIR DISCOMFORT.
WHAT IS IT?
DRALN MINDHUNTERS. THEY'RE LOOKING FOR US.
CLEAR YOUR HEAD AND FOLLOW CLOSE.
WE CAN'T STOP HERE!
WE'RE OUT OF RANGE. IT'S OKAY.
CAMPING AND SPORTING GOODS ON THE THIRD FLOOR.
WE GRAB SUPPLIES, SOME FREEZE-DRIED FOOD, AND HEAD OUT IN THE MORNING.

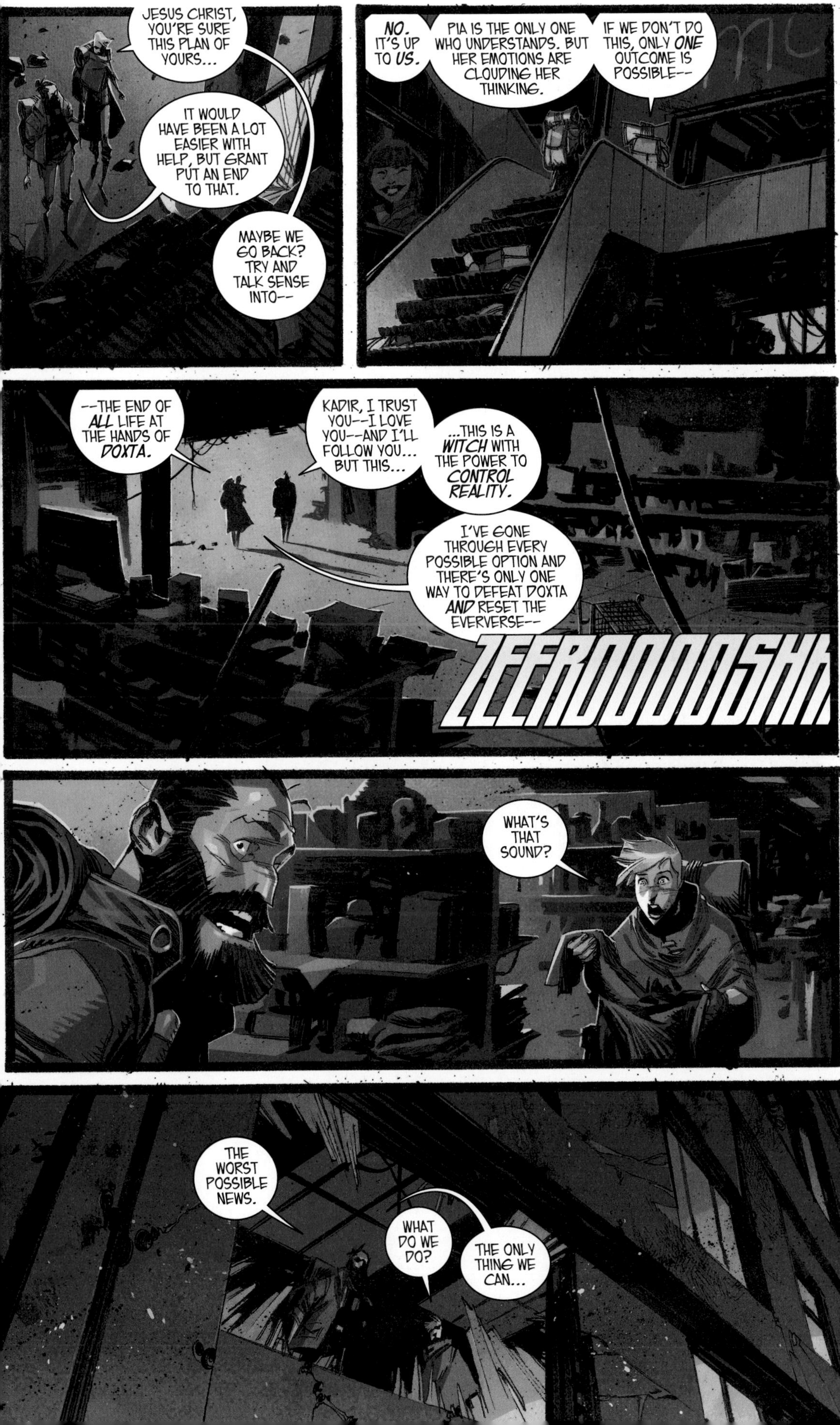
JESUS CHRIST, YOU'RE SURE THIS PLAN OF YOURS...
IT WOULD HAVE BEEN A LOT EASIER WITH HELP, BUT GRANT PUT AN END TO THAT.
MAYBE WE GO BACK? TRY AND TALK SENSE INTO--
NO. IT'S UP TO US.
PIA IS THE ONLY ONE WHO UNDERSTANDS. BUT HER EMOTIONS ARE CLOUDING HER THINKING.
IF WE DON'T DO THIS, ONLY ONE OUTCOME IS POSSIBLE--
--THE END OF ALL LIFE AT THE HANDS OF DOXTA.
KADIR, I TRUST YOU--I LOVE YOU--AND I'LL FOLLOW YOU... BUT THIS...
...THIS IS A WITCH WITH THE POWER TO CONTROL REALITY.
I'VE GONE THROUGH EVERY POSSIBLE OPTION AND THERE'S ONLY ONE WAY TO DEFEAT DOXTA AND RESET THE EVERVERSE--
ZEEROOOOOSHH
WHAT'S THAT SOUND?
THE WORST POSSIBLE NEWS.
WHAT DO WE DO?
THE ONLY THING WE CAN...

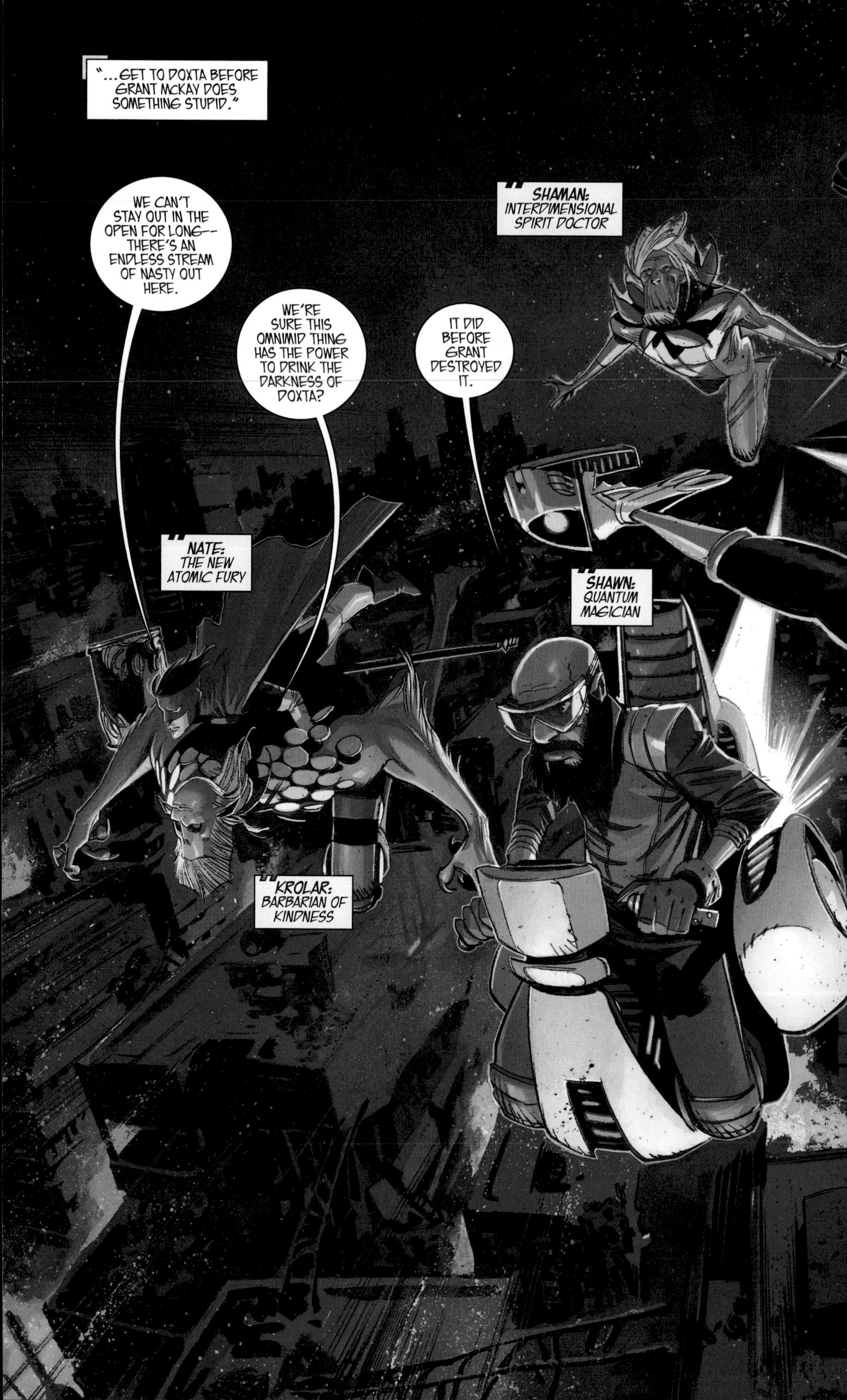
"...GET TO DOXTA BEFORE GRANT McKAY DOES SOMETHING STUPID."
WE CAN'T STAY OUT IN THE OPEN FOR LONG-- THERE'S AN ENDLESS STREAM OF NASTY OUT HERE.
WE'RE SURE THIS OMNIMID THING HAS THE POWER TO DRINK THE DARKNESS OF DOXTA?
IT DID BEFORE GRANT DESTROYED IT.
SHAMAN: INTERDIMENSIONAL SPIRIT DOCTOR
NATE: THE NEW ATOMIC FURY
SHAWN: QUANTUM MAGICIAN
KROLAR: BARBARIAN OF KINDNESS

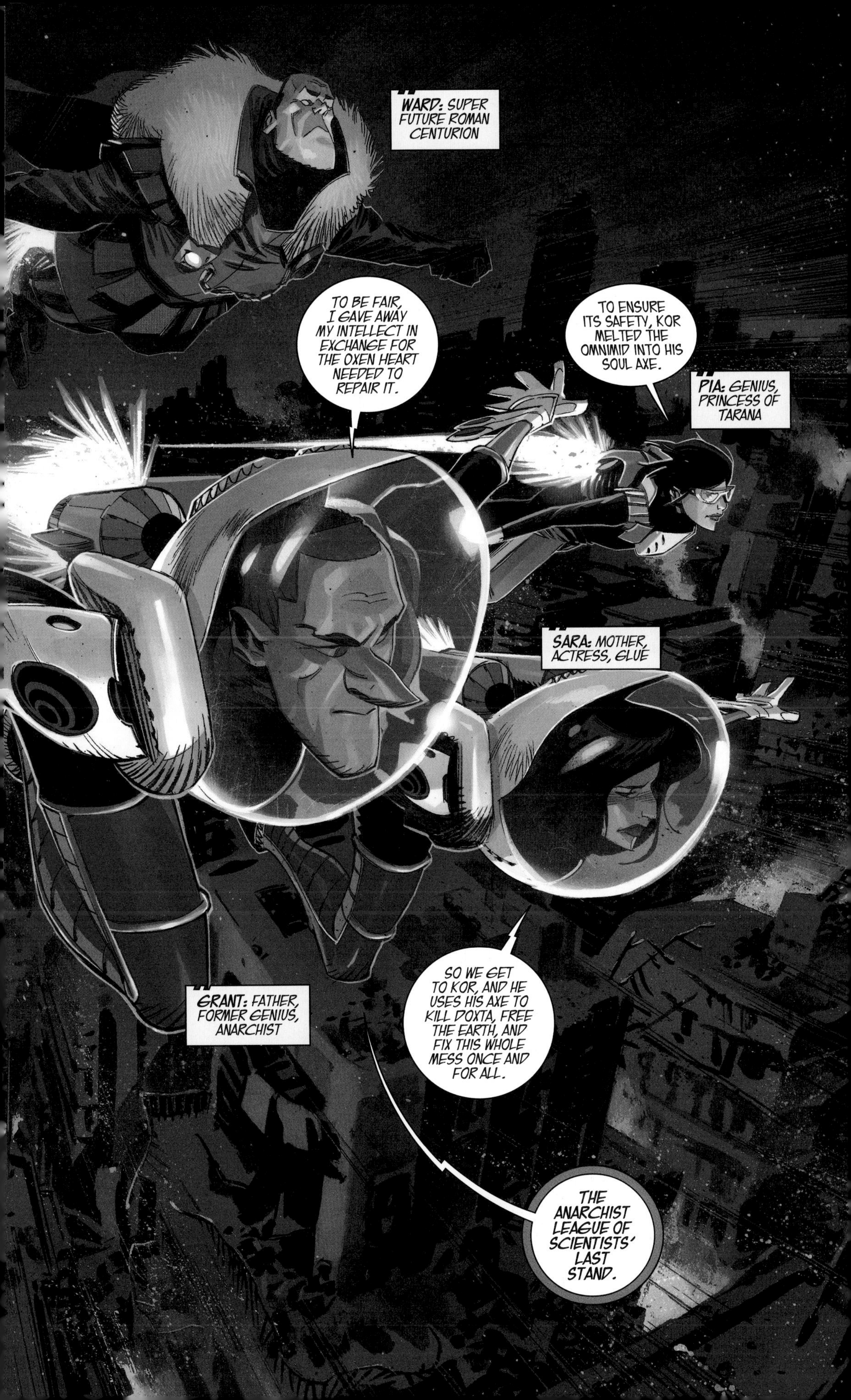
WARD: SUPER FUTURE ROMAN CENTURION
TO BE FAIR, I GAVE AWAY MY INTELLECT IN EXCHANGE FOR THE OXEN HEART NEEDED TO REPAIR IT.
TO ENSURE ITS SAFETY, KOR MELTED THE OMNIMID INTO HIS SOUL AXE.
PIA: GENIUS, PRINCESS OF TARANA
SARA: MOTHER, ACTRESS, GLUE
GRANT: FATHER, FORMER GENIUS, ANARCHIST
SO WE GET TO KOR, AND HE USES HIS AXE TO KILL DOXTA, FREE THE EARTH, AND FIX THIS WHOLE MESS ONCE AND FOR ALL.
THE ANARCHIST LEAGUE OF SCIENTISTS' LAST STAND.

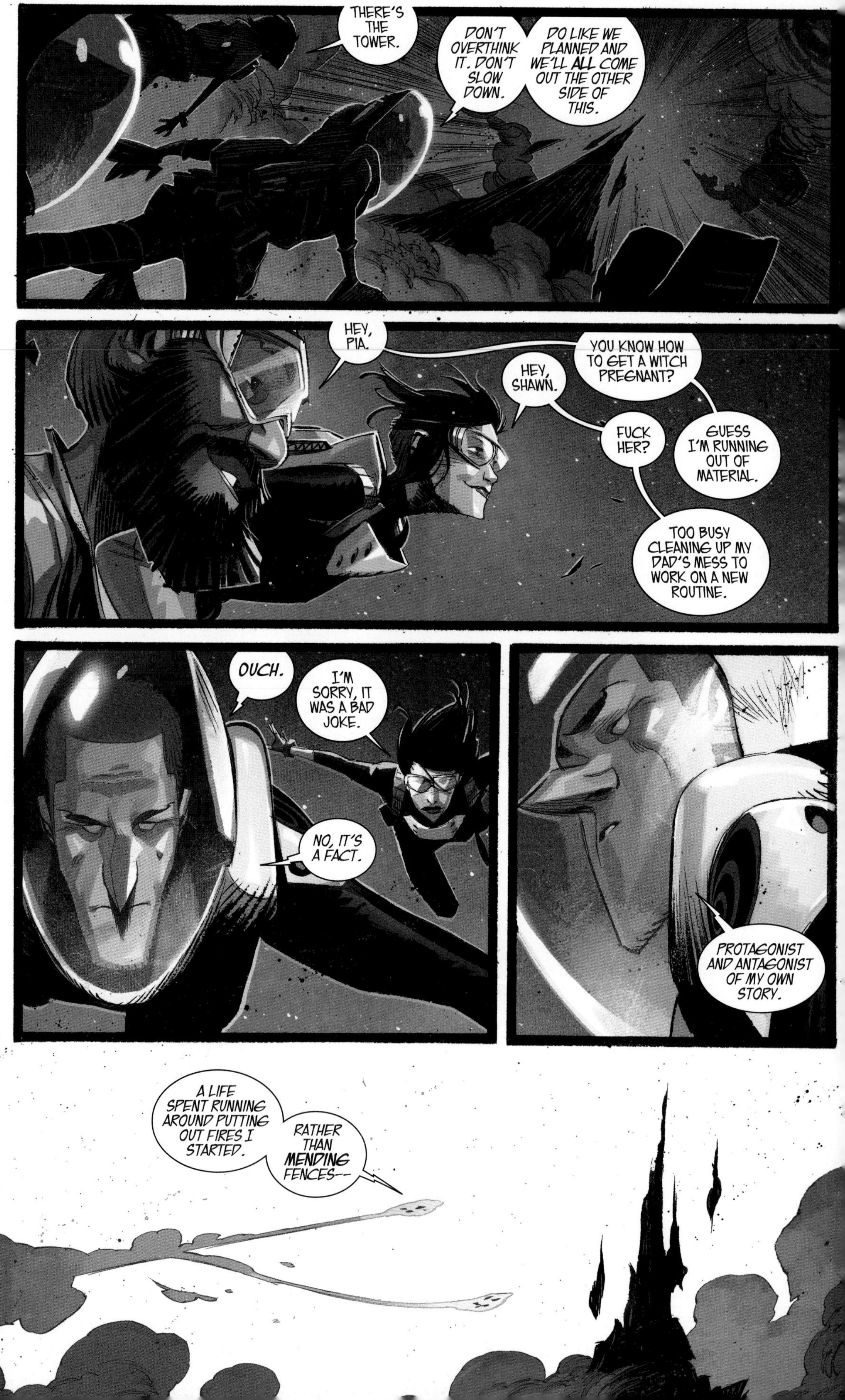
THERE'S THE TOWER.
DON'T OVERTHINK IT. DON'T SLOW DOWN.
DO LIKE WE PLANNED AND WE'LL ALL COME OUT THE OTHER SIDE OF THIS.
HEY, PIA.
YOU KNOW HOW TO GET A WITCH PREGNANT?
HEY, SHAWN.
FUCK HER?
GUESS I'M RUNNING OUT OF MATERIAL.
TOO BUSY CLEANING UP MY DAD'S MESS TO WORK ON A NEW ROUTINE.
OUCH.
I'M SORRY, IT WAS A BAD JOKE.
NO, IT'S A FACT.
PROTAGONIST AND ANTAGONIST OF MY OWN STORY.
A LIFE SPENT RUNNING AROUND PUTTING OUT FIRES I STARTED.
RATHER THAN MENDING FENCES--

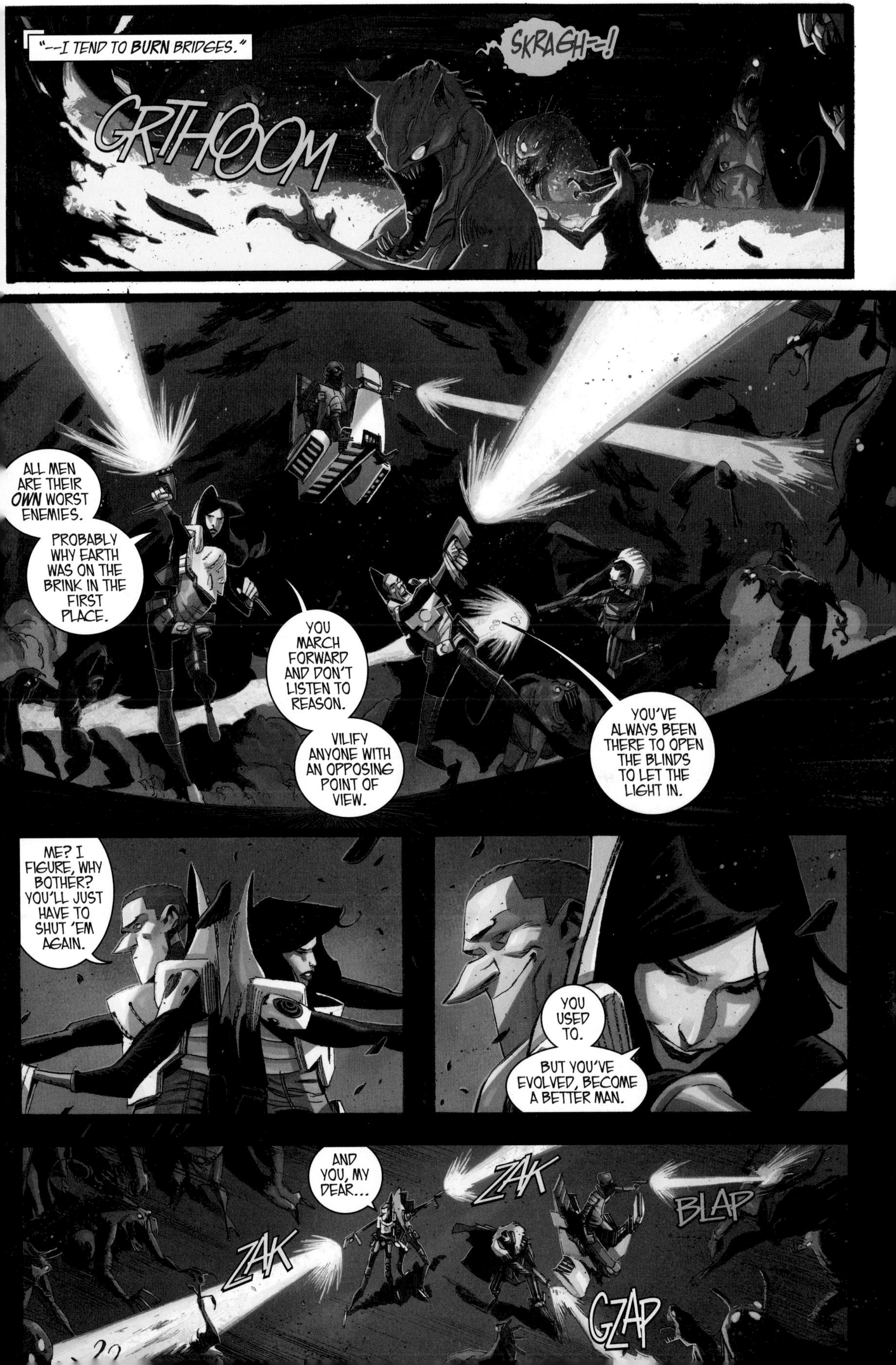
"--I TEND TO BURN BRIDGES."
SKRAGH--!
GRTHOOM
ALL MEN ARE THEIR OWN WORST ENEMIES.
PROBABLY WHY EARTH WAS ON THE BRINK IN THE FIRST PLACE.
YOU MARCH FORWARD AND DON'T LISTEN TO REASON.
VILIFY ANYONE WITH AN OPPOSING POINT OF VIEW.
YOU'VE ALWAYS BEEN THERE TO OPEN THE BLINDS TO LET THE LIGHT IN.
ME? I FIGURE, WHY BOTHER? YOU'LL JUST HAVE TO SHUT 'EM AGAIN.
YOU USED TO.
BUT YOU'VE EVOLVED, BECOME A BETTER MAN.
AND YOU, MY DEAR...
ZAK
BLAP
ZAK
GZAP

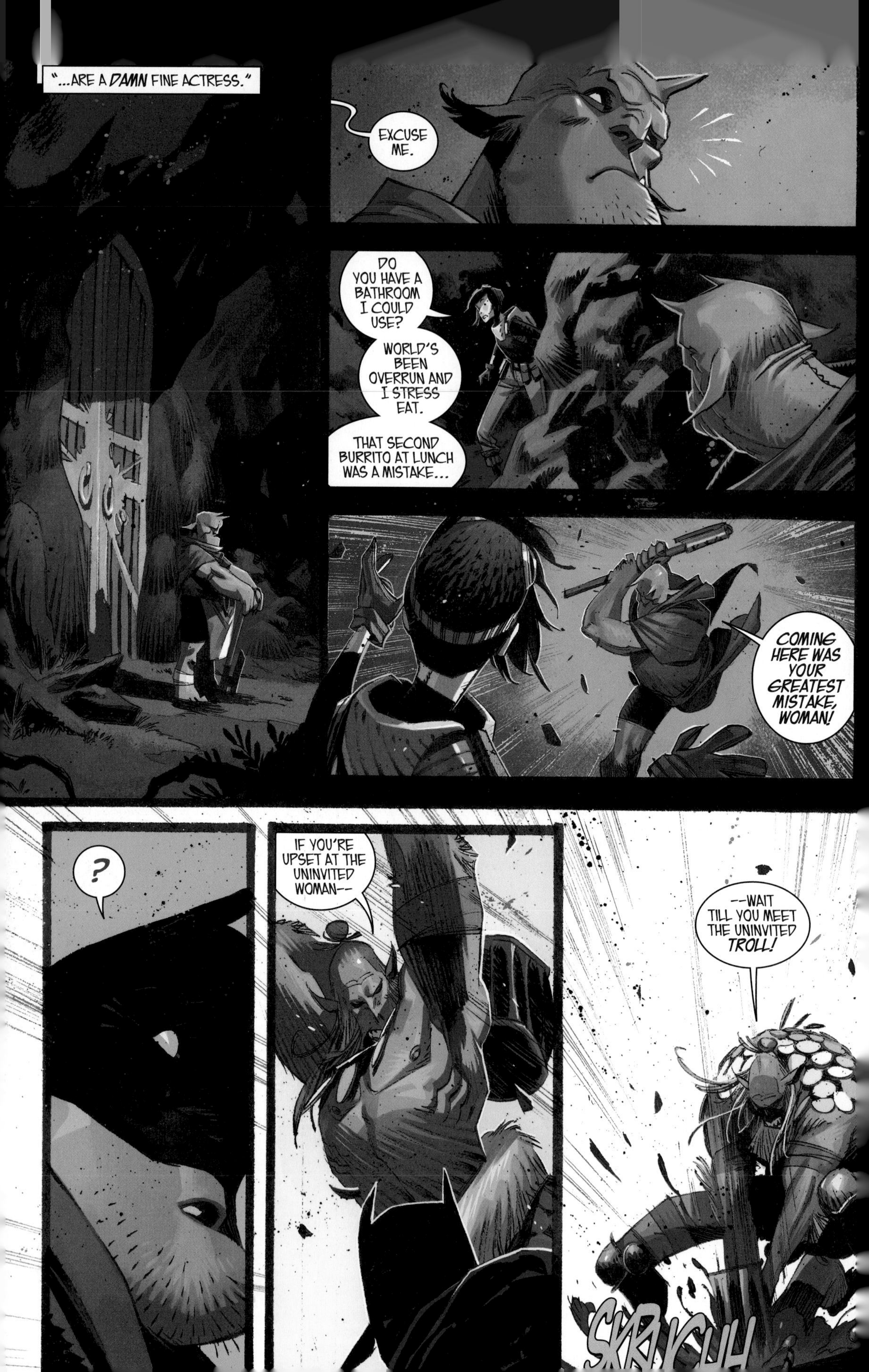
"...ARE A DAMN FINE ACTRESS."
EXCUSE ME.
DO YOU HAVE A BATHROOM I COULD USE?
WORLD'S BEEN OVERRUN AND I STRESS EAT.
THAT SECOND BURRITO AT LUNCH WAS A MISTAKE...
COMING HERE WAS YOUR GREATEST MISTAKE, WOMAN!
?
IF YOU'RE UPSET AT THE UNINVITED WOMAN--
--WAIT TILL YOU MEET THE UNINVITED TROLL!
SKRUNCH

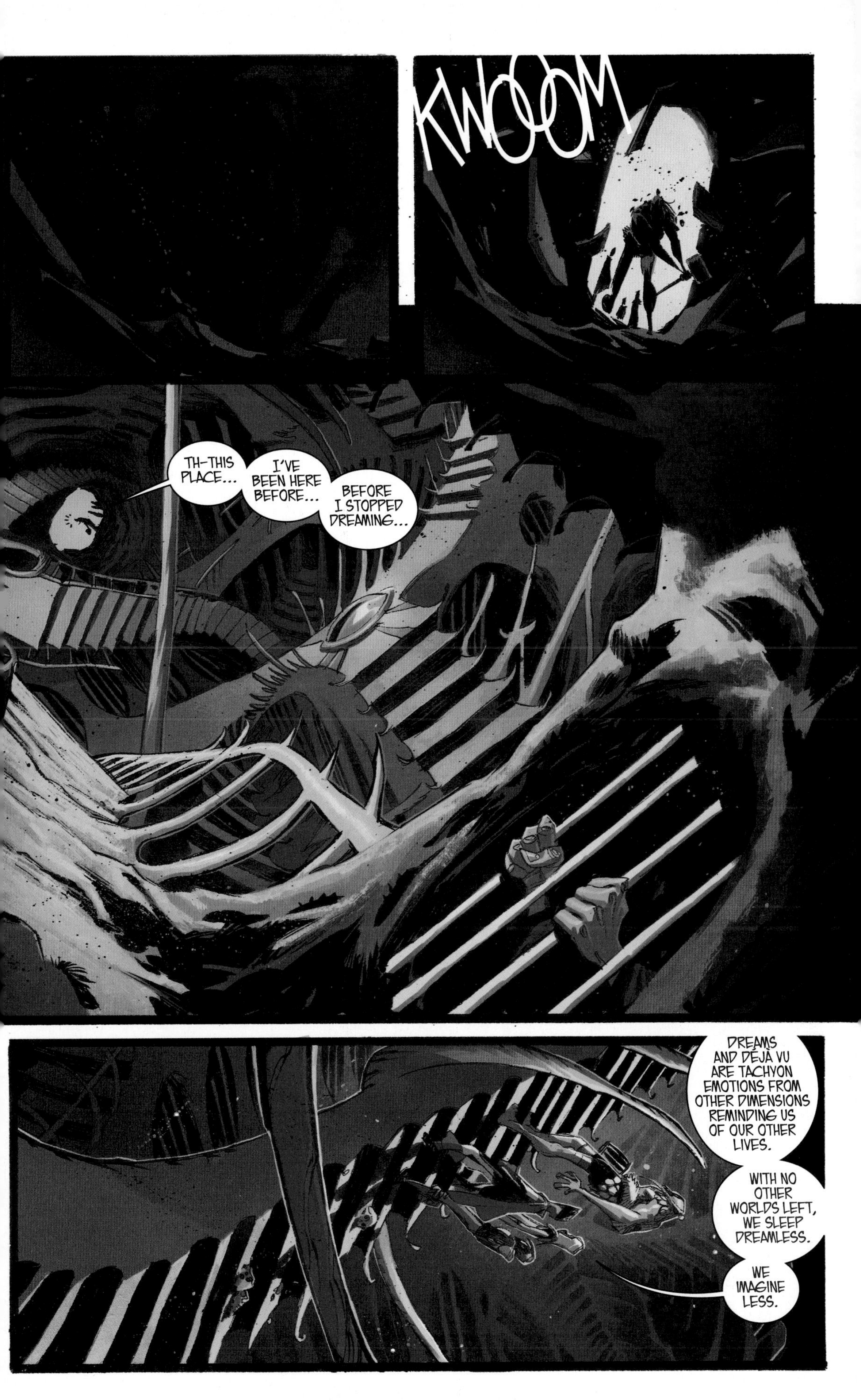
KWOOM
TH-THIS PLACE...
I'VE BEEN HERE BEFORE...
BEFORE I STOPPED DREAMING...
DREAMS AND DÉJÀ VU ARE TACHYON EMOTIONS FROM OTHER DIMENSIONS REMINDING US OF OUR OTHER LIVES.
WITH NO OTHER WORLDS LEFT, WE SLEEP DREAMLESS.
WE IMAGINE LESS.

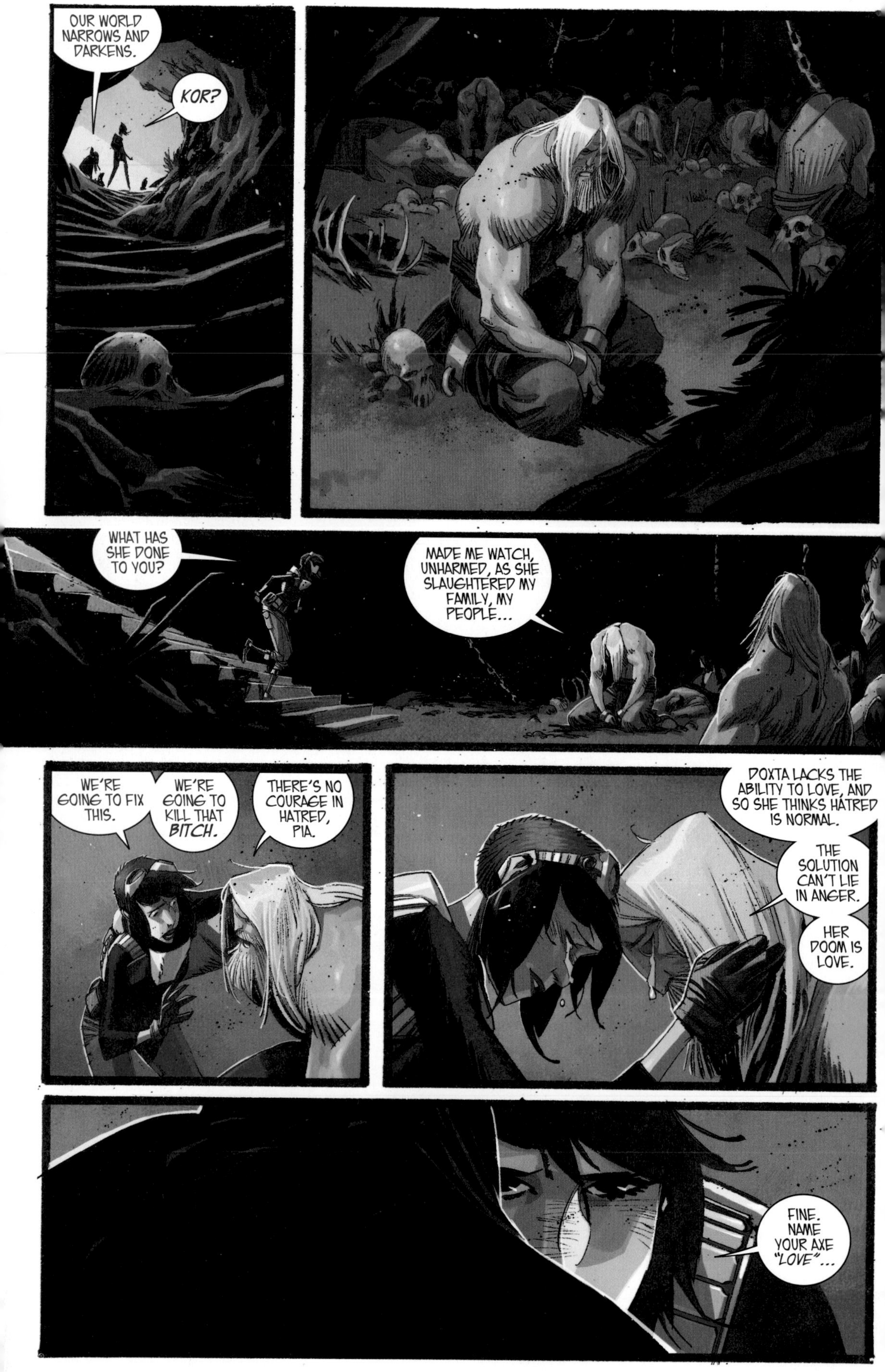
OUR WORLD NARROWS AND DARKENS.
KOR?
WHAT HAS SHE DONE TO YOU?
MADE ME WATCH, UNHARMED, AS SHE SLAUGHTERED MY FAMILY, MY PEOPLE...
WE'RE GOING TO FIX THIS.
WE'RE GOING TO KILL THAT *BITCH*.
THERE'S NO COURAGE IN HATRED, PIA.
DOXTA LACKS THE ABILITY TO LOVE, AND SO SHE THINKS HATRED IS NORMAL.
THE SOLUTION CAN'T LIE IN ANGER.
HER DOOM IS LOVE.
FINE. NAME YOUR AXE *"LOVE"*...

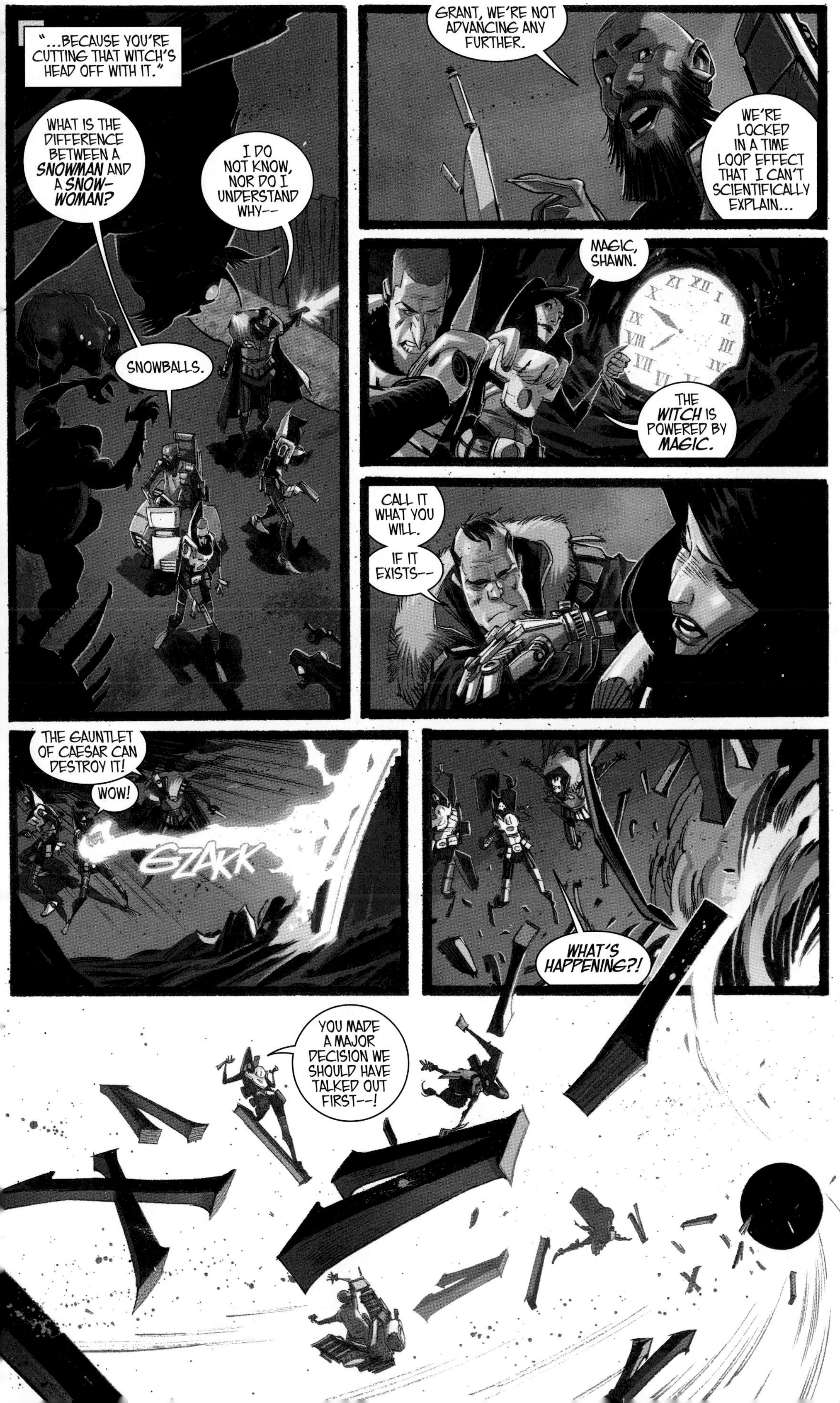
"...BECAUSE YOU'RE CUTTING THAT WITCH'S HEAD OFF WITH IT."
WHAT IS THE DIFFERENCE BETWEEN A SNOWMAN AND A SNOW-WOMAN?
I DO NOT KNOW, NOR DO I UNDERSTAND WHY--
SNOWBALLS.
GRANT, WE'RE NOT ADVANCING ANY FURTHER.
WE'RE LOCKED IN A TIME LOOP EFFECT THAT I CAN'T SCIENTIFICALLY EXPLAIN...
MAGIC, SHAWN.
THE WITCH IS POWERED BY MAGIC.
CALL IT WHAT YOU WILL.
IF IT EXISTS--
THE GAUNTLET OF CAESAR CAN DESTROY IT!
WOW!
GZAKK
WHAT'S HAPPENING?!
YOU MADE A MAJOR DECISION WE SHOULD HAVE TALKED OUT FIRST--!

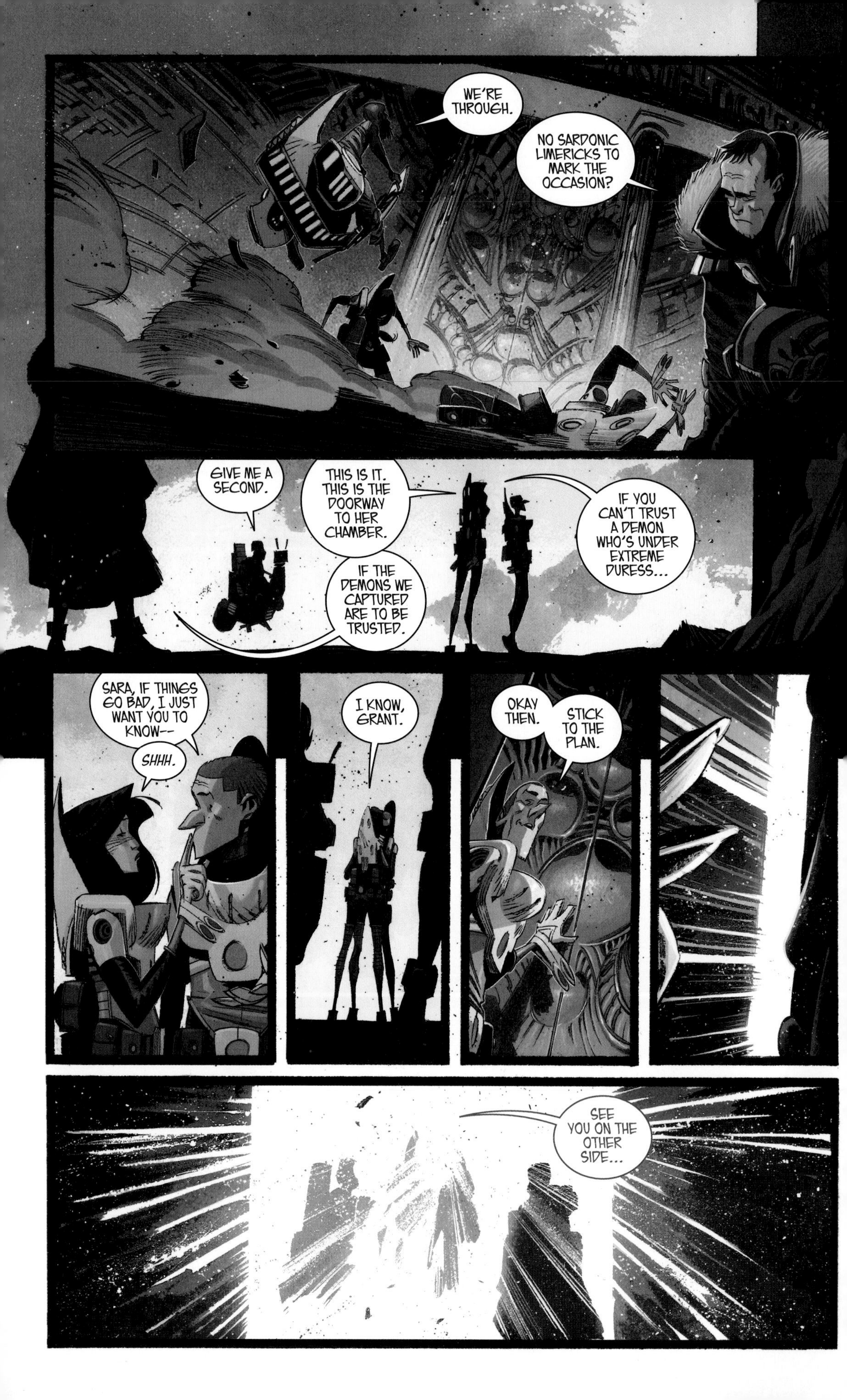
WE'RE THROUGH.
NO SARDONIC LIMERICKS TO MARK THE OCCASION?
GIVE ME A SECOND.
THIS IS IT. THIS IS THE DOORWAY TO HER CHAMBER.
IF THE DEMONS WE CAPTURED ARE TO BE TRUSTED.
IF YOU CAN'T TRUST A DEMON WHO'S UNDER EXTREME DURESS...
SARA, IF THINGS GO BAD, I JUST WANT YOU TO KNOW--
SHHH.
I KNOW, GRANT.
OKAY THEN.
STICK TO THE PLAN.
SEE YOU ON THE OTHER SIDE...

THEY SAY YOU NEVER HEAL.
YOU JUST MOVE ON.

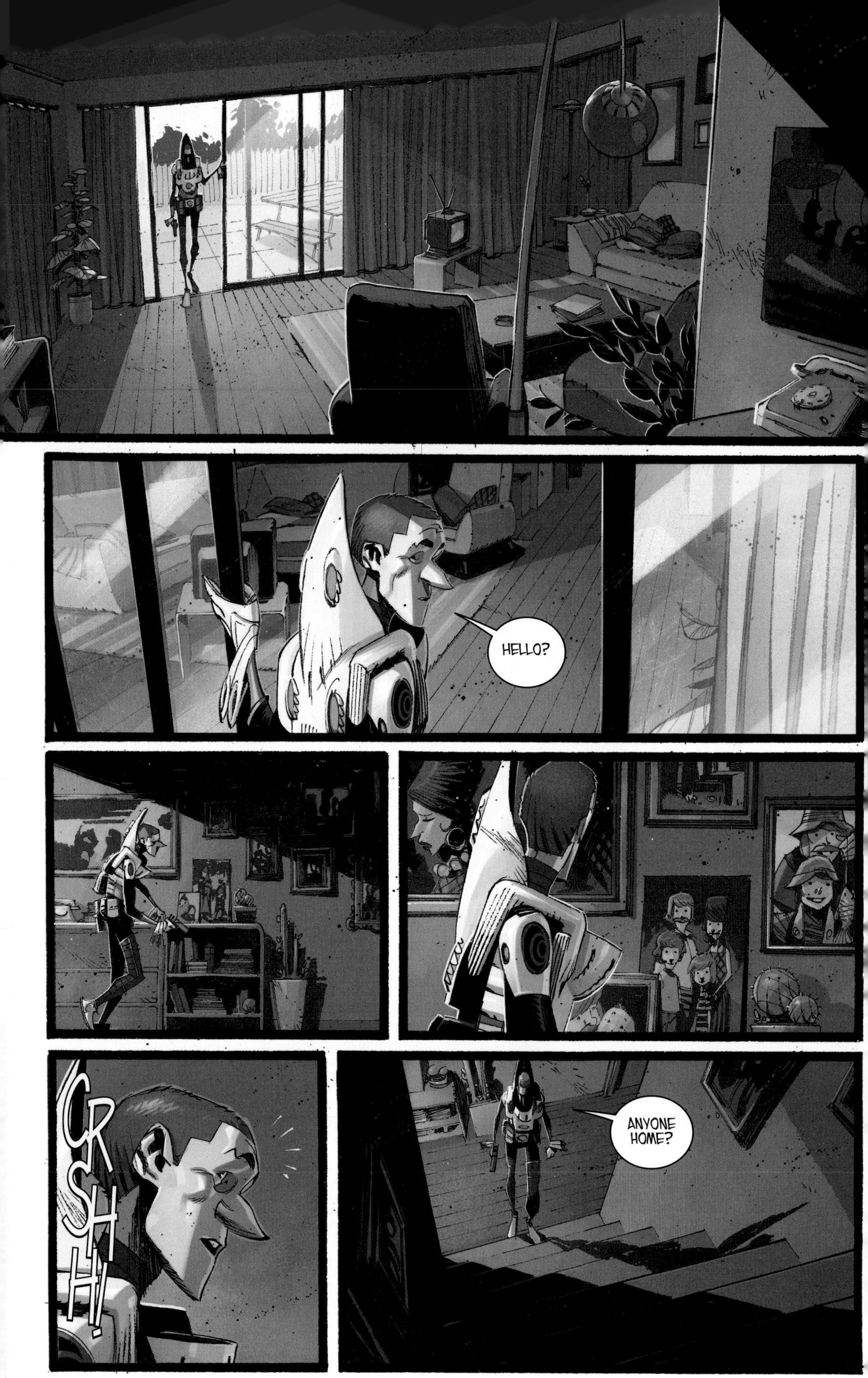
HELLO?
CRSHH!
ANYONE HOME?

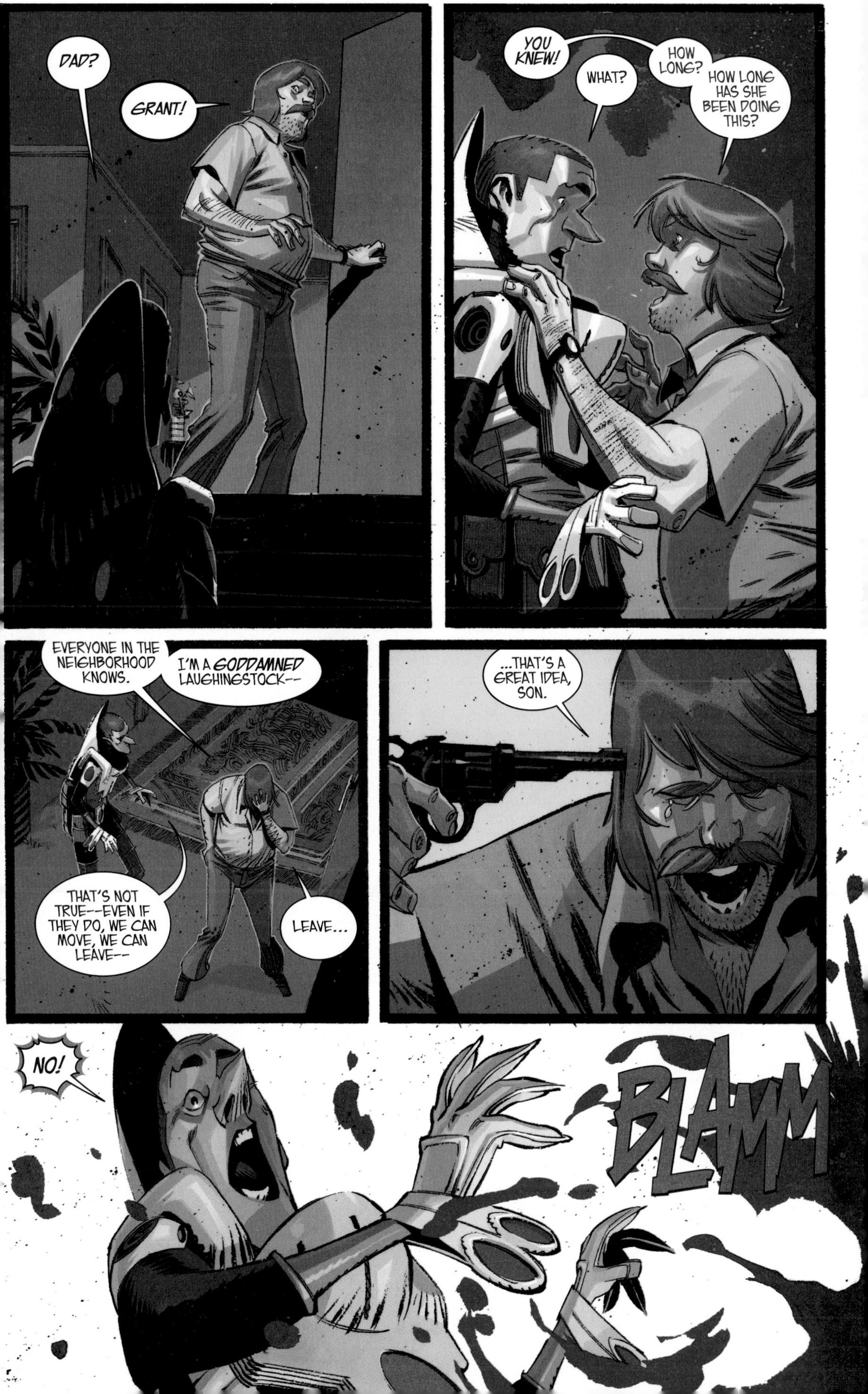
DAD?
GRANT!
YOU KNEW!
WHAT?
HOW LONG?
HOW LONG HAS SHE BEEN DOING THIS?
EVERYONE IN THE NEIGHBORHOOD KNOWS.
I'M A GODDAMNED LAUGHINGSTOCK--
THAT'S NOT TRUE--EVEN IF THEY DO, WE CAN MOVE, WE CAN LEAVE--
LEAVE...
...THAT'S A GREAT IDEA, SON.
NO!
BLAMM

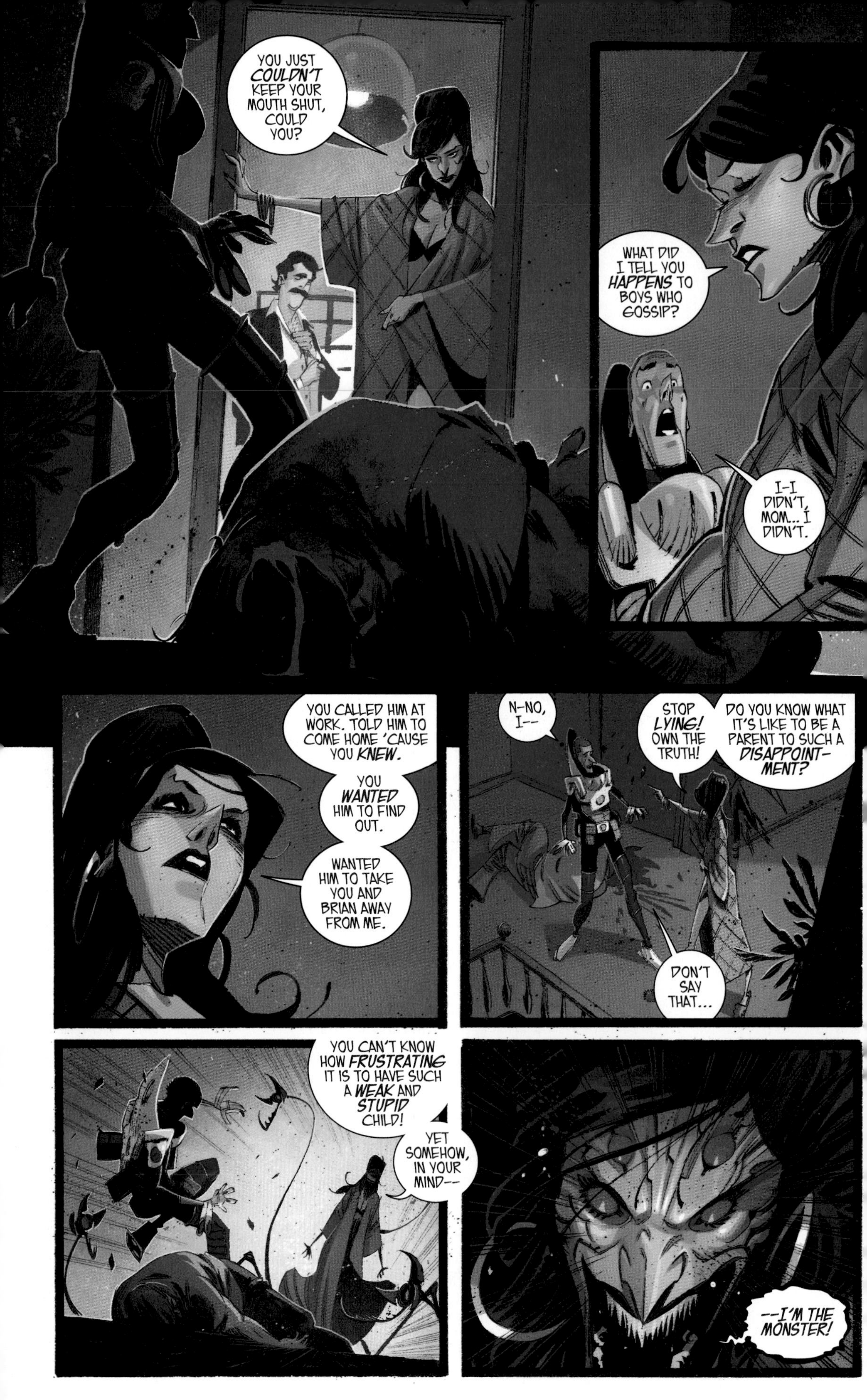
YOU JUST COULDN'T KEEP YOUR MOUTH SHUT, COULD YOU?
WHAT DID I TELL YOU HAPPENS TO BOYS WHO GOSSIP?
I-I DIDN'T, MOM... I DIDN'T.
YOU CALLED HIM AT WORK. TOLD HIM TO COME HOME 'CAUSE YOU KNEW.
YOU WANTED HIM TO FIND OUT.
WANTED HIM TO TAKE YOU AND BRIAN AWAY FROM ME.
N-NO, I--
STOP LYING! OWN THE TRUTH!
DO YOU KNOW WHAT IT'S LIKE TO BE A PARENT TO SUCH A DISAPPOINT-MENT?
DON'T SAY THAT...
YOU CAN'T KNOW HOW FRUSTRATING IT IS TO HAVE SUCH A WEAK AND STUPID CHILD!
YET SOMEHOW, IN YOUR MIND--
--I'M THE MONSTER!

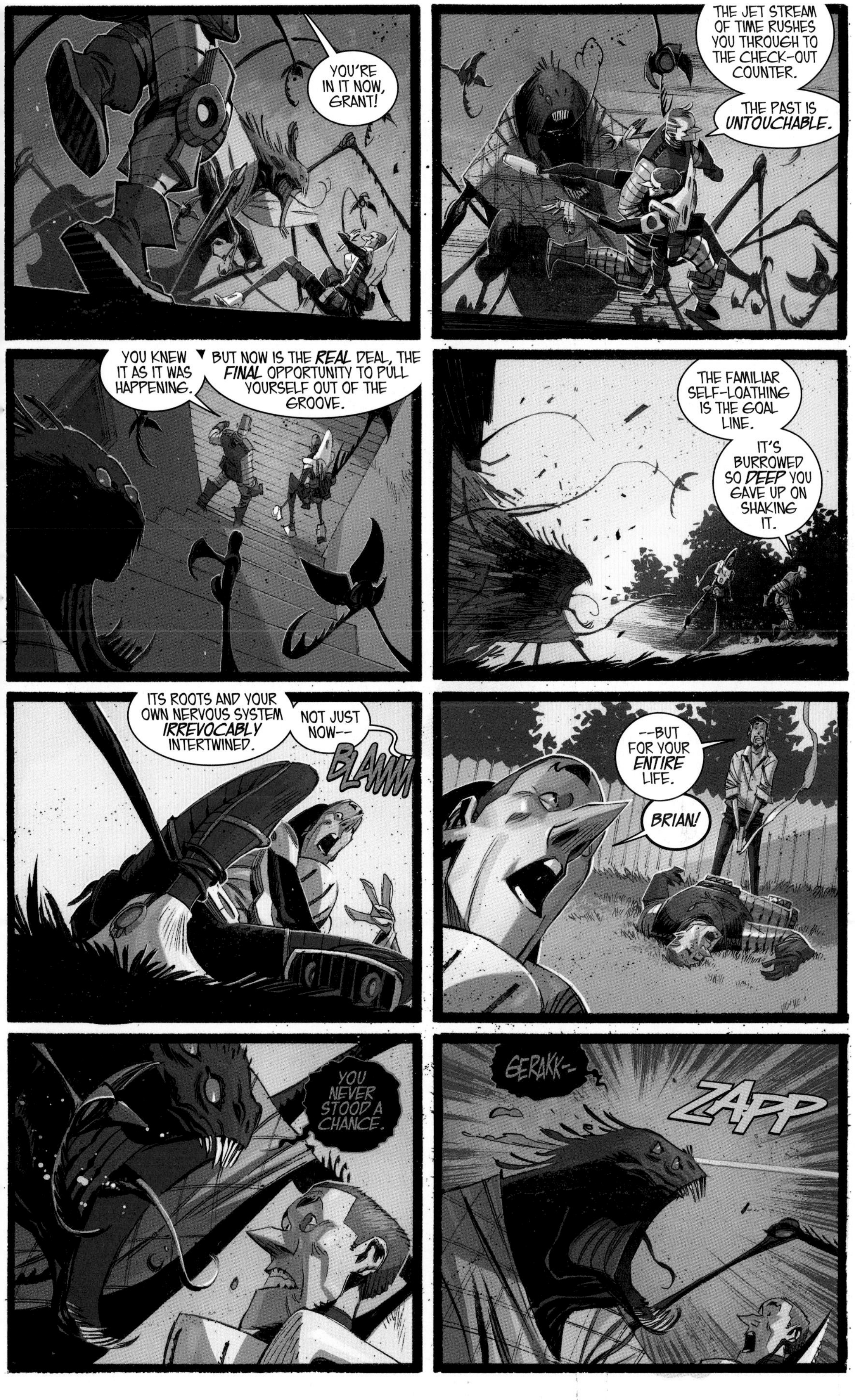
YOU'RE IN IT NOW, GRANT!
THE JET STREAM OF TIME RUSHES YOU THROUGH TO THE CHECK-OUT COUNTER.
THE PAST IS *UNTOUCHABLE.*
YOU KNEW IT AS IT WAS HAPPENING.
BUT NOW IS THE *REAL* DEAL, THE *FINAL* OPPORTUNITY TO PULL YOURSELF OUT OF THE GROOVE.
THE FAMILIAR SELF-LOATHING IS THE GOAL LINE.
IT'S BURROWED SO *DEEP* YOU GAVE UP ON SHAKING IT.
ITS ROOTS AND YOUR OWN NERVOUS SYSTEM *IRREVOCABLY* INTERTWINED.
NOT JUST NOW--
BLAMM
--BUT FOR YOUR *ENTIRE* LIFE.
BRIAN!
YOU NEVER STOOD A CHANCE.
GERAKK--
ZAPP

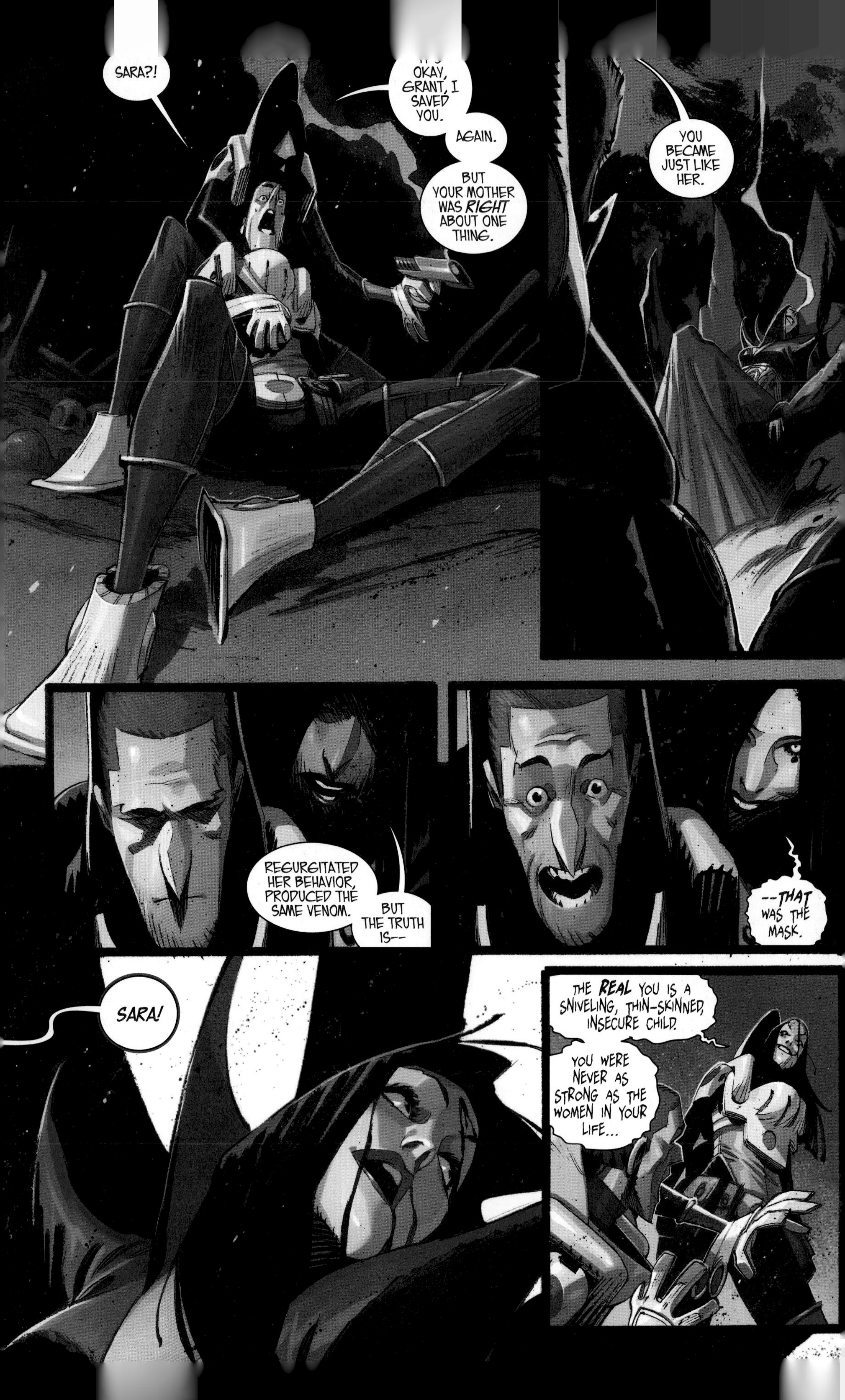
SARA?!
OKAY, GRANT, I SAVED YOU.
AGAIN.
BUT YOUR MOTHER WAS *RIGHT* ABOUT ONE THING.
YOU BECAME JUST LIKE HER.
REGURGITATED HER BEHAVIOR, PRODUCED THE SAME VENOM.
BUT THE TRUTH IS--
--*THAT* WAS THE MASK.
SARA!
THE *REAL* YOU IS A SNIVELING, THIN-SKINNED, INSECURE CHILD.
YOU WERE NEVER AS STRONG AS THE WOMEN IN YOUR LIFE...

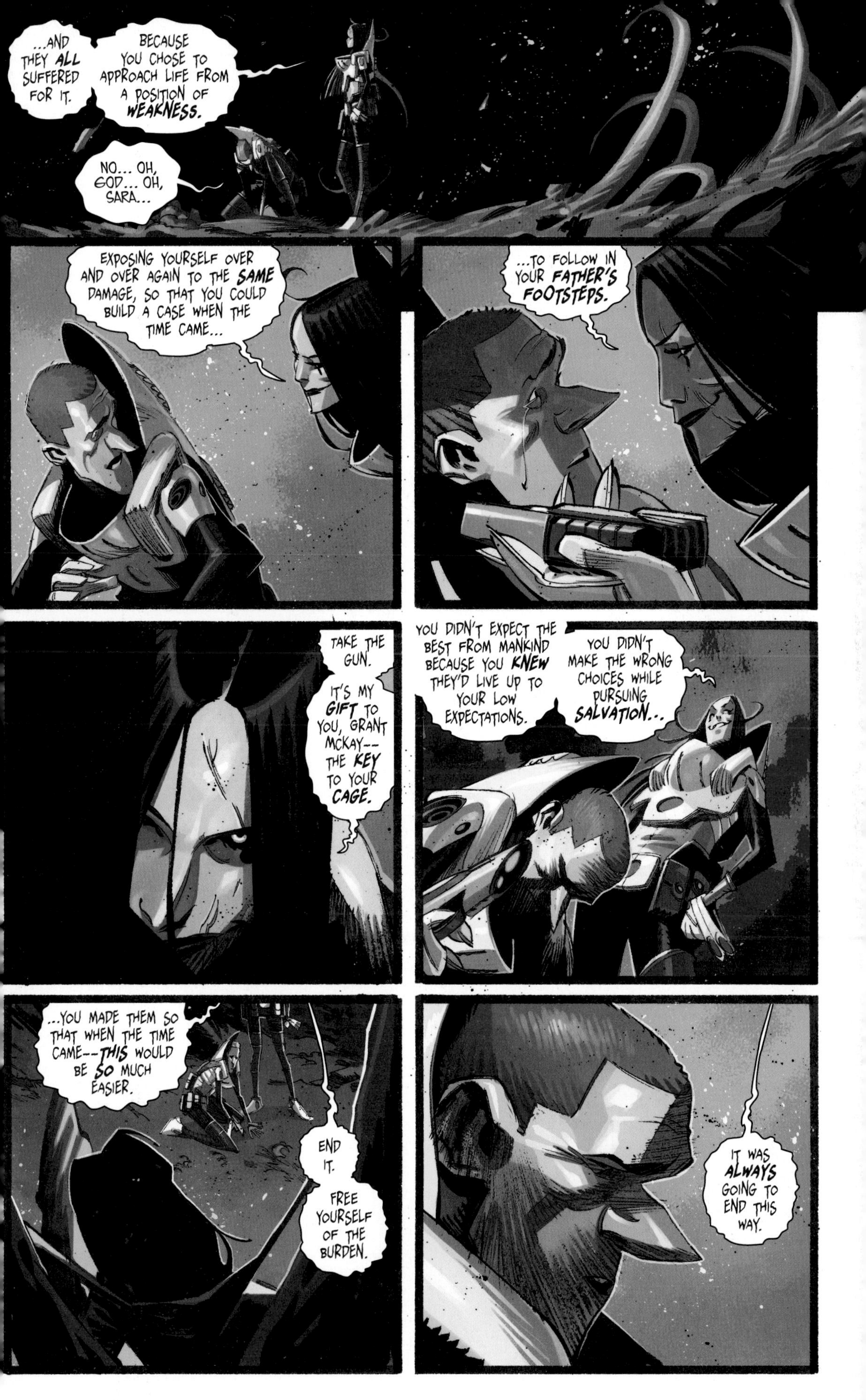

...AND THEY ALL SUFFERED FOR IT.
BECAUSE YOU CHOSE TO APPROACH LIFE FROM A POSITION OF WEAKNESS.
NO... OH, GOD... OH, SARA...
EXPOSING YOURSELF OVER AND OVER AGAIN TO THE SAME DAMAGE, SO THAT YOU COULD BUILD A CASE WHEN THE TIME CAME...
...TO FOLLOW IN YOUR FATHER'S FOOTSTEPS.
TAKE THE GUN.
IT'S MY GIFT TO YOU, GRANT MCKAY-- THE KEY TO YOUR CAGE.
YOU DIDN'T EXPECT THE BEST FROM MANKIND BECAUSE YOU KNEW THEY'D LIVE UP TO YOUR LOW EXPECTATIONS.
YOU DIDN'T MAKE THE WRONG CHOICES WHILE PURSUING SALVATION...
...YOU MADE THEM SO THAT WHEN THE TIME CAME--THIS WOULD BE SO MUCH EASIER.
END IT.
FREE YOURSELF OF THE BURDEN.
IT WAS ALWAYS GOING TO END THIS WAY.

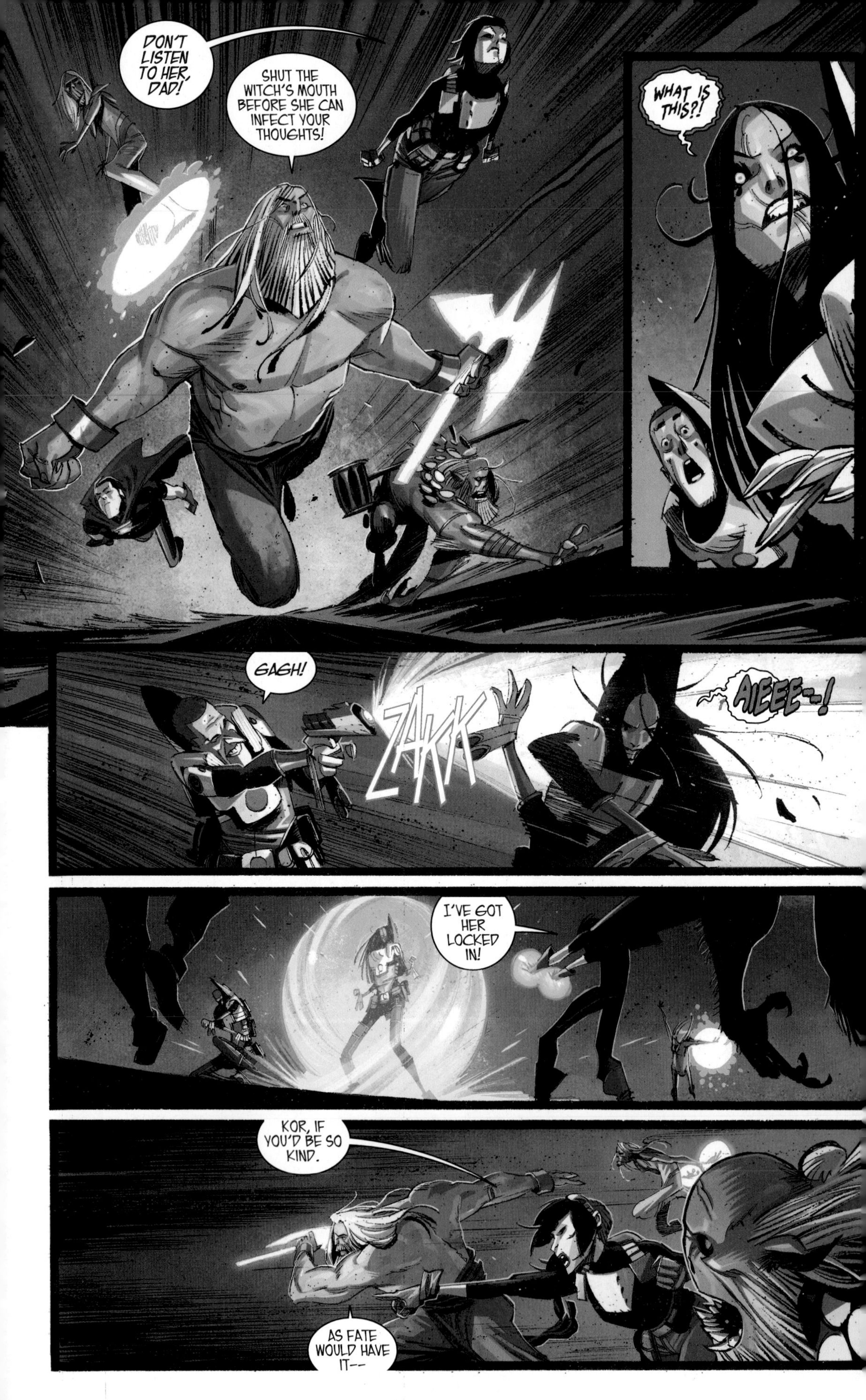

DON'T LISTEN TO HER, DAD!
SHUT THE WITCH'S MOUTH BEFORE SHE CAN INFECT YOUR THOUGHTS!
WHAT IS THIS?!
GAGH!
ZAKK
AIEEE--!
I'VE GOT HER LOCKED IN!
KOR, IF YOU'D BE SO KIND.
AS FATE WOULD HAVE IT--

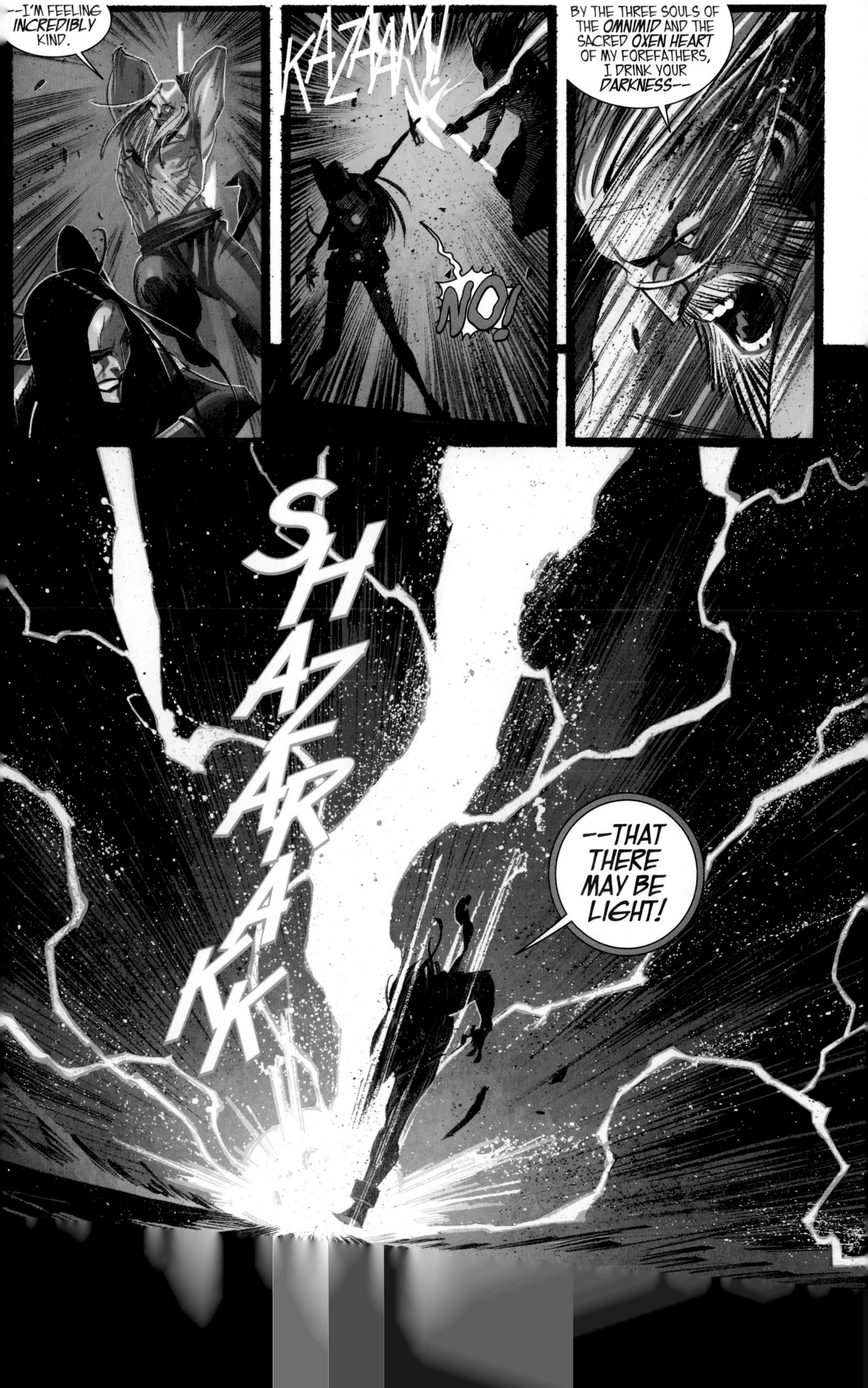
--I'M FEELING INCREDIBLY KIND.
KAZAAM!
NO!
BY THE THREE SOULS OF THE OMNIMID AND THE SACRED OXEN HEART OF MY FOREFATHERS, I DRINK YOUR DARKNESS--
SHAZARAKK
--THAT THERE MAY BE LIGHT!

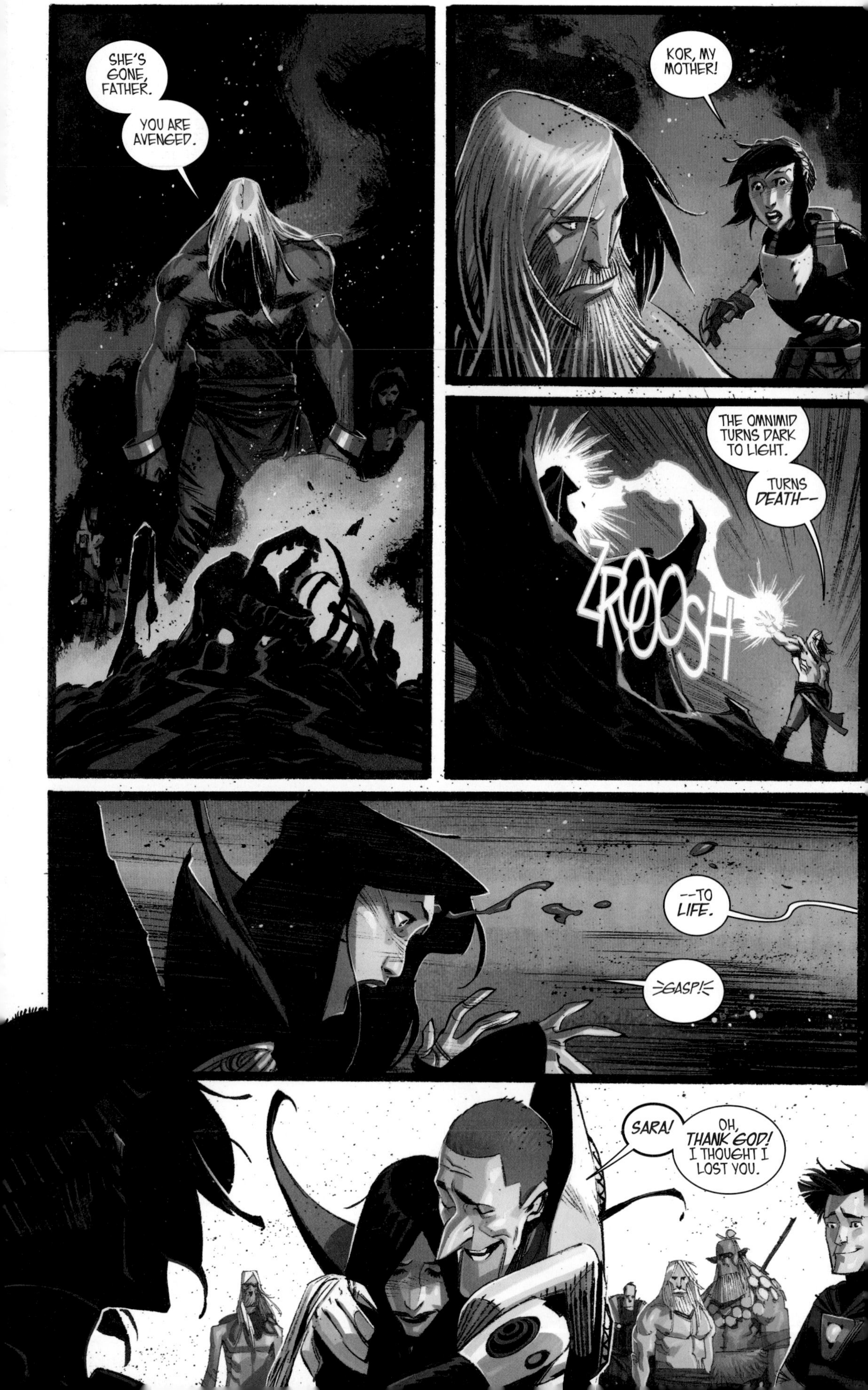

SHE'S GONE, FATHER.
YOU ARE AVENGED.
KOR, MY MOTHER!
THE OMNIMID TURNS DARK TO LIGHT.
TURNS DEATH--
ZROOSH
--TO LIFE.
GASP!
SARA!
OH, THANK GOD! I THOUGHT I LOST YOU.

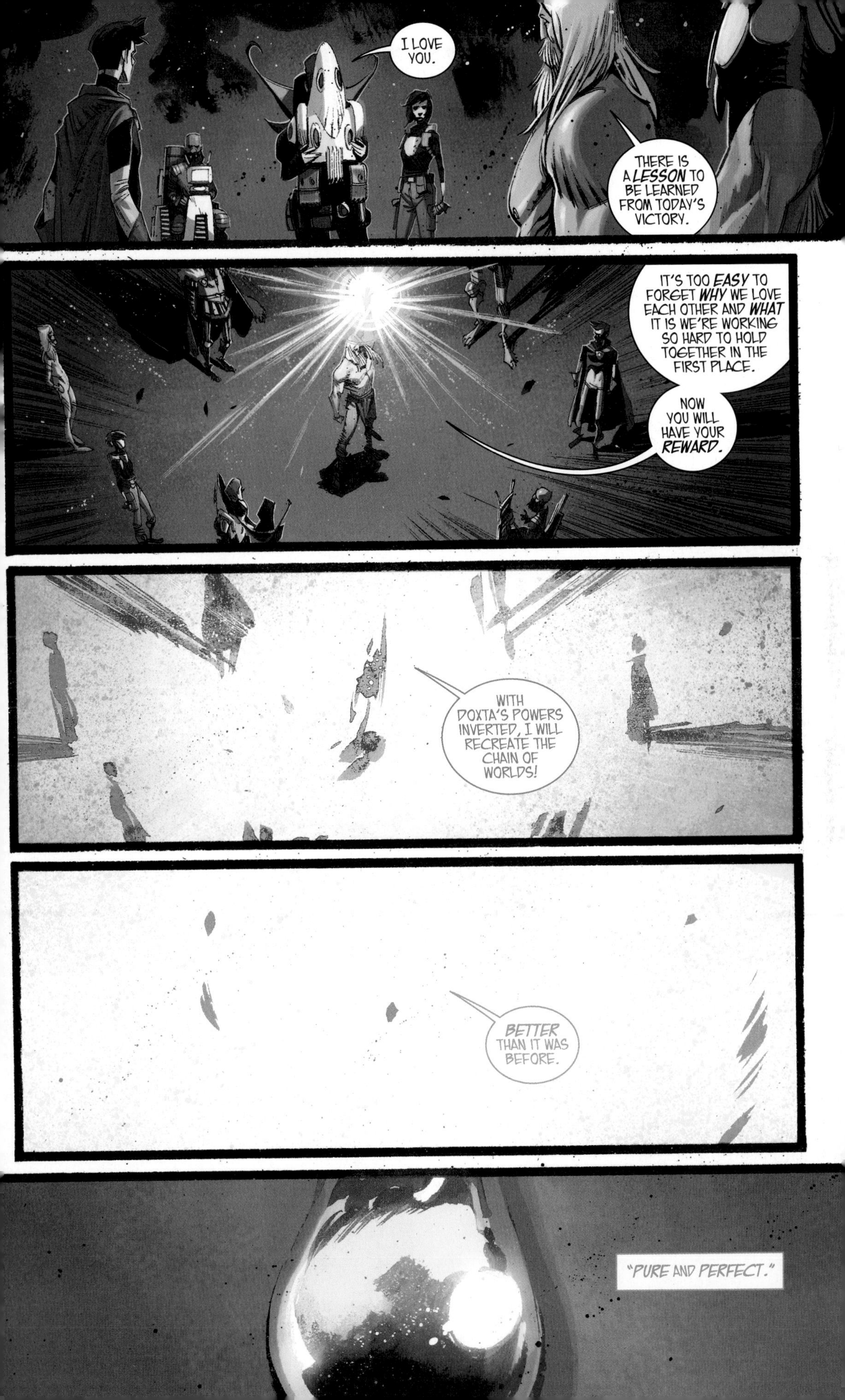
I LOVE YOU.
THERE IS A *LESSON* TO BE LEARNED FROM TODAY'S VICTORY.
IT'S TOO *EASY* TO FORGET *WHY* WE LOVE EACH OTHER AND *WHAT* IT IS WE'RE WORKING SO HARD TO HOLD TOGETHER IN THE FIRST PLACE.
NOW YOU WILL HAVE YOUR *REWARD*.
WITH DOXTA'S POWERS INVERTED, I WILL RECREATE THE CHAIN OF WORLDS!
BETTER THAN IT WAS BEFORE.
"*PURE* AND *PERFECT*."

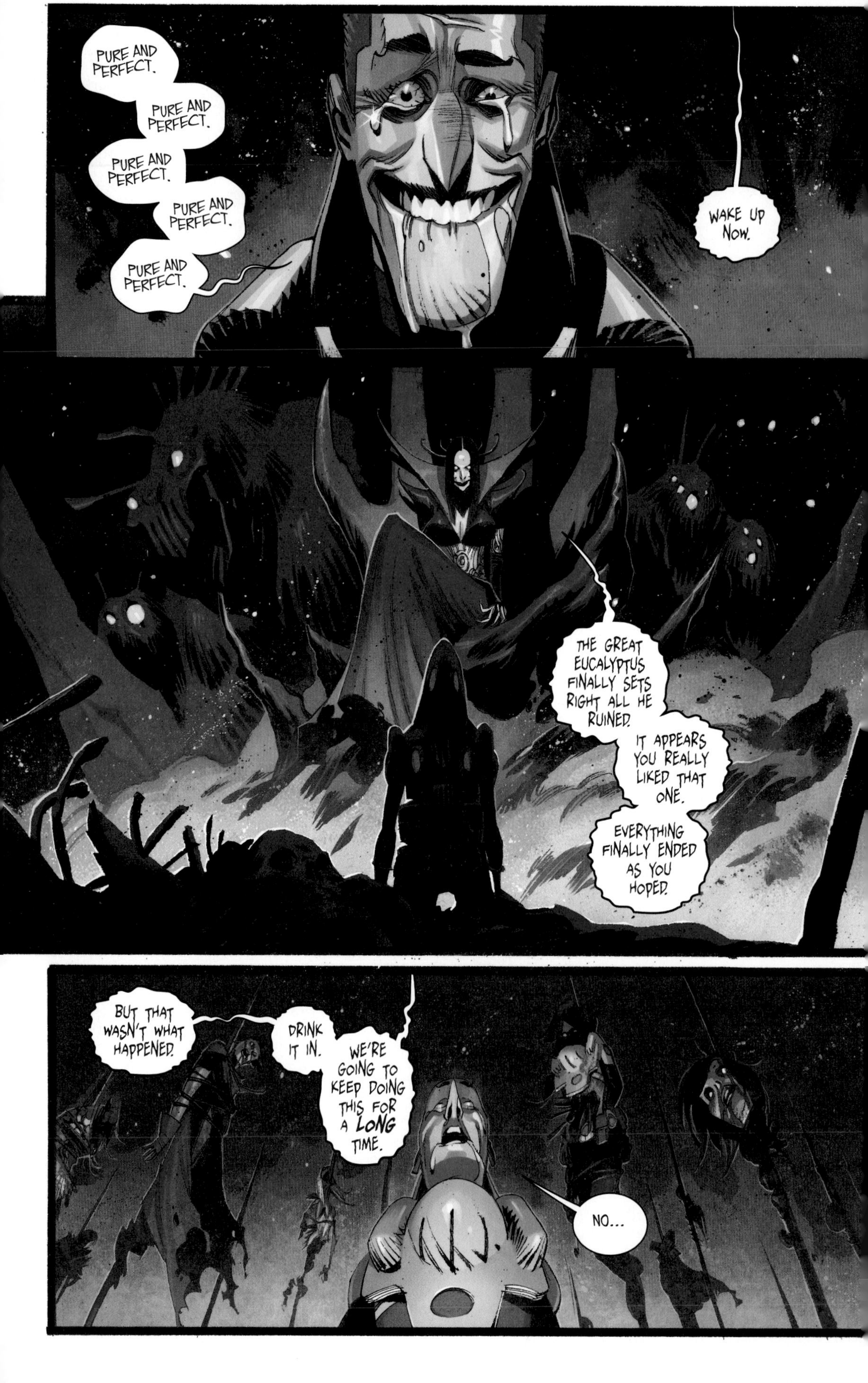
PURE AND PERFECT.
PURE AND PERFECT.
PURE AND PERFECT.
PURE AND PERFECT.
PURE AND PERFECT.
WAKE UP NOW.
THE GREAT EUCALYPTUS FINALLY SETS RIGHT ALL HE RUINED.
IT APPEARS YOU REALLY LIKED THAT ONE.
EVERYTHING FINALLY ENDED AS YOU HOPED.
BUT THAT WASN'T WHAT HAPPENED.
DRINK IT IN.
WE'RE GOING TO KEEP DOING THIS FOR A LONG TIME.
NO...

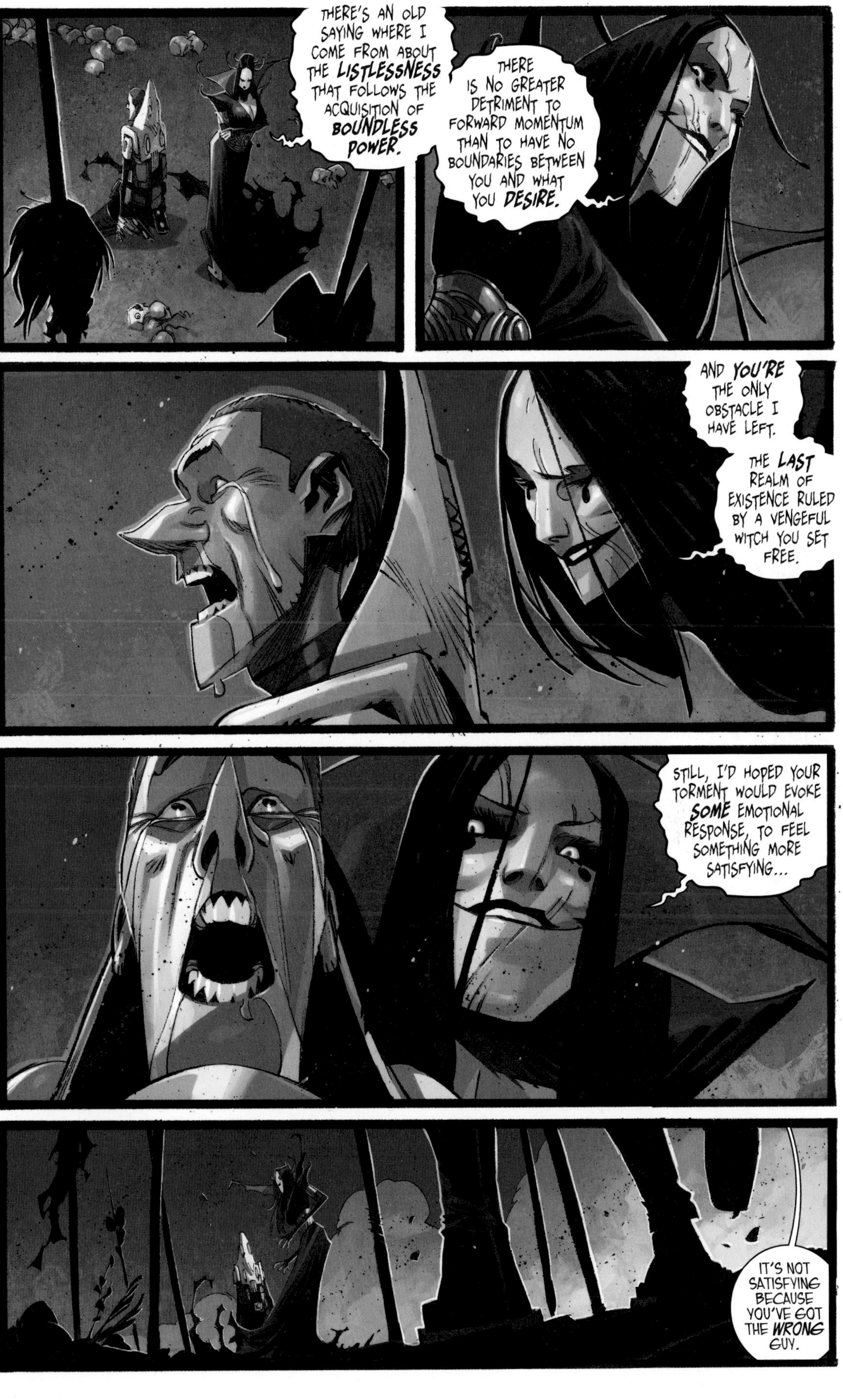
THERE'S AN OLD SAYING WHERE I COME FROM ABOUT THE LISTLESSNESS THAT FOLLOWS THE ACQUISITION OF BOUNDLESS POWER.
THERE IS NO GREATER DETRIMENT TO FORWARD MOMENTUM THAN TO HAVE NO BOUNDARIES BETWEEN YOU AND WHAT YOU DESIRE.
AND YOU'RE THE ONLY OBSTACLE I HAVE LEFT.
THE LAST REALM OF EXISTENCE RULED BY A VENGEFUL WITCH YOU SET FREE.
STILL, I'D HOPED YOUR TORMENT WOULD EVOKE SOME EMOTIONAL RESPONSE, TO FEEL SOMETHING MORE SATISFYING...
IT'S NOT SATISFYING BECAUSE YOU'VE GOT THE WRONG GUY.

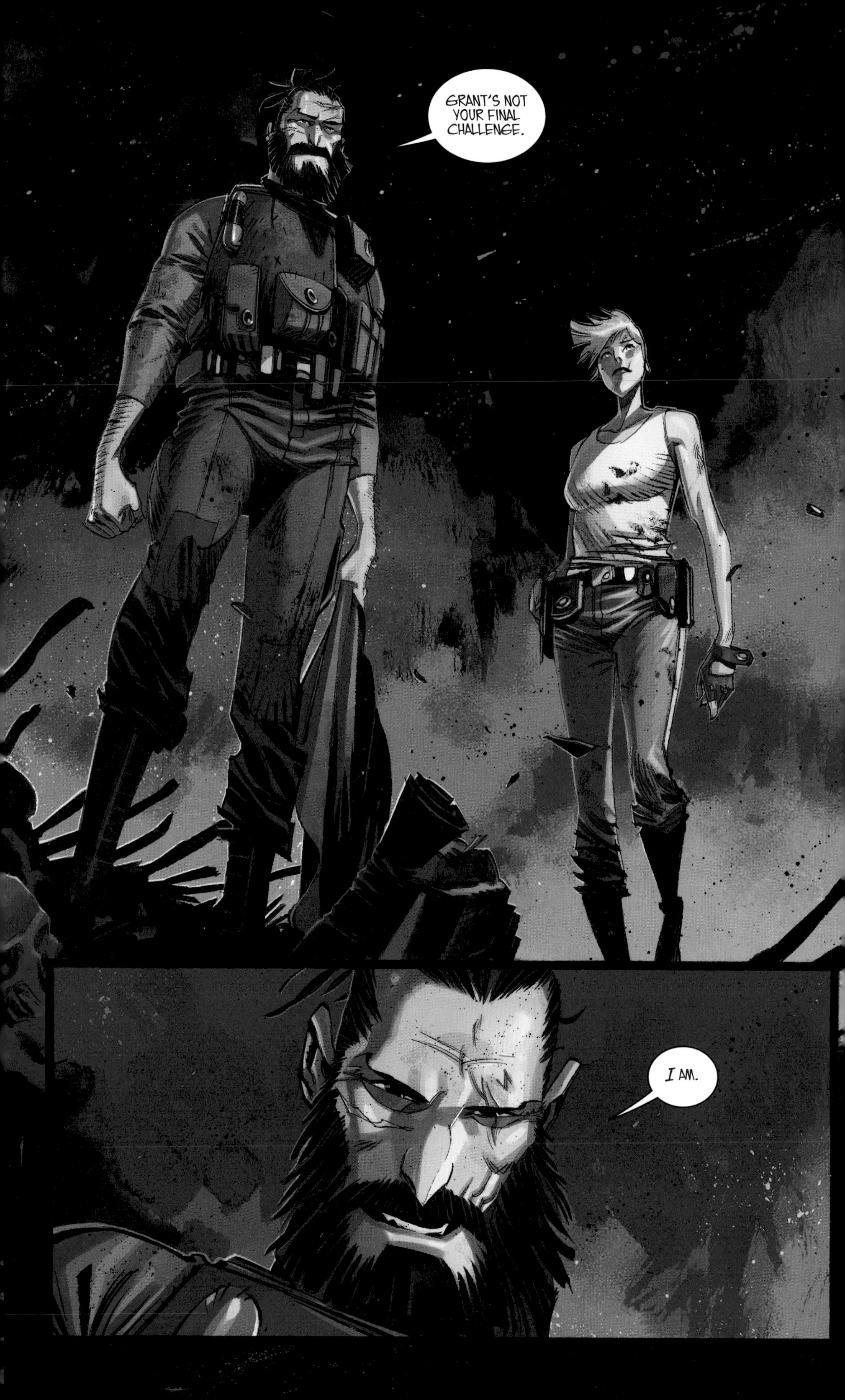
GRANT'S NOT YOUR FINAL CHALLENGE.
I AM.

41

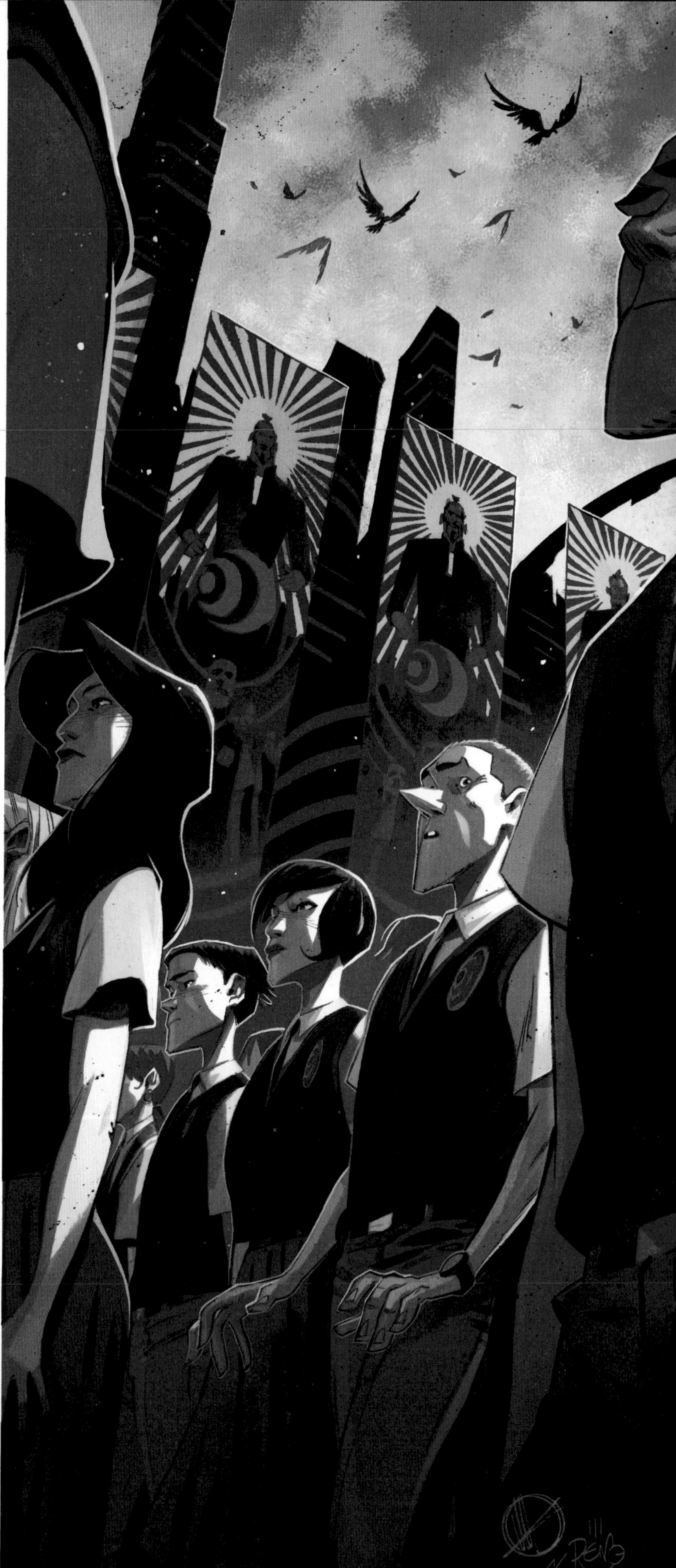

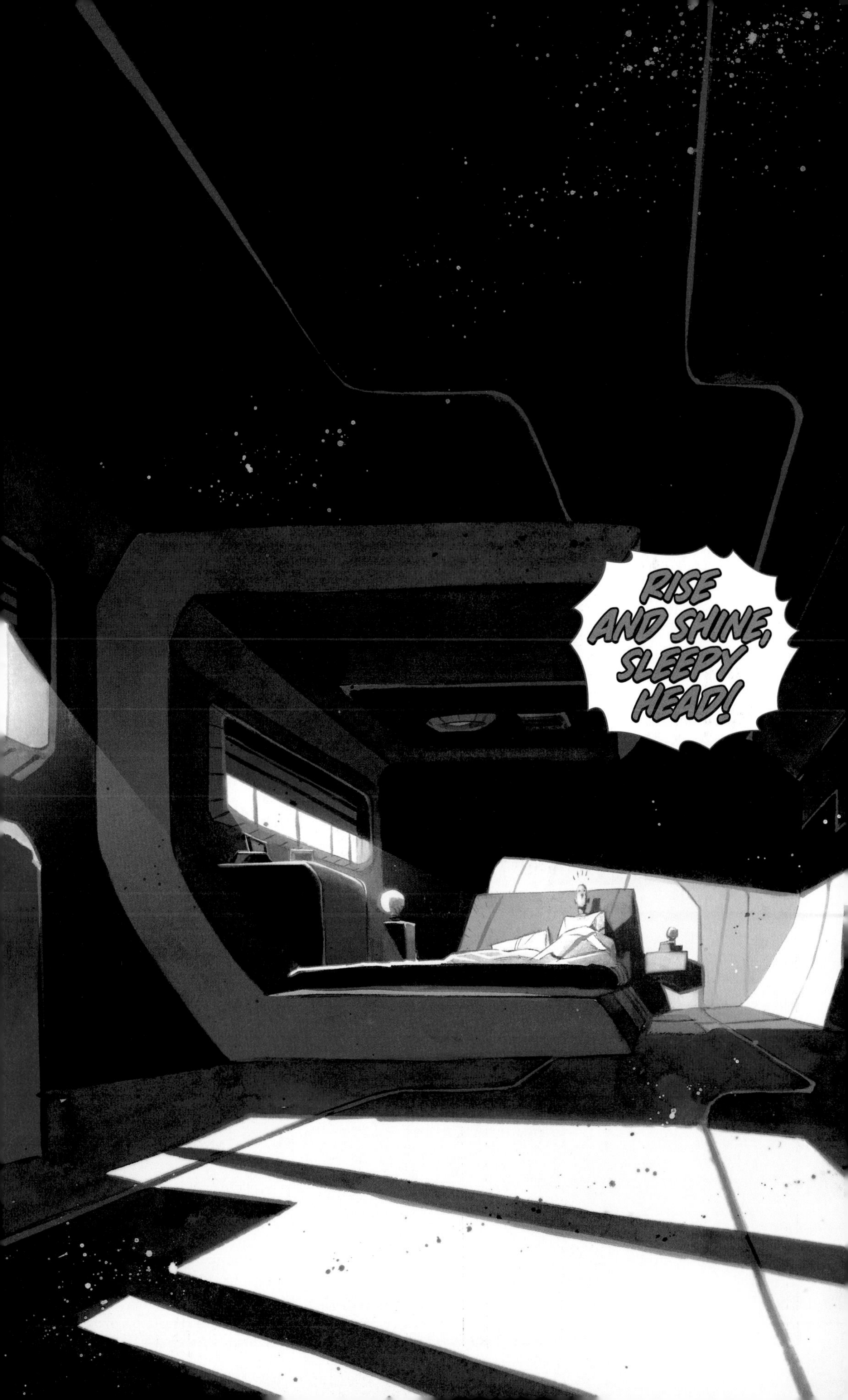
RISE AND SHINE, SLEEPY HEAD!

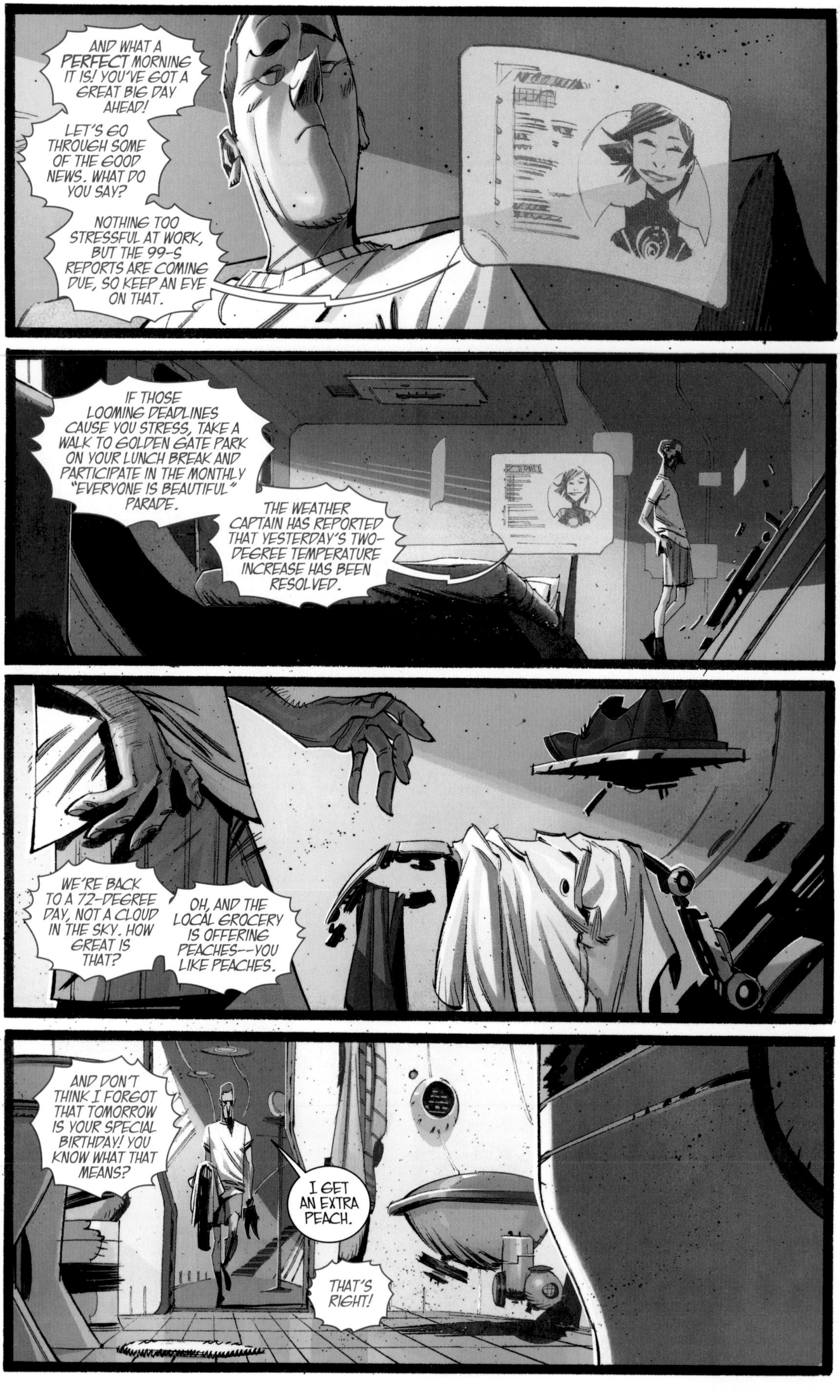
AND WHAT A PERFECT MORNING IT IS! YOU'VE GOT A GREAT BIG DAY AHEAD!
LET'S GO THROUGH SOME OF THE GOOD NEWS. WHAT DO YOU SAY?
NOTHING TOO STRESSFUL AT WORK, BUT THE 99-S REPORTS ARE COMING DUE, SO KEEP AN EYE ON THAT.
IF THOSE LOOMING DEADLINES CAUSE YOU STRESS, TAKE A WALK TO GOLDEN GATE PARK ON YOUR LUNCH BREAK AND PARTICIPATE IN THE MONTHLY "EVERYONE IS BEAUTIFUL" PARADE.
THE WEATHER CAPTAIN HAS REPORTED THAT YESTERDAY'S TWO-DEGREE TEMPERATURE INCREASE HAS BEEN RESOLVED.
WE'RE BACK TO A 72-DEGREE DAY, NOT A CLOUD IN THE SKY. HOW GREAT IS THAT?
OH, AND THE LOCAL GROCERY IS OFFERING PEACHES--YOU LIKE PEACHES.
AND DON'T THINK I FORGOT THAT TOMORROW IS YOUR SPECIAL BIRTHDAY! YOU KNOW WHAT THAT MEANS?
I GET AN EXTRA PEACH.
THAT'S RIGHT!

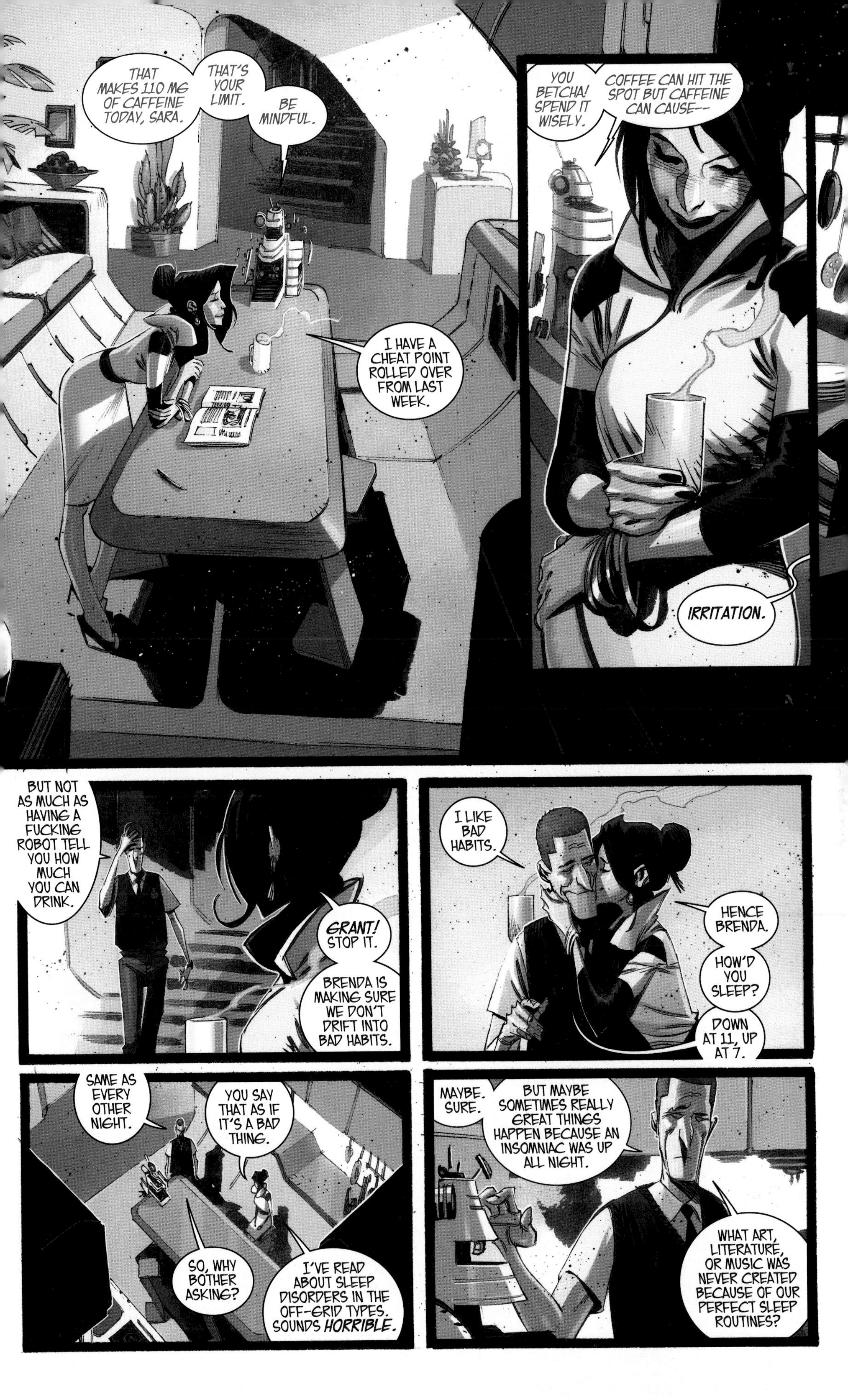
THAT MAKES 110 MG OF CAFFEINE TODAY, SARA.
THAT'S YOUR LIMIT.
BE MINDFUL.
I HAVE A CHEAT POINT ROLLED OVER FROM LAST WEEK.
YOU BETCHA! SPEND IT WISELY.
COFFEE CAN HIT THE SPOT BUT CAFFEINE CAN CAUSE--
IRRITATION.
BUT NOT AS MUCH AS HAVING A FUCKING ROBOT TELL YOU HOW MUCH YOU CAN DRINK.
GRANT! STOP IT.
BRENDA IS MAKING SURE WE DON'T DRIFT INTO BAD HABITS.
I LIKE BAD HABITS.
HENCE BRENDA.
HOW'D YOU SLEEP?
DOWN AT 11, UP AT 7.
SAME AS EVERY OTHER NIGHT.
YOU SAY THAT AS IF IT'S A BAD THING.
SO, WHY BOTHER ASKING?
I'VE READ ABOUT SLEEP DISORDERS IN THE OFF-GRID TYPES. SOUNDS HORRIBLE.
MAYBE. SURE.
BUT MAYBE SOMETIMES REALLY GREAT THINGS HAPPEN BECAUSE AN INSOMNIAC WAS UP ALL NIGHT.
WHAT ART, LITERATURE, OR MUSIC WAS NEVER CREATED BECAUSE OF OUR PERFECT SLEEP ROUTINES?

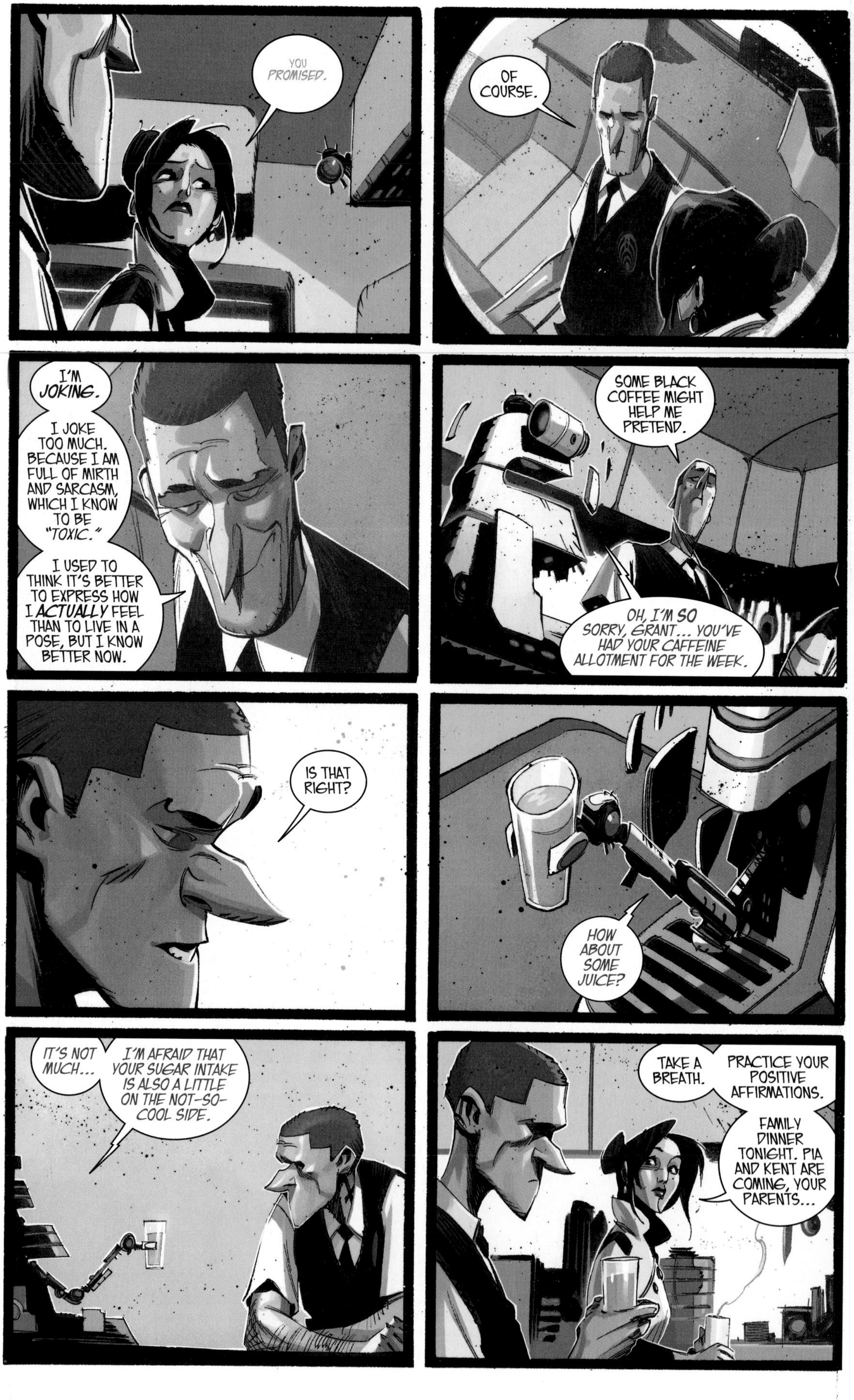
YOU PROMISED.
OF COURSE.
I'M JOKING.
I JOKE TOO MUCH. BECAUSE I AM FULL OF MIRTH AND SARCASM, WHICH I KNOW TO BE "TOXIC."
I USED TO THINK IT'S BETTER TO EXPRESS HOW I ACTUALLY FEEL THAN TO LIVE IN A POSE, BUT I KNOW BETTER NOW.
SOME BLACK COFFEE MIGHT HELP ME PRETEND.
OH, I'M SO SORRY, GRANT... YOU'VE HAD YOUR CAFFEINE ALLOTMENT FOR THE WEEK.
IS THAT RIGHT?
HOW ABOUT SOME JUICE?
IT'S NOT MUCH...
I'M AFRAID THAT YOUR SUGAR INTAKE IS ALSO A LITTLE ON THE NOT-SO-COOL SIDE.
TAKE A BREATH.
PRACTICE YOUR POSITIVE AFFIRMATIONS.
FAMILY DINNER TONIGHT. PIA AND KENT ARE COMING, YOUR PARENTS...

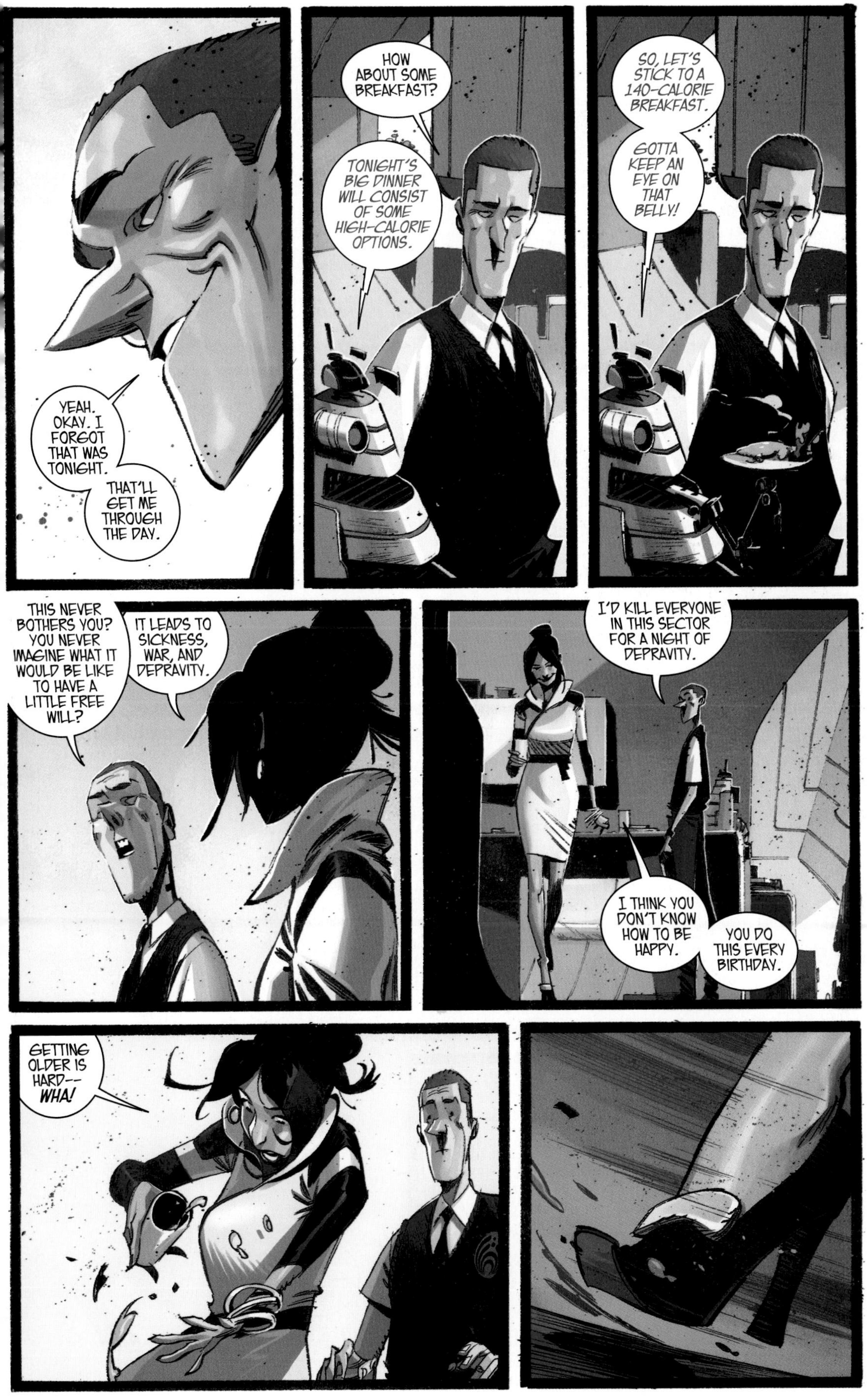
YEAH. OKAY. I FORGOT THAT WAS TONIGHT.
THAT'LL GET ME THROUGH THE DAY.
HOW ABOUT SOME BREAKFAST?
TONIGHT'S BIG DINNER WILL CONSIST OF SOME HIGH-CALORIE OPTIONS.
SO, LET'S STICK TO A 140-CALORIE BREAKFAST.
GOTTA KEEP AN EYE ON THAT BELLY!
THIS NEVER BOTHERS YOU? YOU NEVER IMAGINE WHAT IT WOULD BE LIKE TO HAVE A LITTLE FREE WILL?
IT LEADS TO SICKNESS, WAR, AND DEPRAVITY.
I'D KILL EVERYONE IN THIS SECTOR FOR A NIGHT OF DEPRAVITY.
I THINK YOU DON'T KNOW HOW TO BE HAPPY.
YOU DO THIS EVERY BIRTHDAY.
GETTING OLDER IS HARD-- WHA!

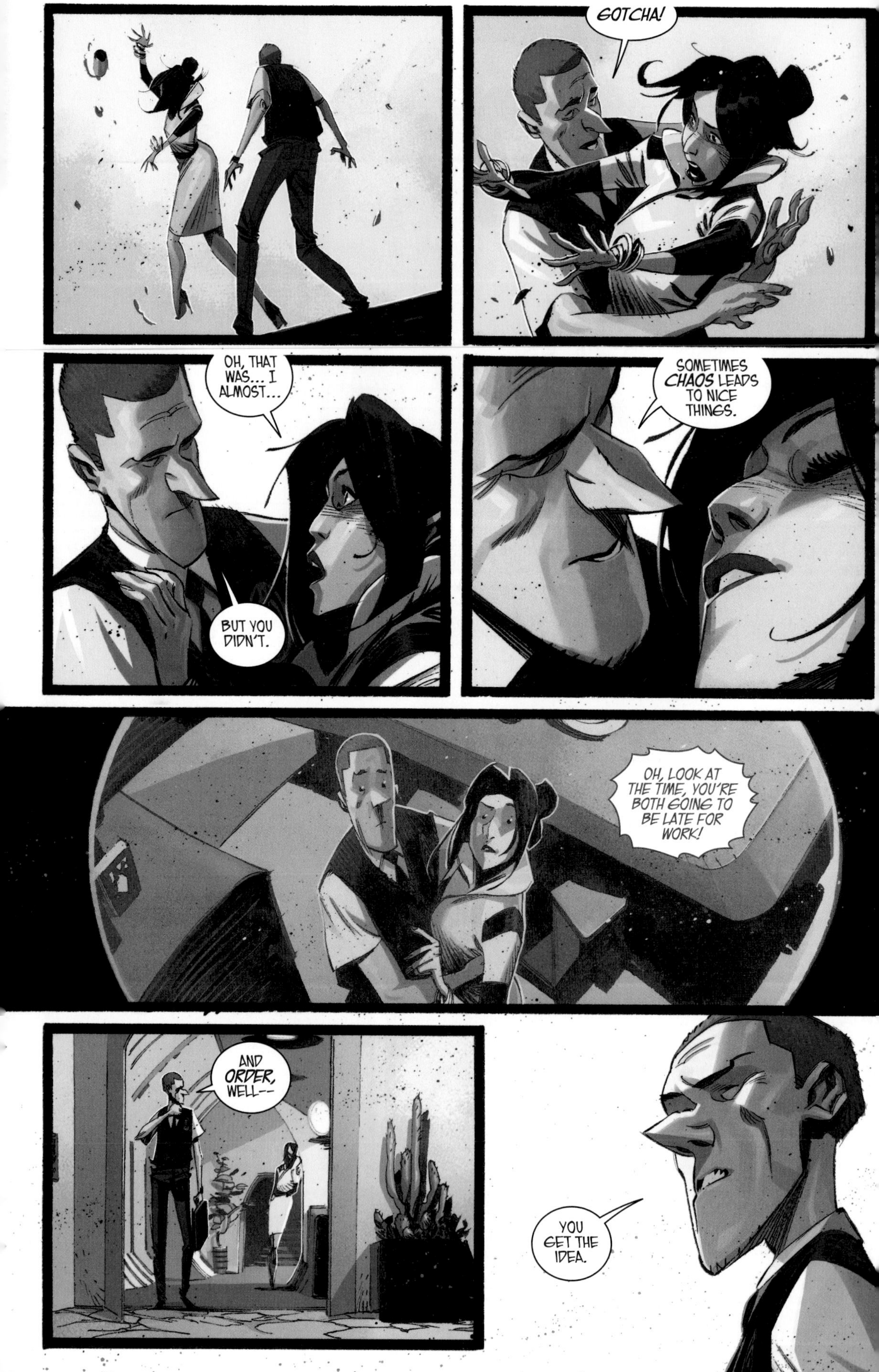
GOTCHA!
OH, THAT WAS... I ALMOST...
BUT YOU DIDN'T.
SOMETIMES CHAOS LEADS TO NICE THINGS.
OH, LOOK AT THE TIME, YOU'RE BOTH GOING TO BE LATE FOR WORK!
AND ORDER, WELL--
YOU GET THE IDEA.

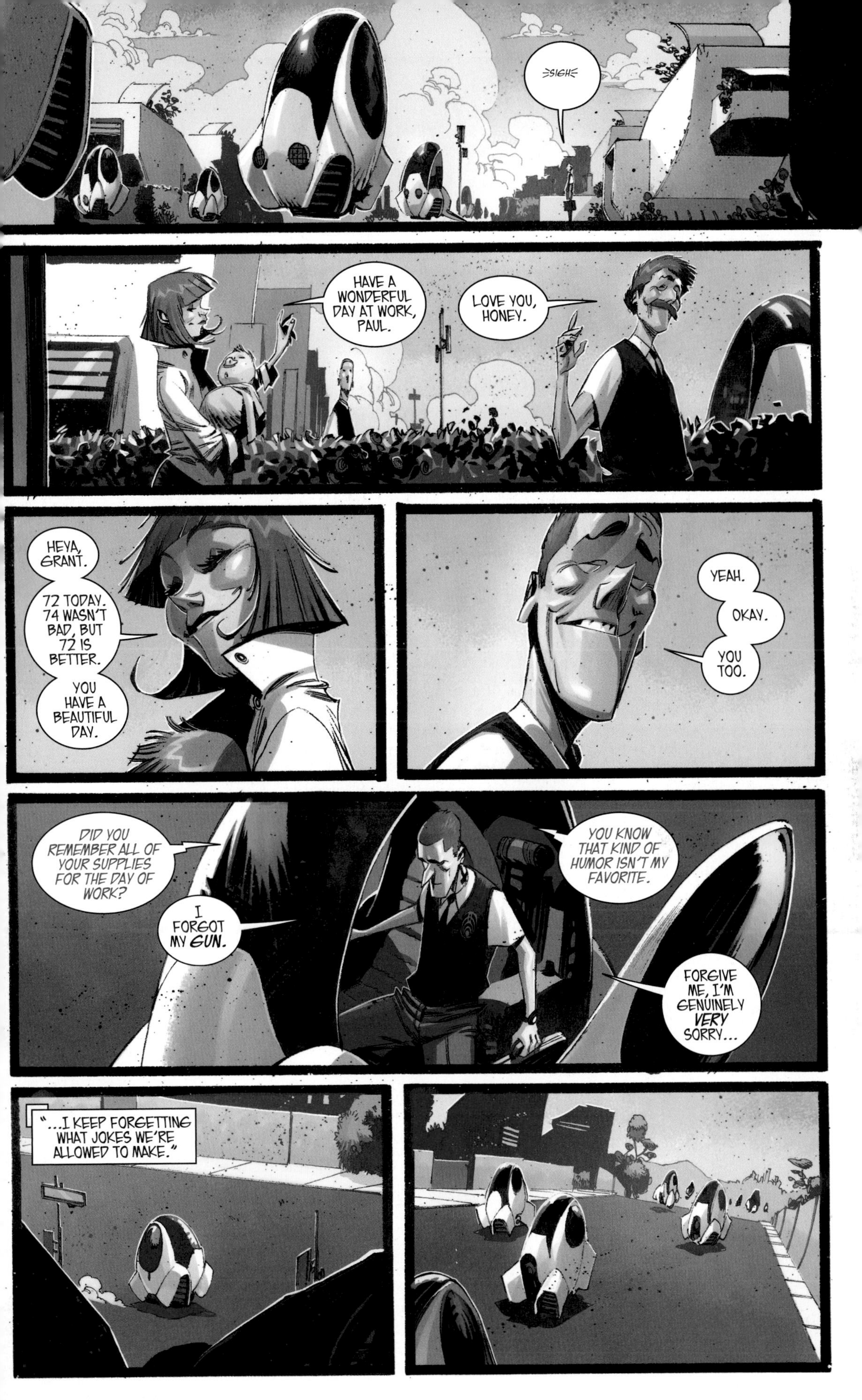

≥SIGH≤
HAVE A WONDERFUL DAY AT WORK, PAUL.
LOVE YOU, HONEY.
HEYA, GRANT.
72 TODAY. 74 WASN'T BAD, BUT 72 IS BETTER.
YOU HAVE A BEAUTIFUL DAY.
YEAH.
OKAY.
YOU TOO.
DID YOU REMEMBER ALL OF YOUR SUPPLIES FOR THE DAY OF WORK?
I FORGOT MY GUN.
YOU KNOW THAT KIND OF HUMOR ISN'T MY FAVORITE.
FORGIVE ME, I'M GENUINELY VERY SORRY...
"...I KEEP FORGETTING WHAT JOKES WE'RE ALLOWED TO MAKE."

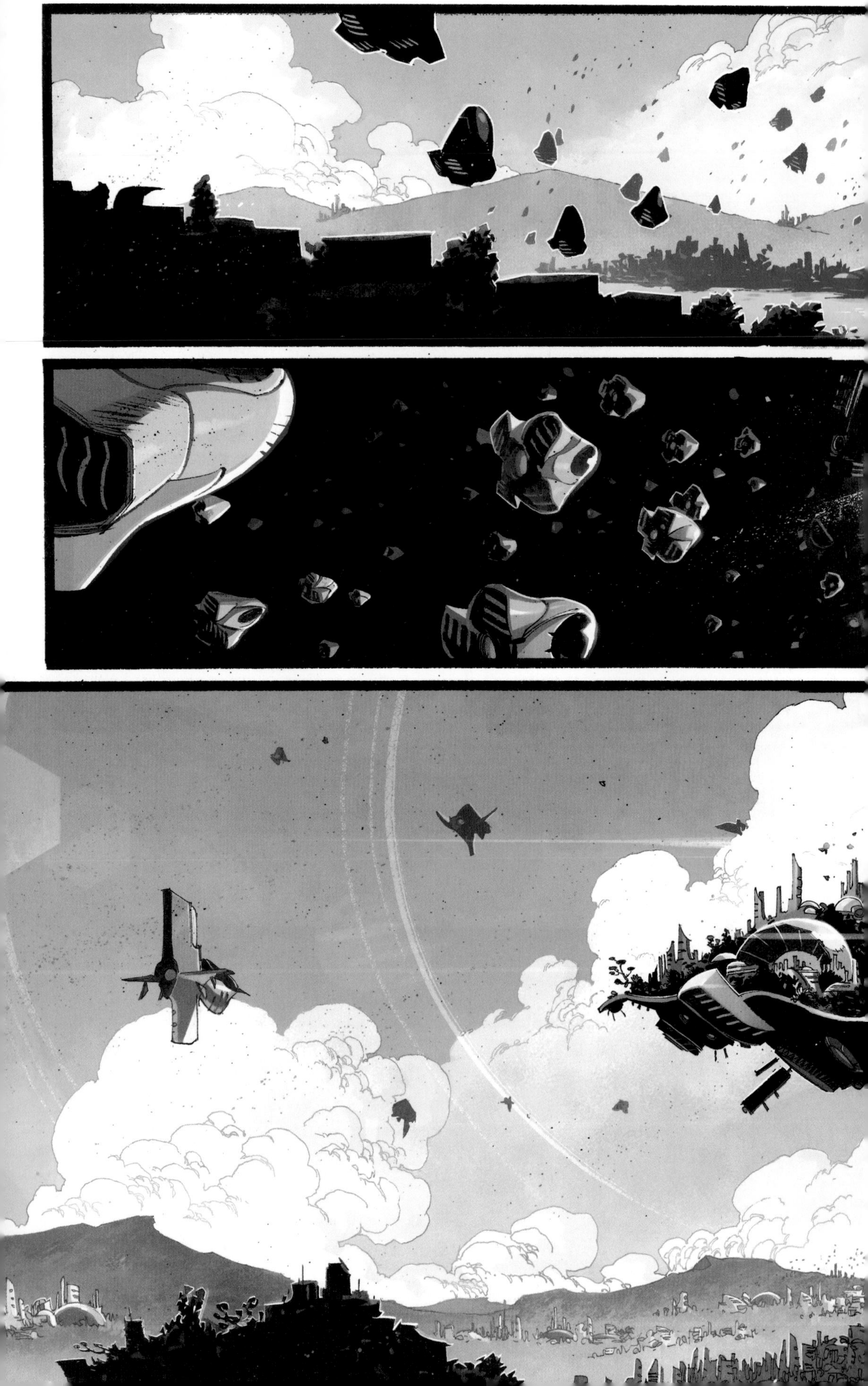

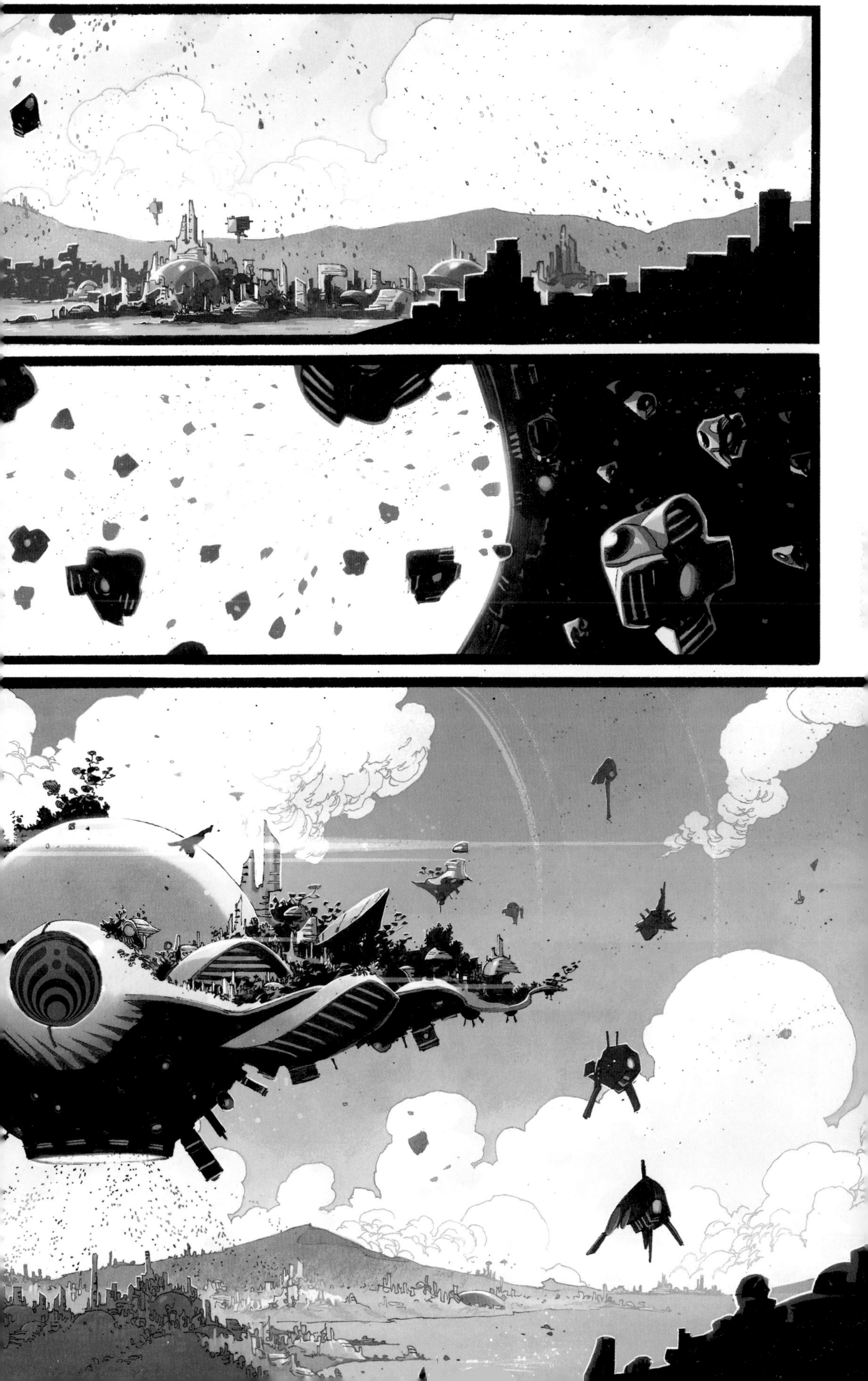

--SO, LET'S KEEP THAT *POSITIVE* ATTITUDE GOING. GREAT NEWS-- WE HAVEN'T HAD A *SINGLE* INAPPROPRIATE COMMENT OR INTERACTION REPORTED ALL WEEK.

THE WORK WEEK IS *ALMOST* OVER, SO LET'S HIT A *PERFECT* CIVILITY SCORE.

IF YOU'RE FEELING DOWN AFTER LUNCH, HIT THE GYM.

IT'LL OXYGENATE YOUR BRAIN, IMPROVE WELL-BEING, AND GIVE YOU A 60% INCREASE IN PROBLEM-SOLVING SKILLS.

PLUS, IT'S THE BEST WAY TO COMBAT EXHAUSTION.

SOME OF YOUR WELLNESS CHARTS WORRY ME.

I WORRY ABOUT YOU, BECAUSE I *CARE* ABOUT EACH AND EVERY ONE OF YOU AND WANT YOU TO HAVE A *PERFECT* DAY.

I TRULY DO.

HEYA, WARD.

HOW YOU DOIN' THIS MORNIN', GRANT?

YOU KNOW ME.

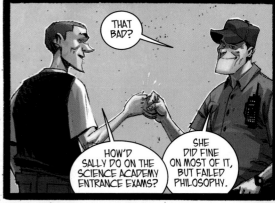

THAT *BAD?*

HOW'D SALLY DO ON THE SCIENCE ACADEMY ENTRANCE EXAMS?

SHE DID FINE ON MOST OF IT, BUT FAILED PHILOSOPHY.

THAT'S OKAY. SCIENTISTS ARE *EXPLORERS...*

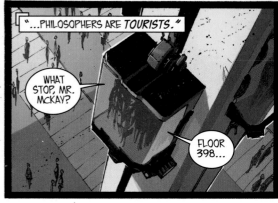

"...PHILOSOPHERS ARE *TOURISTS.*"

WHAT STOP, MR. MCKAY?

FLOOR 398...

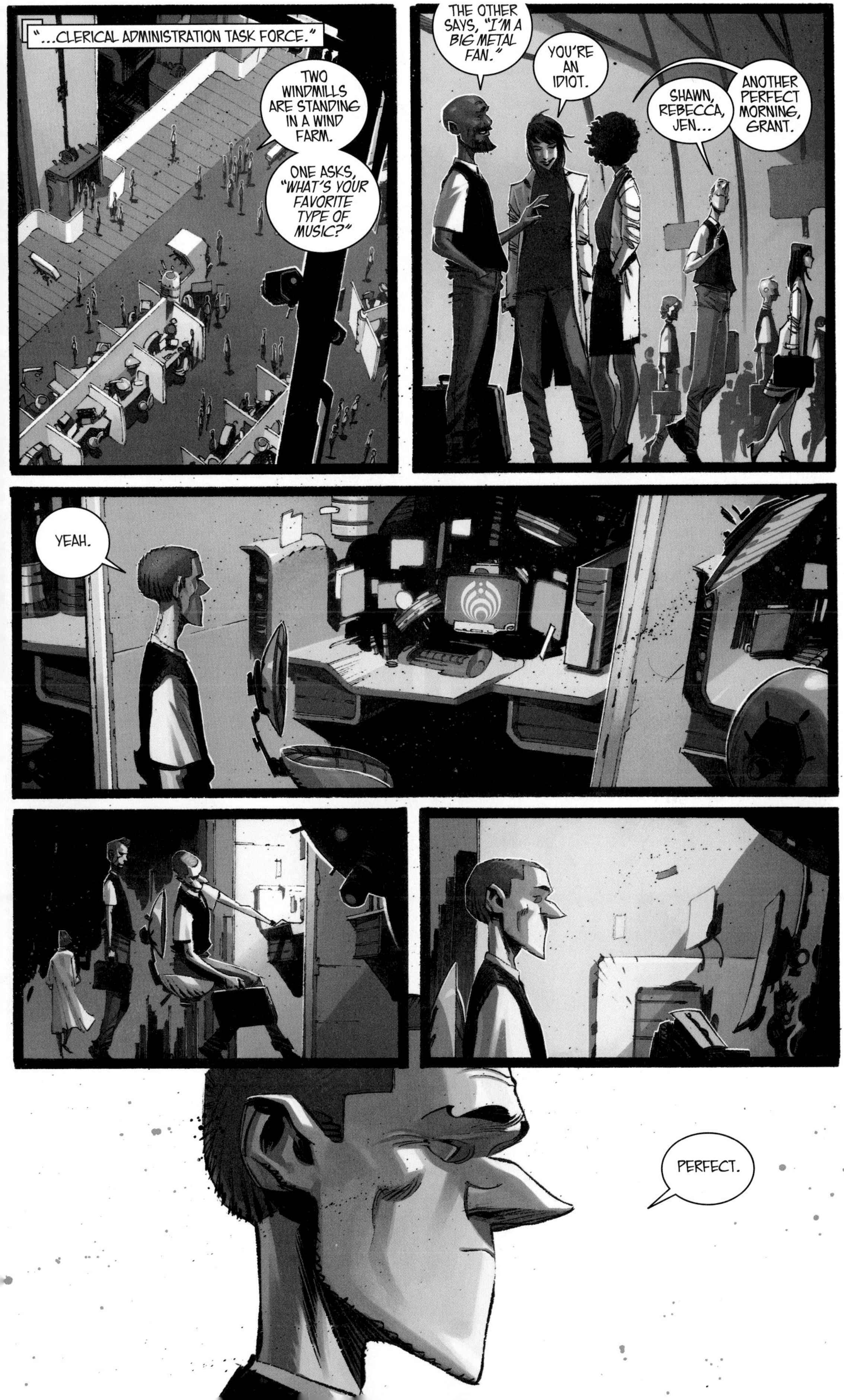
"...CLERICAL ADMINISTRATION TASK FORCE."
TWO WINDMILLS ARE STANDING IN A WIND FARM.
ONE ASKS, "WHAT'S YOUR FAVORITE TYPE OF MUSIC?"
THE OTHER SAYS, "I'M A BIG METAL FAN."
YOU'RE AN IDIOT.
ANOTHER PERFECT MORNING, GRANT.
SHAWN, REBECCA, JEN...
YEAH.
PERFECT.

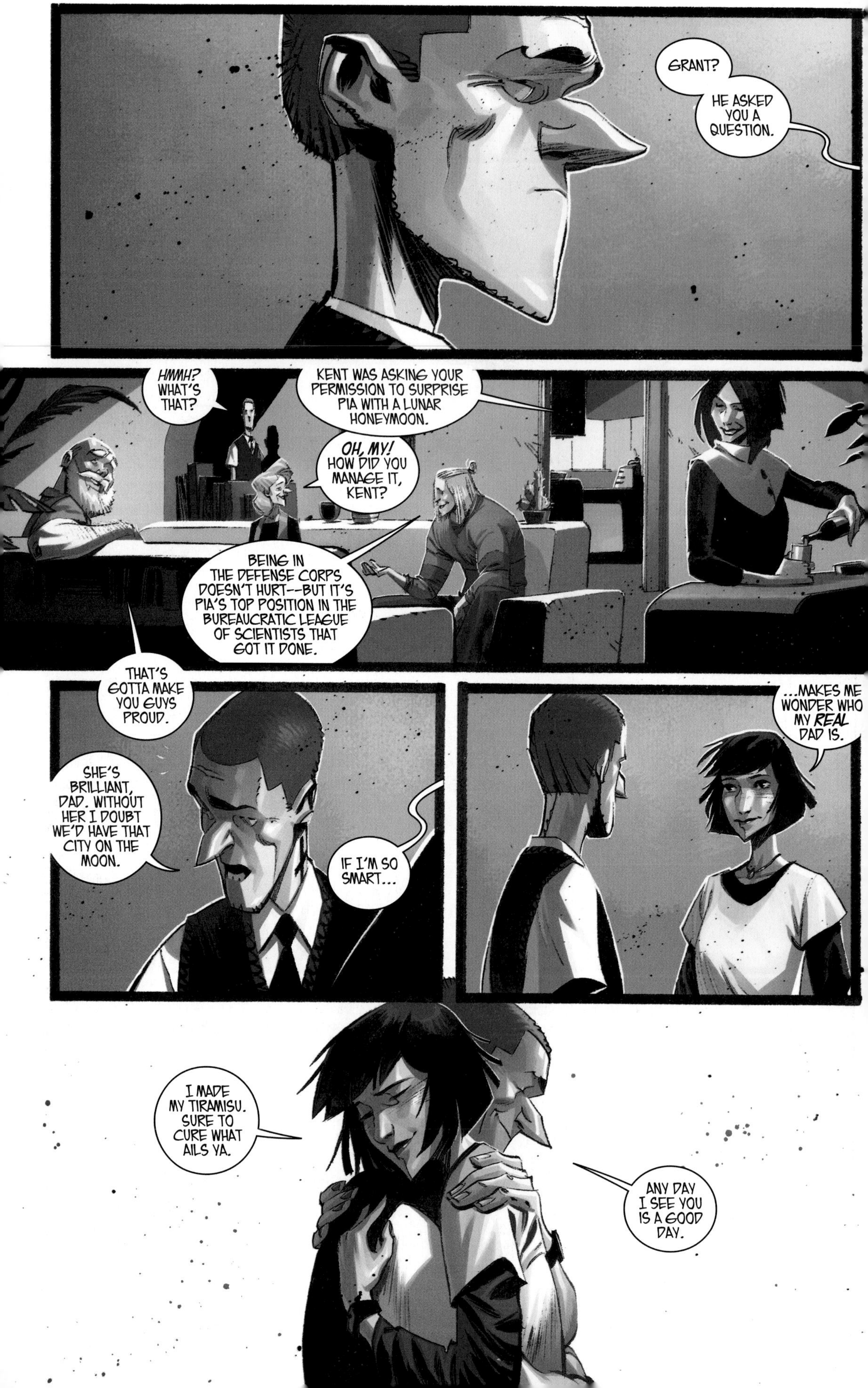
GRANT?
HE ASKED YOU A QUESTION.
HMMH? WHAT'S THAT?
KENT WAS ASKING YOUR PERMISSION TO SURPRISE PIA WITH A LUNAR HONEYMOON.
OH, MY! HOW DID YOU MANAGE IT, KENT?
BEING IN THE DEFENSE CORPS DOESN'T HURT--BUT IT'S PIA'S TOP POSITION IN THE BUREAUCRATIC LEAGUE OF SCIENTISTS THAT GOT IT DONE.
THAT'S GOTTA MAKE YOU GUYS PROUD.
SHE'S BRILLIANT, DAD. WITHOUT HER I DOUBT WE'D HAVE THAT CITY ON THE MOON.
IF I'M SO SMART...
...MAKES ME WONDER WHO MY REAL DAD IS.
I MADE MY TIRAMISU. SURE TO CURE WHAT AILS YA.
ANY DAY I SEE YOU IS A GOOD DAY.

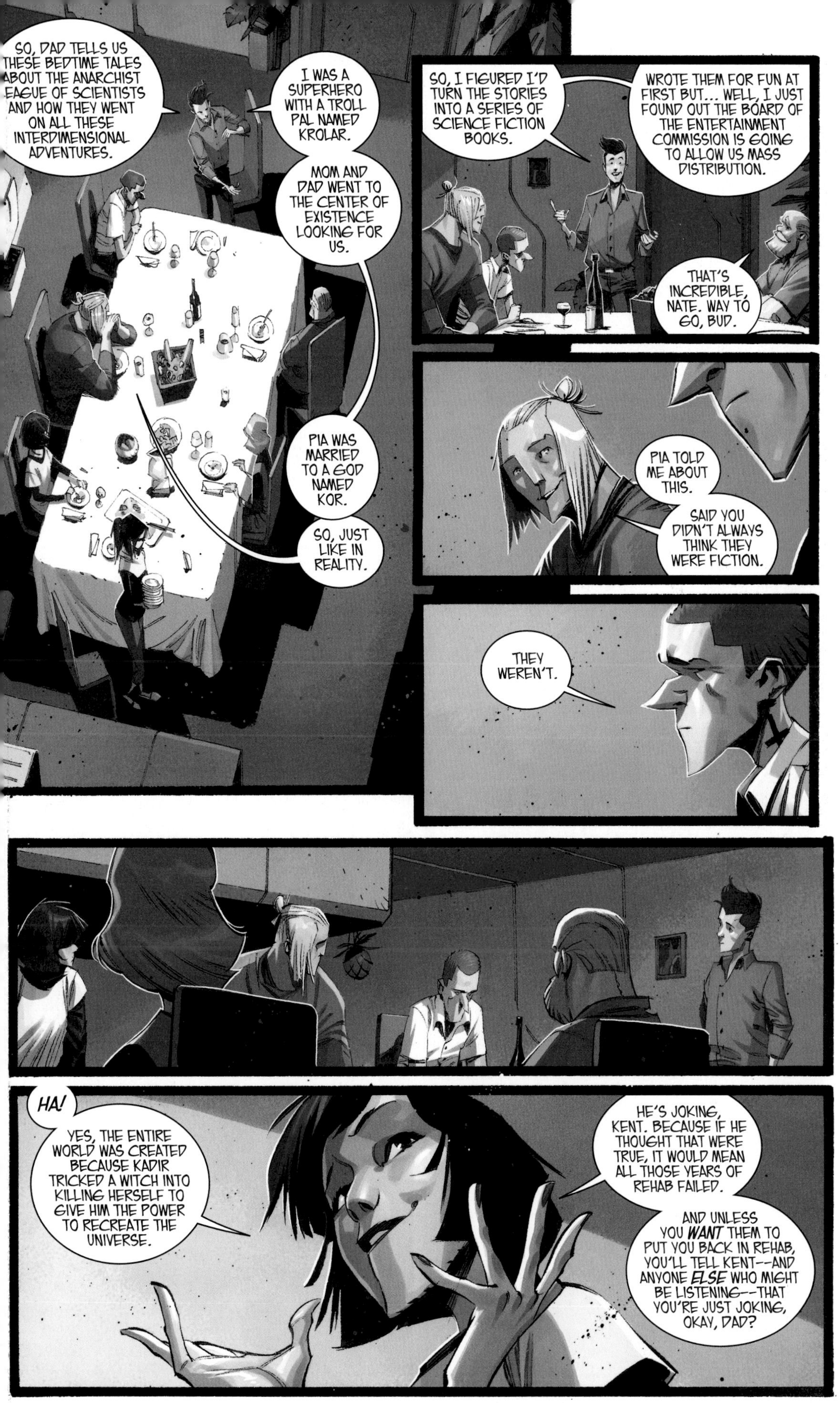
SO, DAD TELLS US THESE BEDTIME TALES ABOUT THE ANARCHIST LEAGUE OF SCIENTISTS AND HOW THEY WENT ON ALL THESE INTERDIMENSIONAL ADVENTURES.
I WAS A SUPERHERO WITH A TROLL PAL NAMED KROLAR.
MOM AND DAD WENT TO THE CENTER OF EXISTENCE LOOKING FOR US.
PIA WAS MARRIED TO A GOD NAMED KOR.
SO, JUST LIKE IN REALITY.
SO, I FIGURED I'D TURN THE STORIES INTO A SERIES OF SCIENCE FICTION BOOKS.
WROTE THEM FOR FUN AT FIRST BUT... WELL, I JUST FOUND OUT THE BOARD OF THE ENTERTAINMENT COMMISSION IS GOING TO ALLOW US MASS DISTRIBUTION.
THAT'S INCREDIBLE, NATE. WAY TO GO, BUD.
PIA TOLD ME ABOUT THIS.
SAID YOU DIDN'T ALWAYS THINK THEY WERE FICTION.
THEY WEREN'T.
HA!
YES, THE ENTIRE WORLD WAS CREATED BECAUSE KADIR TRICKED A WITCH INTO KILLING HERSELF TO GIVE HIM THE POWER TO RECREATE THE UNIVERSE.
HE'S JOKING, KENT. BECAUSE IF HE THOUGHT THAT WERE TRUE, IT WOULD MEAN ALL THOSE YEARS OF REHAB FAILED.
AND UNLESS YOU *WANT* THEM TO PUT YOU BACK IN REHAB, YOU'LL TELL KENT--AND ANYONE *ELSE* WHO MIGHT BE LISTENING--THAT YOU'RE JUST JOKING, OKAY, DAD?

GRANT?

HMMH? OH, RIGHT. YEAH. SORRY.

I'M SUCH A *GOOF!* WHAT KIND OF A CRAZY *ASSHOLE* WOULD BELIEVE OUR UNIVERSE WAS CREATED BY WITCHERY?

NOT ME.

ALL OF THE THERAPY WORKED WONDERS ON MY DELUSIONS AND MENTAL ILLNESS.

DAD'S NOT CRAZY ANYMORE.

EVERYTHING IS *GREAT.*

BRENDA, MAKE ME A BLACK COFFEE.

YIKES, AFRAID I CAN'T, GRANT.

YOU'RE OVER THE LIMIT THIS WEEK.

MAKE ME A FUCKING COFFEE.

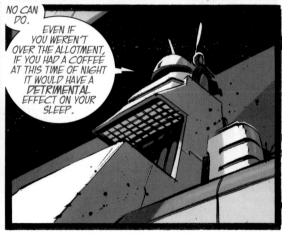

NO CAN DO.

EVEN IF YOU WEREN'T OVER THE ALLOTMENT, IF YOU HAD A *COFFEE* AT THIS TIME OF NIGHT IT WOULD HAVE A *DETRIMENTAL* EFFECT ON YOUR SLEEP.

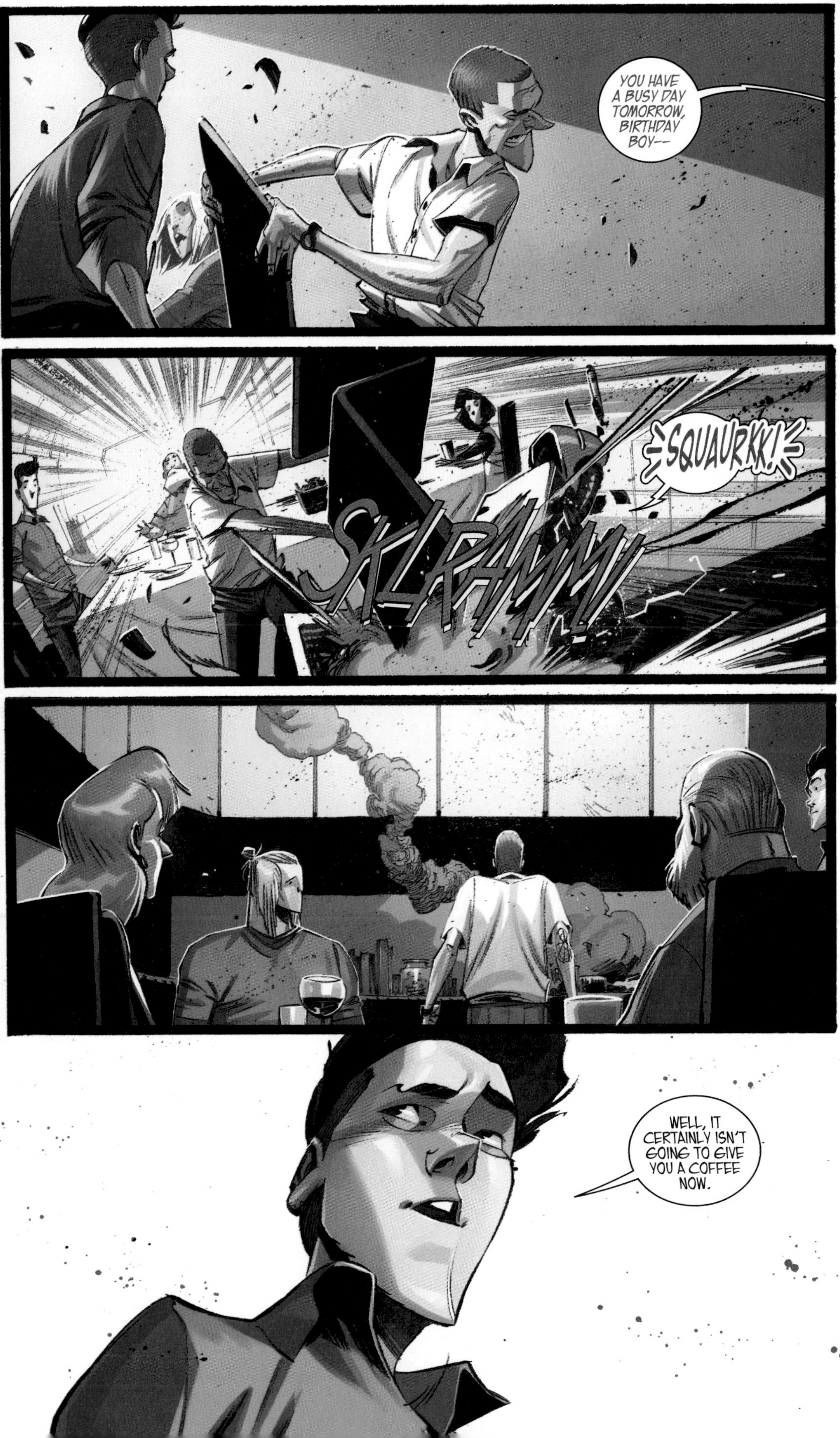
YOU HAVE A BUSY DAY TOMORROW, BIRTHDAY BOY--
SQUAURKK!
SKLRAMM!
WELL, IT CERTAINLY ISN'T GOING TO GIVE YOU A COFFEE NOW.

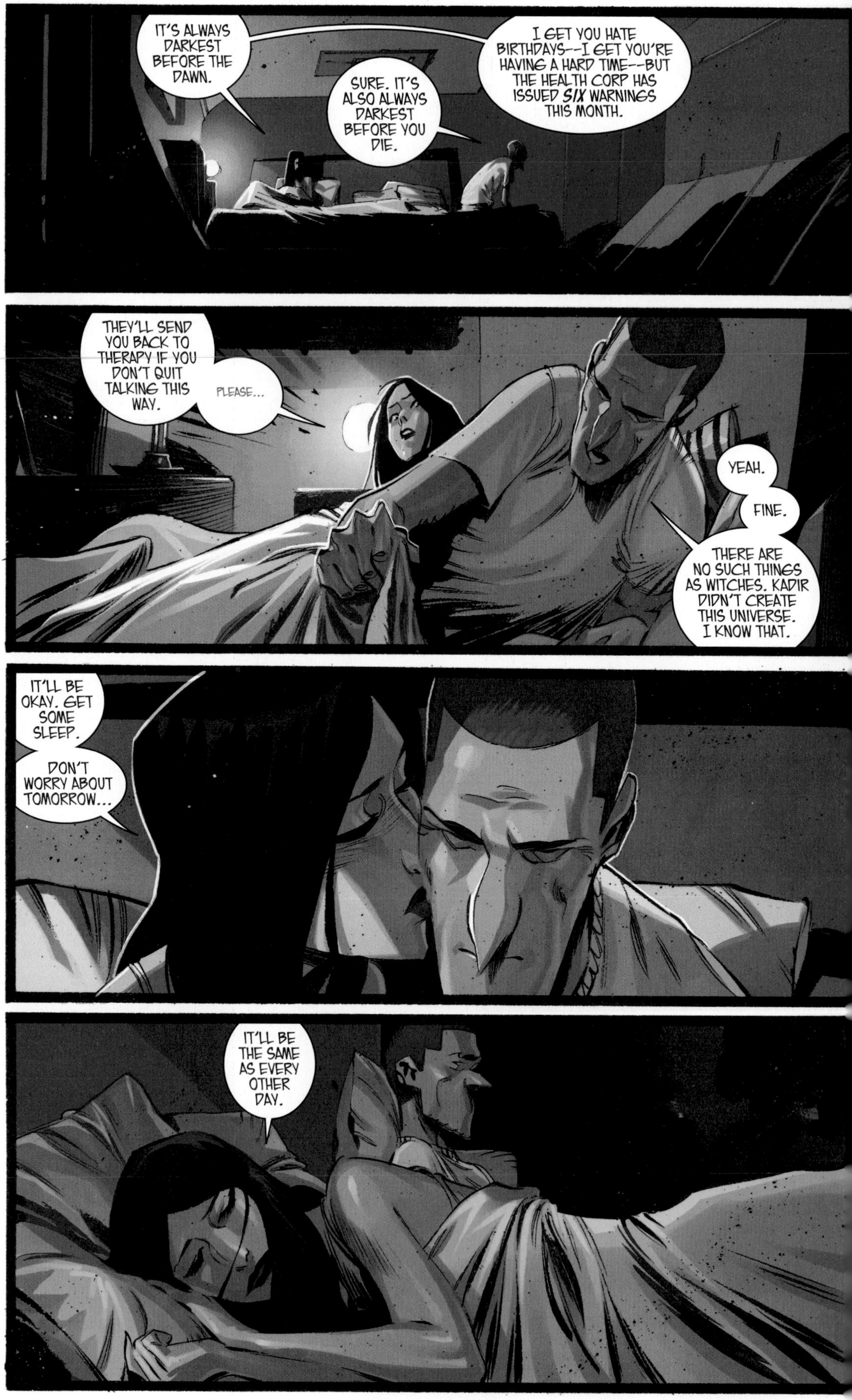

IT'S ALWAYS DARKEST BEFORE THE DAWN.
SURE. IT'S ALSO ALWAYS DARKEST BEFORE YOU DIE.
I GET YOU HATE BIRTHDAYS--I GET YOU'RE HAVING A HARD TIME--BUT THE HEALTH CORP HAS ISSUED **SIX** WARNINGS THIS MONTH.
THEY'LL SEND YOU BACK TO THERAPY IF YOU DON'T QUIT TALKING THIS WAY.
PLEASE...
YEAH.
FINE.
THERE ARE NO SUCH THINGS AS WITCHES. KADIR DIDN'T CREATE THIS UNIVERSE. I KNOW THAT.
IT'LL BE OKAY. GET SOME SLEEP.
DON'T WORRY ABOUT TOMORROW...
IT'LL BE THE SAME AS EVERY OTHER DAY.

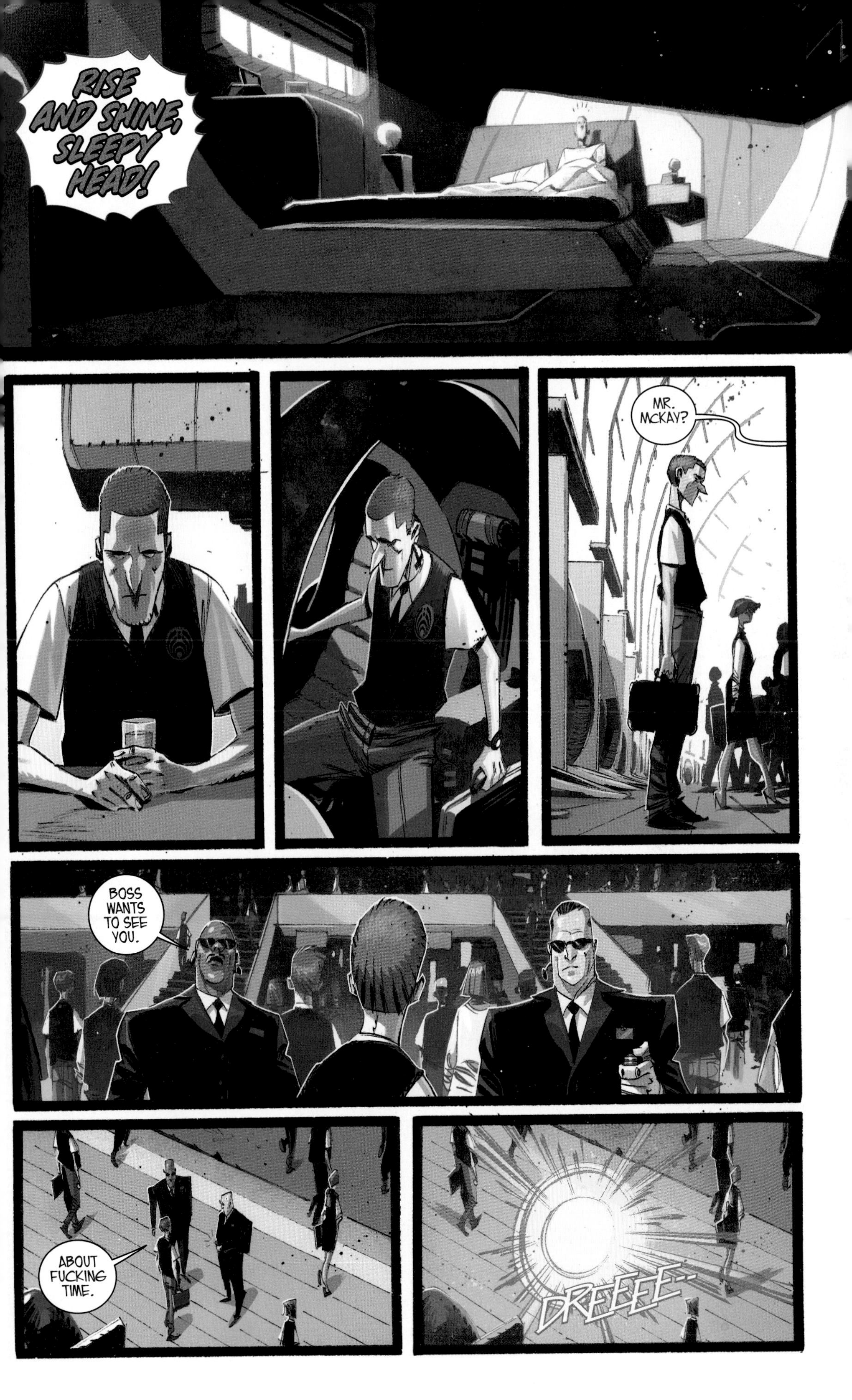
RISE AND SHINE, SLEEPY HEAD!
MR. MCKAY?
BOSS WANTS TO SEE YOU.
ABOUT FUCKING TIME.
DREEEE-

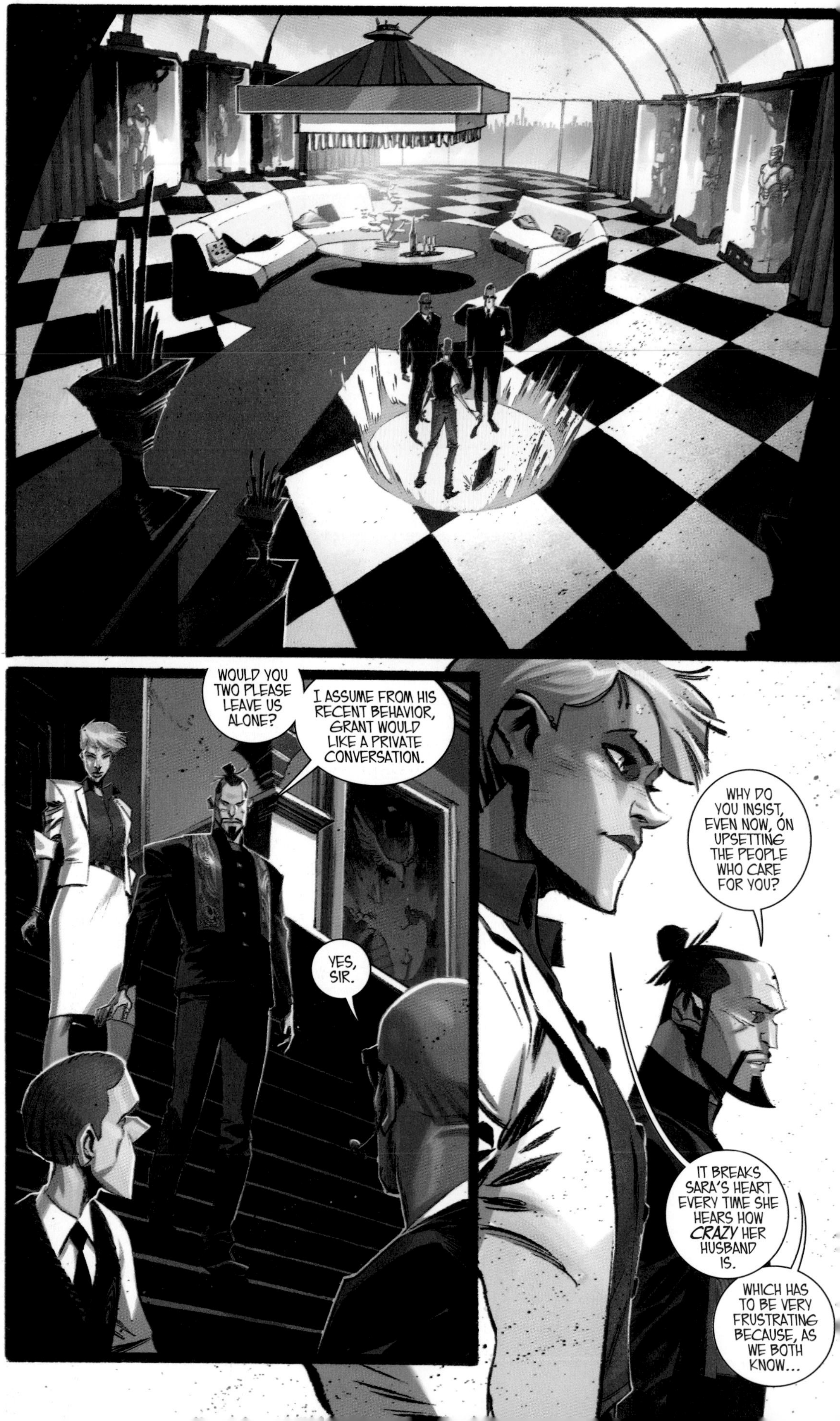

WOULD YOU TWO PLEASE LEAVE US ALONE?
I ASSUME FROM HIS RECENT BEHAVIOR, GRANT WOULD LIKE A PRIVATE CONVERSATION.
YES, SIR.
WHY DO YOU INSIST, EVEN NOW, ON UPSETTING THE PEOPLE WHO CARE FOR YOU?
IT BREAKS SARA'S HEART EVERY TIME SHE HEARS HOW *CRAZY* HER HUSBAND IS.
WHICH HAS TO BE VERY FRUSTRATING BECAUSE, AS WE BOTH KNOW...

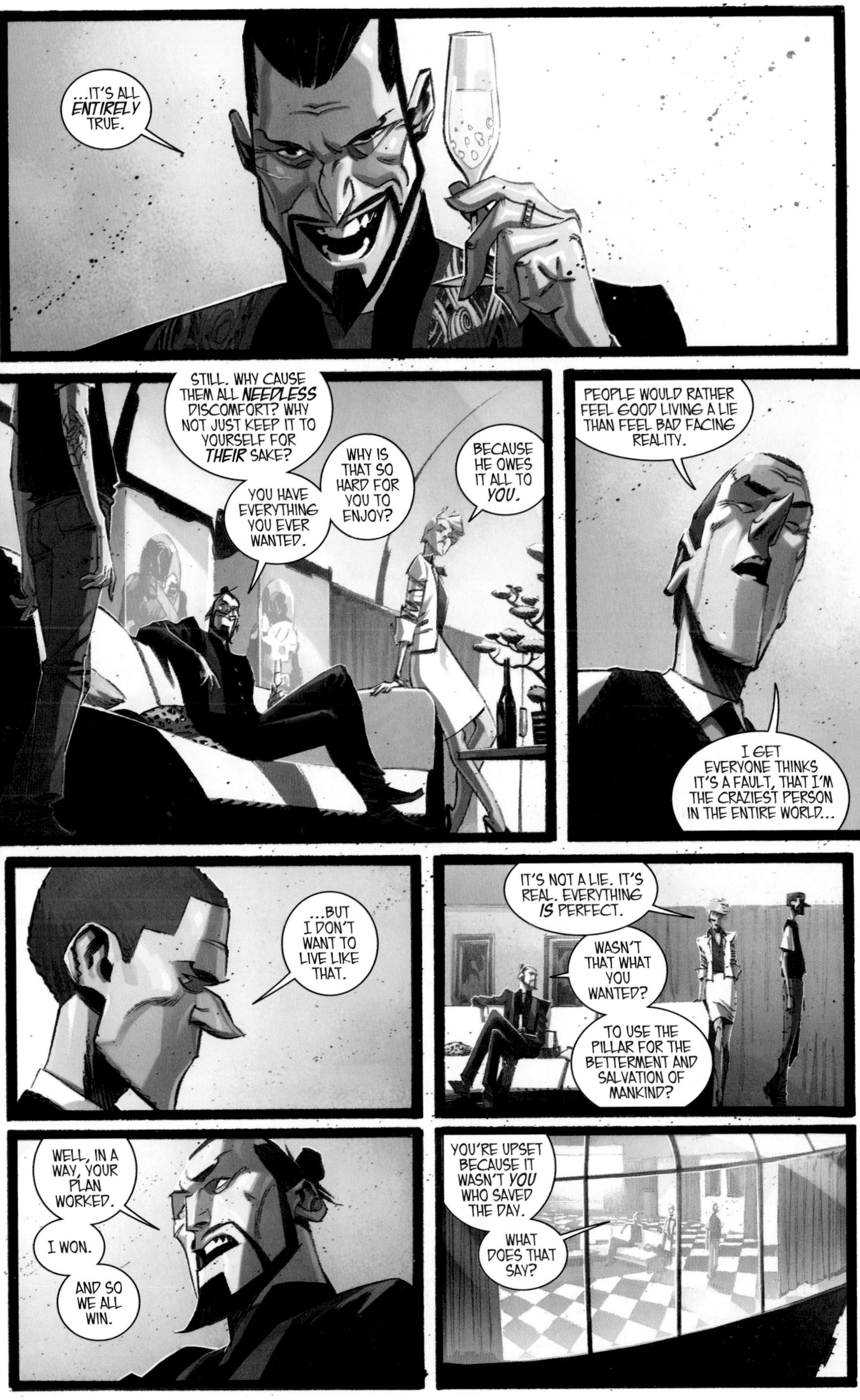

...IT'S ALL ENTIRELY TRUE.
STILL. WHY CAUSE THEM ALL NEEDLESS DISCOMFORT? WHY NOT JUST KEEP IT TO YOURSELF FOR THEIR SAKE?
YOU HAVE EVERYTHING YOU EVER WANTED.
WHY IS THAT SO HARD FOR YOU TO ENJOY?
BECAUSE HE OWES IT ALL TO YOU.
PEOPLE WOULD RATHER FEEL GOOD LIVING A LIE THAN FEEL BAD FACING REALITY.
I GET EVERYONE THINKS IT'S A FAULT, THAT I'M THE CRAZIEST PERSON IN THE ENTIRE WORLD...
...BUT I DON'T WANT TO LIVE LIKE THAT.
IT'S NOT A LIE. IT'S REAL. EVERYTHING IS PERFECT.
WASN'T THAT WHAT YOU WANTED?
TO USE THE PILLAR FOR THE BETTERMENT AND SALVATION OF MANKIND?
WELL, IN A WAY, YOUR PLAN WORKED.
I WON.
AND SO WE ALL WIN.
YOU'RE UPSET BECAUSE IT WASN'T YOU WHO SAVED THE DAY.
WHAT DOES THAT SAY?

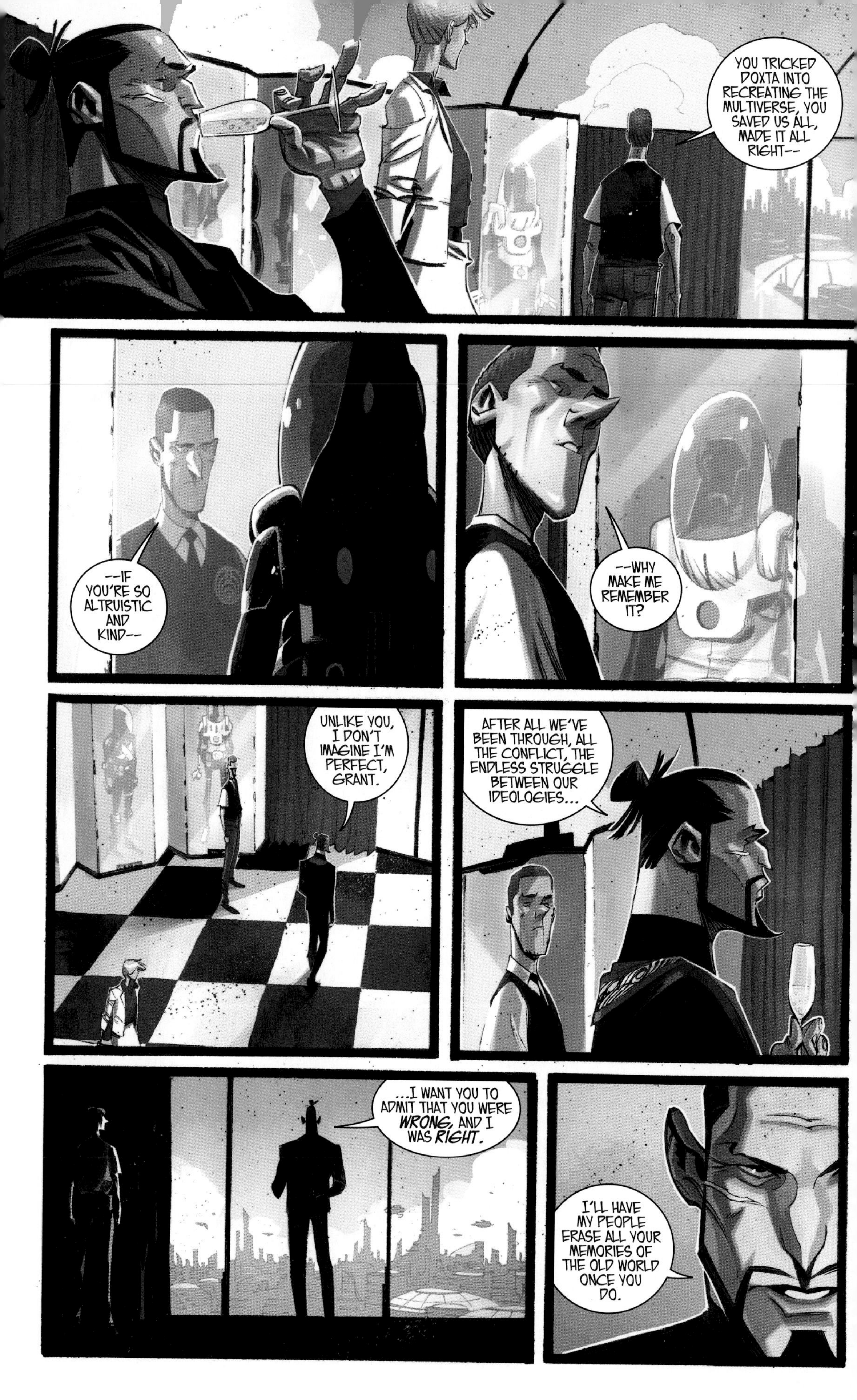
YOU TRICKED DOXTA INTO RECREATING THE MULTIVERSE, YOU SAVED US ALL, MADE IT ALL RIGHT--
--IF YOU'RE SO ALTRUISTIC AND KIND--
--WHY MAKE ME REMEMBER IT?
UNLIKE YOU, I DON'T IMAGINE I'M PERFECT, GRANT.
AFTER ALL WE'VE BEEN THROUGH, ALL THE CONFLICT, THE ENDLESS STRUGGLE BETWEEN OUR IDEOLOGIES...
...I WANT YOU TO ADMIT THAT YOU WERE *WRONG*, AND I WAS *RIGHT*.
I'LL HAVE MY PEOPLE ERASE ALL YOUR MEMORIES OF THE OLD WORLD ONCE YOU DO.

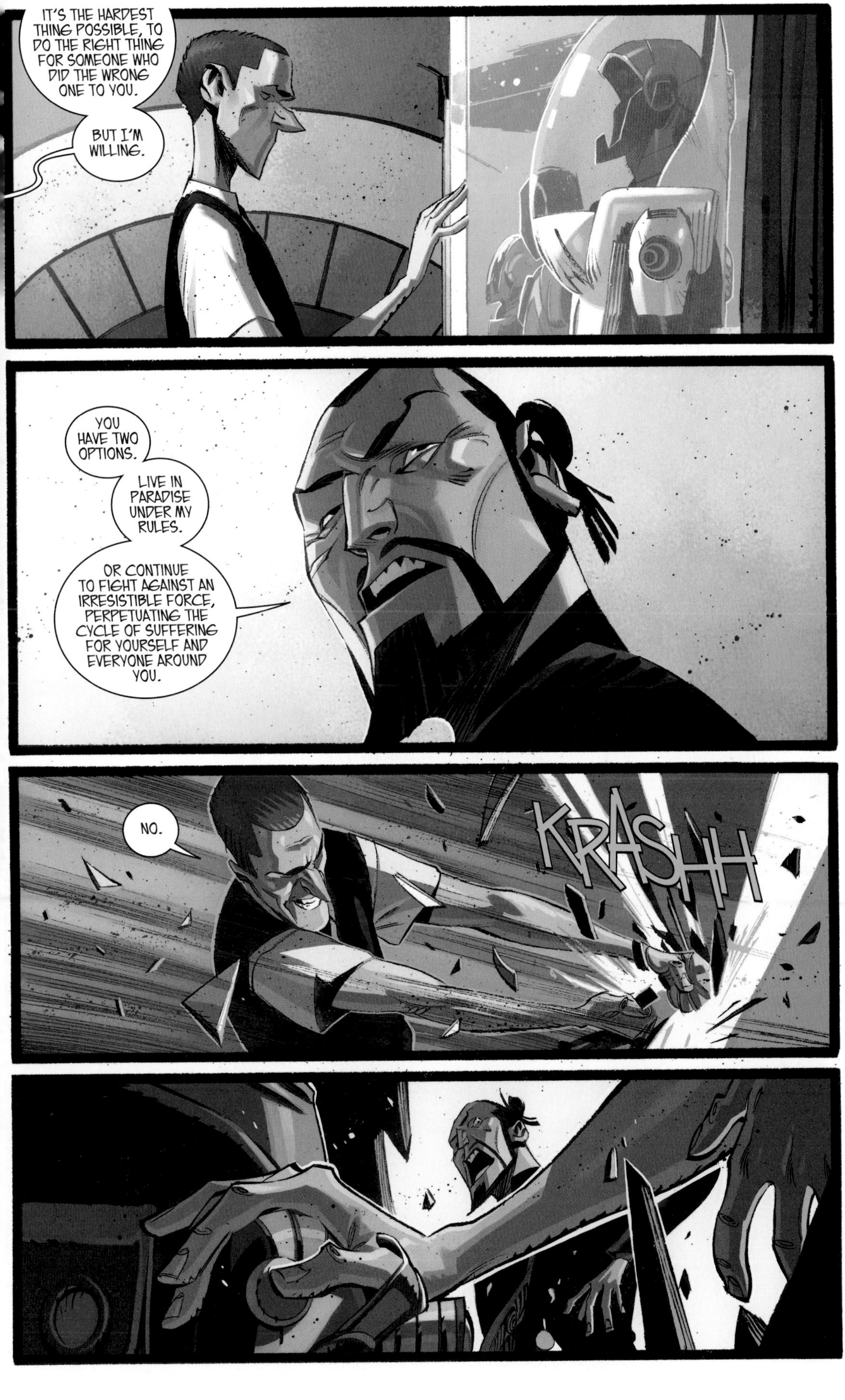
IT'S THE HARDEST THING POSSIBLE, TO DO THE RIGHT THING FOR SOMEONE WHO DID THE WRONG ONE TO YOU.
BUT I'M WILLING.
YOU HAVE TWO OPTIONS.
LIVE IN PARADISE UNDER MY RULES.
OR CONTINUE TO FIGHT AGAINST AN IRRESISTIBLE FORCE, PERPETUATING THE CYCLE OF SUFFERING FOR YOURSELF AND EVERYONE AROUND YOU.
NO.
KRASHH

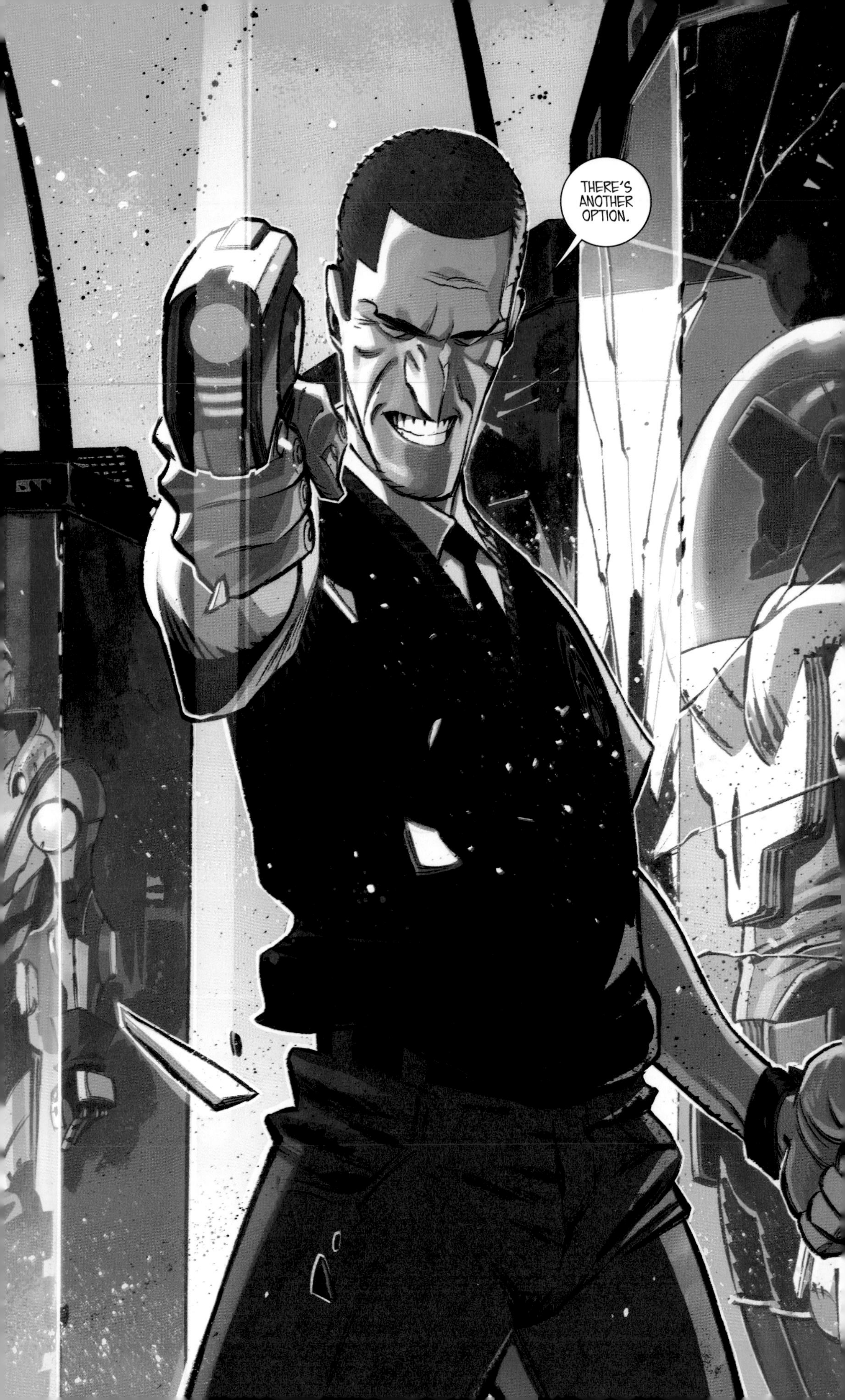
THERE'S ANOTHER OPTION.

42

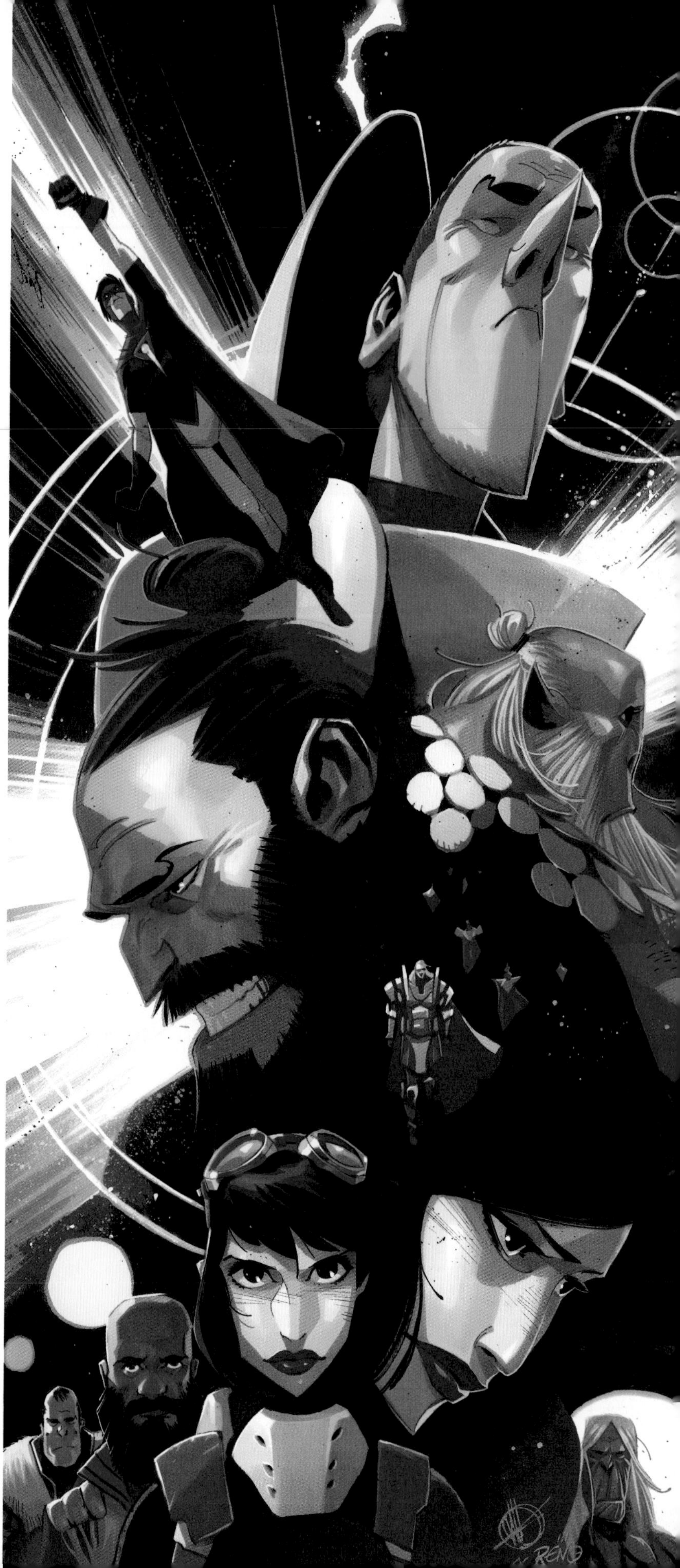

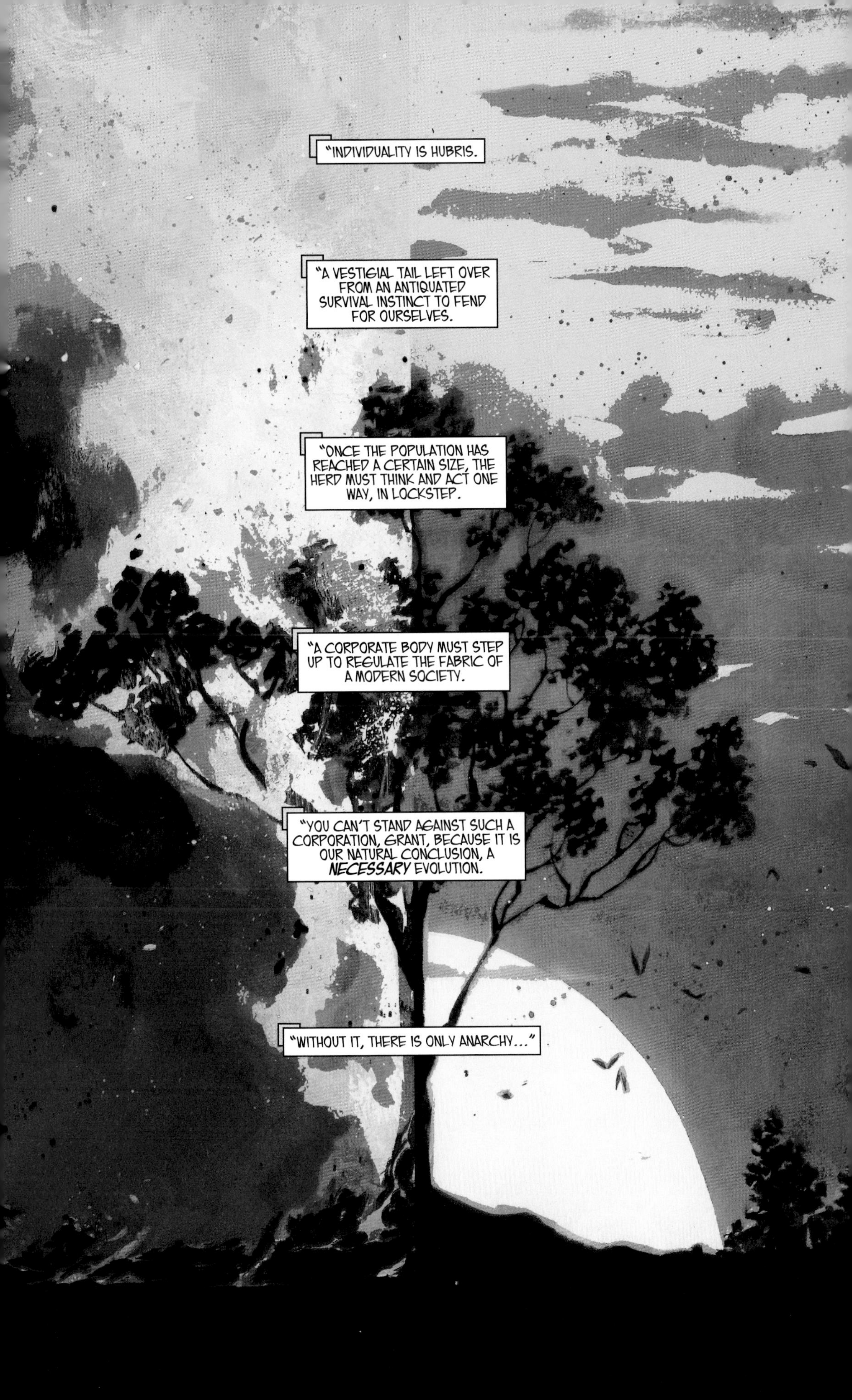
"INDIVIDUALITY IS HUBRIS.
"A VESTIGIAL TAIL LEFT OVER FROM AN ANTIQUATED SURVIVAL INSTINCT TO FEND FOR OURSELVES.
"ONCE THE POPULATION HAS REACHED A CERTAIN SIZE, THE HERD MUST THINK AND ACT ONE WAY, IN LOCKSTEP.
"A CORPORATE BODY MUST STEP UP TO REGULATE THE FABRIC OF A MODERN SOCIETY.
"YOU CAN'T STAND AGAINST SUCH A CORPORATION, GRANT, BECAUSE IT IS OUR NATURAL CONCLUSION, A ***NECESSARY*** EVOLUTION.
"WITHOUT IT, THERE IS ONLY ANARCHY..."

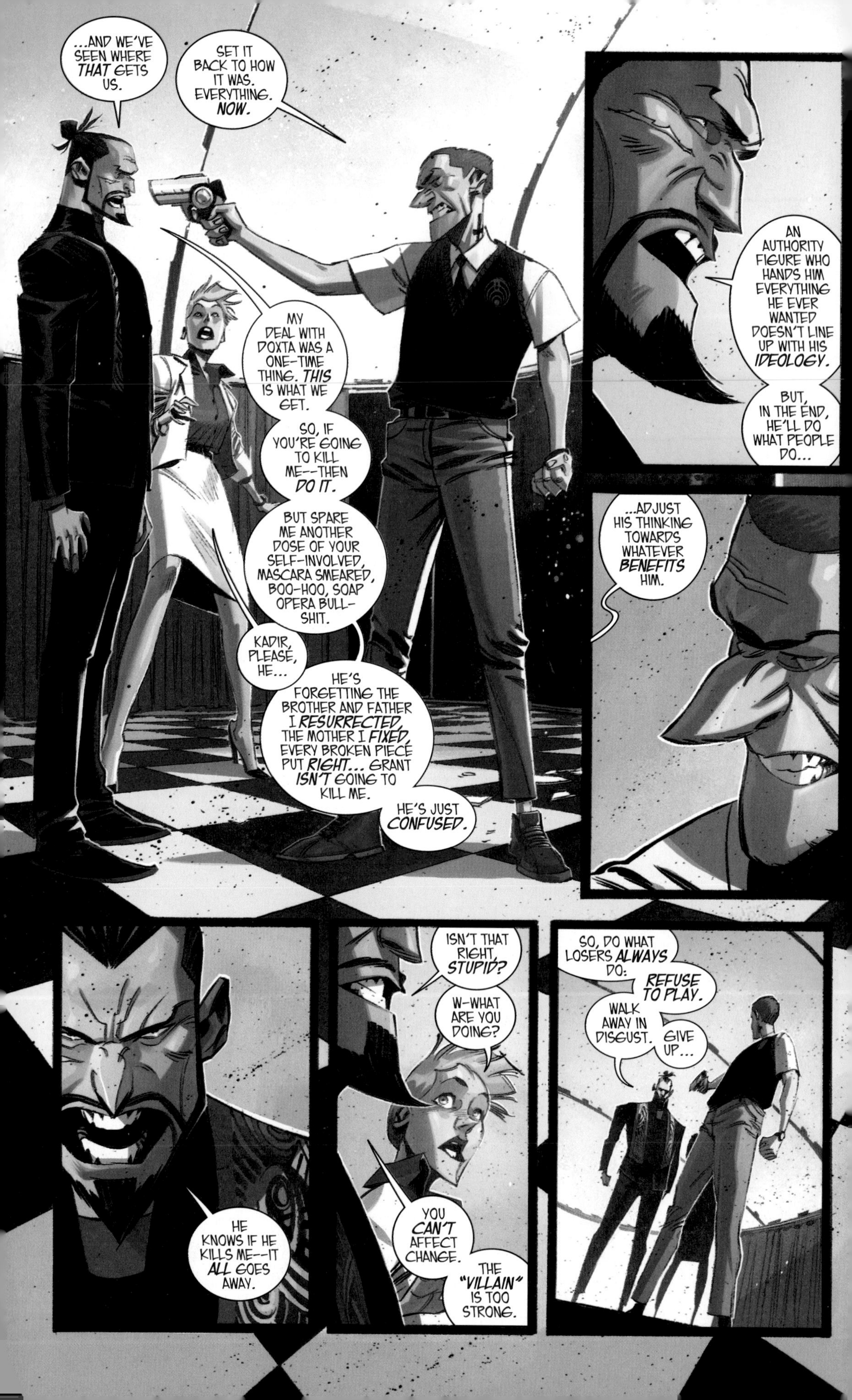
...AND WE'VE SEEN WHERE THAT GETS US.
SET IT BACK TO HOW IT WAS. EVERYTHING. NOW.
MY DEAL WITH DOXTA WAS A ONE-TIME THING. THIS IS WHAT WE GET.
SO, IF YOU'RE GOING TO KILL ME--THEN DO IT.
BUT SPARE ME ANOTHER DOSE OF YOUR SELF-INVOLVED, MASCARA SMEARED, BOO-HOO, SOAP OPERA BULL-SHIT.
KADIR, PLEASE, HE...
HE'S FORGETTING THE BROTHER AND FATHER I RESURRECTED, THE MOTHER I FIXED, EVERY BROKEN PIECE PUT RIGHT... GRANT ISN'T GOING TO KILL ME.
HE'S JUST CONFUSED.
AN AUTHORITY FIGURE WHO HANDS HIM EVERYTHING HE EVER WANTED DOESN'T LINE UP WITH HIS IDEOLOGY.
BUT, IN THE END, HE'LL DO WHAT PEOPLE DO...
...ADJUST HIS THINKING TOWARDS WHATEVER BENEFITS HIM.
HE KNOWS IF HE KILLS ME--IT ALL GOES AWAY.
ISN'T THAT RIGHT, STUPID?
W-WHAT ARE YOU DOING?
YOU CAN'T AFFECT CHANGE.
THE "VILLAIN" IS TOO STRONG.
SO, DO WHAT LOSERS ALWAYS DO:
REFUSE TO PLAY.
WALK AWAY IN DISGUST.
GIVE UP...

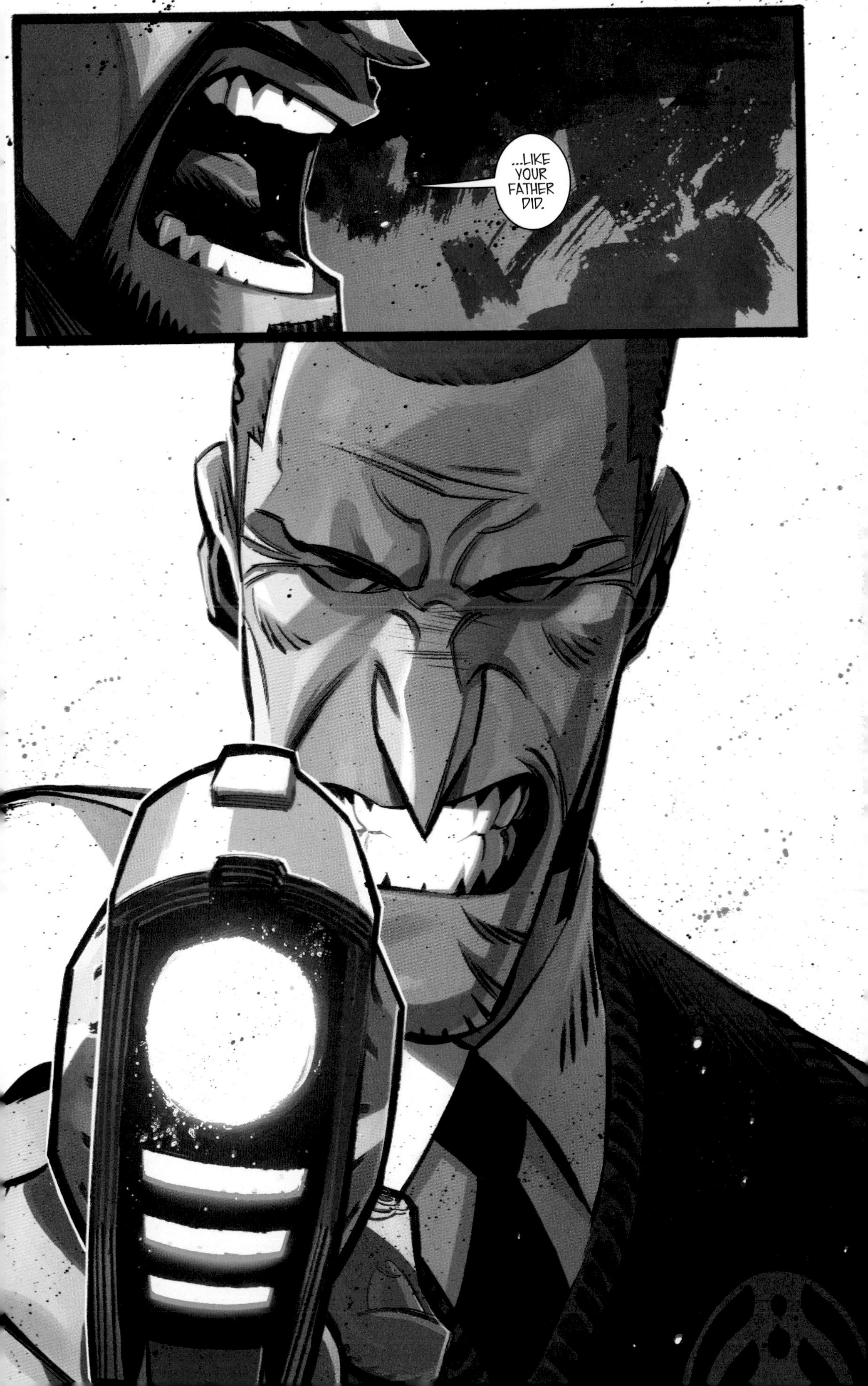
...LIKE YOUR FATHER DID.

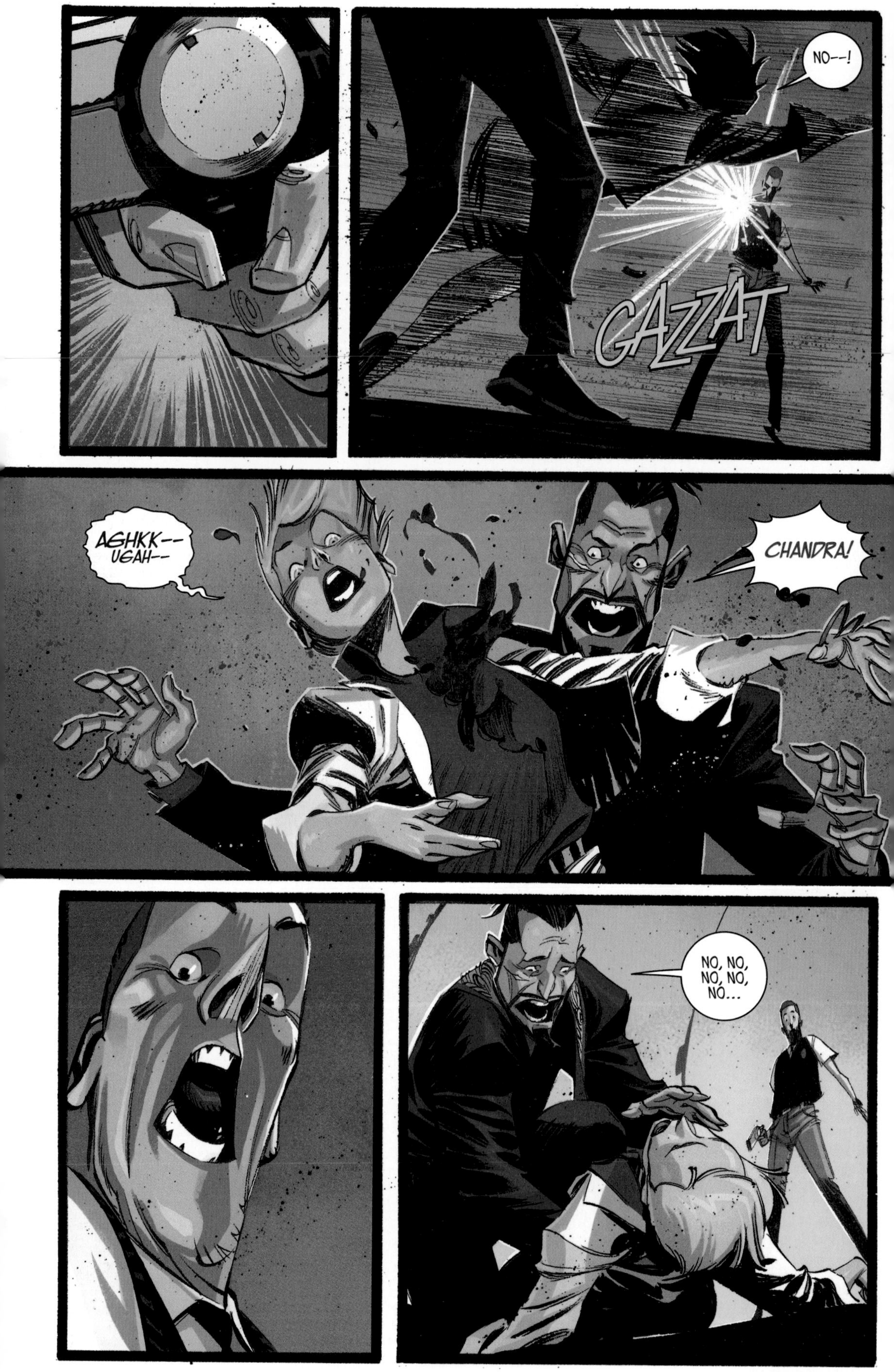
NO--!
GAZZAT
AGHKK--
UGAH--
CHANDRA!
NO, NO,
NO, NO,
NO...

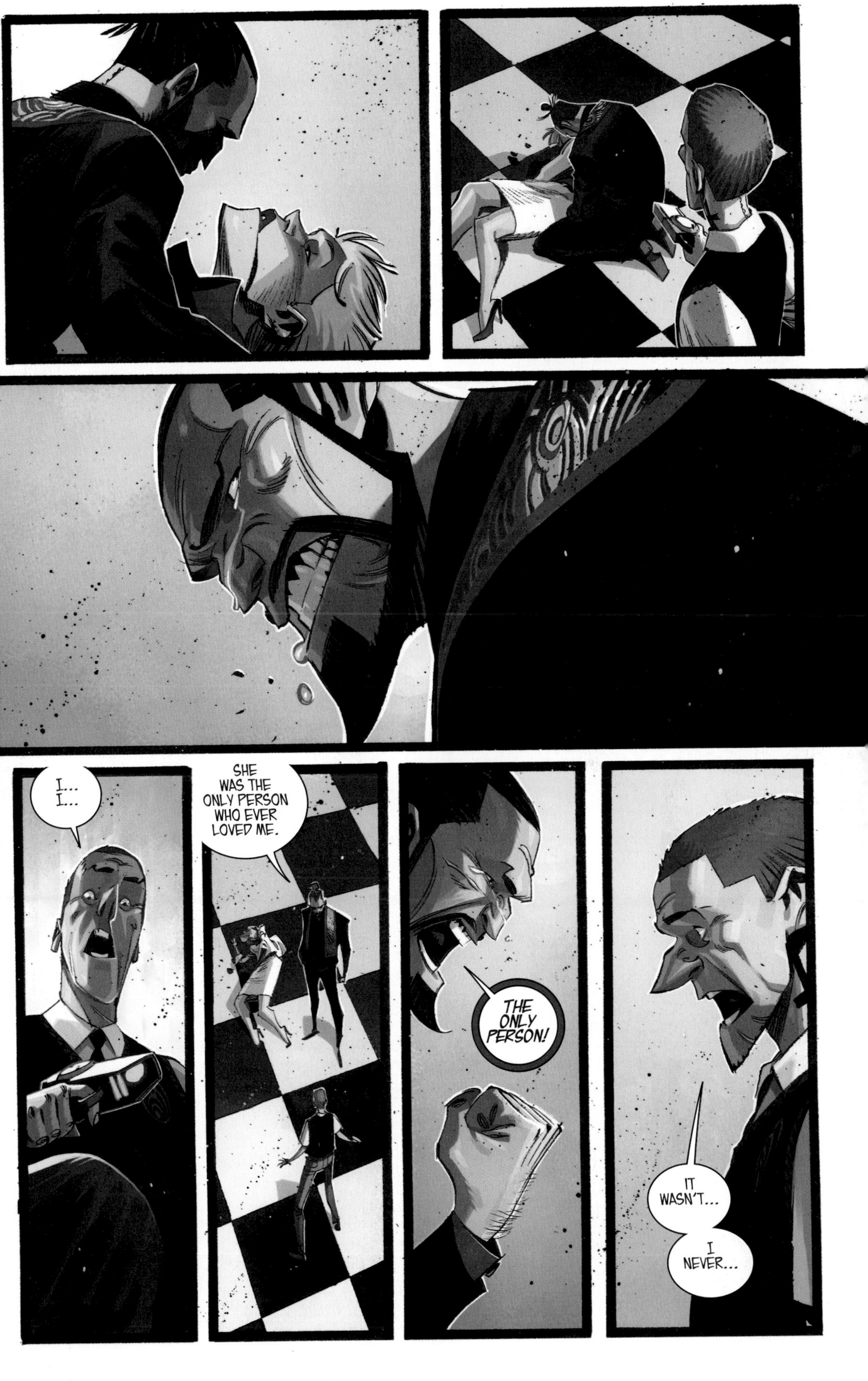
I...
I...
SHE WAS THE ONLY PERSON WHO EVER LOVED ME.
THE ONLY PERSON!
IT WASN'T...
I NEVER...

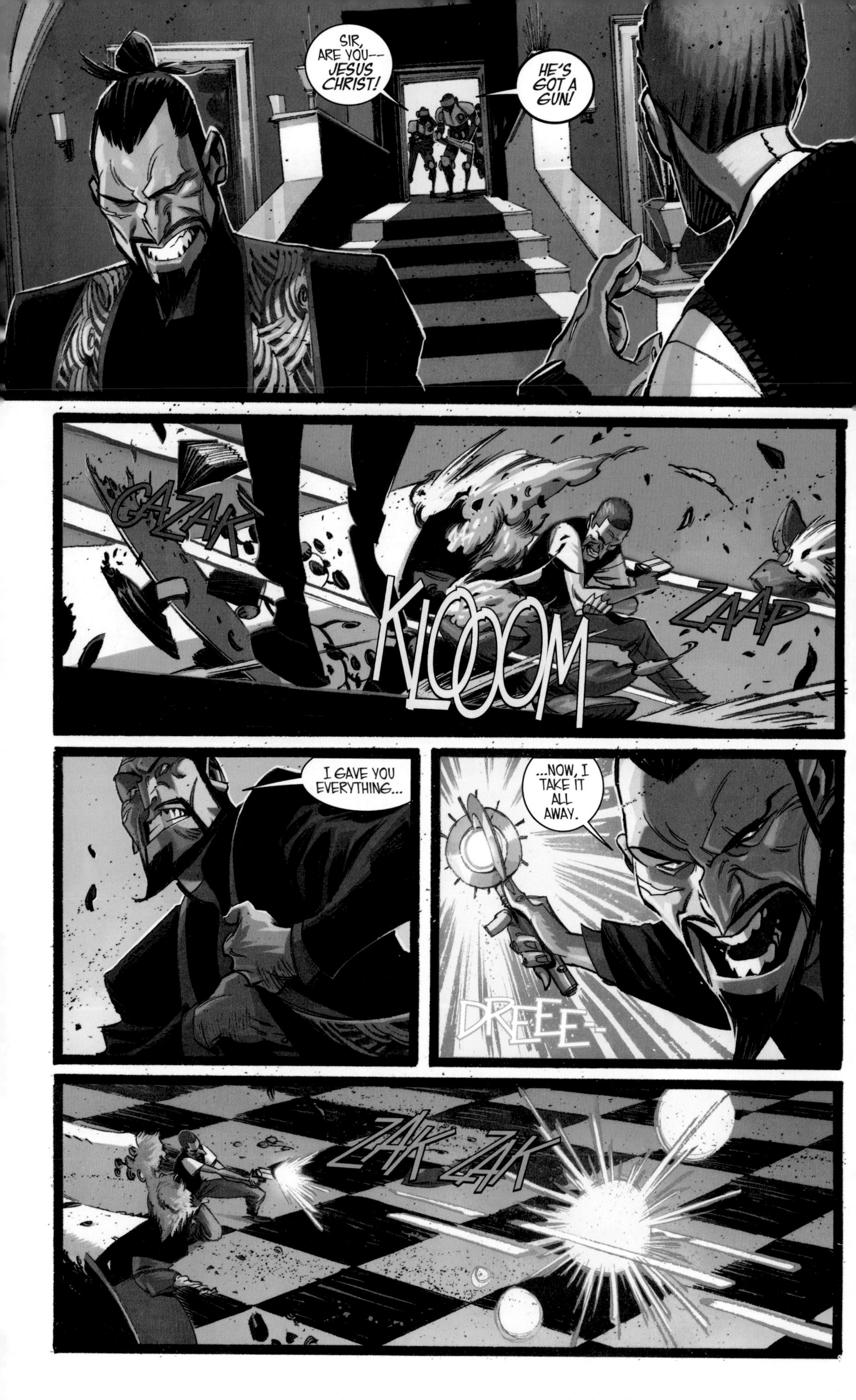
SIR, ARE YOU-- JESUS CHRIST!
HE'S GOT A GUN!
GAZAK
KLOOOM
ZAAP
I GAVE YOU EVERYTHING...
...NOW, I TAKE IT ALL AWAY.
DREEEE--
ZAK ZAK

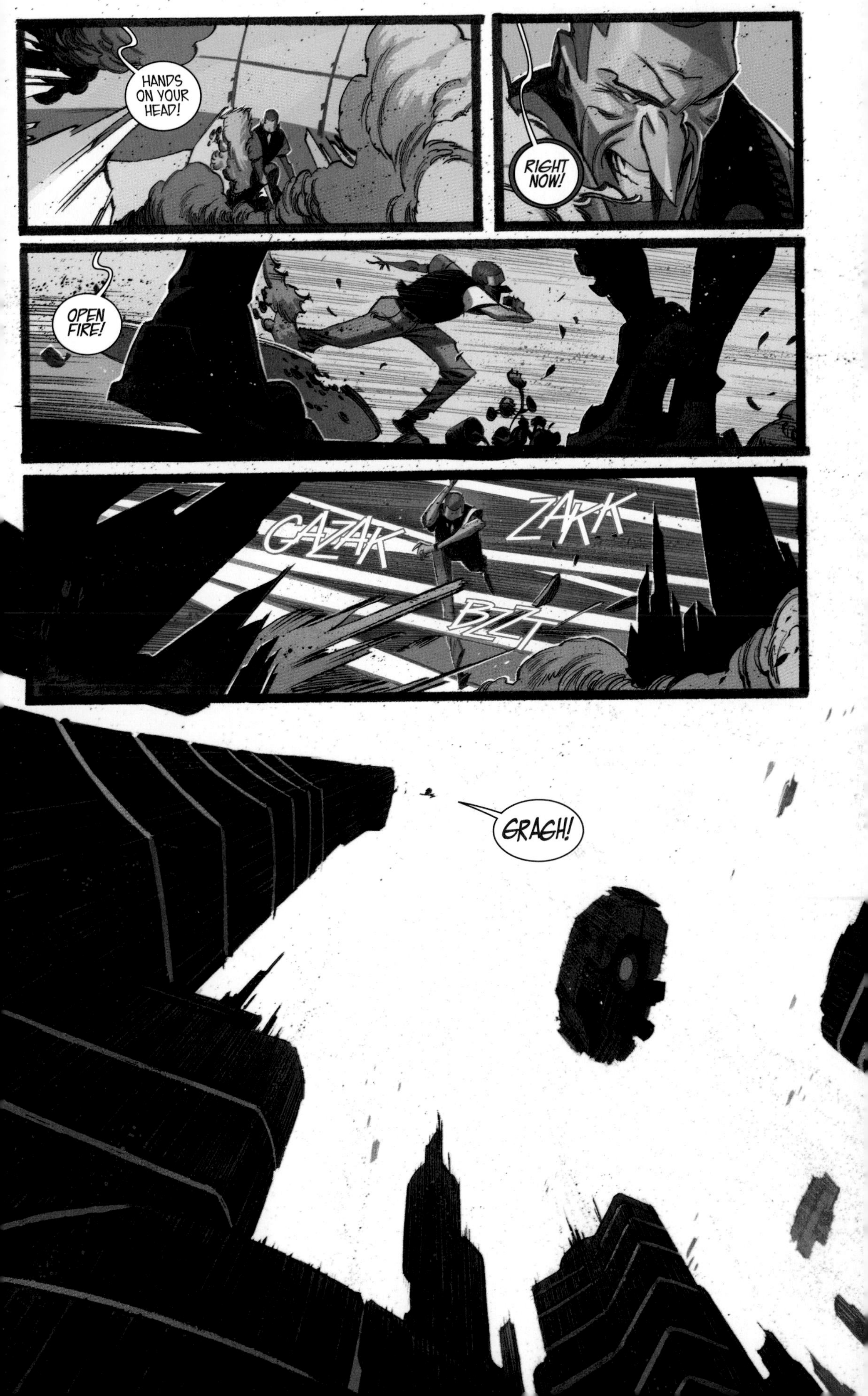
HANDS ON YOUR HEAD!
RIGHT NOW!
OPEN FIRE!
GAZAK
ZAKK
BZZT
GRAGH!

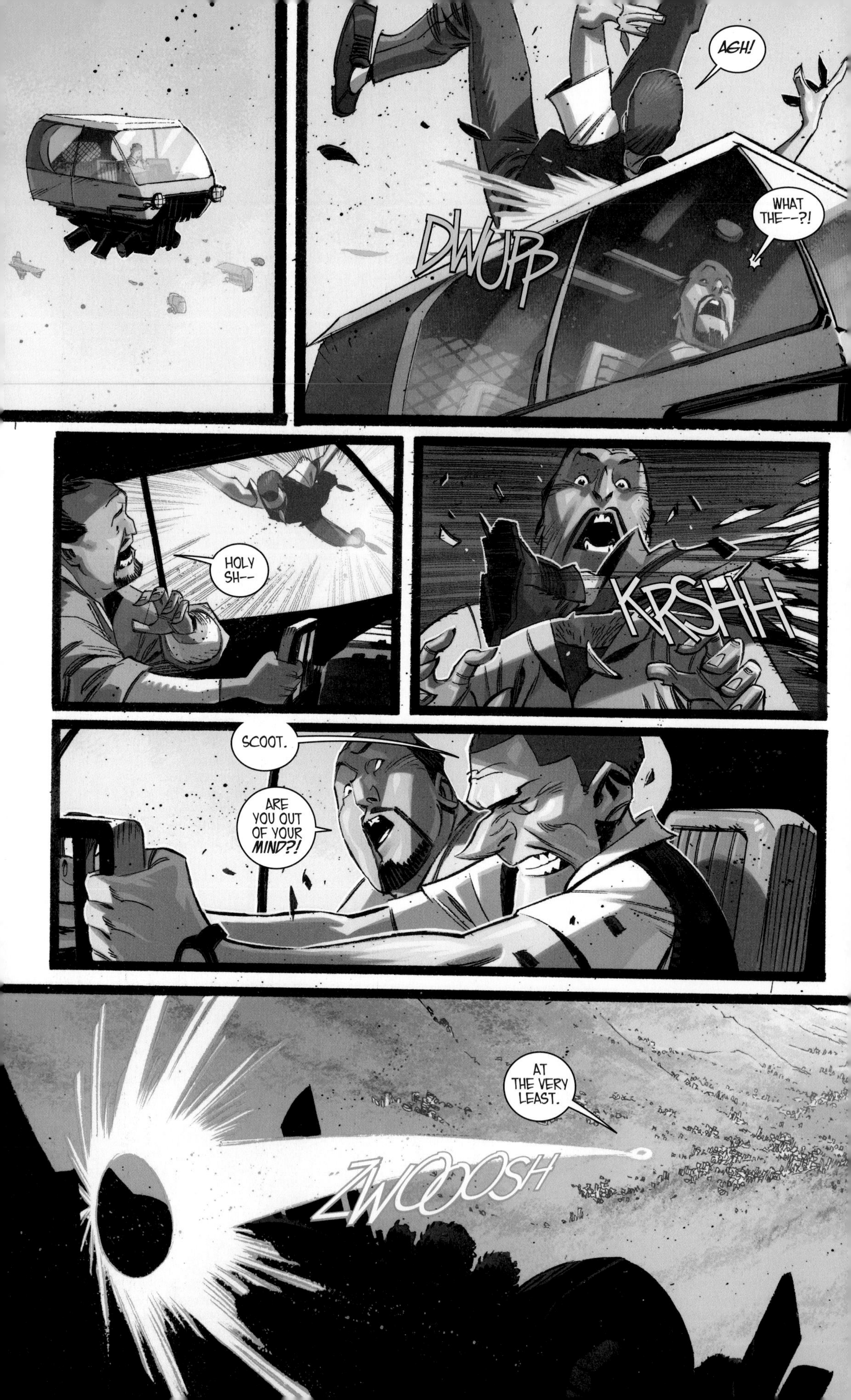
AGH!
DWUPP
WHAT THE--?!
HOLY SH--
KRSHH
SCOOT.
ARE YOU OUT OF YOUR *MIND?!*
AT THE VERY LEAST.
ZWOOOSH

"YOU CAN'T BEAT SUCH A CORPORATION, GRANT, BECAUSE IT IS OUR NATURAL CONCLUSION, A *NECESSARY* EVOLUTION.

"WITHOUT IT, THERE IS ONLY ANARCHY..."

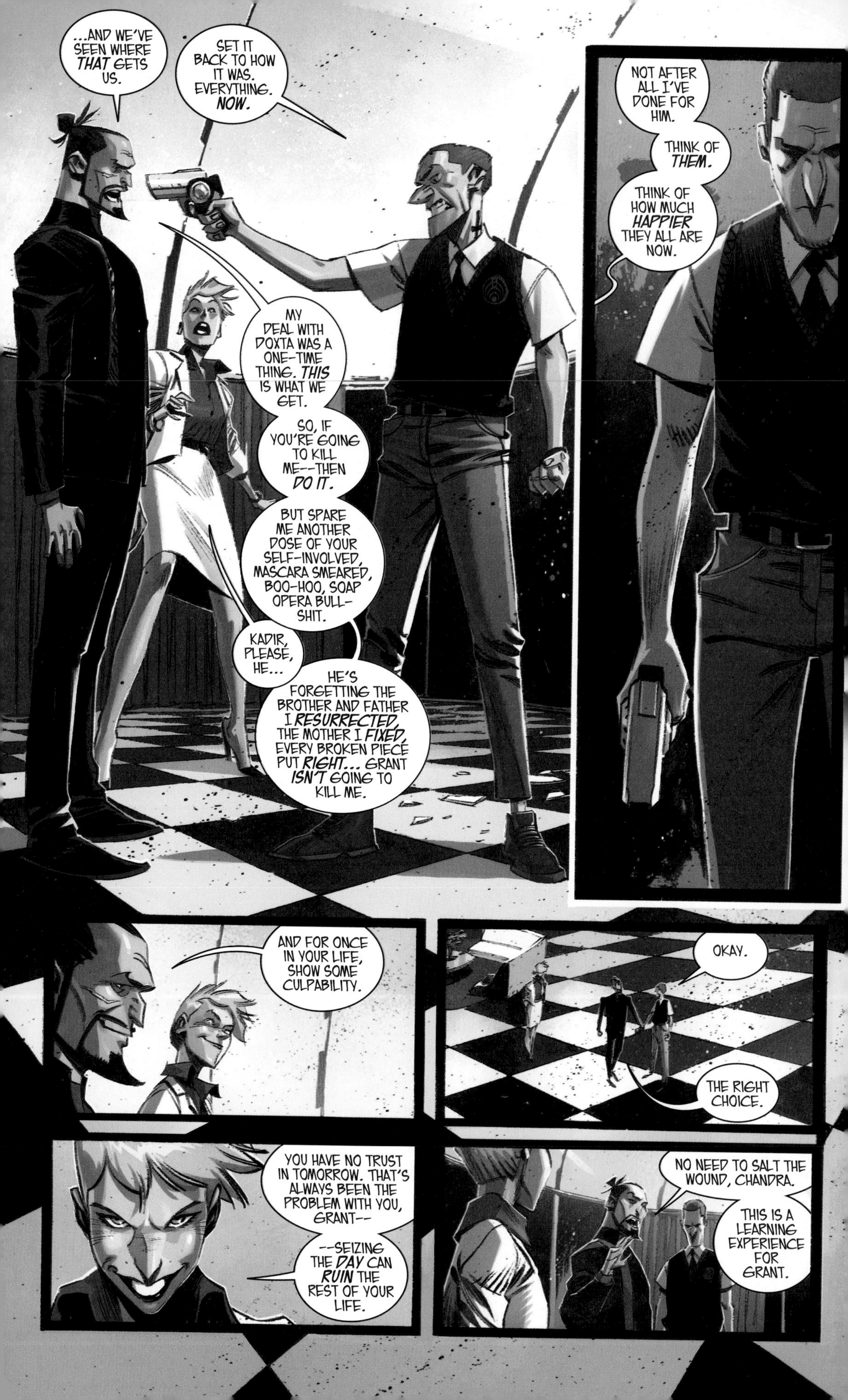
...AND WE'VE SEEN WHERE THAT GETS US.
SET IT BACK TO HOW IT WAS. EVERYTHING. NOW.
MY DEAL WITH DOXTA WAS A ONE-TIME THING. THIS IS WHAT WE GET.
SO, IF YOU'RE GOING TO KILL ME--THEN DO IT.
BUT SPARE ME ANOTHER DOSE OF YOUR SELF-INVOLVED, MASCARA SMEARED, BOO-HOO, SOAP OPERA BULL-SHIT.
KADIR, PLEASE, HE...
HE'S FORGETTING THE BROTHER AND FATHER I RESURRECTED, THE MOTHER I FIXED, EVERY BROKEN PIECE PUT RIGHT... GRANT ISN'T GOING TO KILL ME.
NOT AFTER ALL I'VE DONE FOR HIM.
THINK OF THEM.
THINK OF HOW MUCH HAPPIER THEY ALL ARE NOW.
AND FOR ONCE IN YOUR LIFE, SHOW SOME CULPABILITY.
OKAY.
THE RIGHT CHOICE.
YOU HAVE NO TRUST IN TOMORROW. THAT'S ALWAYS BEEN THE PROBLEM WITH YOU, GRANT--
--SEIZING THE DAY CAN RUIN THE REST OF YOUR LIFE.
NO NEED TO SALT THE WOUND, CHANDRA.
THIS IS A LEARNING EXPERIENCE FOR GRANT.

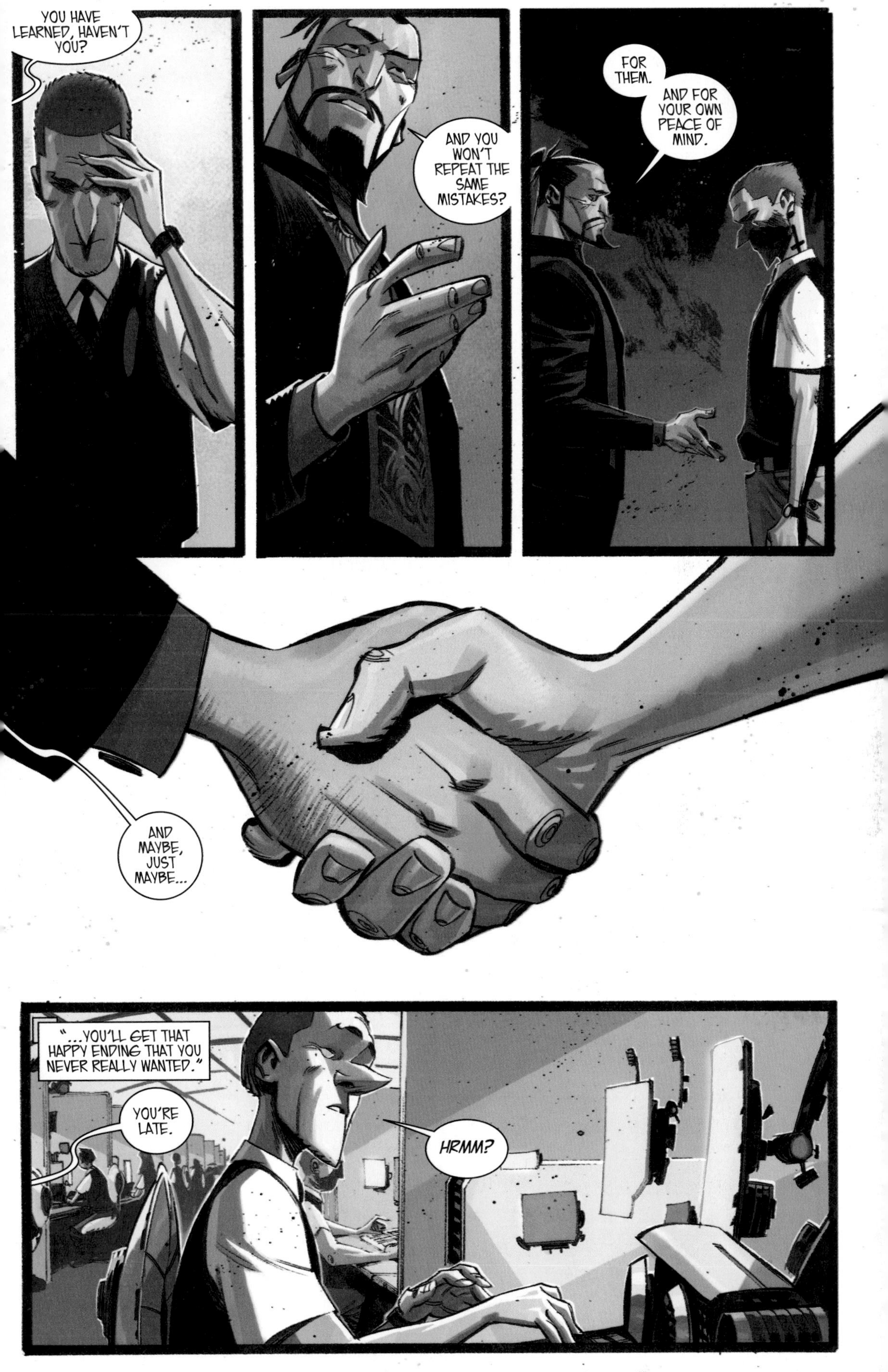
YOU HAVE LEARNED, HAVEN'T YOU?
AND YOU WON'T REPEAT THE SAME MISTAKES?
FOR THEM.
AND FOR YOUR OWN PEACE OF MIND.
AND MAYBE, JUST MAYBE...
"...YOU'LL GET THAT HAPPY ENDING THAT YOU NEVER REALLY WANTED."
YOU'RE LATE.
HRMM?

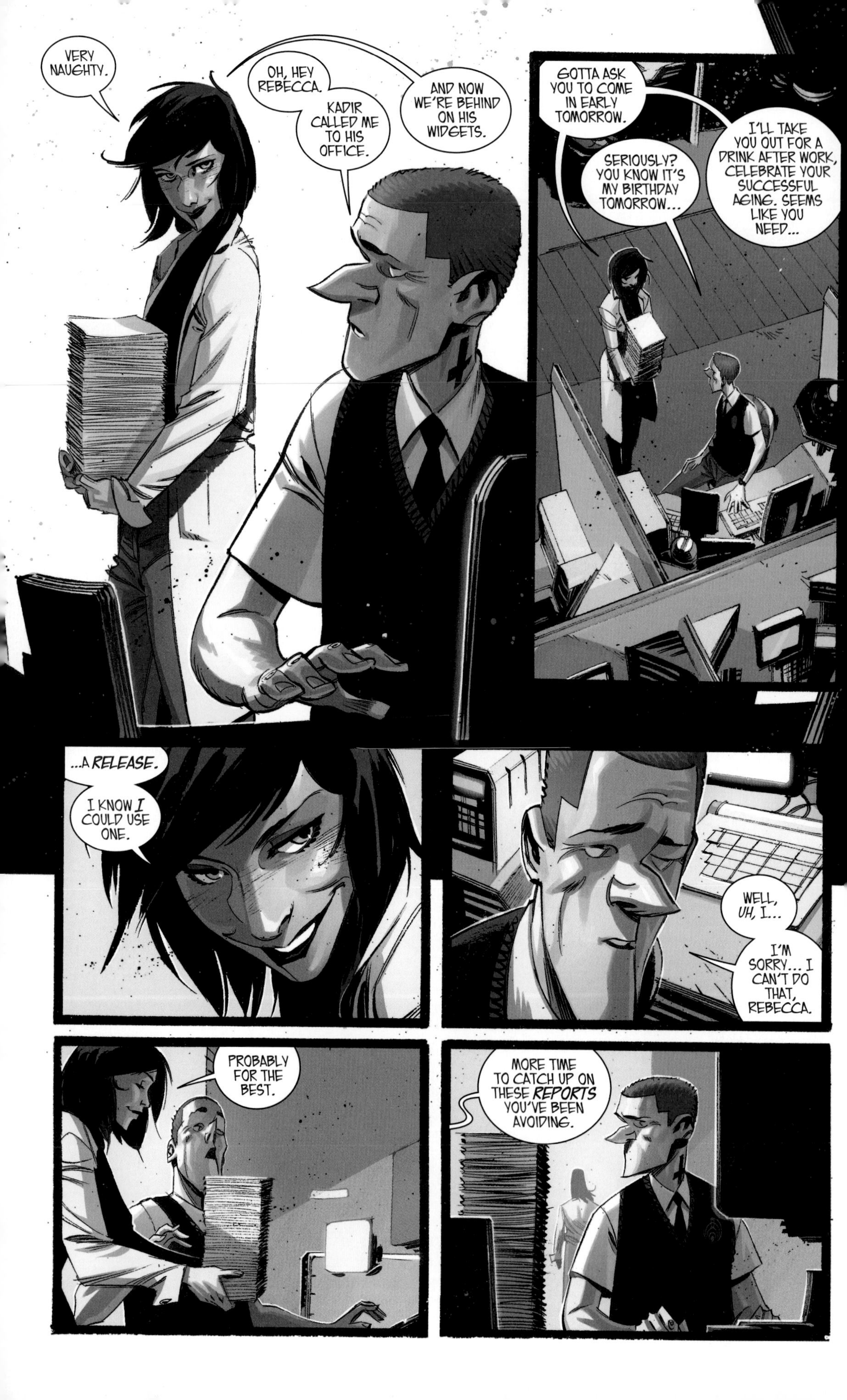
VERY NAUGHTY.
OH, HEY REBECCA.
KADIR CALLED ME TO HIS OFFICE.
AND NOW WE'RE BEHIND ON HIS WIDGETS.
GOTTA ASK YOU TO COME IN EARLY TOMORROW.
SERIOUSLY? YOU KNOW IT'S MY BIRTHDAY TOMORROW...
I'LL TAKE YOU OUT FOR A DRINK AFTER WORK, CELEBRATE YOUR SUCCESSFUL AGING. SEEMS LIKE YOU NEED...
...A *RELEASE*.
I KNOW *I* COULD USE ONE.
WELL, *UH*, I...
I'M SORRY... I CAN'T DO THAT, REBECCA.
PROBABLY FOR THE BEST.
MORE TIME TO CATCH UP ON THESE *REPORTS* YOU'VE BEEN AVOIDING.

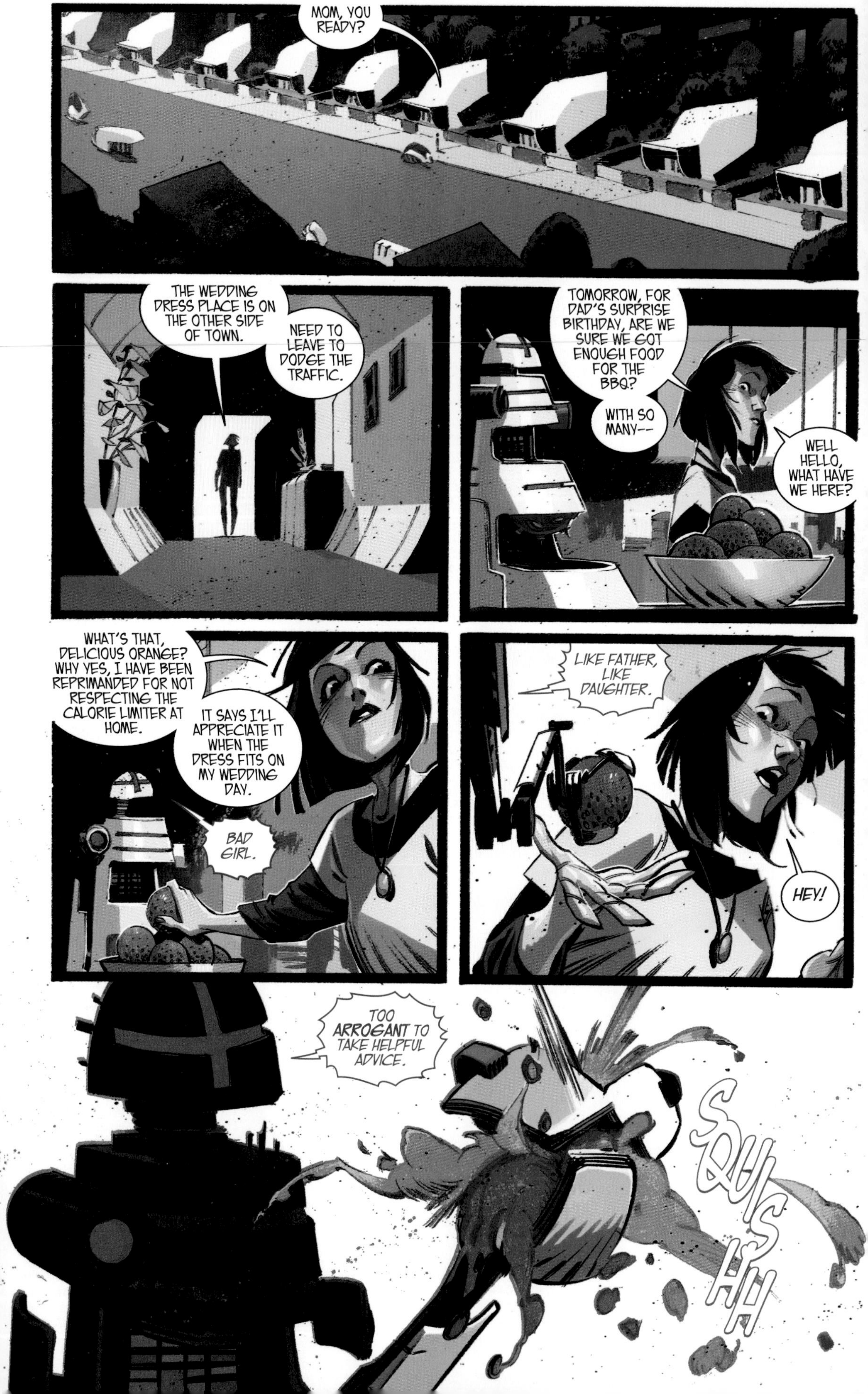
MOM, YOU READY?
THE WEDDING DRESS PLACE IS ON THE OTHER SIDE OF TOWN.
NEED TO LEAVE TO DODGE THE TRAFFIC.
TOMORROW, FOR DAD'S SURPRISE BIRTHDAY, ARE WE SURE WE GOT ENOUGH FOOD FOR THE BBQ?
WITH SO MANY--
WELL HELLO, WHAT HAVE WE HERE?
WHAT'S THAT, DELICIOUS ORANGE? WHY YES, I HAVE BEEN REPRIMANDED FOR NOT RESPECTING THE CALORIE LIMITER AT HOME.
IT SAYS I'LL APPRECIATE IT WHEN THE DRESS FITS ON MY WEDDING DAY.
BAD GIRL.
LIKE FATHER, LIKE DAUGHTER.
HEY!
TOO ARROGANT TO TAKE HELPFUL ADVICE.
SQUISHH

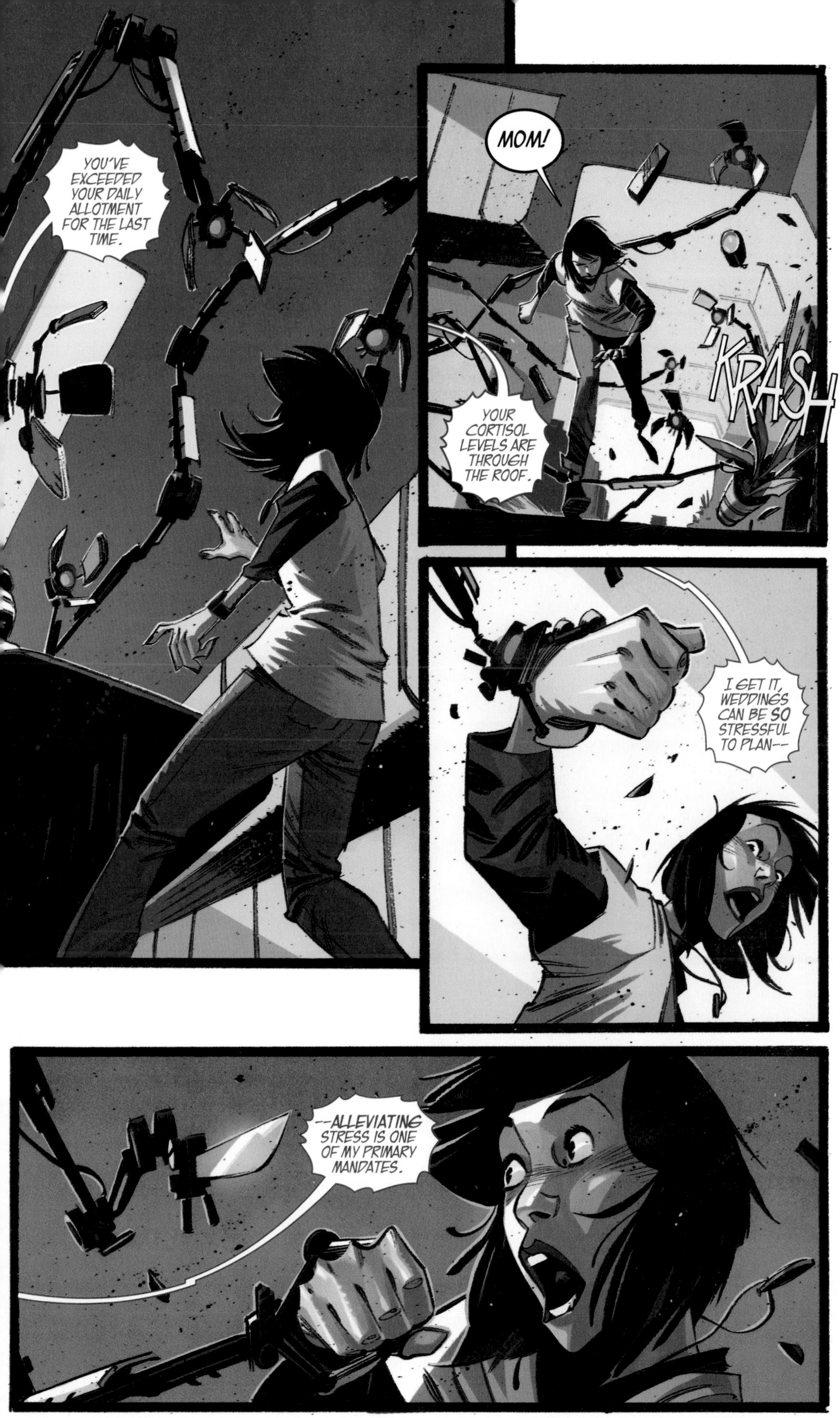
YOU'VE EXCEEDED YOUR DAILY ALLOTMENT FOR THE LAST TIME.
MOM!
KRASH
YOUR CORTISOL LEVELS ARE THROUGH THE ROOF.
I GET IT, WEDDINGS CAN BE SO STRESSFUL TO PLAN--
--ALLEVIATING STRESS IS ONE OF MY PRIMARY MANDATES.

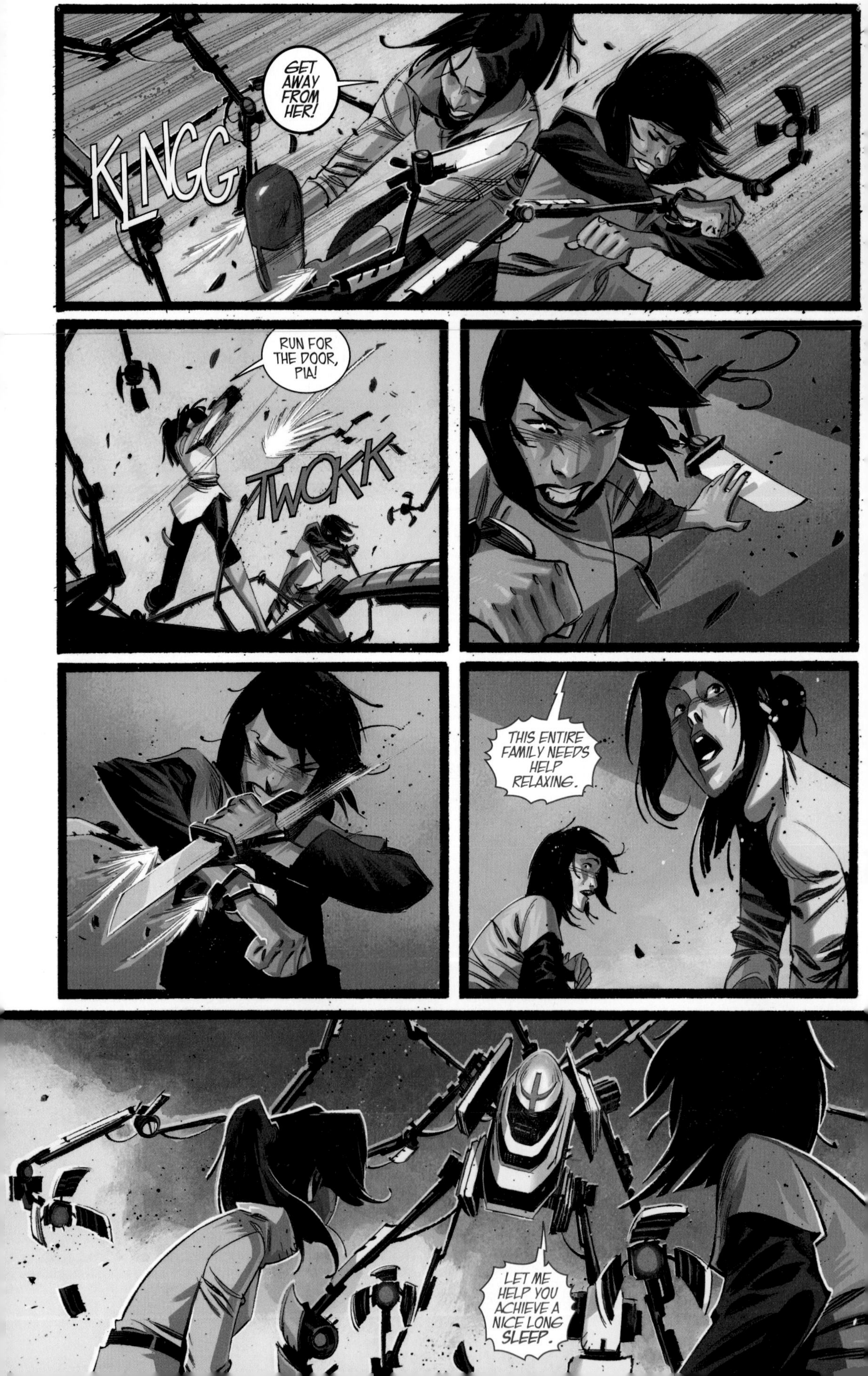
GET AWAY FROM HER!
KLNGG
RUN FOR THE DOOR, PIA!
TWOKK
THIS ENTIRE FAMILY NEEDS HELP RELAXING.
LET ME HELP YOU ACHIEVE A NICE LONG SLEEP.

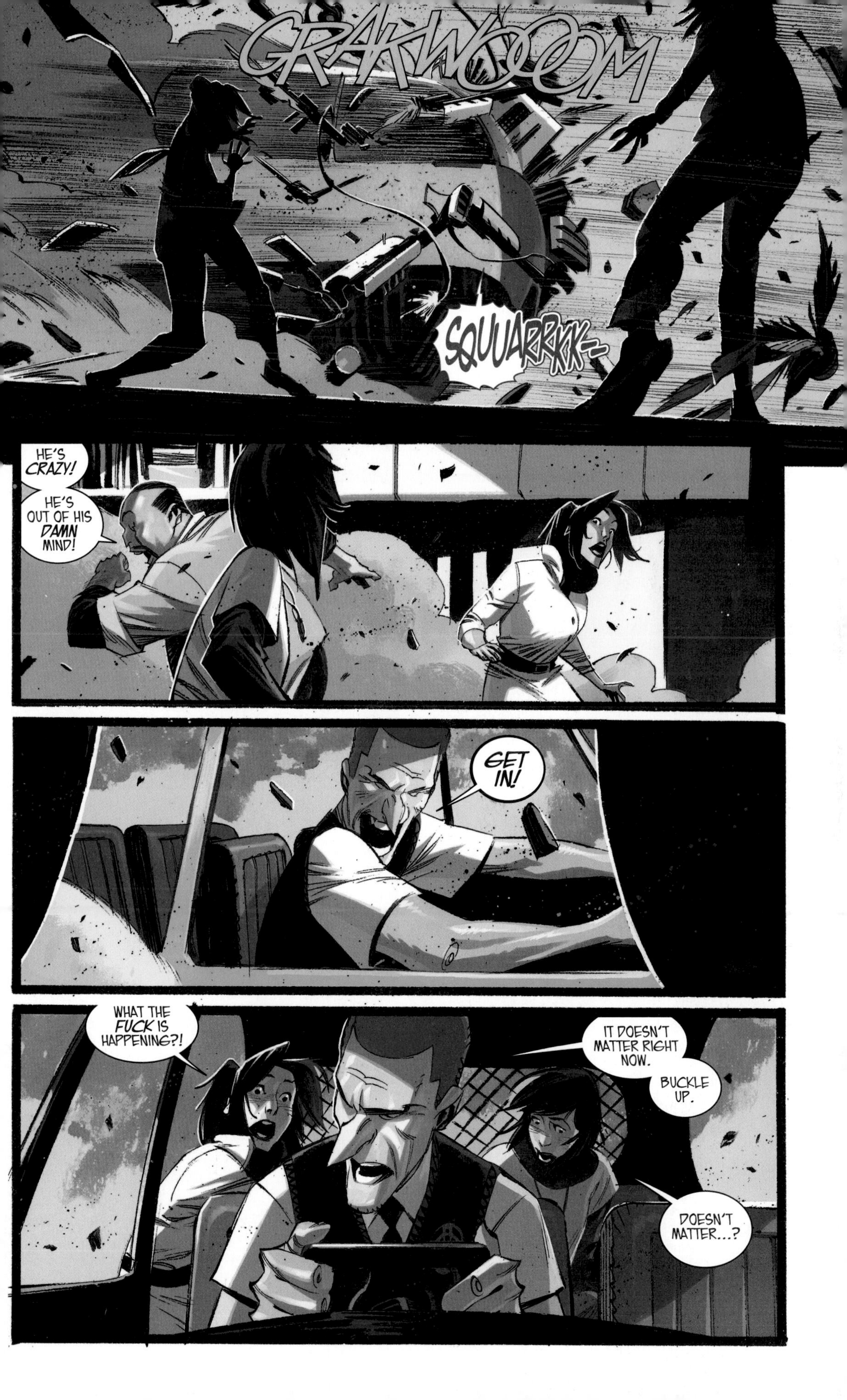
GRAKWOOOM
SQUUARRKKK
HE'S CRAZY!
HE'S OUT OF HIS DAMN MIND!
GET IN!
WHAT THE FUCK IS HAPPENING?!
IT DOESN'T MATTER RIGHT NOW.
BUCKLE UP.
DOESN'T MATTER...?

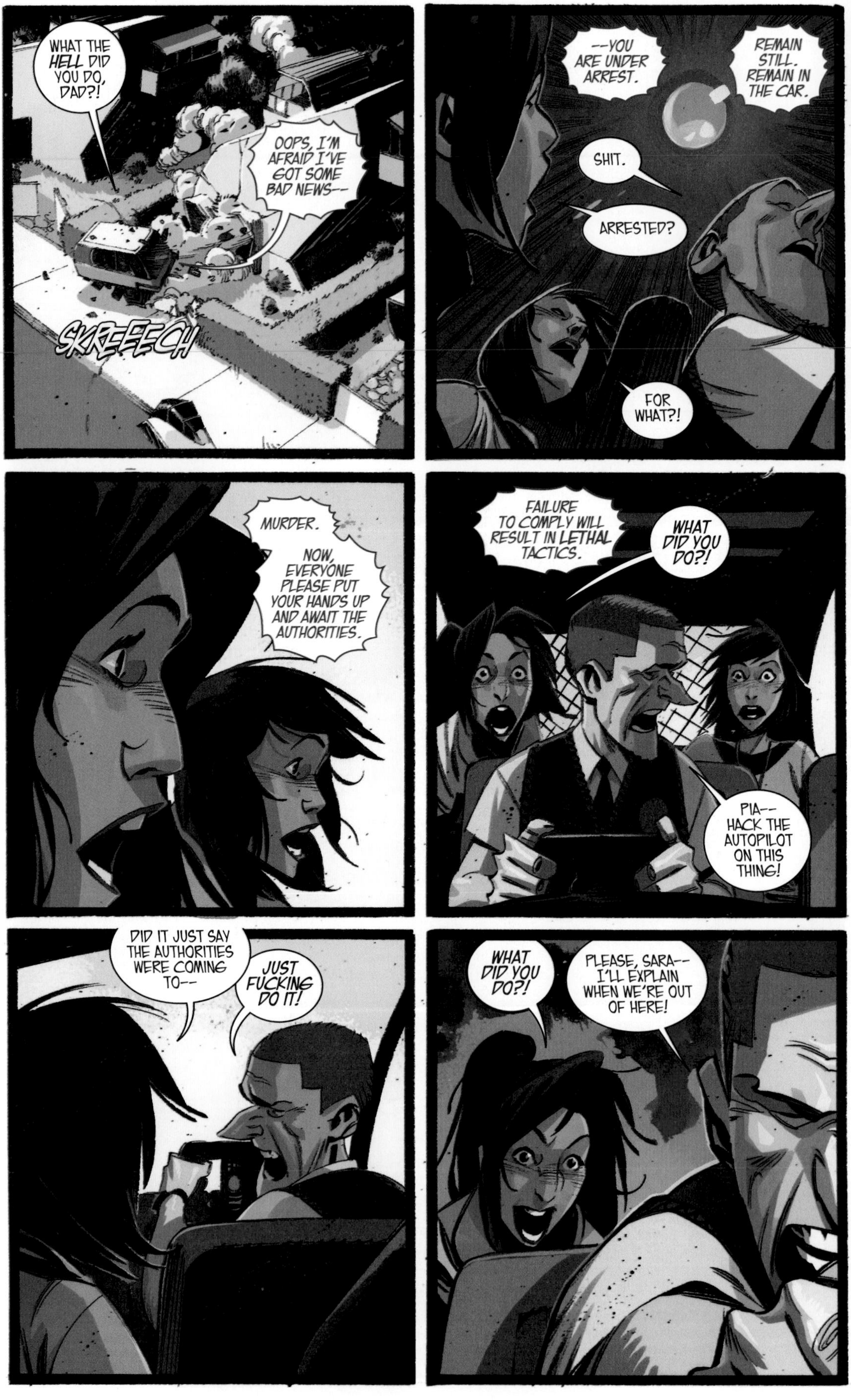
WHAT THE HELL DID YOU DO, DAD?!
OOPS, I'M AFRAID I'VE GOT SOME BAD NEWS--
SKREEEECH
--YOU ARE UNDER ARREST.
REMAIN STILL. REMAIN IN THE CAR.
SHIT.
ARRESTED?
FOR WHAT?!
MURDER.
NOW, EVERYONE PLEASE PUT YOUR HANDS UP AND AWAIT THE AUTHORITIES.
FAILURE TO COMPLY WILL RESULT IN LETHAL TACTICS.
WHAT DID YOU DO?!
PIA-- HACK THE AUTOPILOT ON THIS THING!
DID IT JUST SAY THE AUTHORITIES WERE COMING TO--
JUST FUCKING DO IT!
WHAT DID YOU DO?!
PLEASE, SARA-- I'LL EXPLAIN WHEN WE'RE OUT OF HERE!

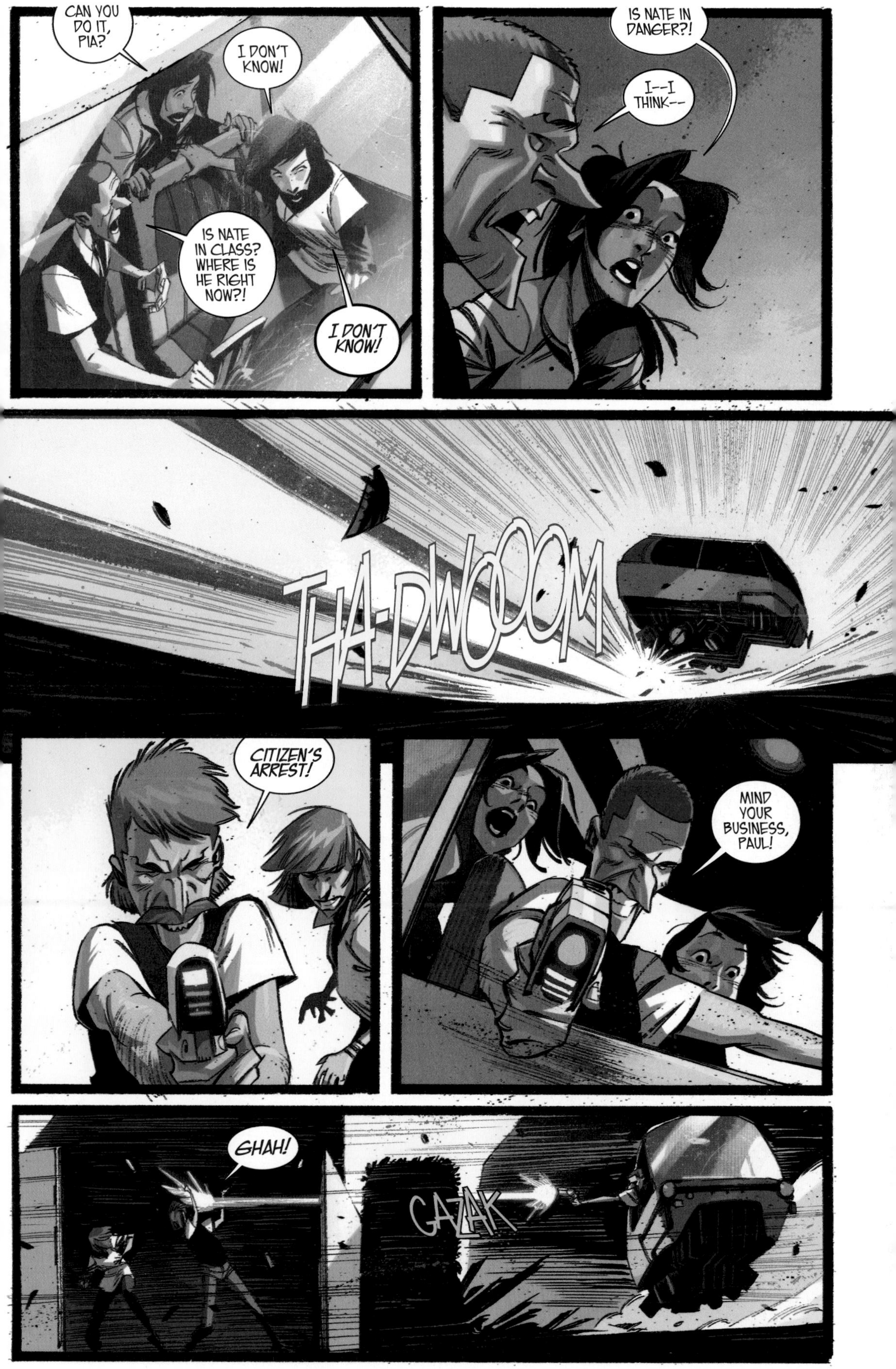
CAN YOU DO IT, PIA?
I DON'T KNOW!
IS NATE IN CLASS? WHERE IS HE RIGHT NOW?!
I DON'T KNOW!
IS NATE IN DANGER?!
I--I THINK--
THA-DWOOOM
CITIZEN'S ARREST!
MIND YOUR BUSINESS, PAUL!
GHAH!
GAZAK

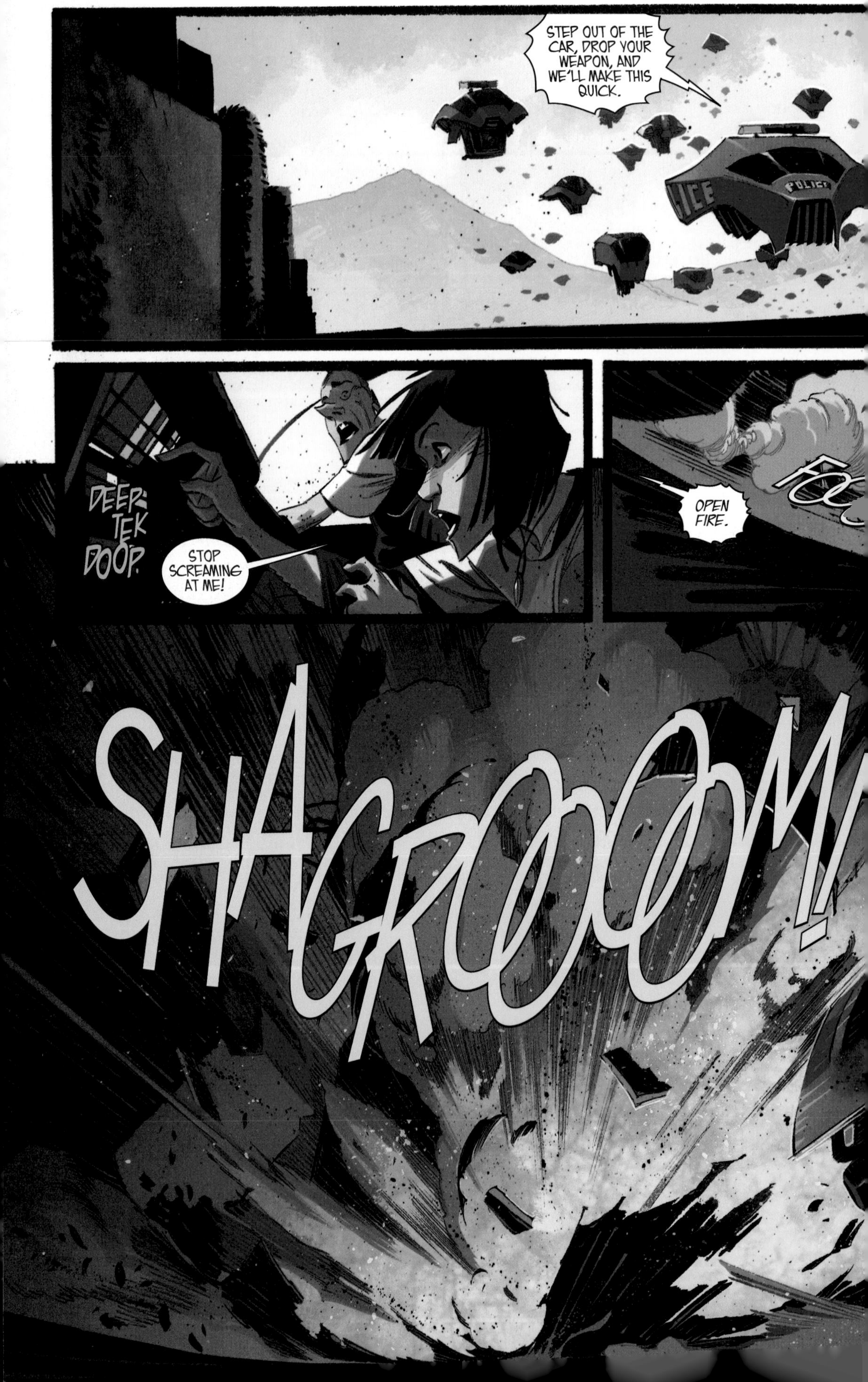
STEP OUT OF THE CAR, DROP YOUR WEAPON, AND WE'LL MAKE THIS QUICK.
DEEP-TEK DOOP.
STOP SCREAMING AT ME!
OPEN FIRE.
SHAGROOOM!!

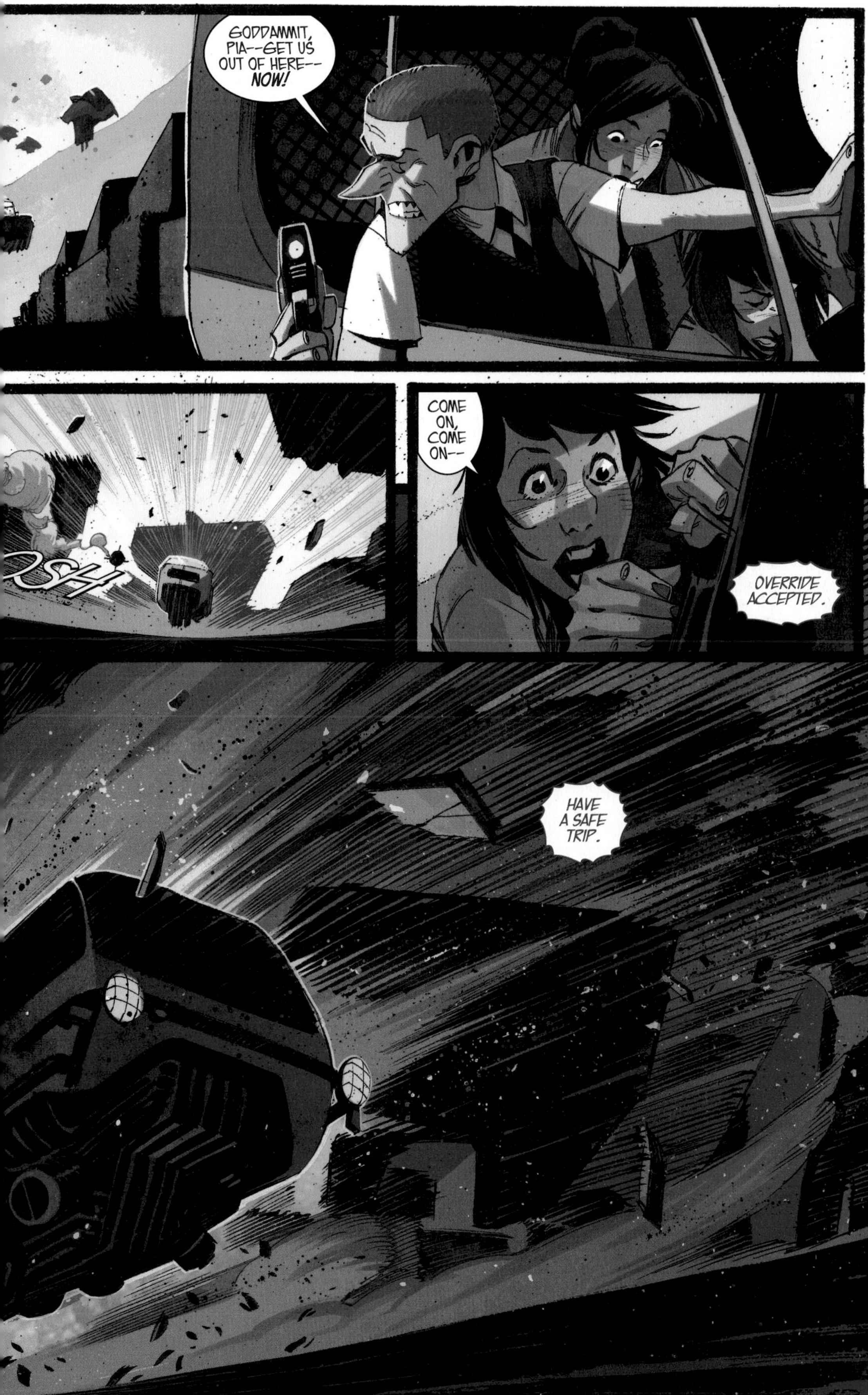
GODDAMMIT, PIA--GET US OUT OF HERE-- NOW!
COME ON, COME ON--
OVERRIDE ACCEPTED.
HAVE A SAFE TRIP.

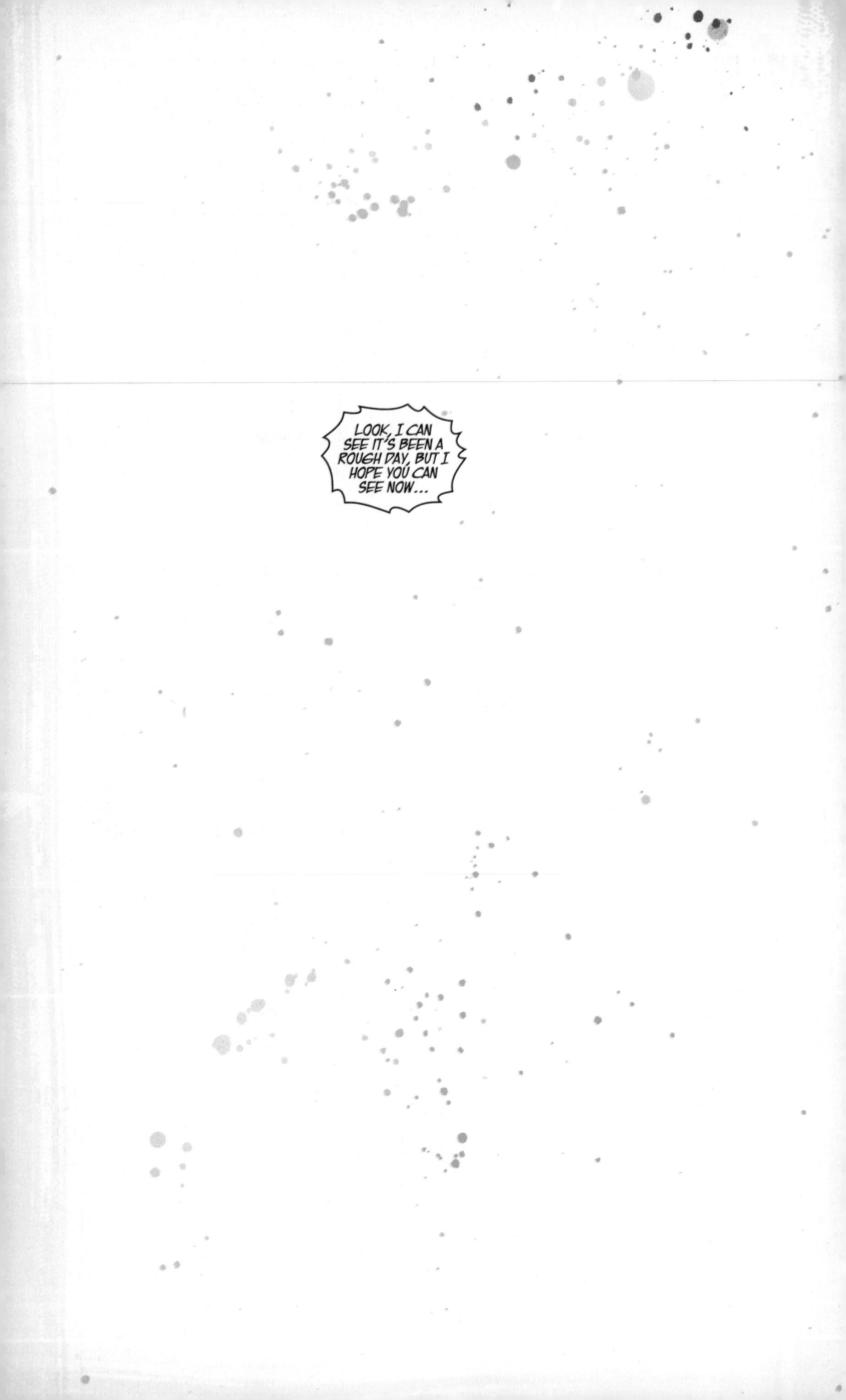
LOOK, I CAN SEE IT'S BEEN A ROUGH DAY, BUT I HOPE YOU CAN SEE NOW...

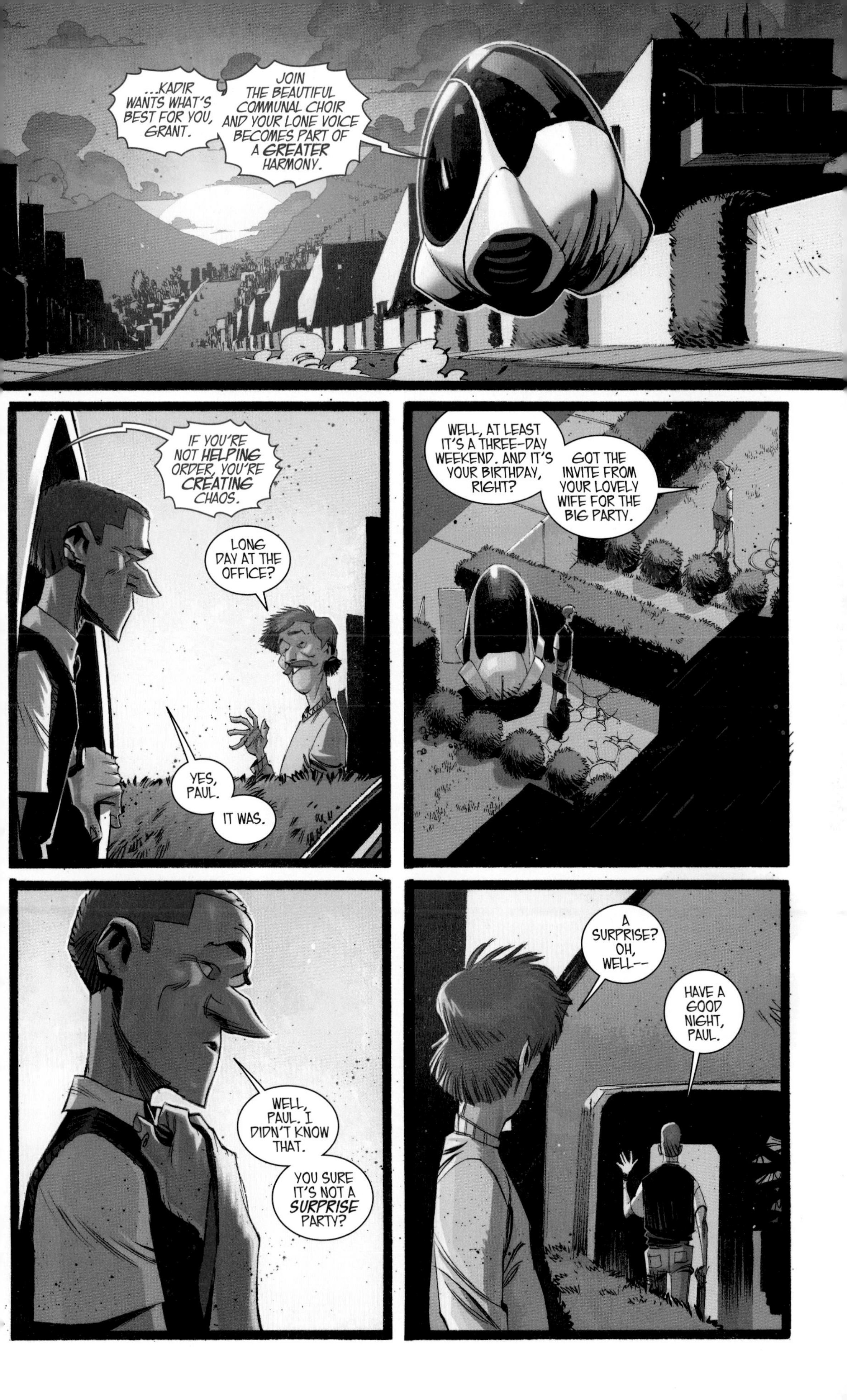
...KADIR WANTS WHAT'S BEST FOR YOU, GRANT.
JOIN THE BEAUTIFUL COMMUNAL CHOIR AND YOUR LONE VOICE BECOMES PART OF A GREATER HARMONY.
IF YOU'RE NOT HELPING ORDER, YOU'RE CREATING CHAOS.
LONG DAY AT THE OFFICE?
YES, PAUL.
IT WAS.
WELL, AT LEAST IT'S A THREE-DAY WEEKEND. AND IT'S YOUR BIRTHDAY, RIGHT?
GOT THE INVITE FROM YOUR LOVELY WIFE FOR THE BIG PARTY.
WELL, PAUL. I DIDN'T KNOW THAT.
YOU SURE IT'S NOT A SURPRISE PARTY?
A SURPRISE? OH, WELL--
HAVE A GOOD NIGHT, PAUL.

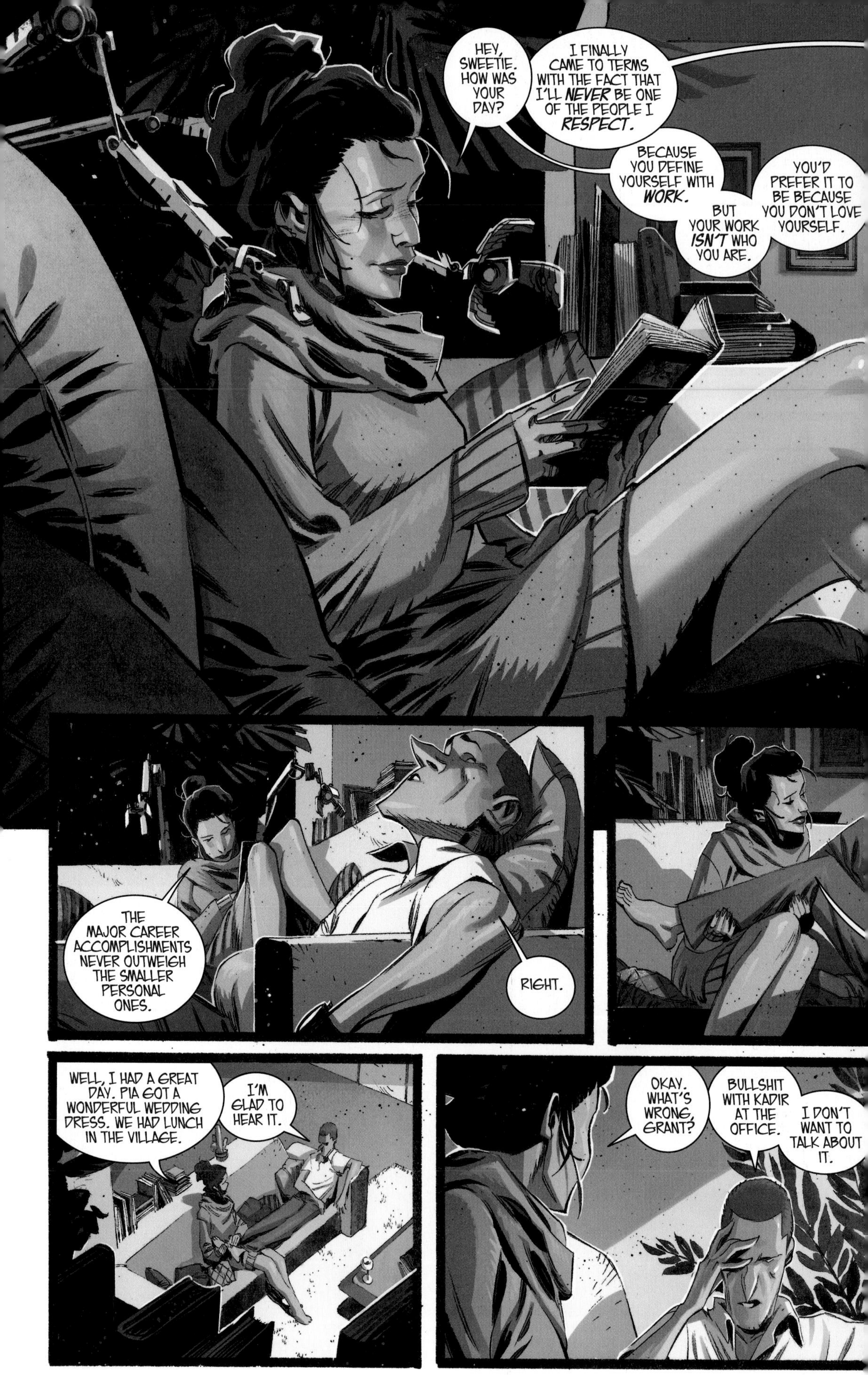
HEY, SWEETIE. HOW WAS YOUR DAY?
I FINALLY CAME TO TERMS WITH THE FACT THAT I'LL NEVER BE ONE OF THE PEOPLE I RESPECT.
BECAUSE YOU DEFINE YOURSELF WITH WORK.
BUT YOUR WORK ISN'T WHO YOU ARE.
YOU'D PREFER IT TO BE BECAUSE YOU DON'T LOVE YOURSELF.
THE MAJOR CAREER ACCOMPLISHMENTS NEVER OUTWEIGH THE SMALLER PERSONAL ONES.
RIGHT.
WELL, I HAD A GREAT DAY. PIA GOT A WONDERFUL WEDDING DRESS. WE HAD LUNCH IN THE VILLAGE.
I'M GLAD TO HEAR IT.
OKAY. WHAT'S WRONG, GRANT?
BULLSHIT WITH KADIR AT THE OFFICE.
I DON'T WANT TO TALK ABOUT IT.

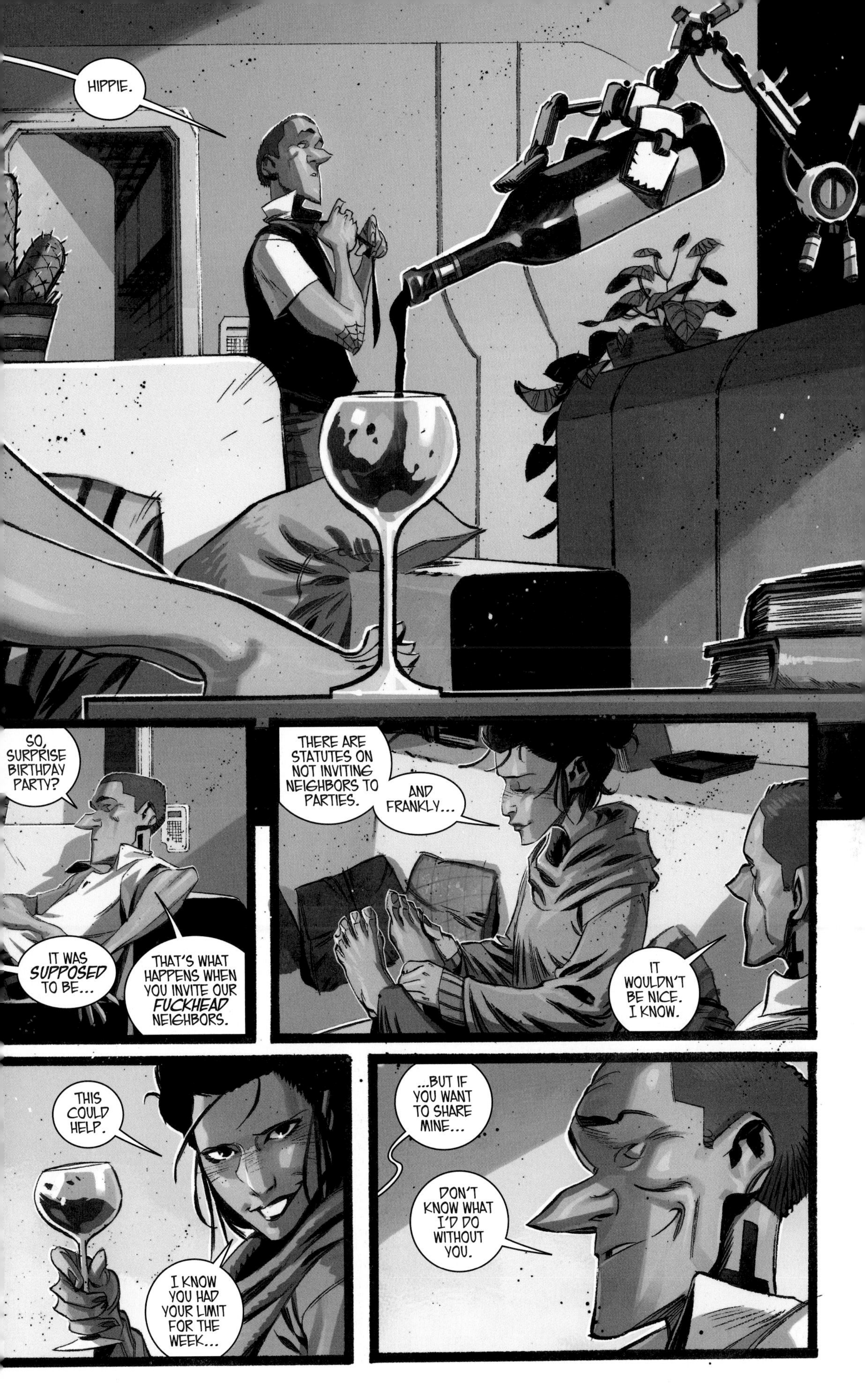
HIPPIE.
SO, SURPRISE BIRTHDAY PARTY?
IT WAS *SUPPOSED* TO BE...
THAT'S WHAT HAPPENS WHEN YOU INVITE OUR *FUCKHEAD* NEIGHBORS.
THERE ARE STATUTES ON NOT INVITING NEIGHBORS TO PARTIES.
AND FRANKLY...
IT WOULDN'T BE NICE. I KNOW.
THIS COULD HELP.
I KNOW YOU HAD YOUR LIMIT FOR THE WEEK...
...BUT IF YOU WANT TO SHARE MINE...
DON'T KNOW WHAT I'D DO WITHOUT YOU.

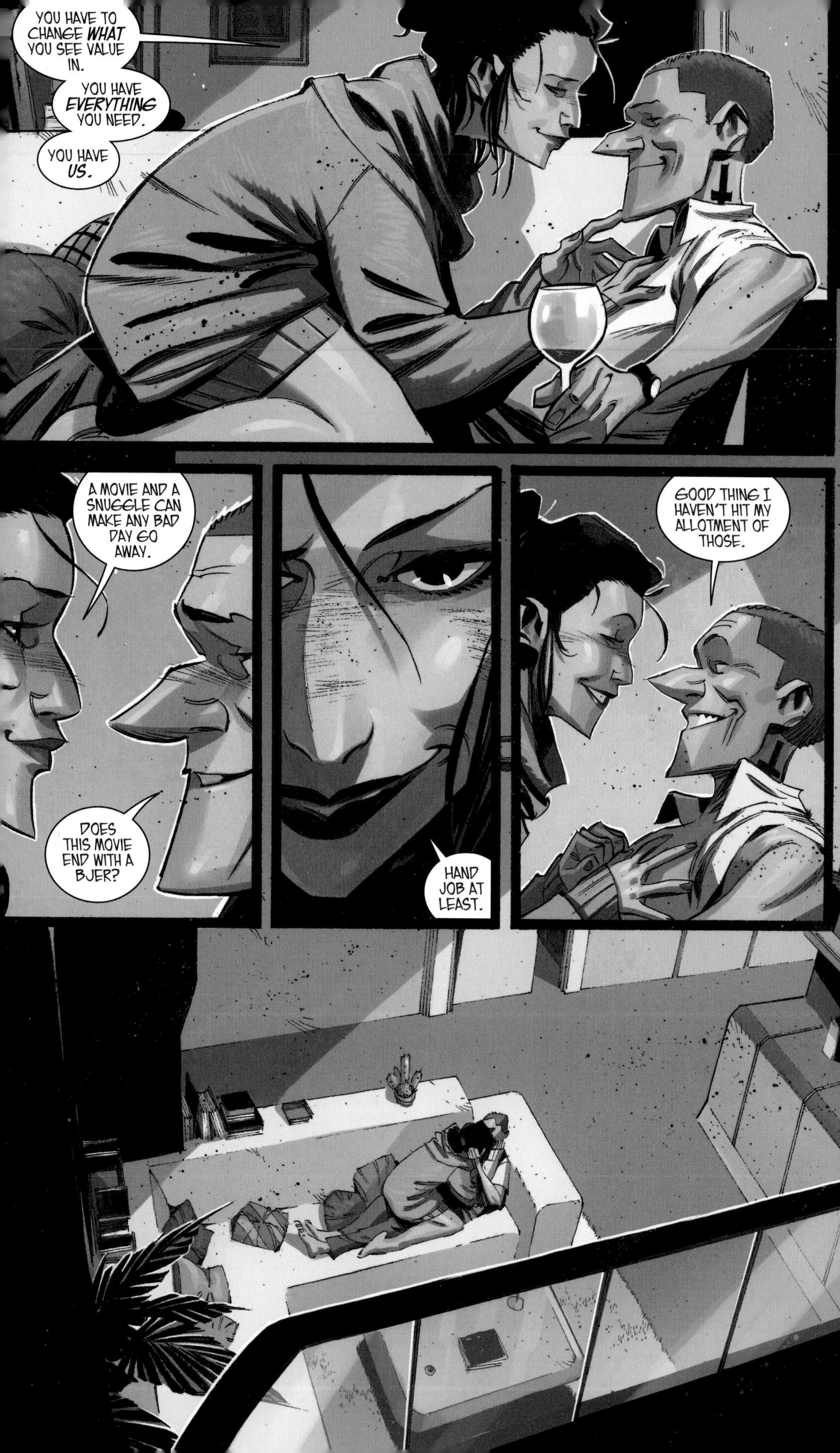
YOU HAVE TO CHANGE WHAT YOU SEE VALUE IN.
YOU HAVE EVERYTHING YOU NEED.
YOU HAVE US.
A MOVIE AND A SNUGGLE CAN MAKE ANY BAD DAY GO AWAY.
DOES THIS MOVIE END WITH A BJER?
HAND JOB AT LEAST.
GOOD THING I HAVEN'T HIT MY ALLOTMENT OF THOSE.

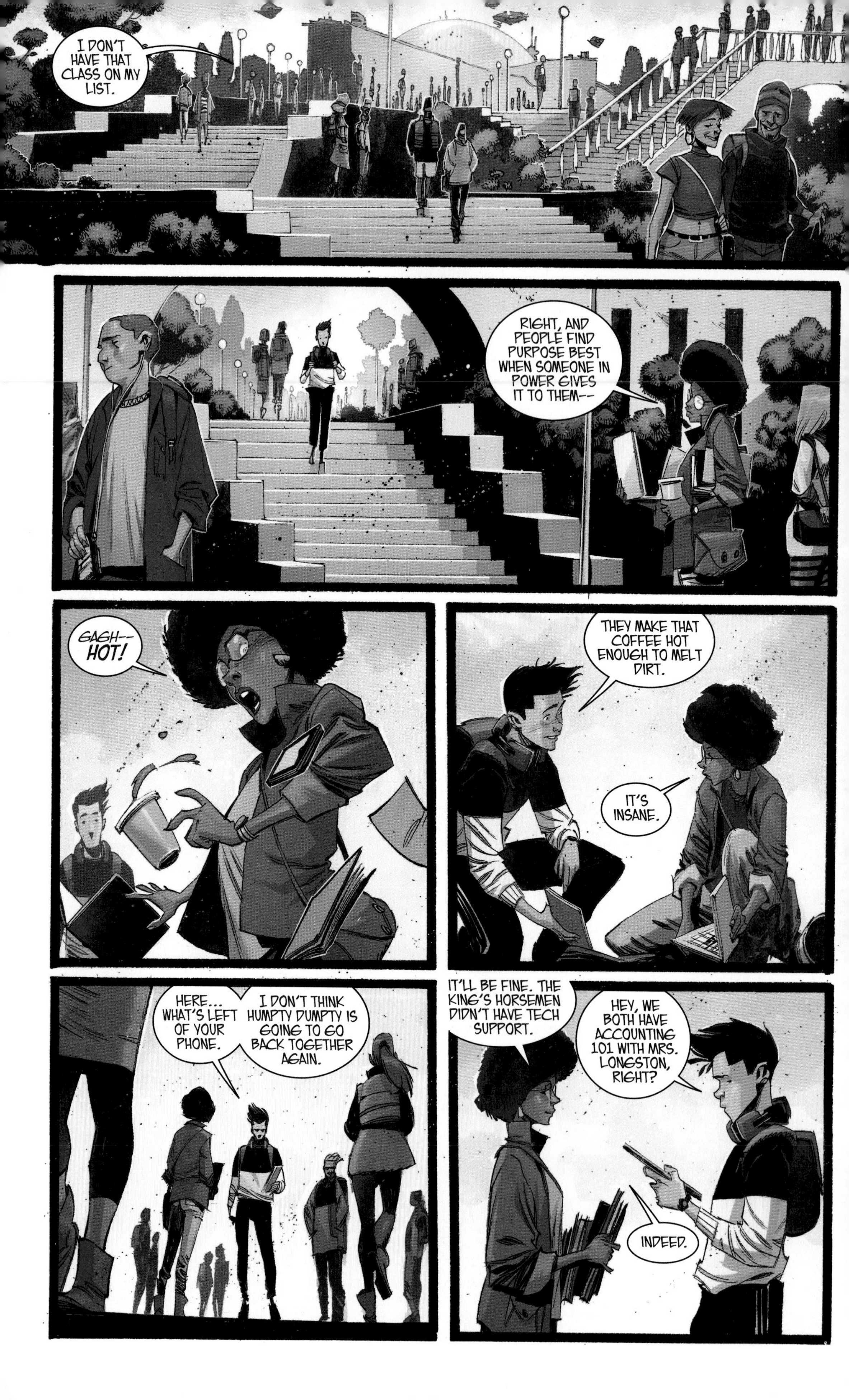

I DON'T HAVE THAT CLASS ON MY LIST.
RIGHT, AND PEOPLE FIND PURPOSE BEST WHEN SOMEONE IN POWER GIVES IT TO THEM--
GAGH-- HOT!
THEY MAKE THAT COFFEE HOT ENOUGH TO MELT DIRT.
IT'S INSANE.
HERE... WHAT'S LEFT OF YOUR PHONE.
I DON'T THINK HUMPTY DUMPTY IS GOING TO GO BACK TOGETHER AGAIN.
IT'LL BE FINE. THE KING'S HORSEMEN DIDN'T HAVE TECH SUPPORT.
HEY, WE BOTH HAVE ACCOUNTING 101 WITH MRS. LONGSTON, RIGHT?
INDEED.

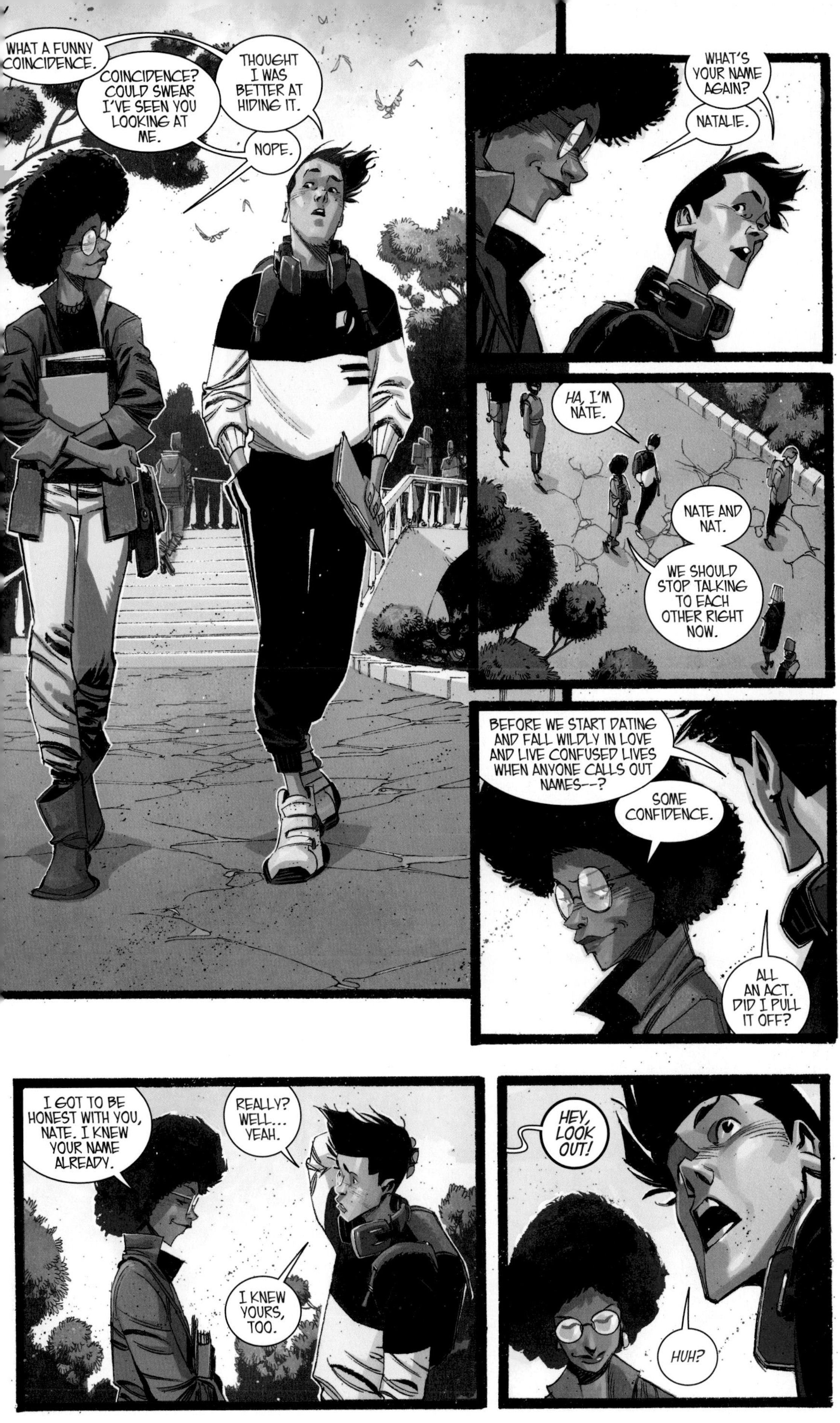
WHAT A FUNNY COINCIDENCE.
COINCIDENCE? COULD SWEAR I'VE SEEN YOU LOOKING AT ME.
THOUGHT I WAS BETTER AT HIDING IT.
NOPE.
WHAT'S YOUR NAME AGAIN?
NATALIE.
HA, I'M NATE.
NATE AND NAT.
WE SHOULD STOP TALKING TO EACH OTHER RIGHT NOW.
BEFORE WE START DATING AND FALL WILDLY IN LOVE AND LIVE CONFUSED LIVES WHEN ANYONE CALLS OUT NAMES--?
SOME CONFIDENCE.
ALL AN ACT. DID I PULL IT OFF?
I GOT TO BE HONEST WITH YOU, NATE. I KNEW YOUR NAME ALREADY.
REALLY? WELL... YEAH.
I KNEW YOURS, TOO.
HEY, LOOK OUT!
HUH?

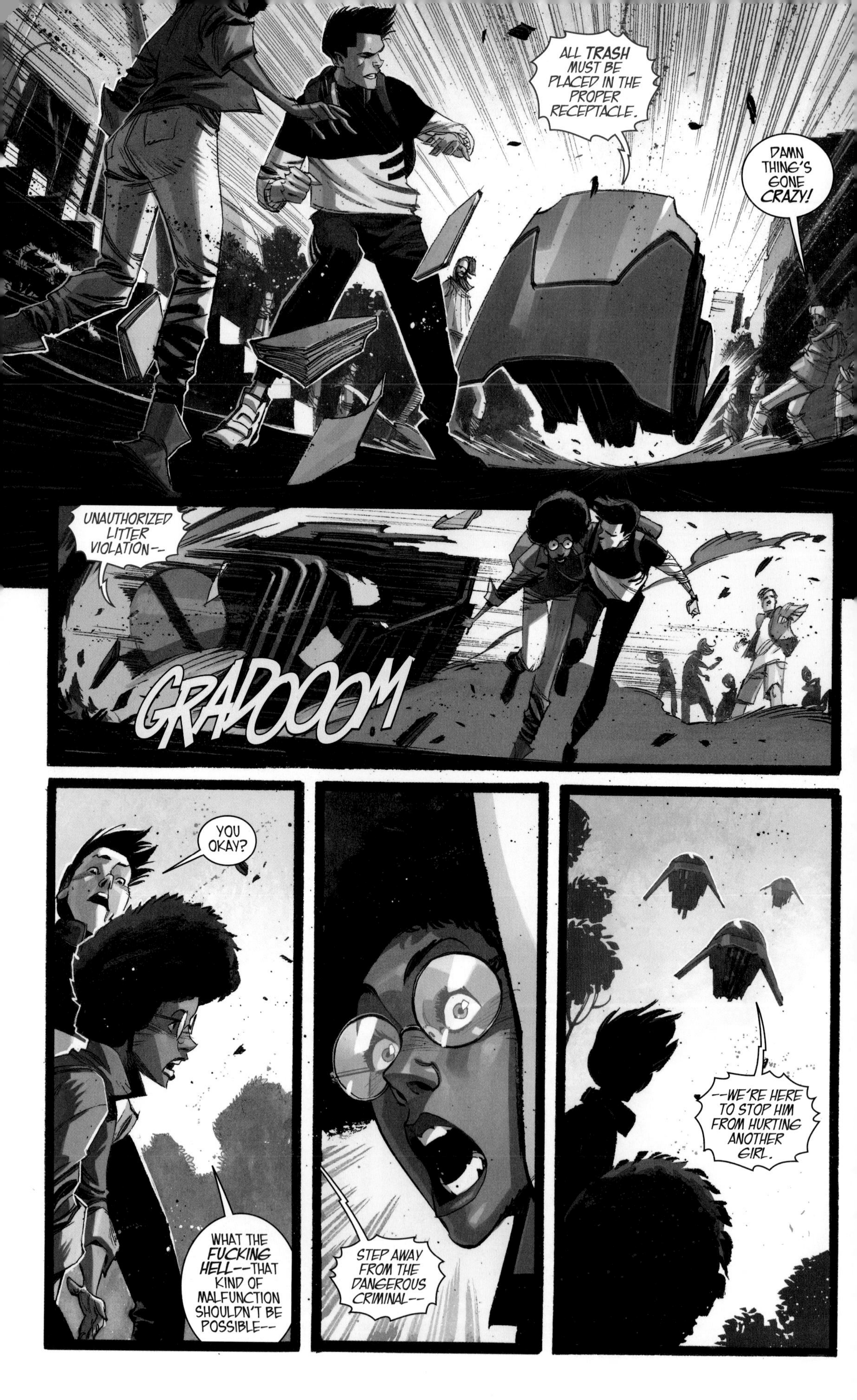
ALL TRASH MUST BE PLACED IN THE PROPER RECEPTACLE.
DAMN THING'S GONE CRAZY!
UNAUTHORIZED LITTER VIOLATION--
GRADOOOM
YOU OKAY?
WHAT THE FUCKING HELL--THAT KIND OF MALFUNCTION SHOULDN'T BE POSSIBLE--
STEP AWAY FROM THE DANGEROUS CRIMINAL--
--WE'RE HERE TO STOP HIM FROM HURTING ANOTHER GIRL.

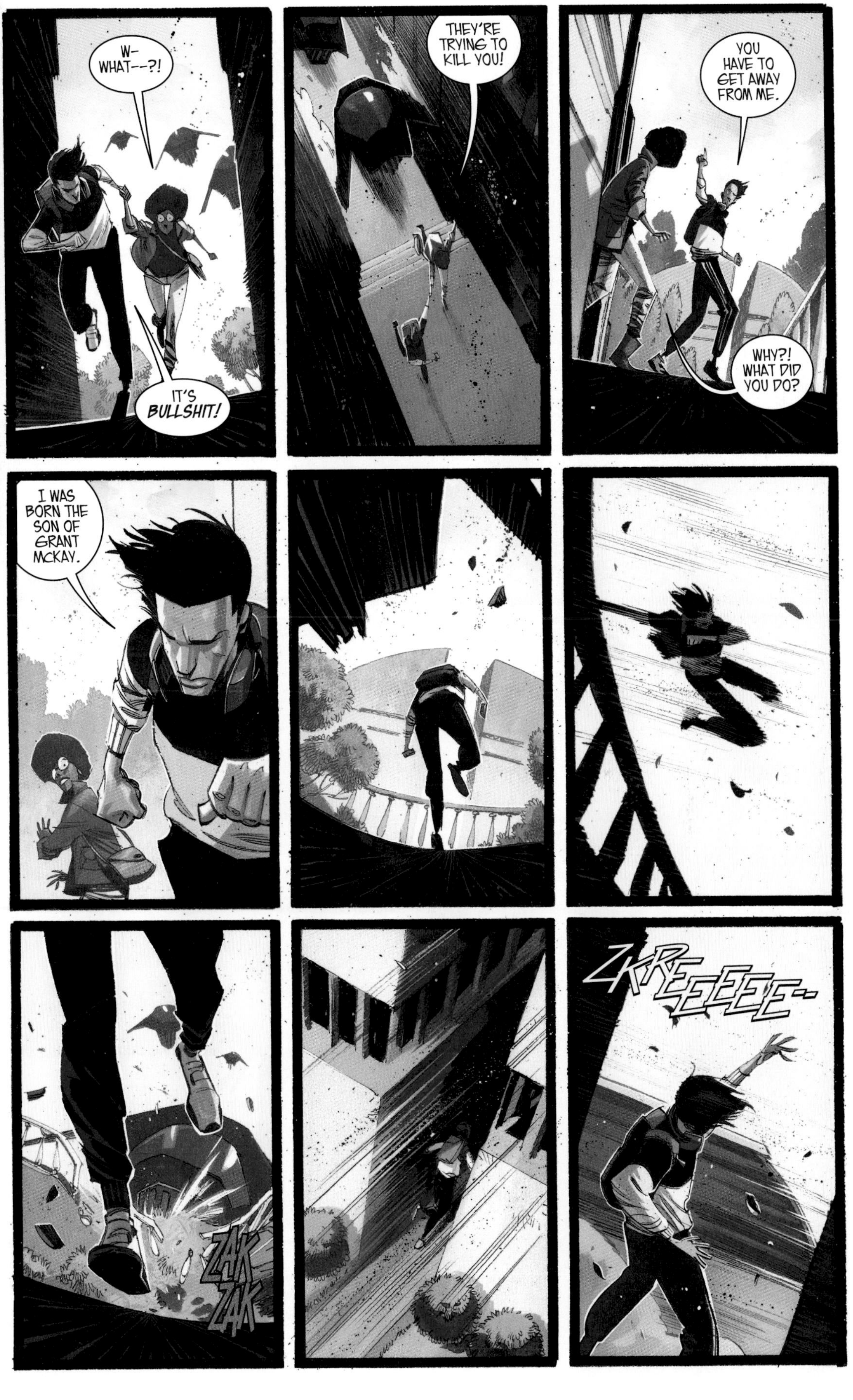
W-
WHAT--?!
IT'S BULLSHIT!
THEY'RE TRYING TO KILL YOU!
YOU HAVE TO GET AWAY FROM ME.
WHY?! WHAT DID YOU DO?
I WAS BORN THE SON OF GRANT MCKAY.
ZAK ZAK
ZKREEEEEE--

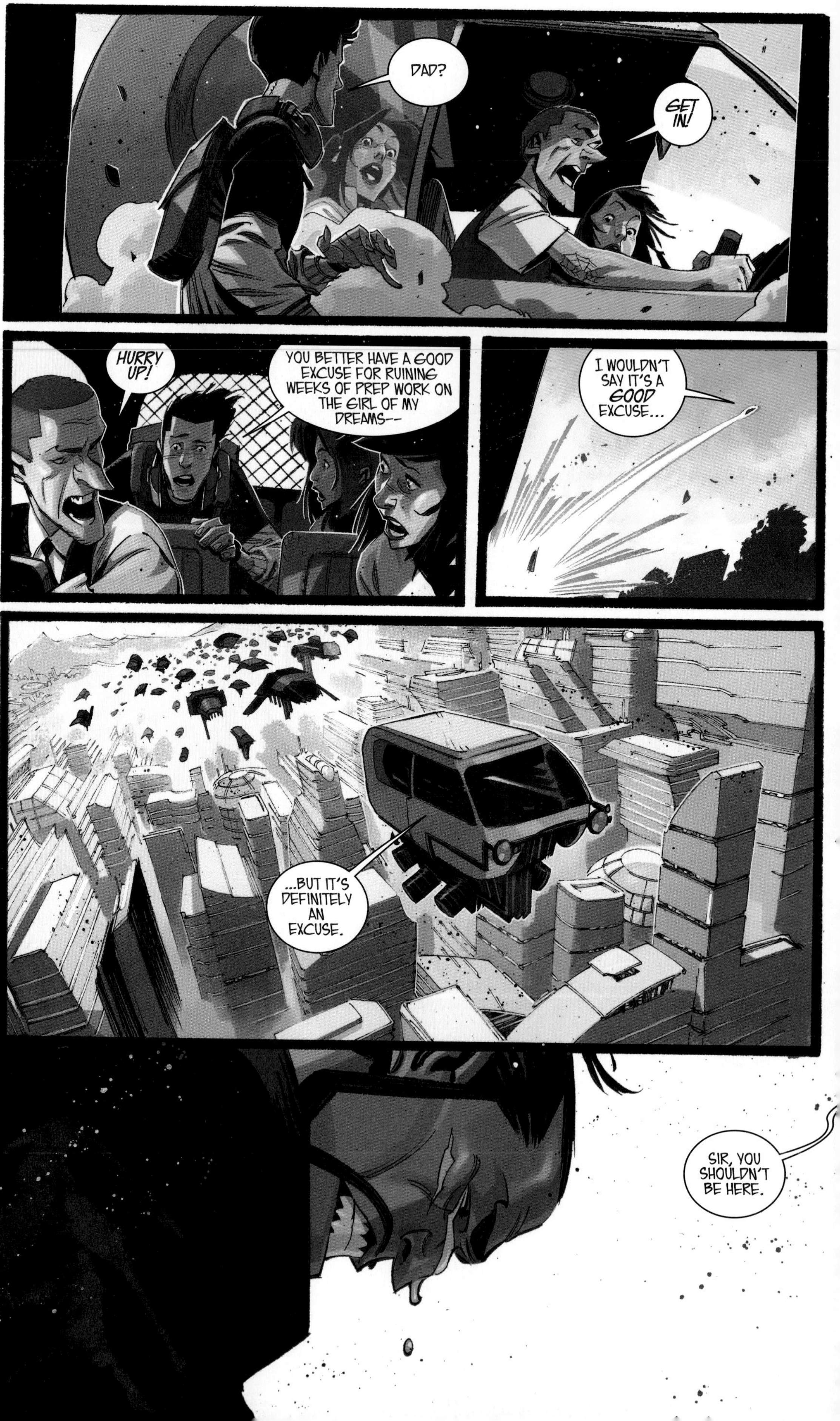
DAD?
GET IN!
HURRY UP!
YOU BETTER HAVE A GOOD EXCUSE FOR RUINING WEEKS OF PREP WORK ON THE GIRL OF MY DREAMS--
I WOULDN'T SAY IT'S A GOOD EXCUSE...
...BUT IT'S DEFINITELY AN EXCUSE.
SIR, YOU SHOULDN'T BE HERE.

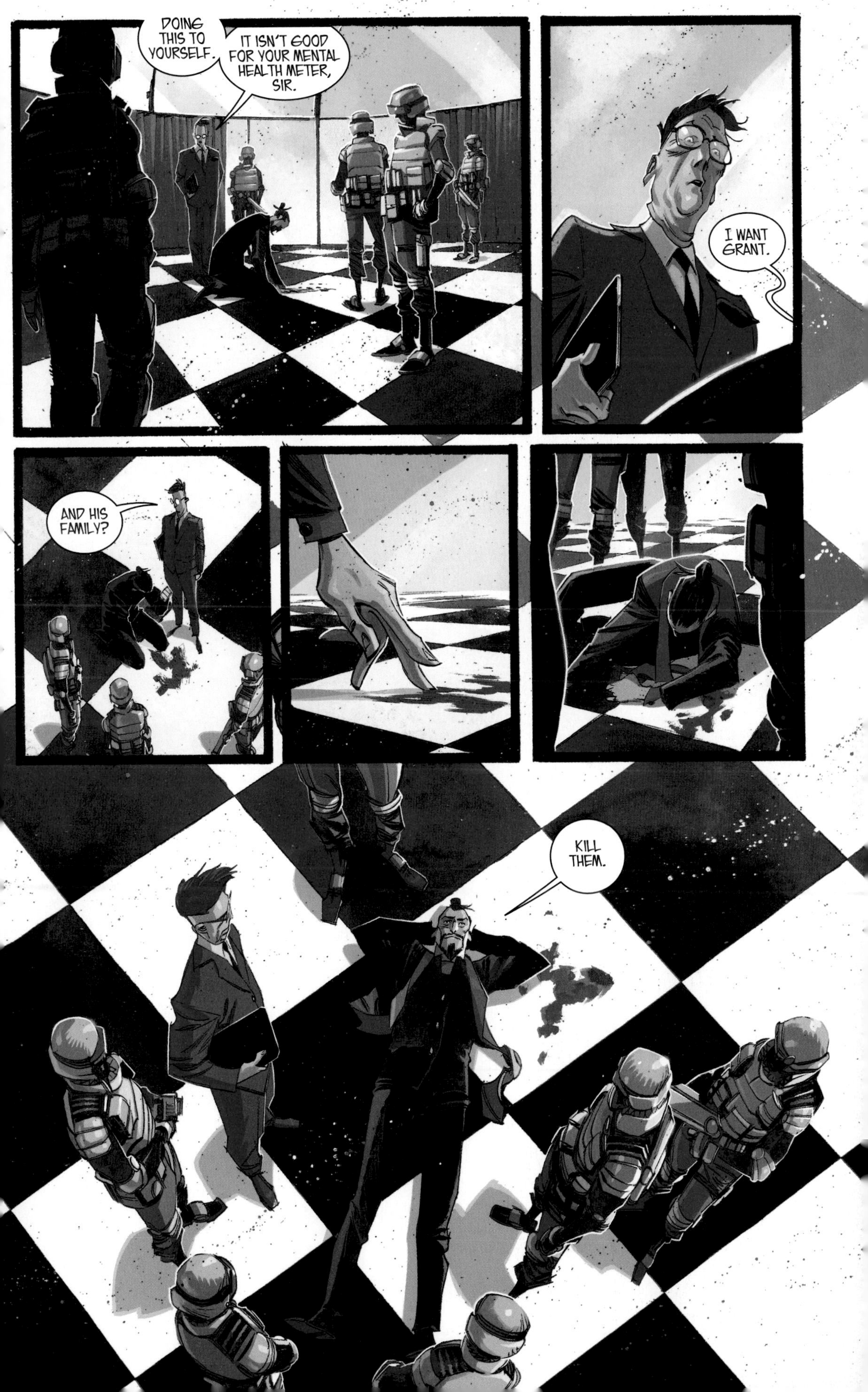
DOING THIS TO YOURSELF.
IT ISN'T GOOD FOR YOUR MENTAL HEALTH METER, SIR.
I WANT GRANT.
AND HIS FAMILY?
KILL THEM.

43

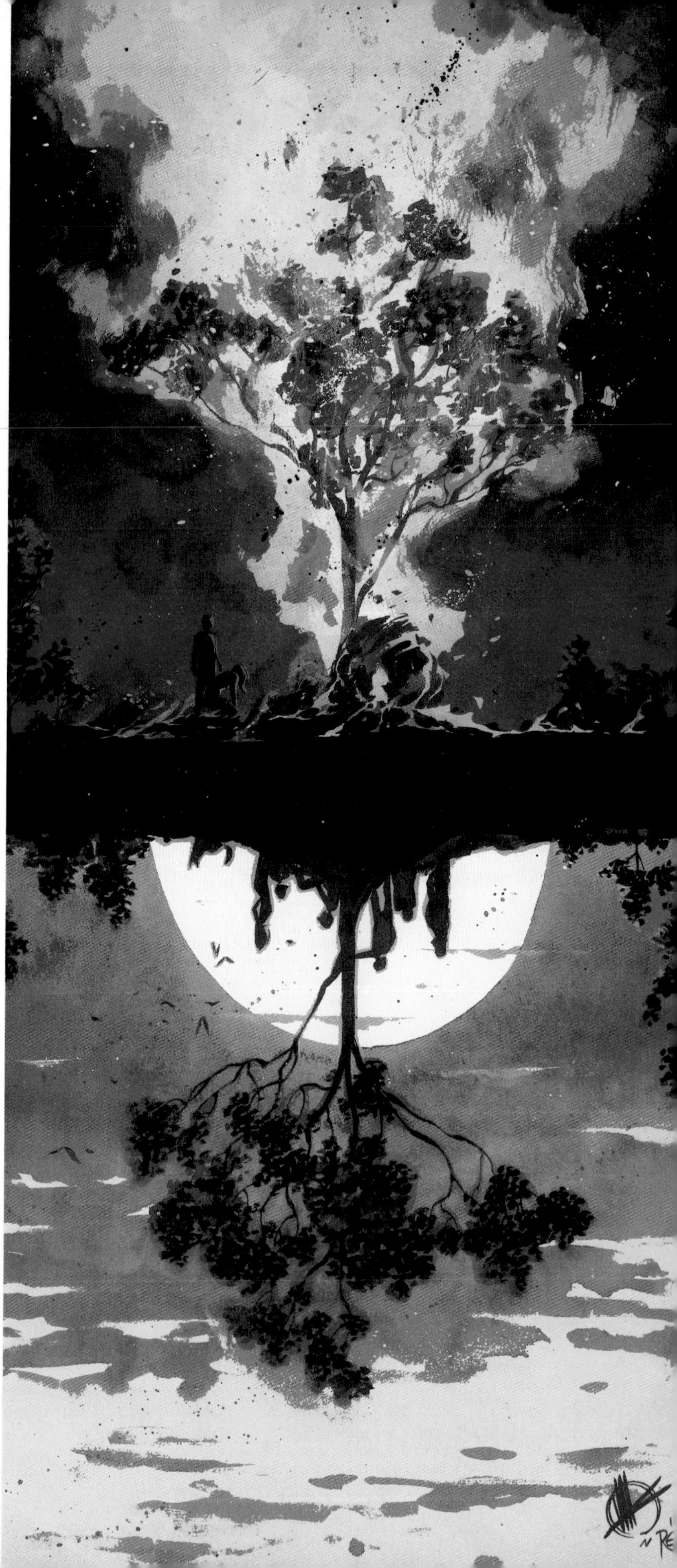

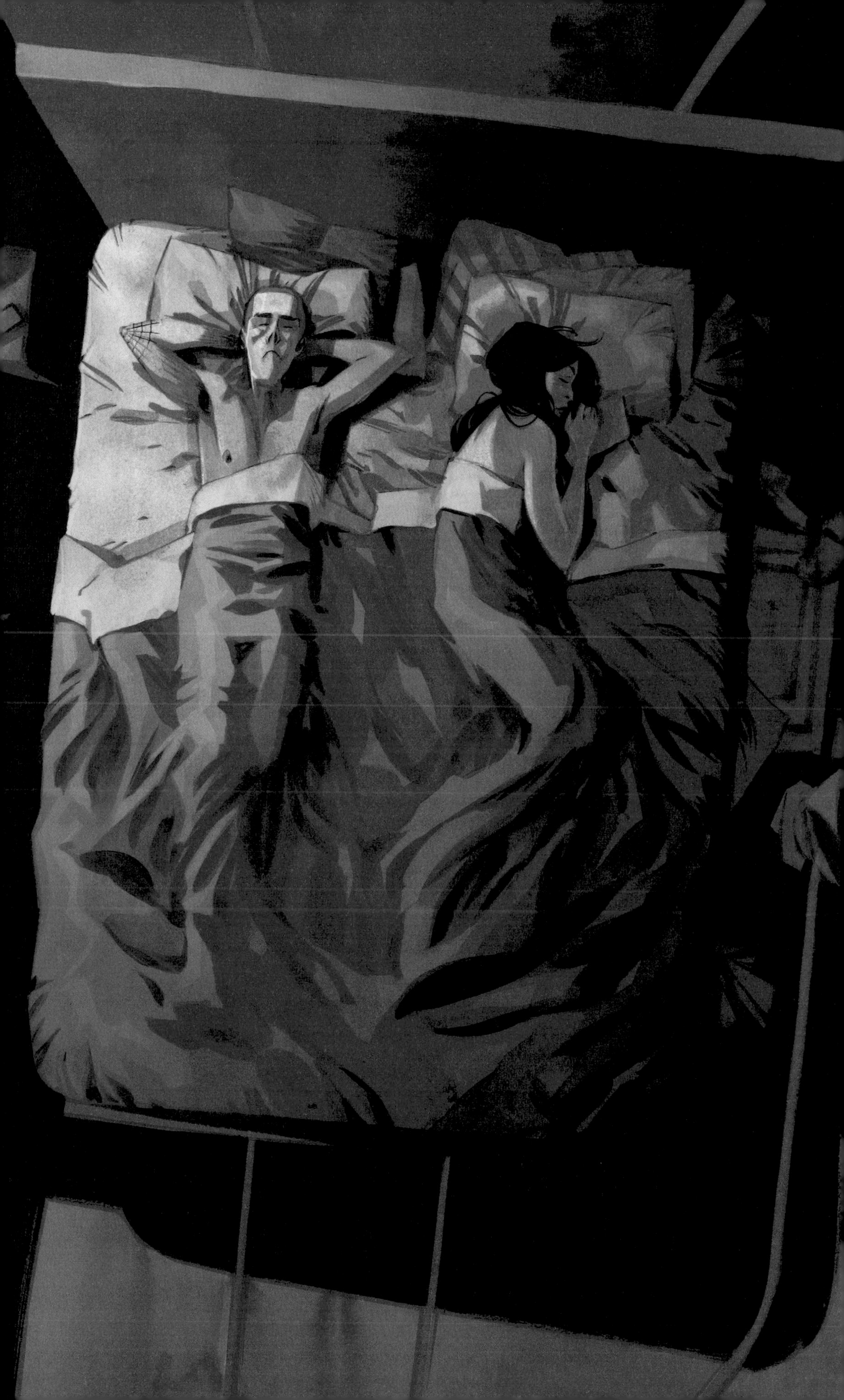

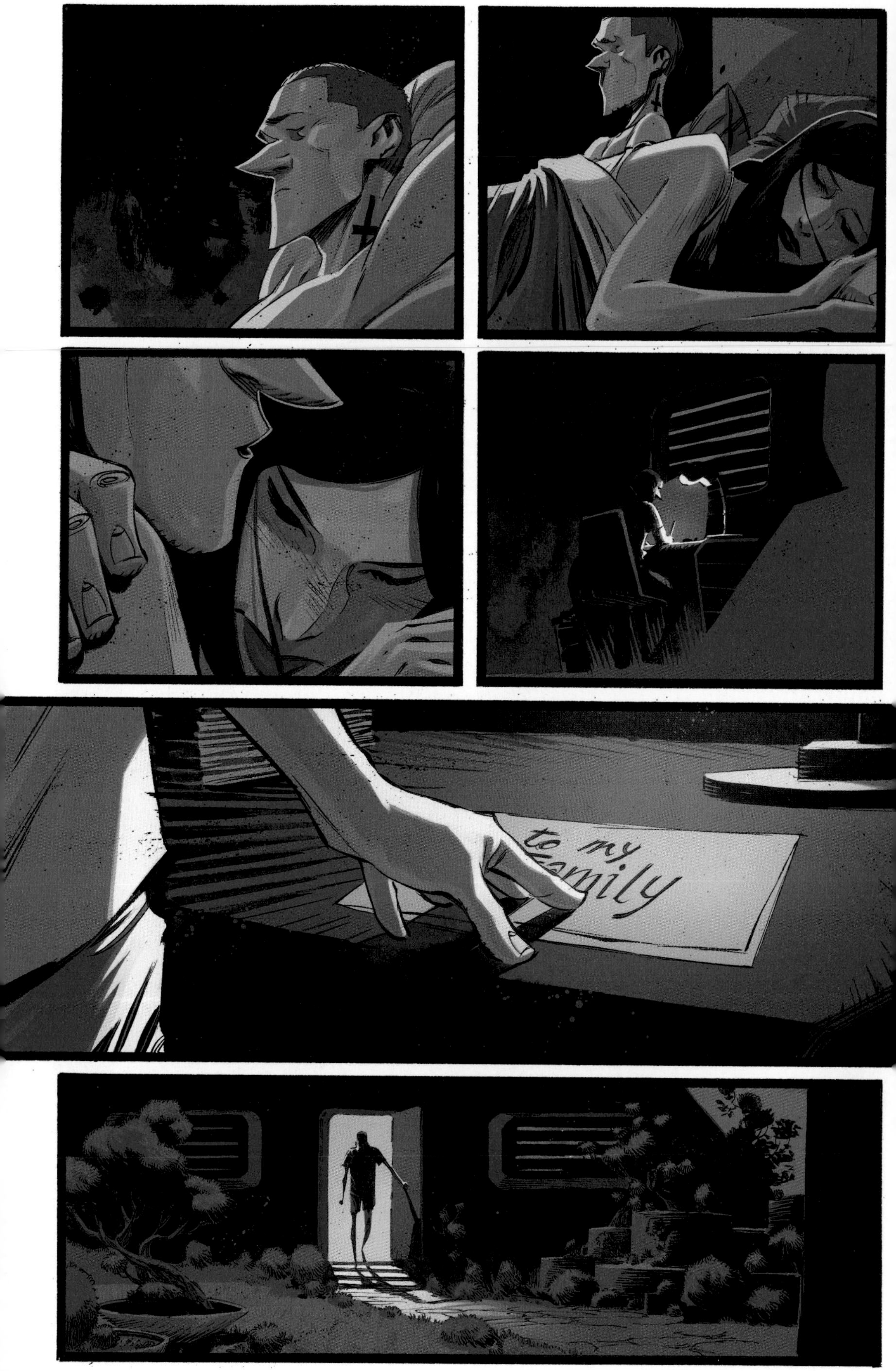
to my family

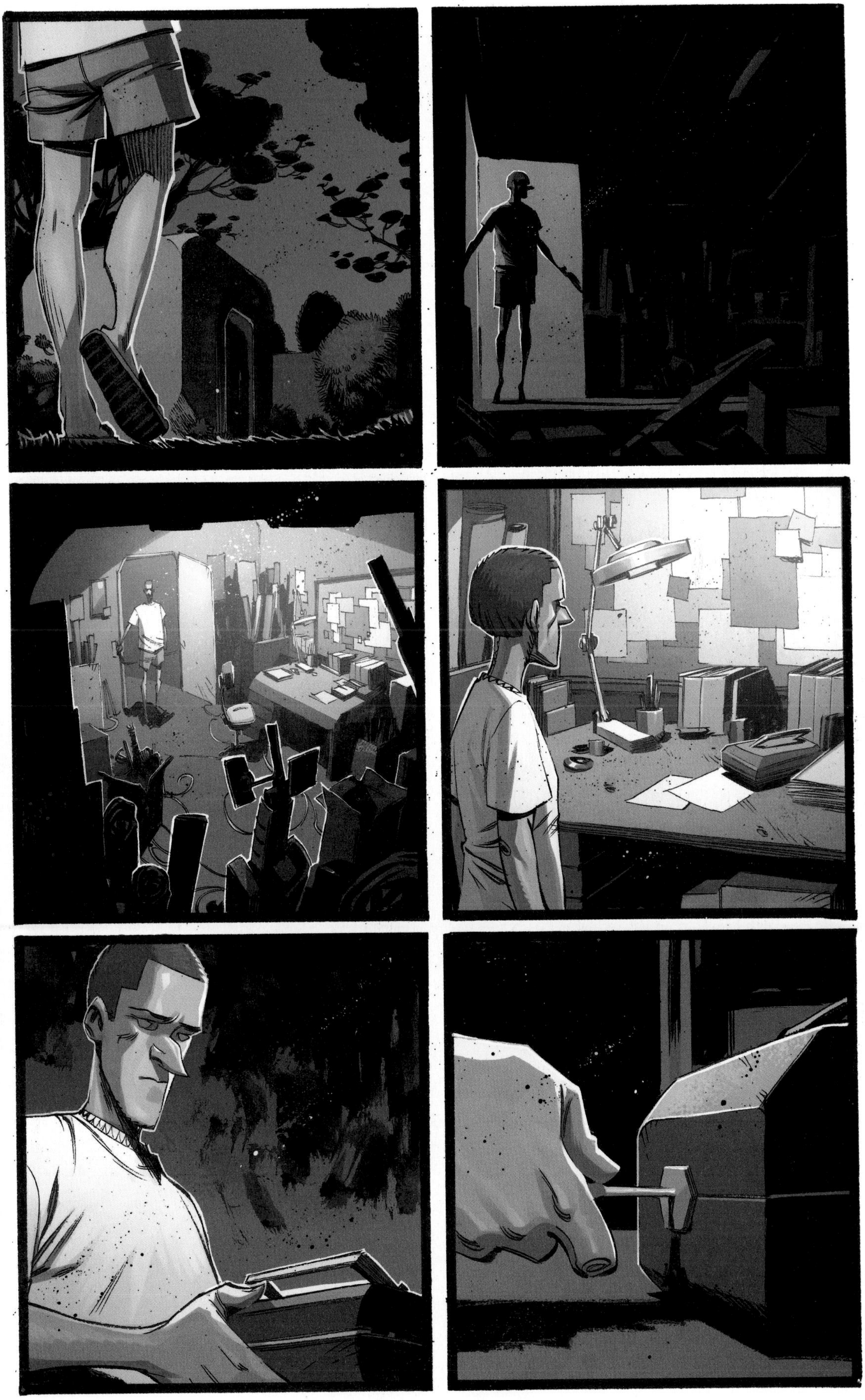

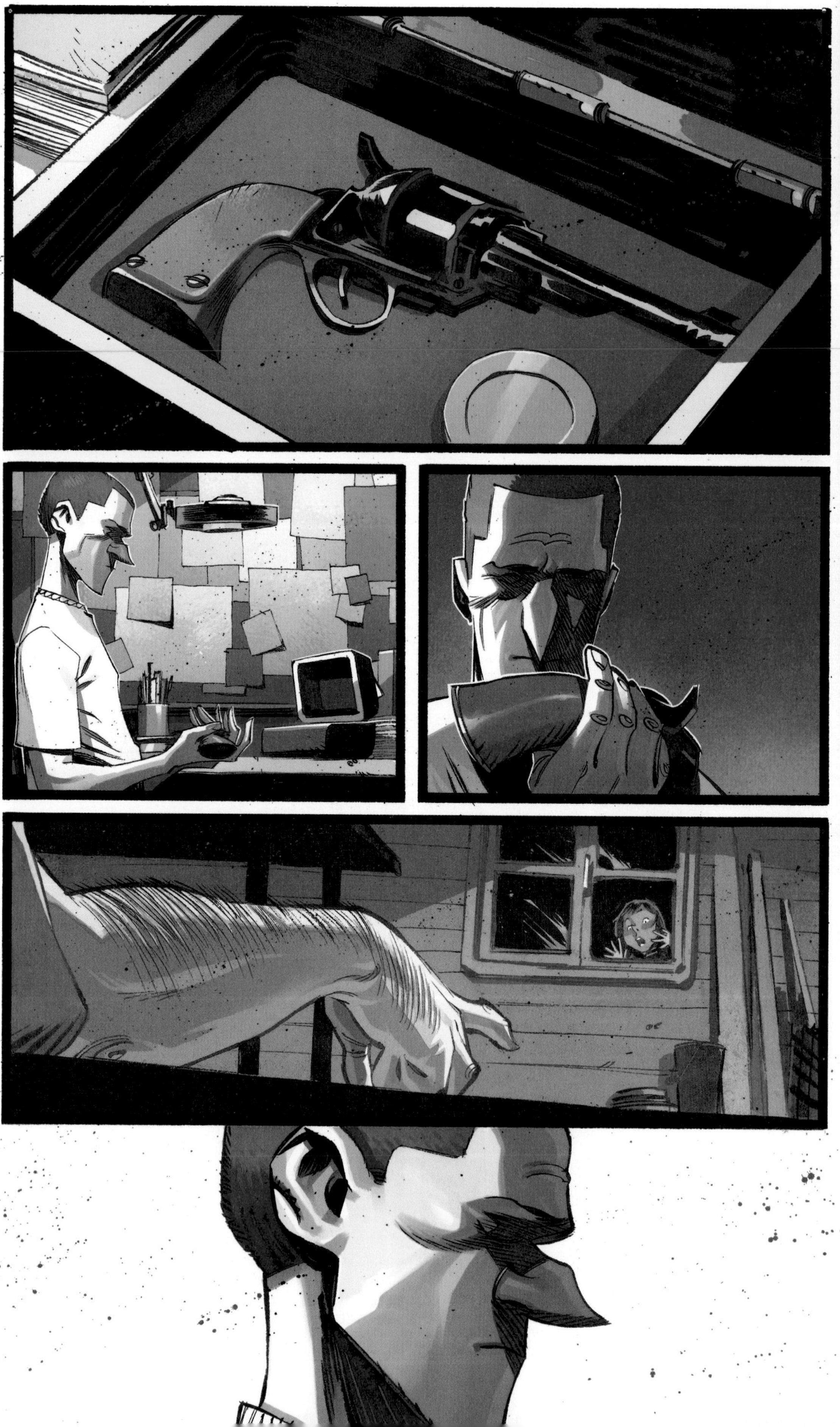

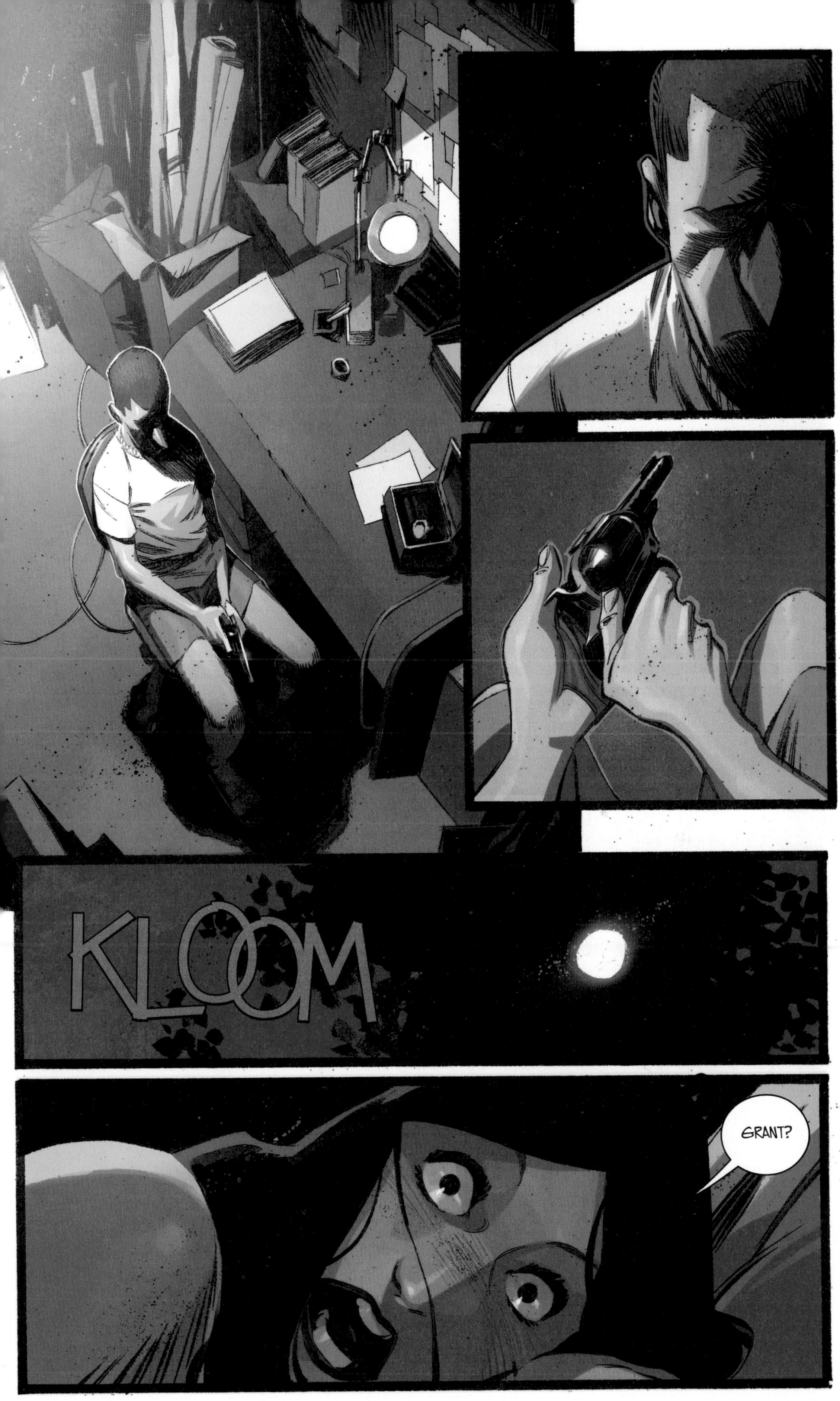
KLOOM
GRANT?

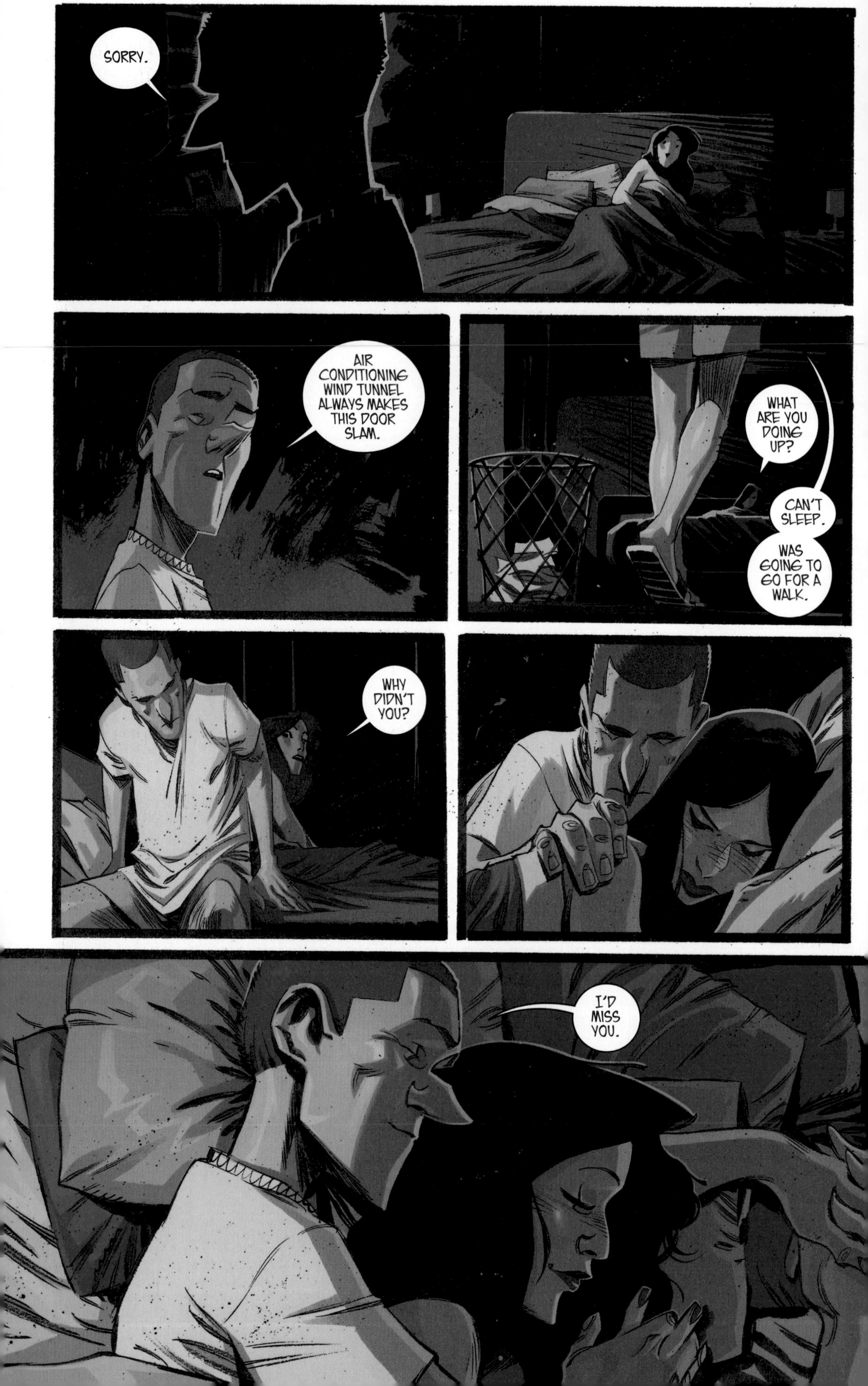
SORRY.
AIR CONDITIONING WIND TUNNEL ALWAYS MAKES THIS DOOR SLAM.
WHAT ARE YOU DOING UP?
CAN'T SLEEP.
WAS GOING TO GO FOR A WALK.
WHY DIDN'T YOU?
I'D MISS YOU.

"WHAT HAVE YOU DONE?!"

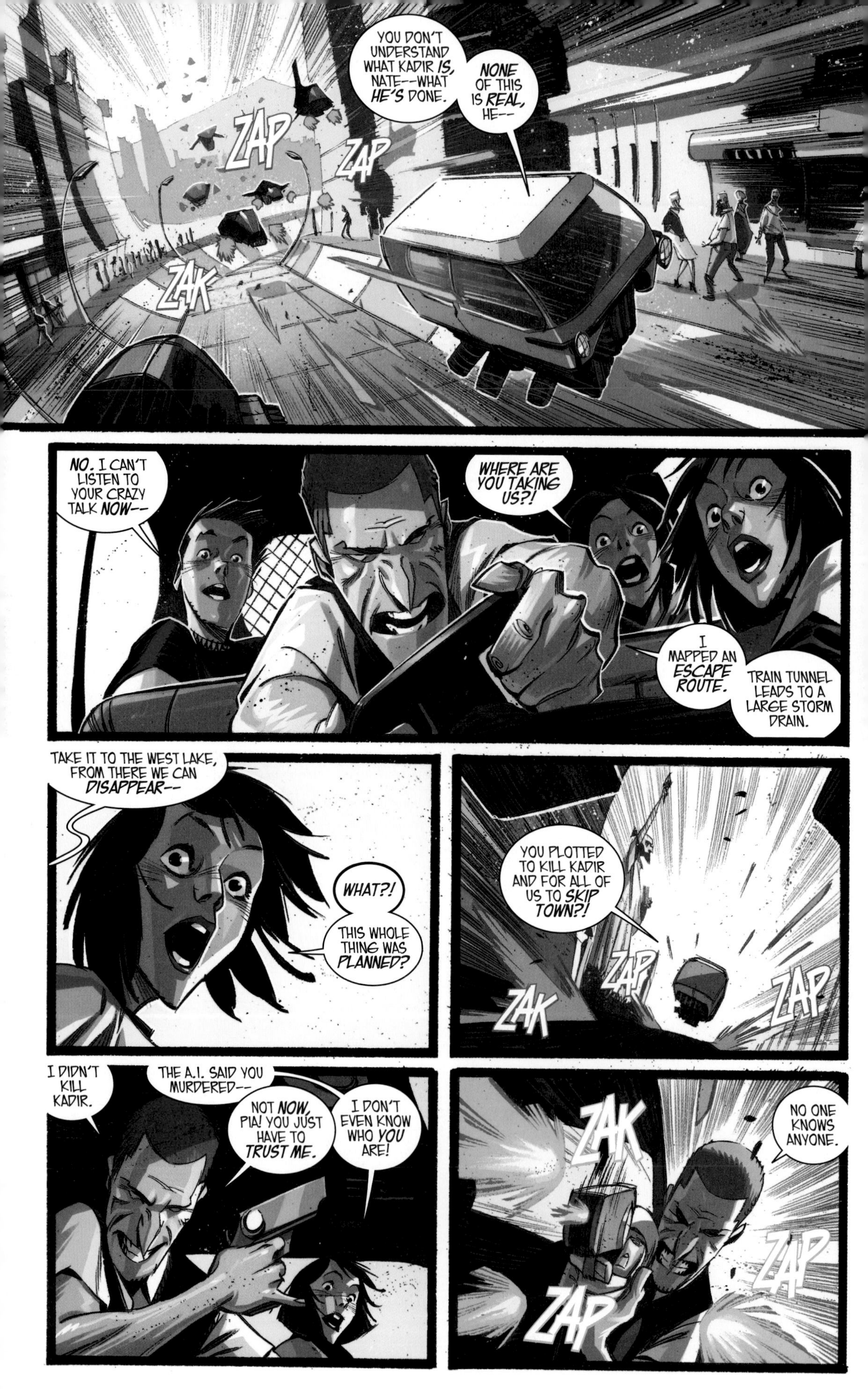
YOU DON'T UNDERSTAND WHAT KADIR IS, NATE--WHAT HE'S DONE.
NONE OF THIS IS REAL, HE--
ZAP
ZAP
ZAK
NO. I CAN'T LISTEN TO YOUR CRAZY TALK NOW--
WHERE ARE YOU TAKING US?!
I MAPPED AN ESCAPE ROUTE.
TRAIN TUNNEL LEADS TO A LARGE STORM DRAIN.
TAKE IT TO THE WEST LAKE, FROM THERE WE CAN DISAPPEAR--
WHAT?!
THIS WHOLE THING WAS PLANNED?
YOU PLOTTED TO KILL KADIR AND FOR ALL OF US TO SKIP TOWN?!
ZAP
ZAK
ZAP
I DIDN'T KILL KADIR.
THE A.I. SAID YOU MURDERED--
NOT NOW, PIA! YOU JUST HAVE TO TRUST ME.
I DON'T EVEN KNOW WHO YOU ARE!
ZAK
NO ONE KNOWS ANYONE.
ZAP
ZAP

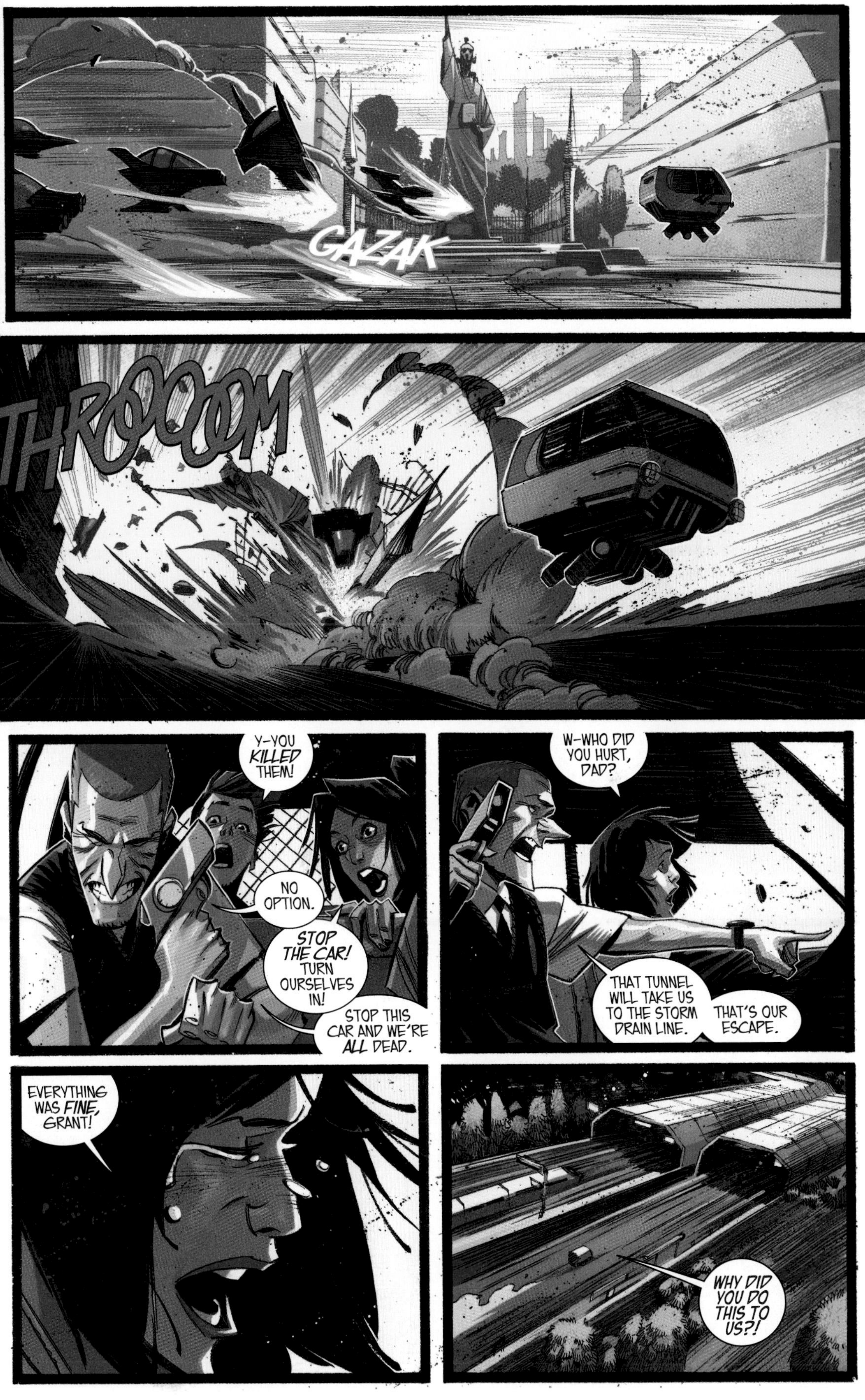
GAZAK
THROOOOM
Y-YOU KILLED THEM!
NO OPTION.
STOP THE CAR! TURN OURSELVES IN!
STOP THIS CAR AND WE'RE ALL DEAD.
W-WHO DID YOU HURT, DAD?
THAT TUNNEL WILL TAKE US TO THE STORM DRAIN LINE.
THAT'S OUR ESCAPE.
EVERYTHING WAS FINE, GRANT!
WHY DID YOU DO THIS TO US?!

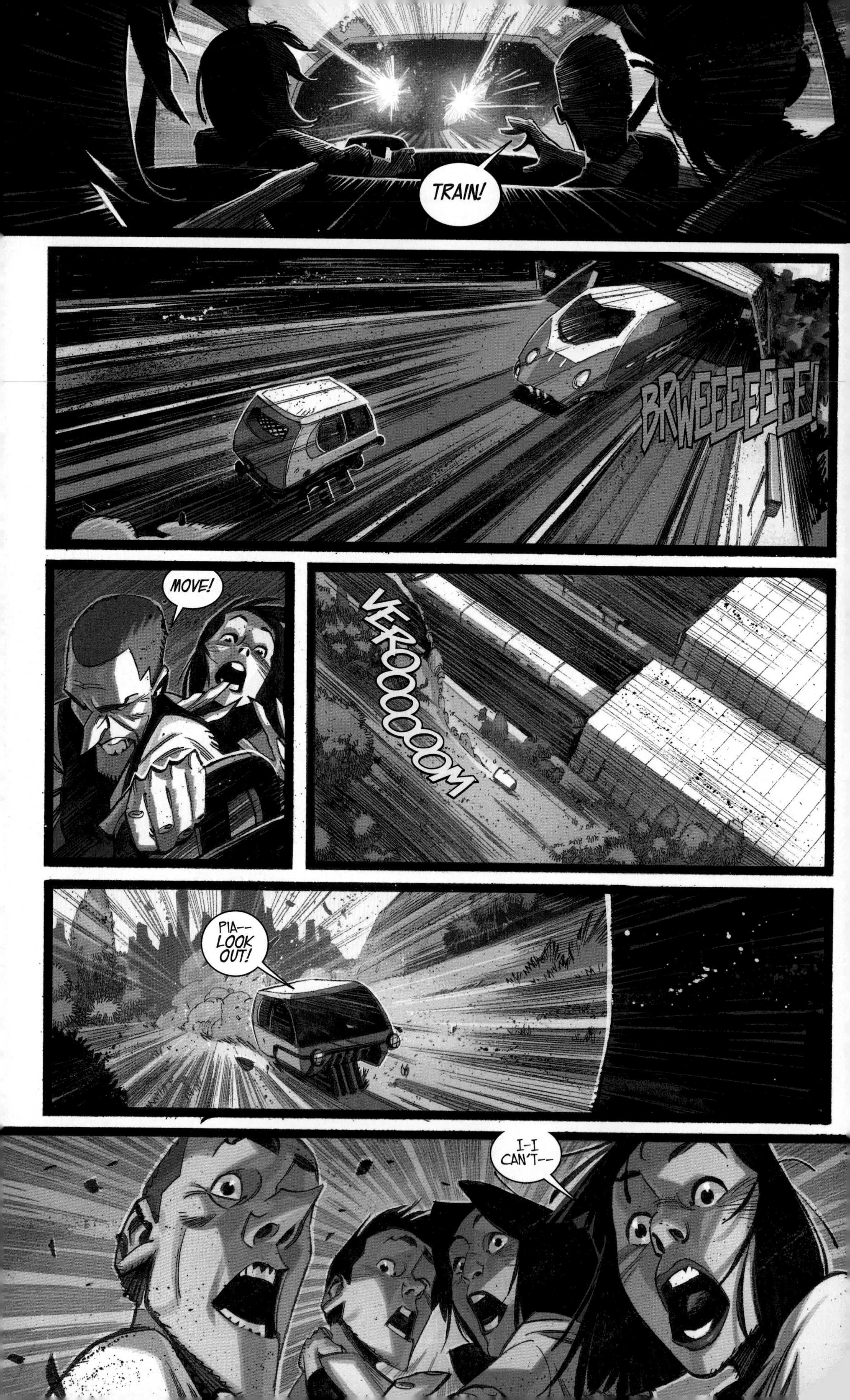
TRAIN!
BRWEEEEEEE!
MOVE!
VEROOOOOOM
PIA-- LOOK OUT!
I-I CAN'T--

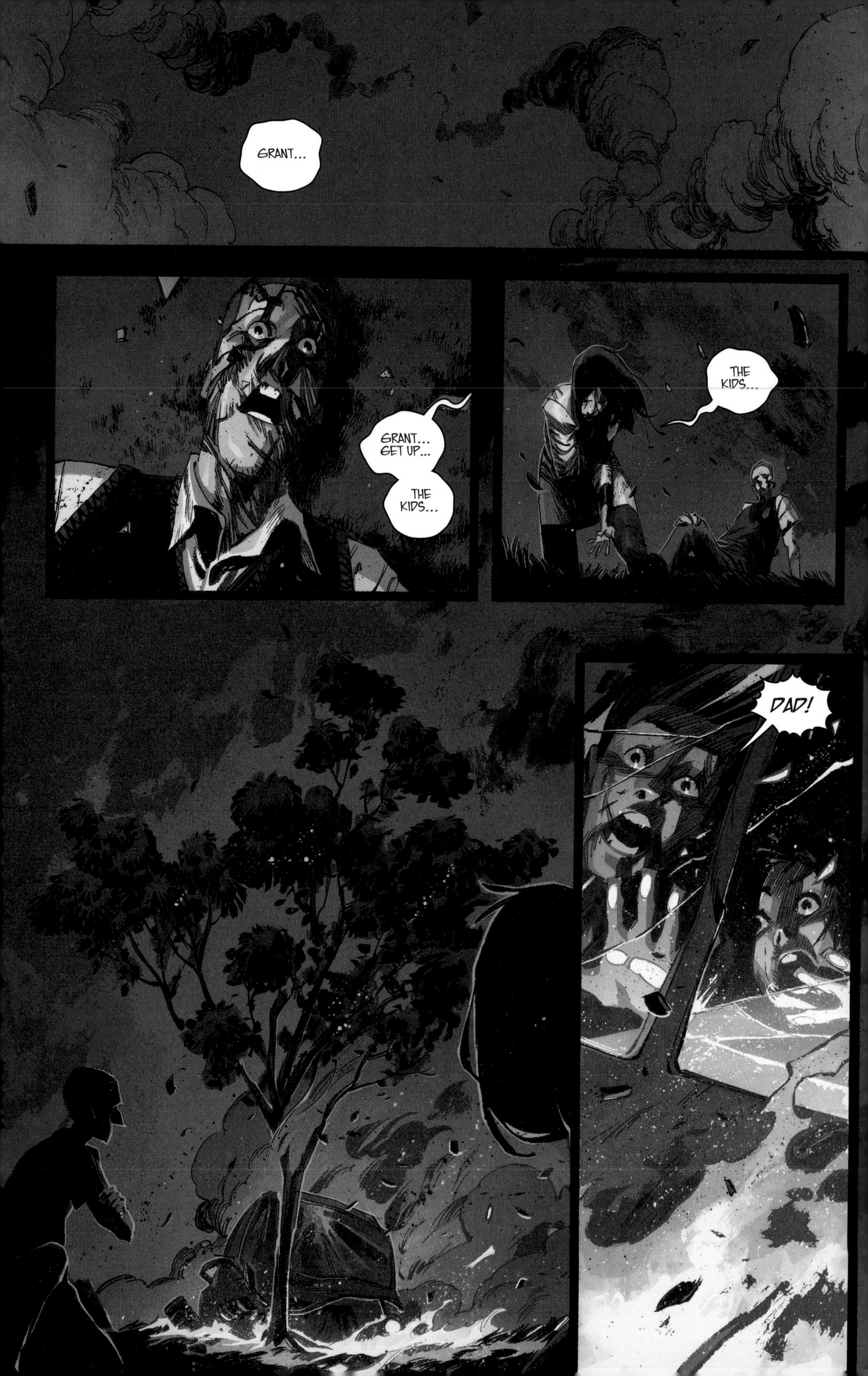
GRANT...
GRANT... GET UP...
THE KIDS...
THE KIDS...
DAD!

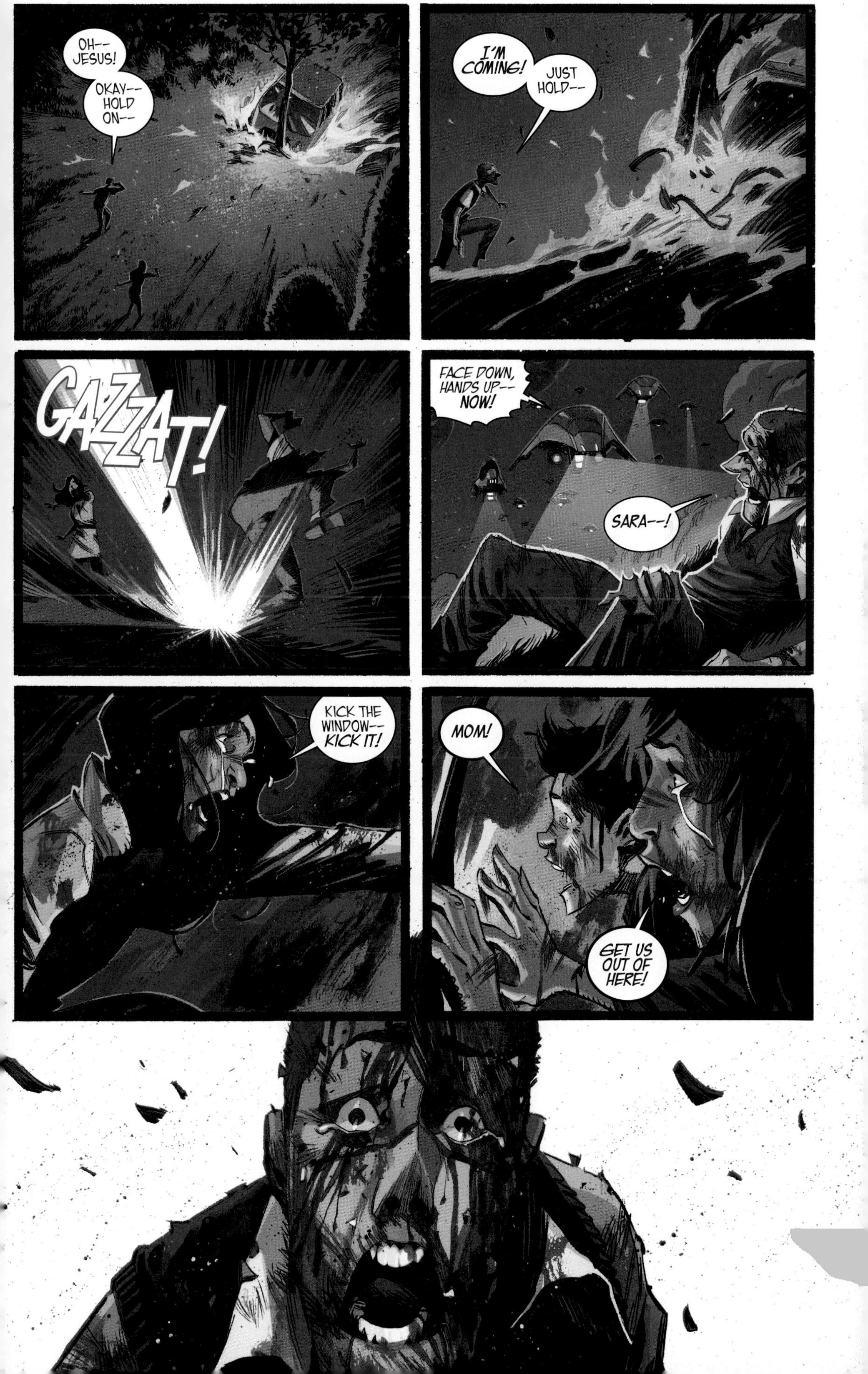
OH-- JESUS!
OKAY-- HOLD ON--
I'M COMING!
JUST HOLD--
GAZZZAT!
FACE DOWN, HANDS UP-- NOW!
SARA--!
KICK THE WINDOW-- KICK IT!
MOM!
GET US OUT OF HERE!

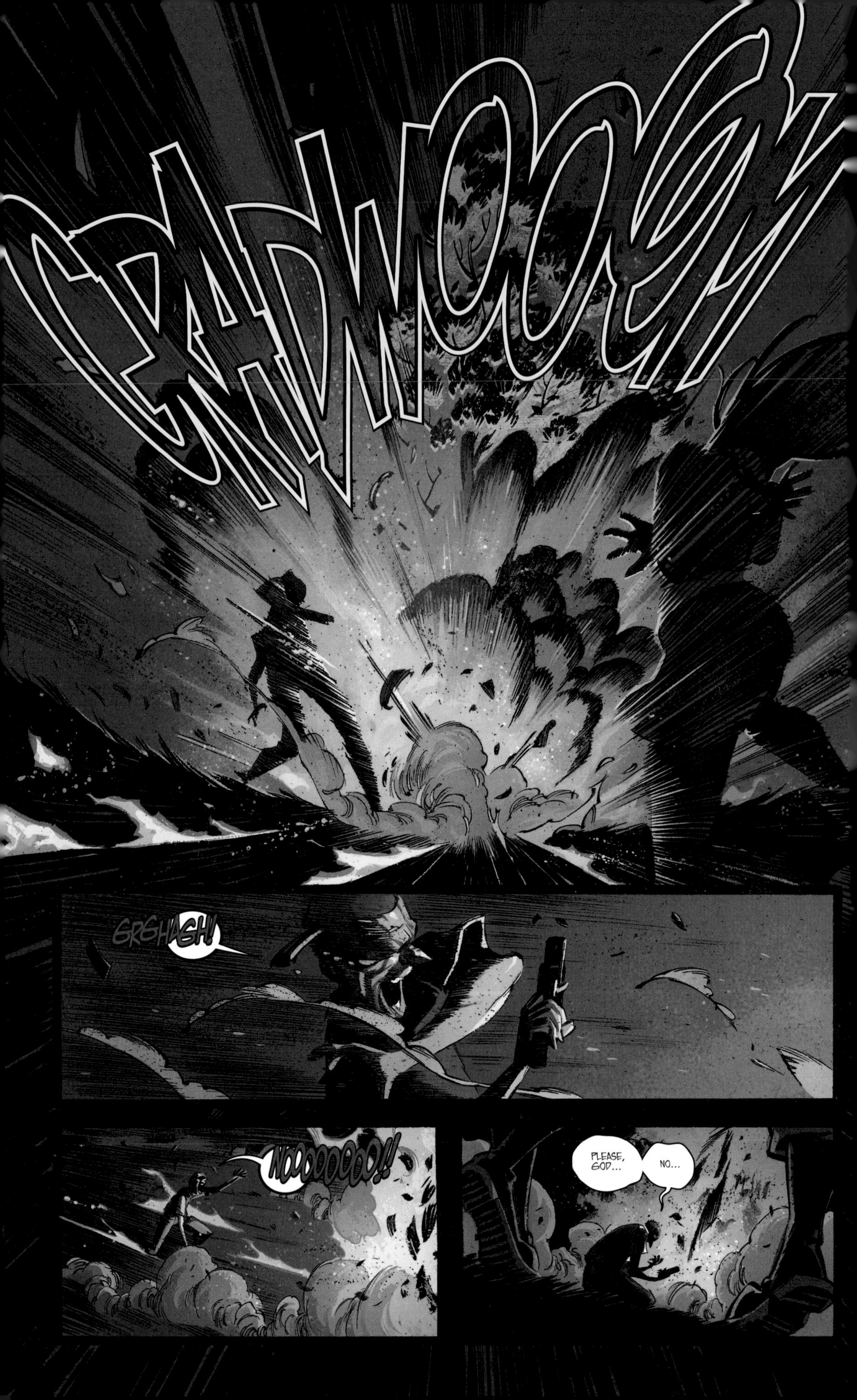
GRSHAGH!
NOOOOOOOO!!
PLEASE, GOD...
NO...

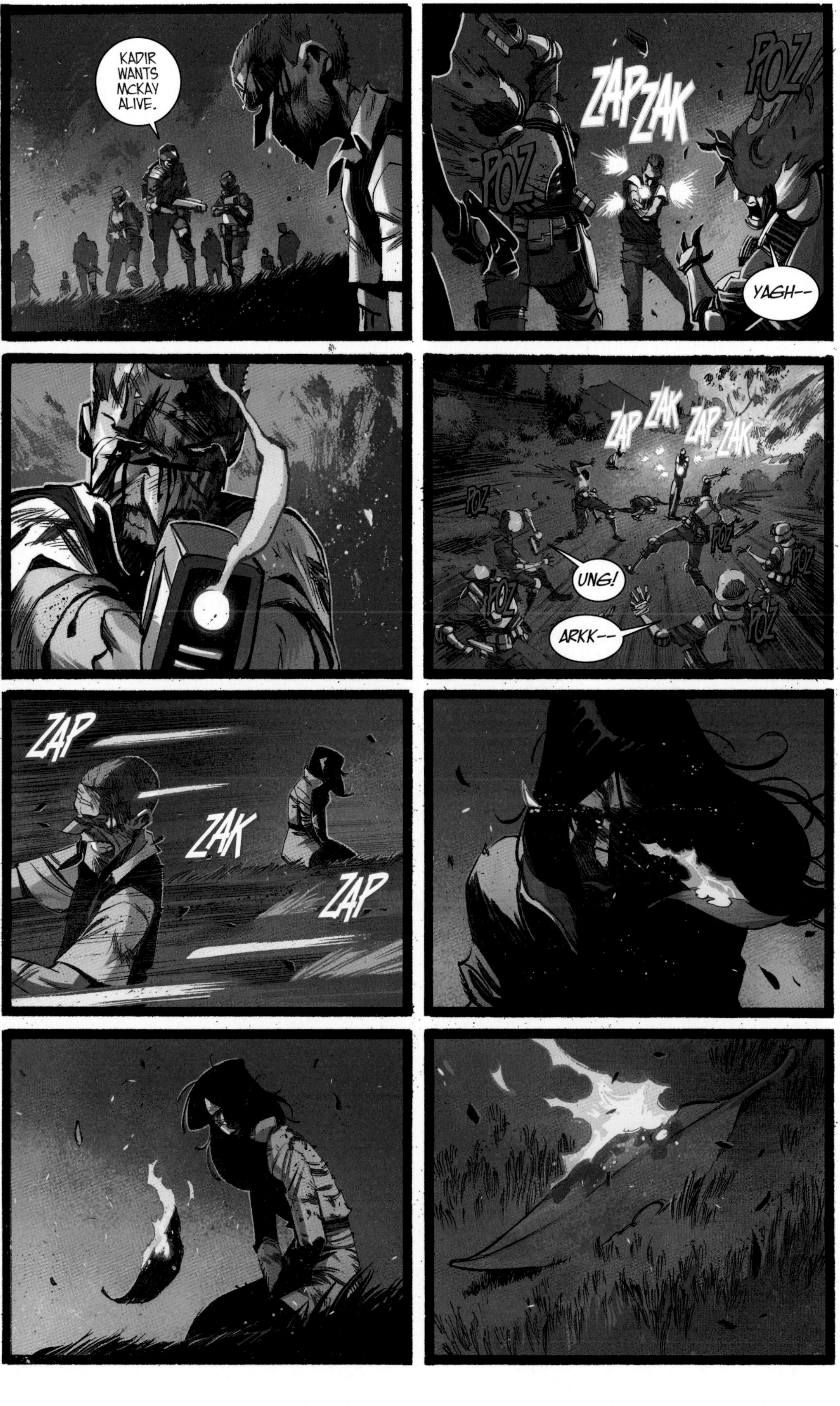
KADIR WANTS MCKAY ALIVE.
ZAP ZAK
POZ
POZ
YAGH--
ZAP ZAK ZAP ZAK
POZ
UNG!
POZ
ARKK--
POZ
POZ
POZ
ZAP
ZAK
ZAP

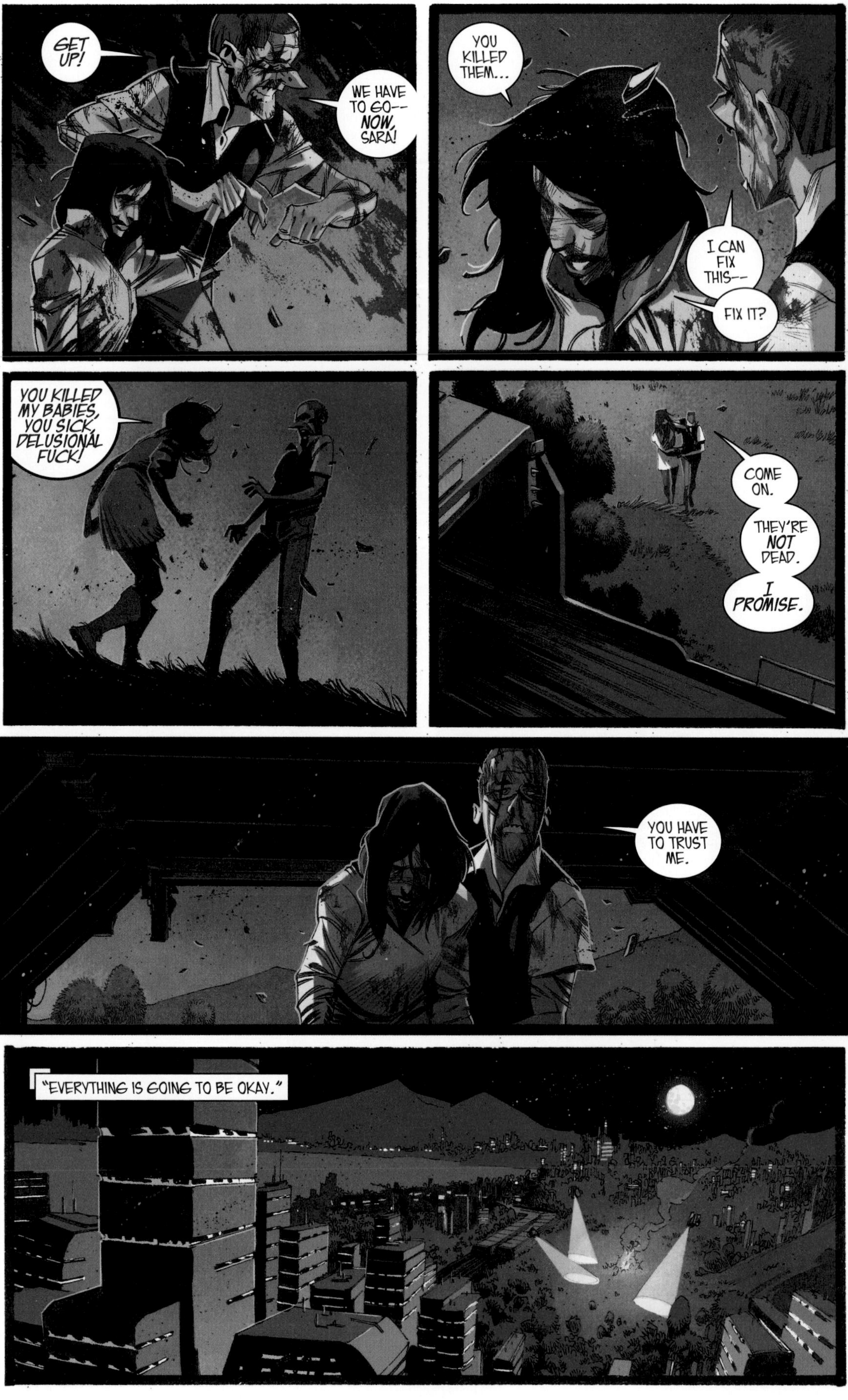
GET UP!
WE HAVE TO GO-- NOW, SARA!
YOU KILLED THEM...
I CAN FIX THIS--
FIX IT?
YOU KILLED MY BABIES, YOU SICK, DELUSIONAL FUCK!
COME ON.
THEY'RE NOT DEAD.
I PROMISE.
YOU HAVE TO TRUST ME.
"EVERYTHING IS GOING TO BE OKAY."

"WHEREVER ARE WE GOING?"

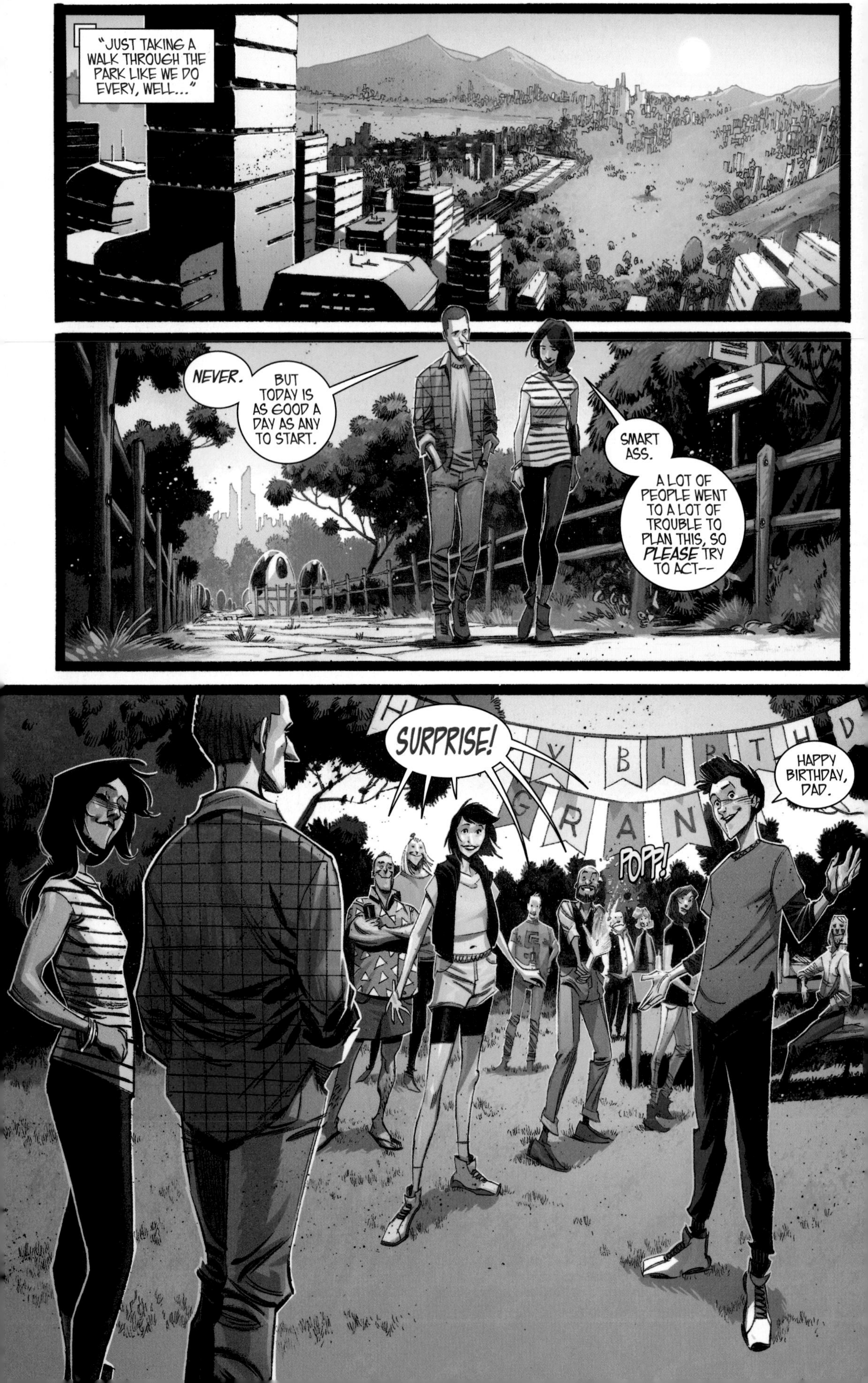
"JUST TAKING A WALK THROUGH THE PARK LIKE WE DO EVERY, WELL..."
NEVER.
BUT TODAY IS AS GOOD A DAY AS ANY TO START.
SMART ASS.
A LOT OF PEOPLE WENT TO A LOT OF TROUBLE TO PLAN THIS, SO *PLEASE* TRY TO ACT--
SURPRISE!
HAPPY BIRTHDAY, DAD.
POPP!

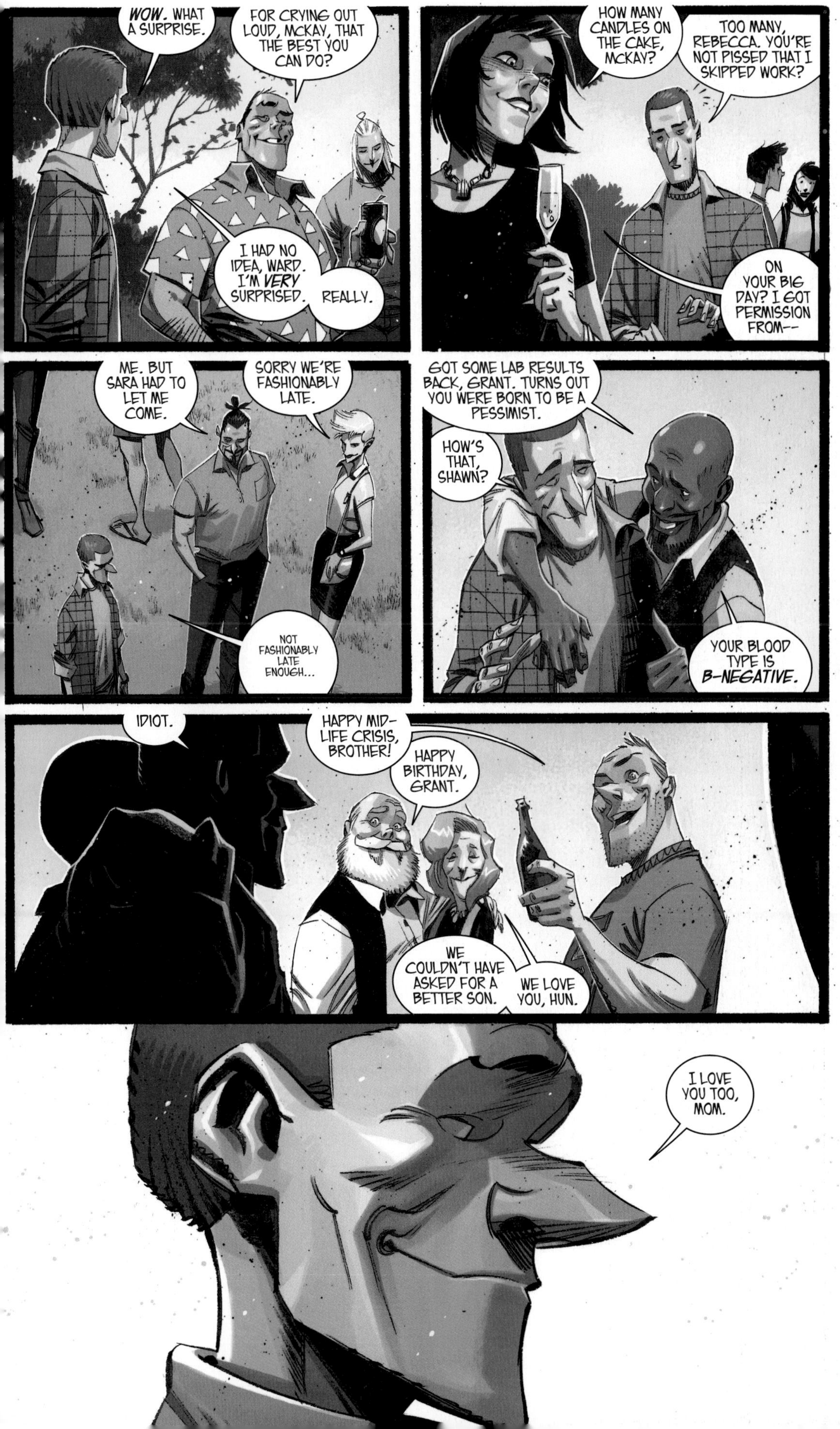
WOW. WHAT A SURPRISE.
FOR CRYING OUT LOUD, MCKAY, THAT THE BEST YOU CAN DO?
I HAD NO IDEA, WARD. I'M VERY SURPRISED.
REALLY.
HOW MANY CANDLES ON THE CAKE, MCKAY?
TOO MANY, REBECCA. YOU'RE NOT PISSED THAT I SKIPPED WORK?
ON YOUR BIG DAY? I GOT PERMISSION FROM--
ME. BUT SARA HAD TO LET ME COME.
SORRY WE'RE FASHIONABLY LATE.
NOT FASHIONABLY LATE ENOUGH...
GOT SOME LAB RESULTS BACK, GRANT. TURNS OUT YOU WERE BORN TO BE A PESSIMIST.
HOW'S THAT, SHAWN?
YOUR BLOOD TYPE IS B-NEGATIVE.
IDIOT.
HAPPY MID-LIFE CRISIS, BROTHER!
HAPPY BIRTHDAY, GRANT.
WE COULDN'T HAVE ASKED FOR A BETTER SON.
WE LOVE YOU, HUN.
I LOVE YOU TOO, MOM.

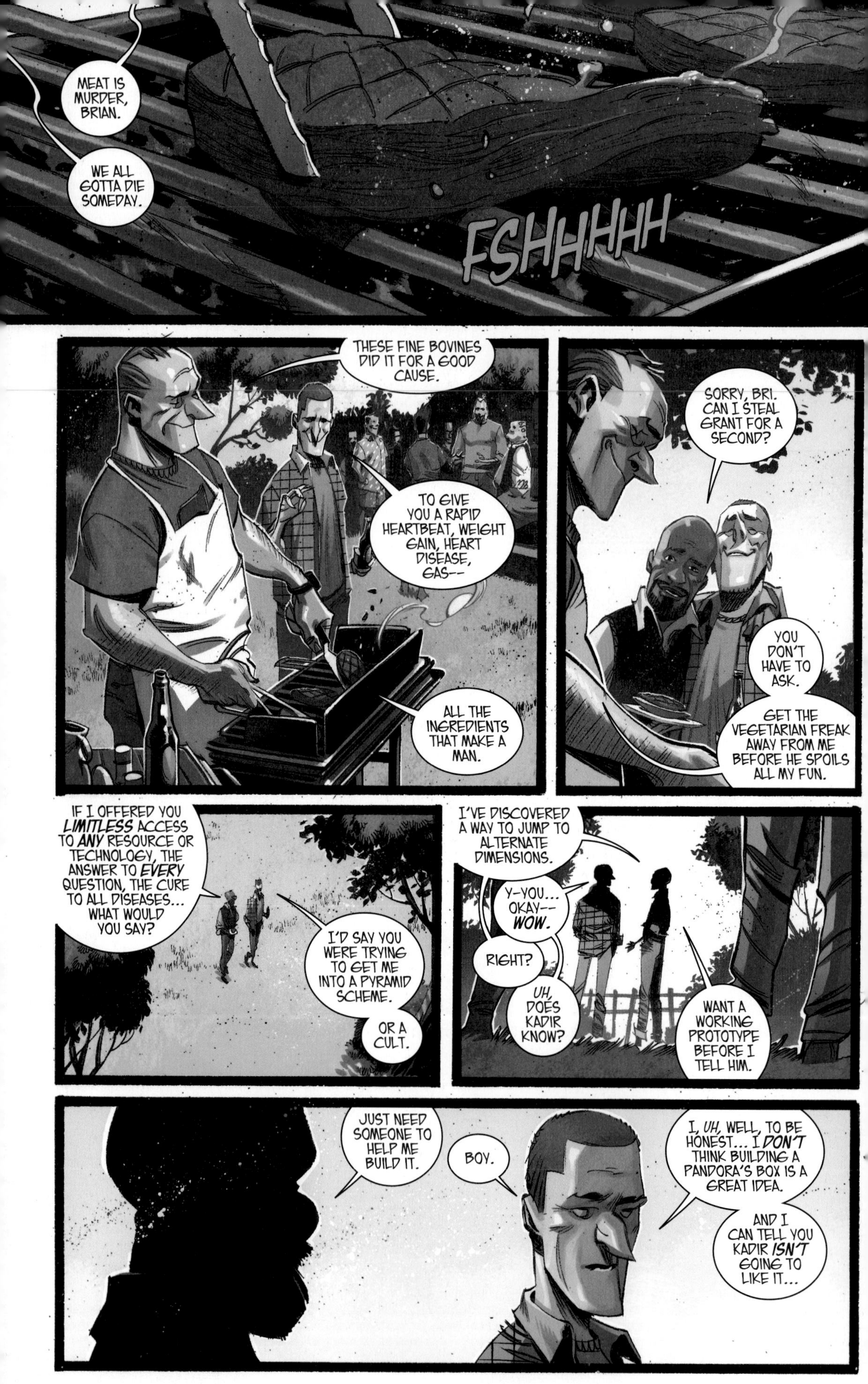
MEAT IS MURDER, BRIAN.
WE ALL GOTTA DIE SOMEDAY.
FSHHHHH
THESE FINE BOVINES DID IT FOR A GOOD CAUSE.
TO GIVE YOU A RAPID HEARTBEAT, WEIGHT GAIN, HEART DISEASE, GAS--
ALL THE INGREDIENTS THAT MAKE A MAN.
SORRY, BRI. CAN I STEAL GRANT FOR A SECOND?
YOU DON'T HAVE TO ASK.
GET THE VEGETARIAN FREAK AWAY FROM ME BEFORE HE SPOILS ALL MY FUN.
IF I OFFERED YOU LIMITLESS ACCESS TO ANY RESOURCE OR TECHNOLOGY, THE ANSWER TO EVERY QUESTION, THE CURE TO ALL DISEASES... WHAT WOULD YOU SAY?
I'D SAY YOU WERE TRYING TO GET ME INTO A PYRAMID SCHEME.
OR A CULT.
I'VE DISCOVERED A WAY TO JUMP TO ALTERNATE DIMENSIONS.
Y-YOU... OKAY-- WOW.
RIGHT?
UH, DOES KADIR KNOW?
WANT A WORKING PROTOTYPE BEFORE I TELL HIM.
JUST NEED SOMEONE TO HELP ME BUILD IT.
BOY.
I, UH, WELL, TO BE HONEST... I DON'T THINK BUILDING A PANDORA'S BOX IS A GREAT IDEA.
AND I CAN TELL YOU KADIR ISN'T GOING TO LIKE IT...

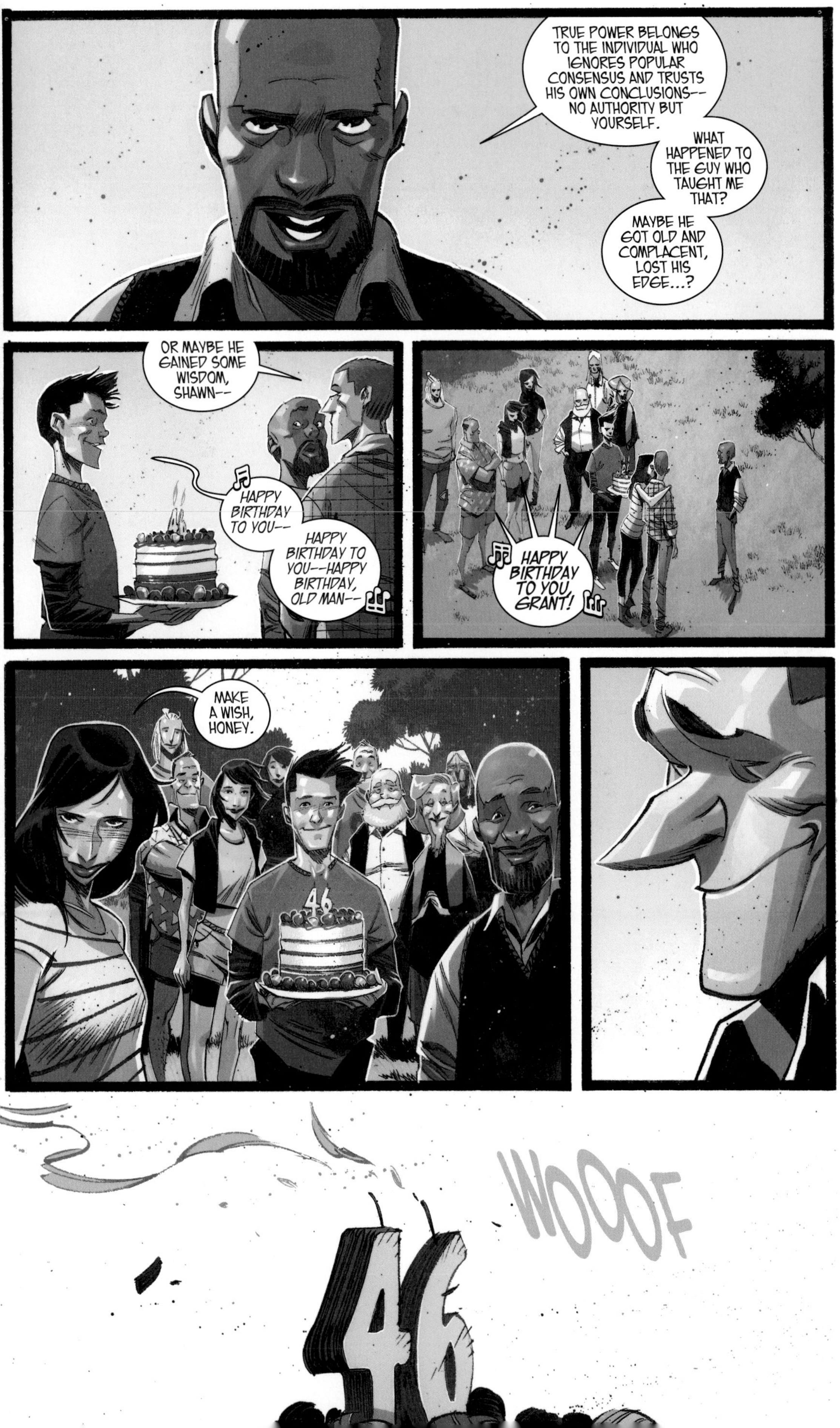
TRUE POWER BELONGS TO THE INDIVIDUAL WHO IGNORES POPULAR CONSENSUS AND TRUSTS HIS OWN CONCLUSIONS-- NO AUTHORITY BUT YOURSELF.
WHAT HAPPENED TO THE GUY WHO TAUGHT ME THAT?
MAYBE HE GOT OLD AND COMPLACENT, LOST HIS EDGE...?
OR MAYBE HE GAINED SOME WISDOM, SHAWN--
HAPPY BIRTHDAY TO YOU--
HAPPY BIRTHDAY TO YOU--HAPPY BIRTHDAY, OLD MAN--
HAPPY BIRTHDAY TO YOU, GRANT!
MAKE A WISH, HONEY.
46
WOOOF

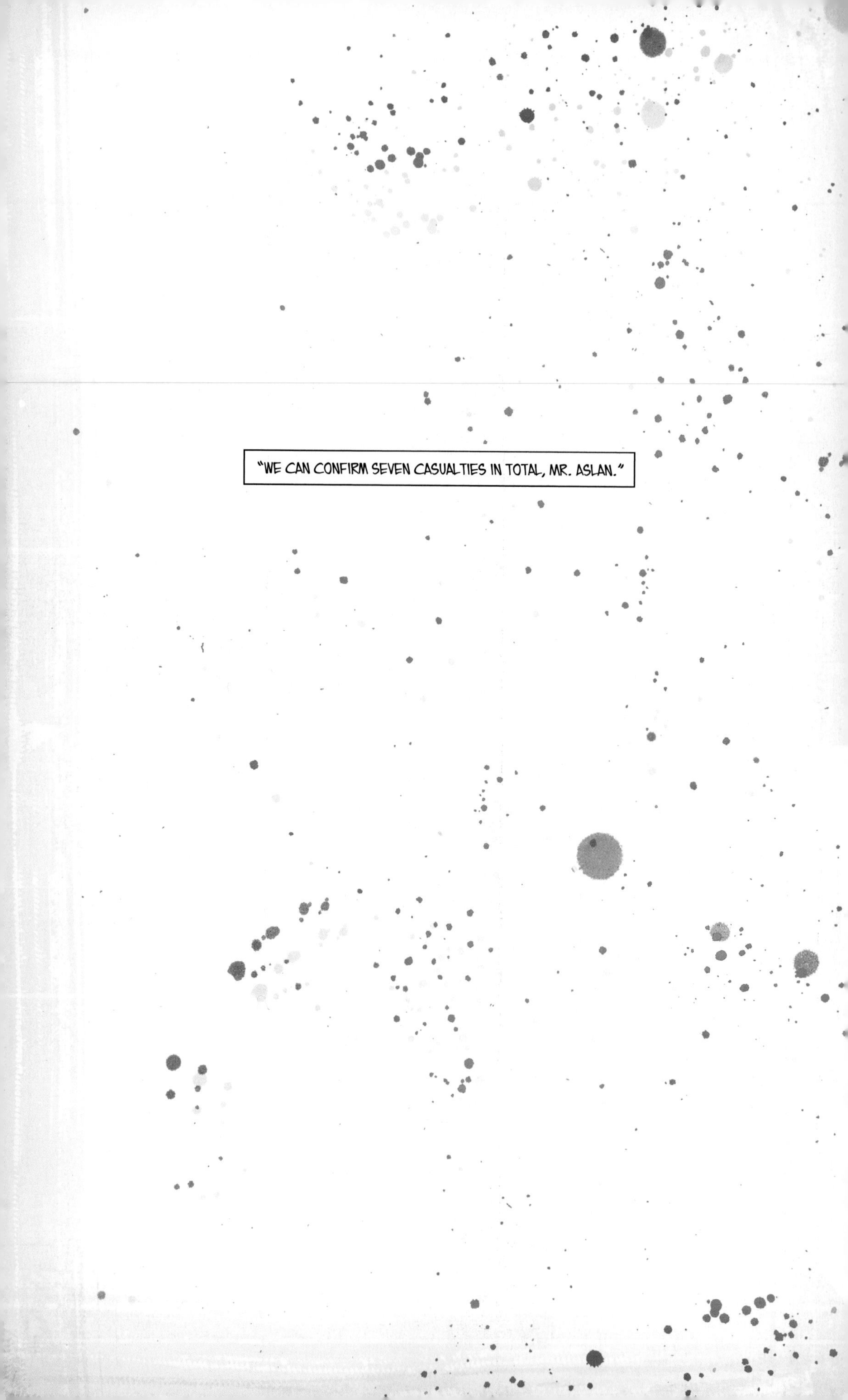
"WE CAN CONFIRM SEVEN CASUALTIES IN TOTAL, MR. ASLAN."

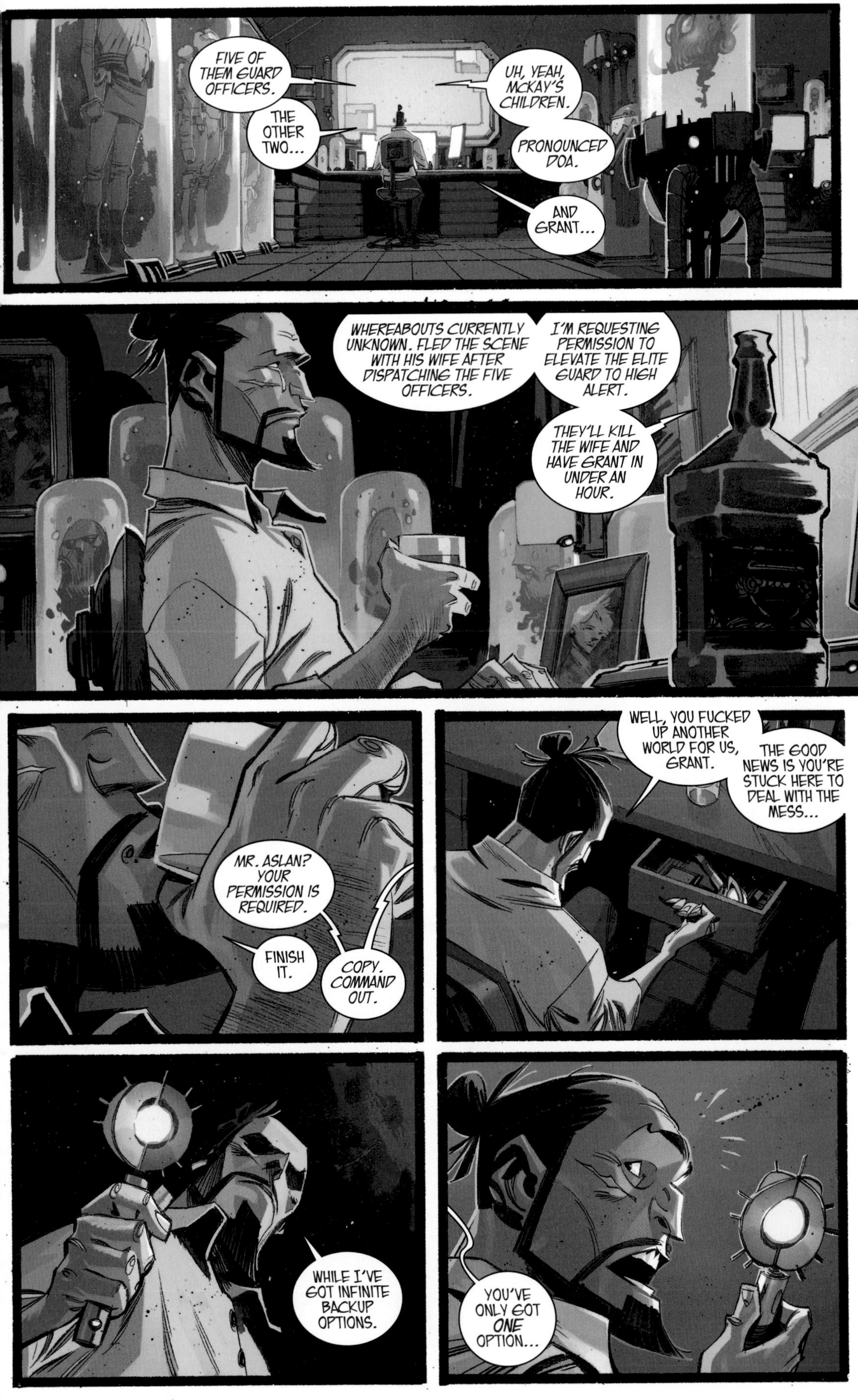
FIVE OF THEM GUARD OFFICERS.
THE OTHER TWO...
UH, YEAH, MCKAY'S CHILDREN.
PRONOUNCED DOA.
AND GRANT...
WHEREABOUTS CURRENTLY UNKNOWN. FLED THE SCENE WITH HIS WIFE AFTER DISPATCHING THE FIVE OFFICERS.
I'M REQUESTING PERMISSION TO ELEVATE THE ELITE GUARD TO HIGH ALERT.
THEY'LL KILL THE WIFE AND HAVE GRANT IN UNDER AN HOUR.
MR. ASLAN? YOUR PERMISSION IS REQUIRED.
FINISH IT.
COPY. COMMAND OUT.
WELL, YOU FUCKED UP ANOTHER WORLD FOR US, GRANT.
THE GOOD NEWS IS YOU'RE STUCK HERE TO DEAL WITH THE MESS...
WHILE I'VE GOT INFINITE BACKUP OPTIONS.
YOU'VE ONLY GOT ONE OPTION...

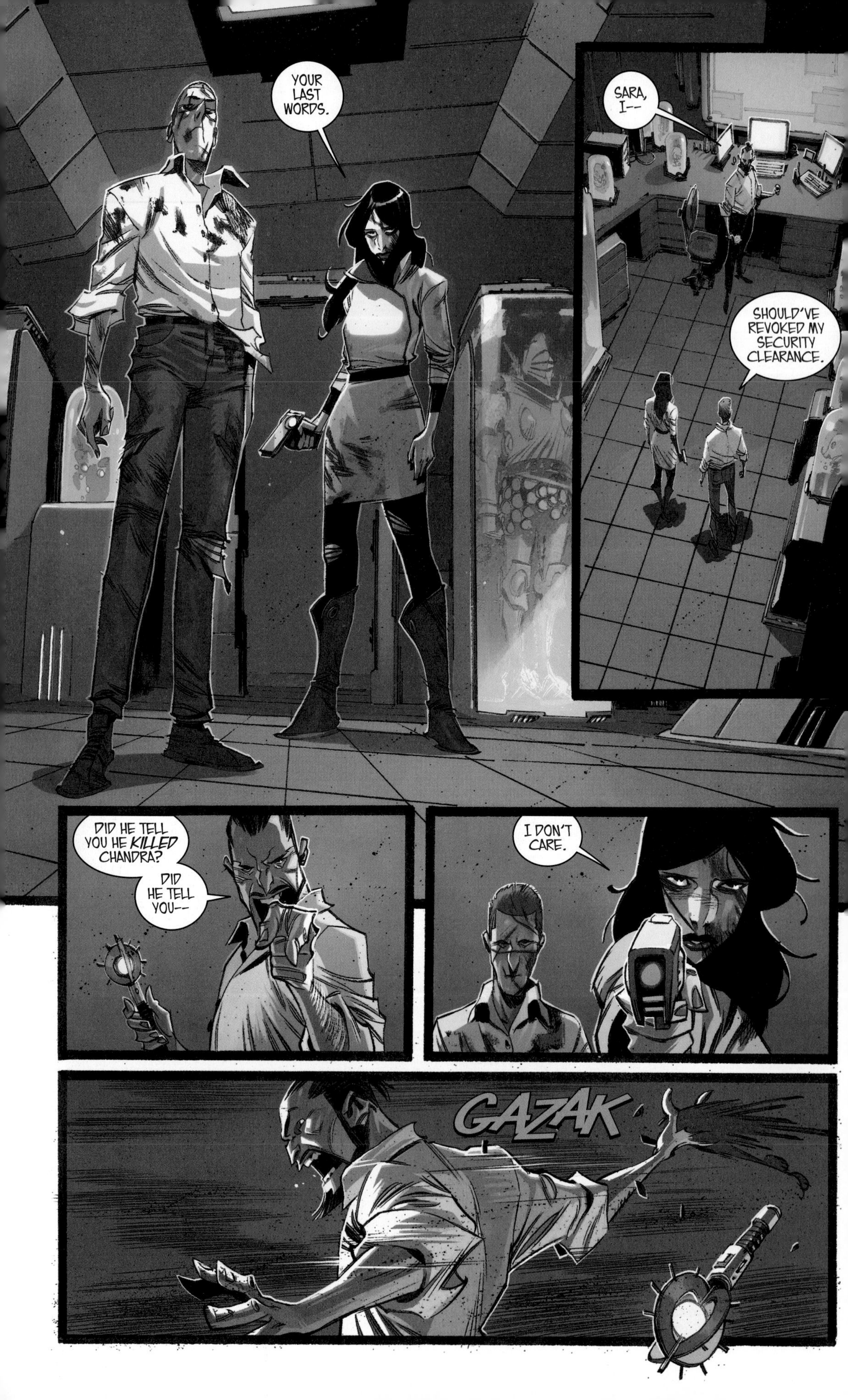
YOUR LAST WORDS.
SARA, I--
SHOULD'VE REVOKED MY SECURITY CLEARANCE.
DID HE TELL YOU HE KILLED CHANDRA?
DID HE TELL YOU--
I DON'T CARE.
GAZAK

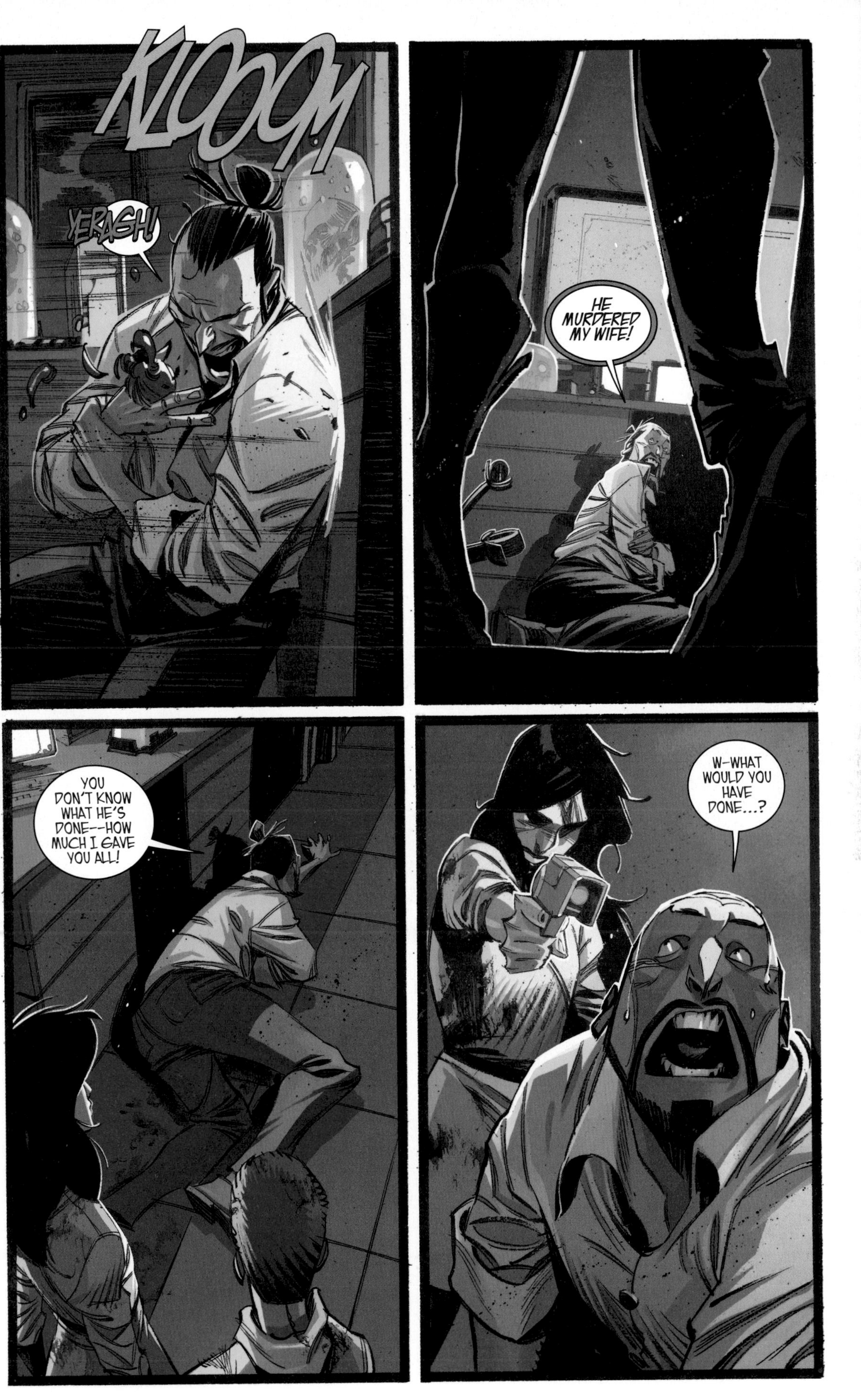
KLOOOM
YERAGH!
HE MURDERED MY WIFE!
YOU DON'T KNOW WHAT HE'S DONE--HOW MUCH I GAVE YOU ALL!
W-WHAT WOULD YOU HAVE DONE...?

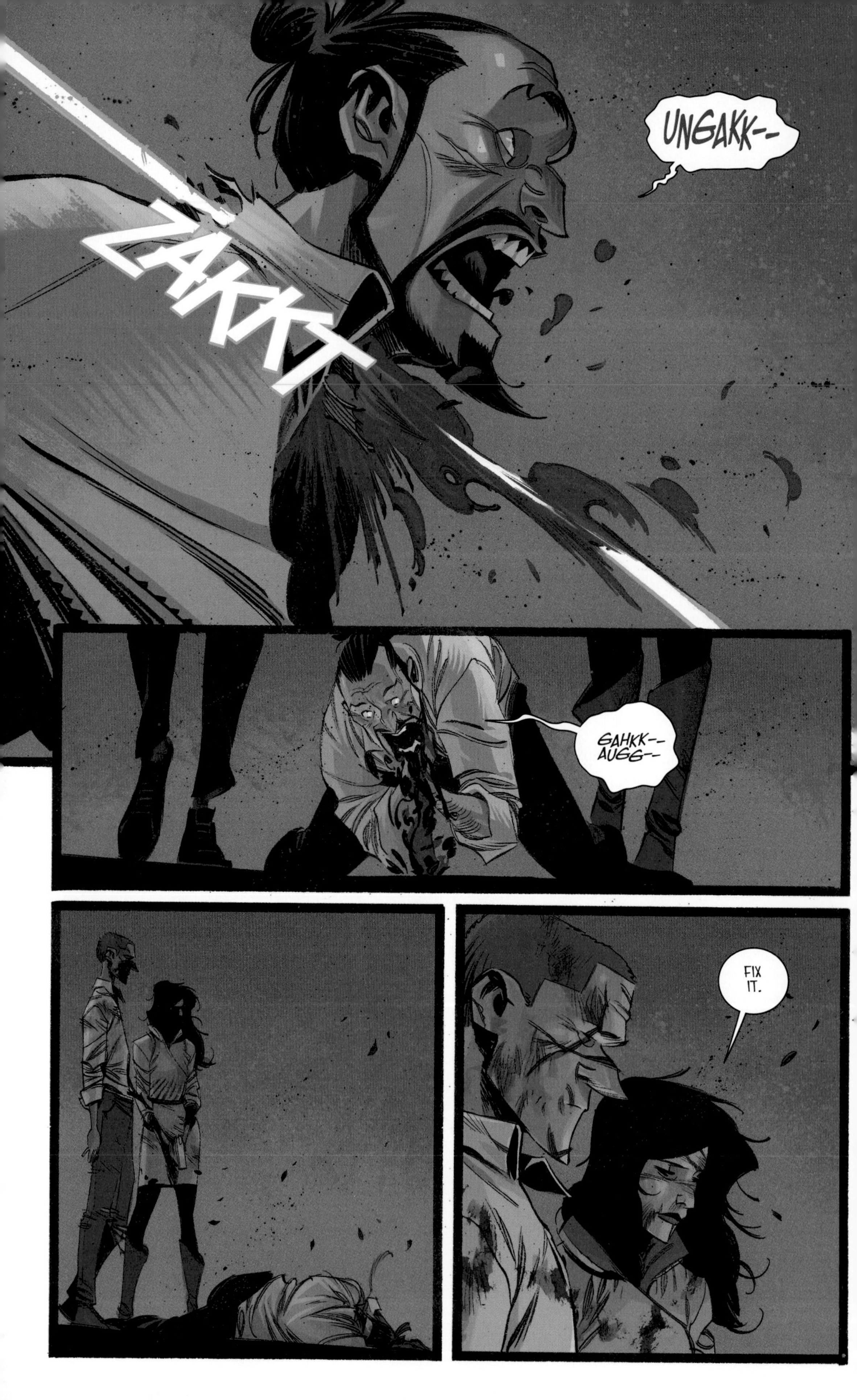
ZAKKT
UNGAKK--
GAHKK--
AUGG--
FIX IT.

"I COME INTO MY OFFICE TO SEE NATE AND PIA HAVE TAKEN THE PAINT FROM THE GARAGE AND JUST COVERED *EVERYTHING* IN SKY BLUE."

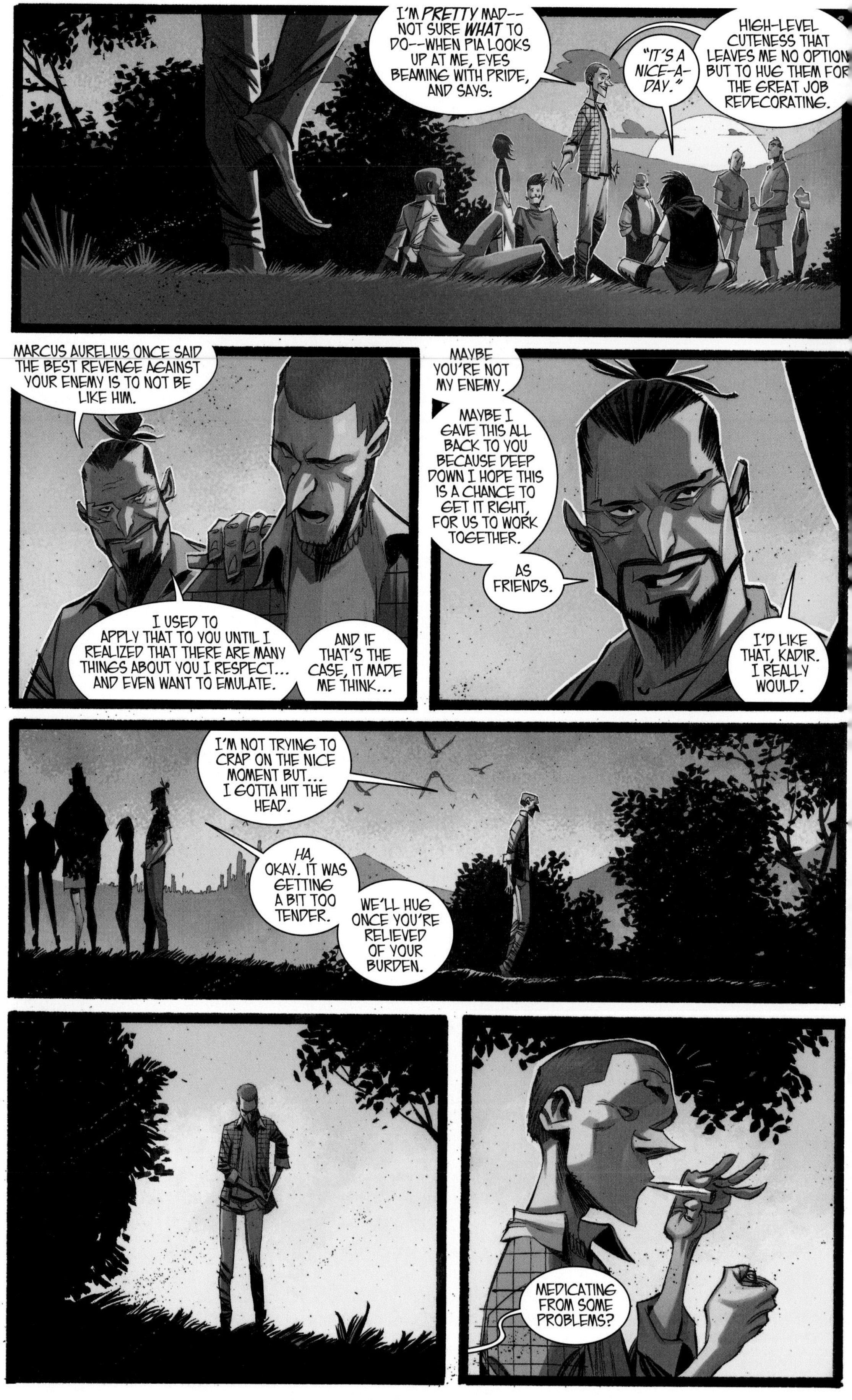
I'M PRETTY MAD-- NOT SURE WHAT TO DO--WHEN PIA LOOKS UP AT ME, EYES BEAMING WITH PRIDE, AND SAYS:
"IT'S A NICE-A-DAY."
HIGH-LEVEL CUTENESS THAT LEAVES ME NO OPTION BUT TO HUG THEM FOR THE GREAT JOB REDECORATING.
MARCUS AURELIUS ONCE SAID THE BEST REVENGE AGAINST YOUR ENEMY IS TO NOT BE LIKE HIM.
I USED TO APPLY THAT TO YOU UNTIL I REALIZED THAT THERE ARE MANY THINGS ABOUT YOU I RESPECT... AND EVEN WANT TO EMULATE.
AND IF THAT'S THE CASE, IT MADE ME THINK...
MAYBE YOU'RE NOT MY ENEMY.
MAYBE I GAVE THIS ALL BACK TO YOU BECAUSE DEEP DOWN I HOPE THIS IS A CHANCE TO GET IT RIGHT, FOR US TO WORK TOGETHER.
AS FRIENDS.
I'D LIKE THAT, KADIR. I REALLY WOULD.
I'M NOT TRYING TO CRAP ON THE NICE MOMENT BUT... I GOTTA HIT THE HEAD.
HA, OKAY. IT WAS GETTING A BIT TOO TENDER.
WE'LL HUG ONCE YOU'RE RELIEVED OF YOUR BURDEN.
MEDICATING FROM SOME PROBLEMS?

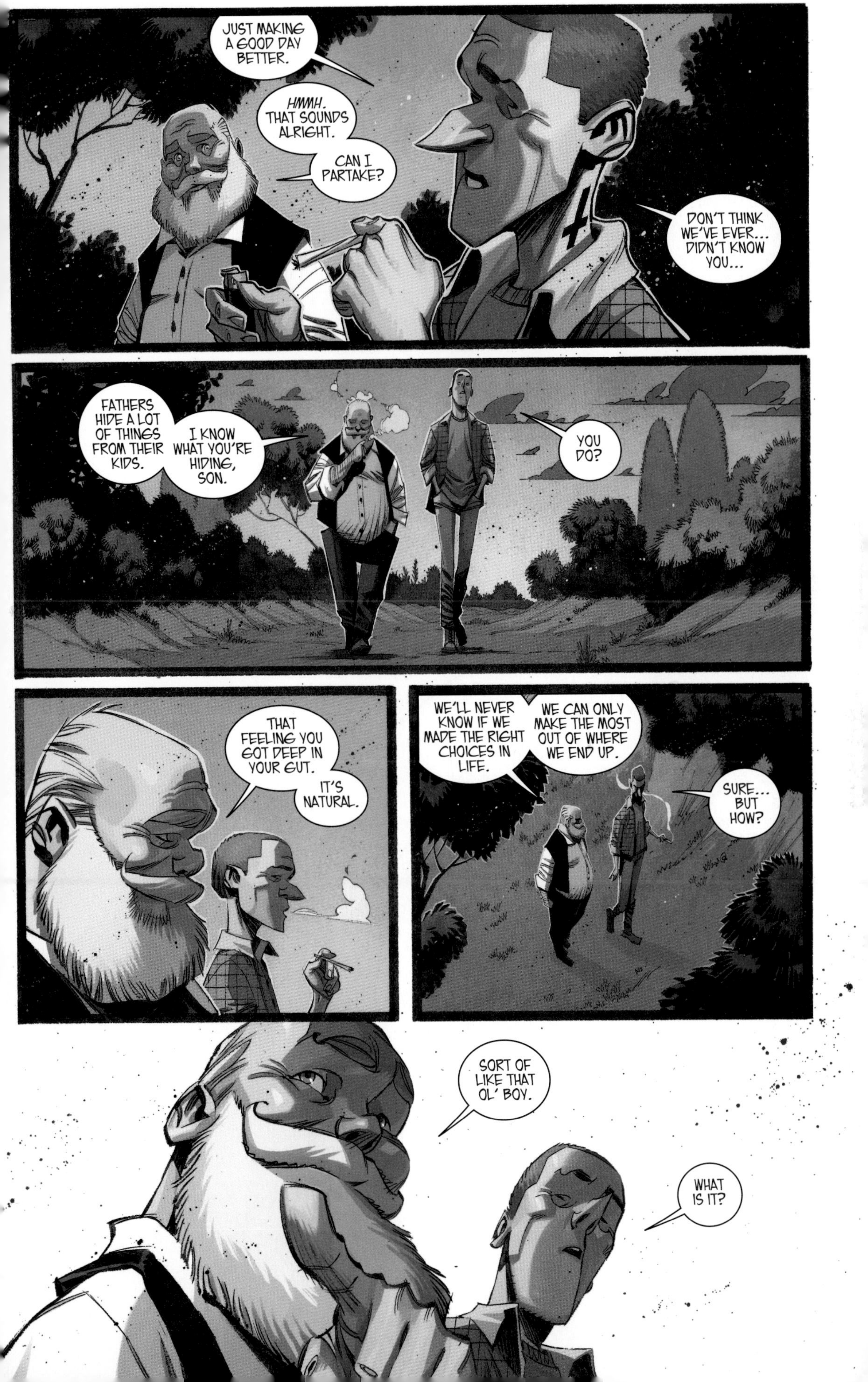
JUST MAKING A GOOD DAY BETTER.
HMMH. THAT SOUNDS ALRIGHT.
CAN I PARTAKE?
DON'T THINK WE'VE EVER... DIDN'T KNOW YOU...
FATHERS HIDE A LOT OF THINGS FROM THEIR KIDS.
I KNOW WHAT YOU'RE HIDING, SON.
YOU DO?
THAT FEELING YOU GOT DEEP IN YOUR GUT.
IT'S NATURAL.
WE'LL NEVER KNOW IF WE MADE THE RIGHT CHOICES IN LIFE.
WE CAN ONLY MAKE THE MOST OUT OF WHERE WE END UP.
SURE... BUT HOW?
SORT OF LIKE THAT OL' BOY.
WHAT IS IT?

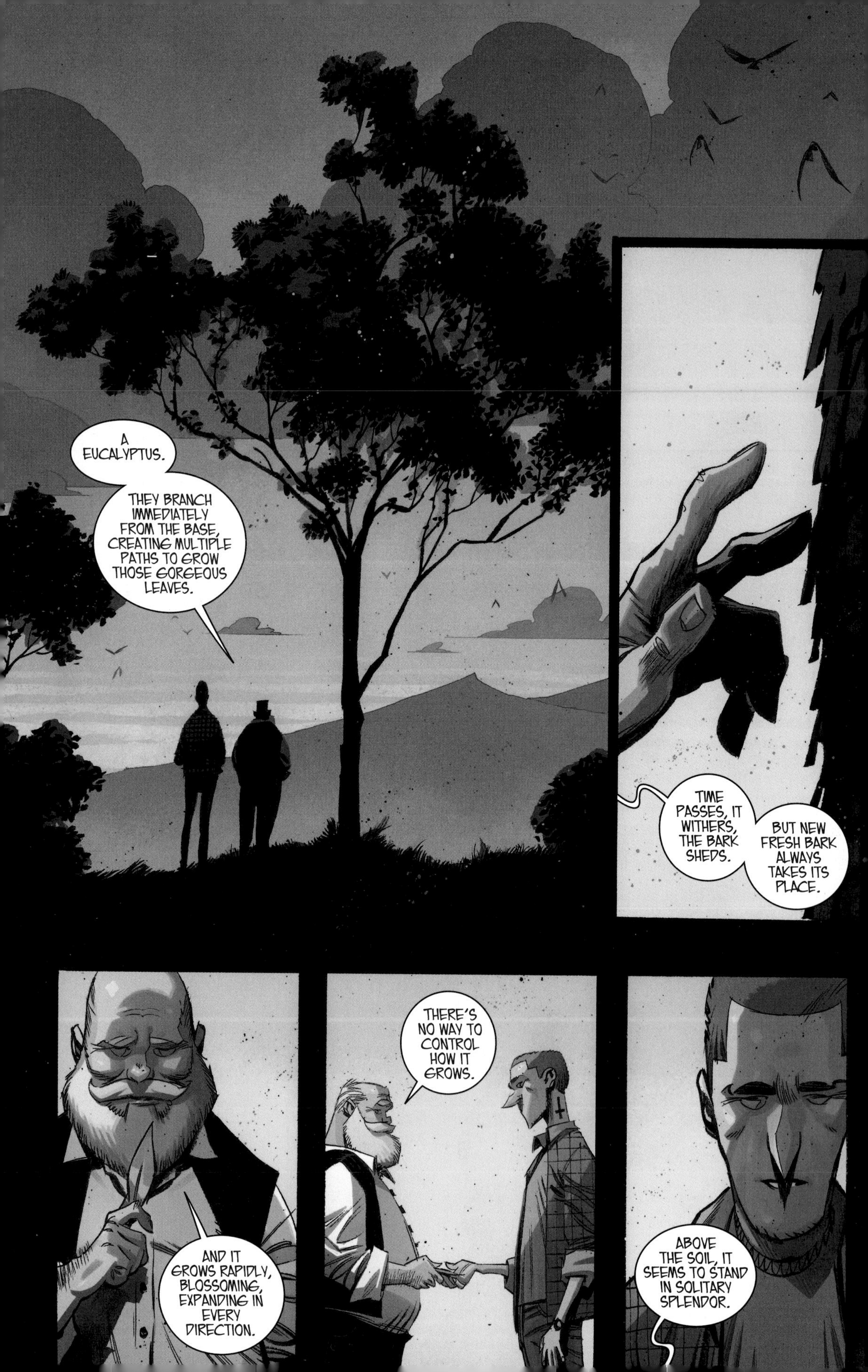
A EUCALYPTUS.
THEY BRANCH IMMEDIATELY FROM THE BASE, CREATING MULTIPLE PATHS TO GROW THOSE GORGEOUS LEAVES.
TIME PASSES, IT WITHERS, THE BARK SHEDS.
BUT NEW FRESH BARK ALWAYS TAKES ITS PLACE.
AND IT GROWS RAPIDLY, BLOSSOMING, EXPANDING IN EVERY DIRECTION.
THERE'S NO WAY TO CONTROL HOW IT GROWS.
ABOVE THE SOIL, IT SEEMS TO STAND IN SOLITARY SPLENDOR.

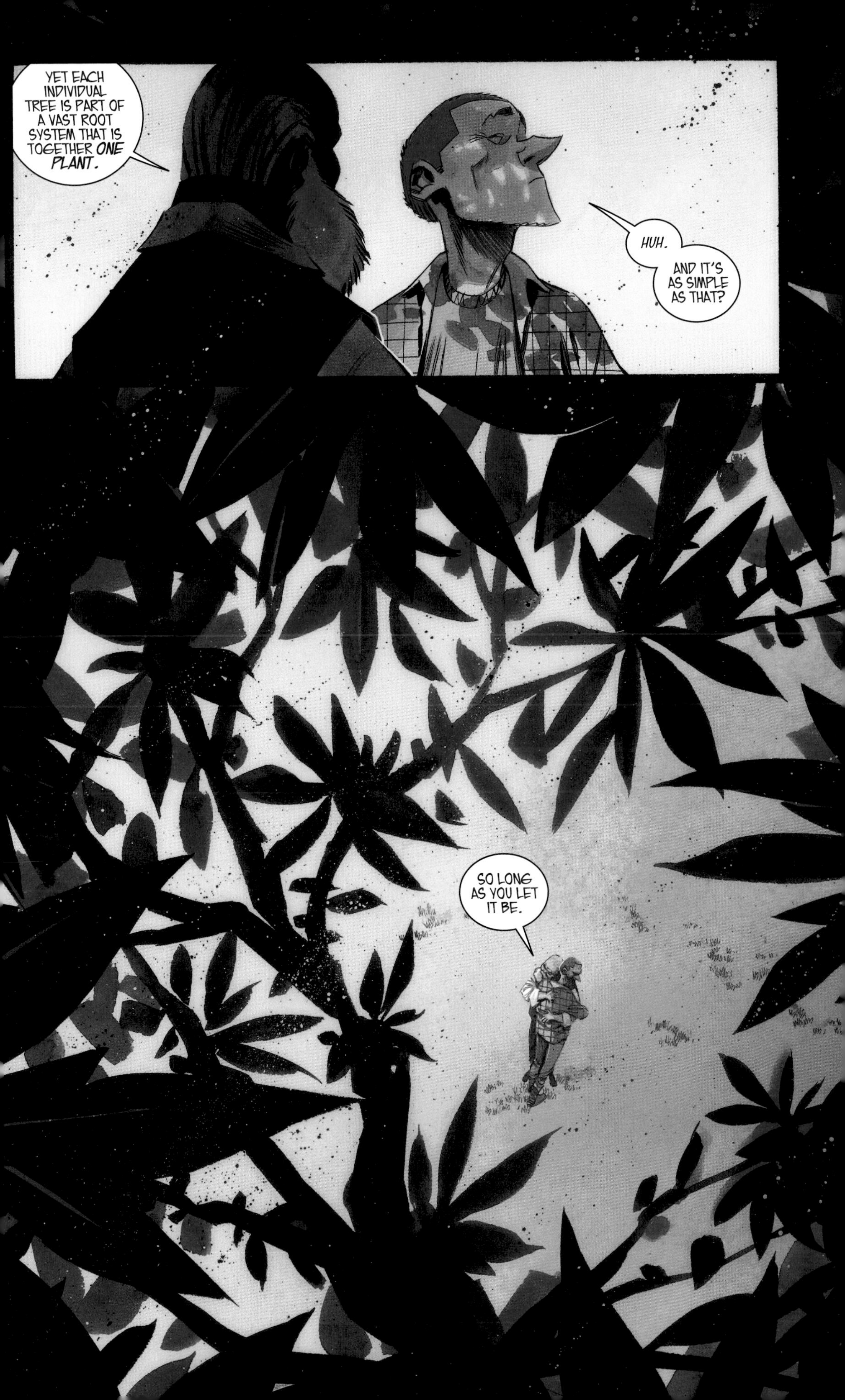
YET EACH INDIVIDUAL TREE IS PART OF A VAST ROOT SYSTEM THAT IS TOGETHER *ONE PLANT*.
HUH.
AND IT'S AS SIMPLE AS THAT?
SO LONG AS YOU LET IT BE.

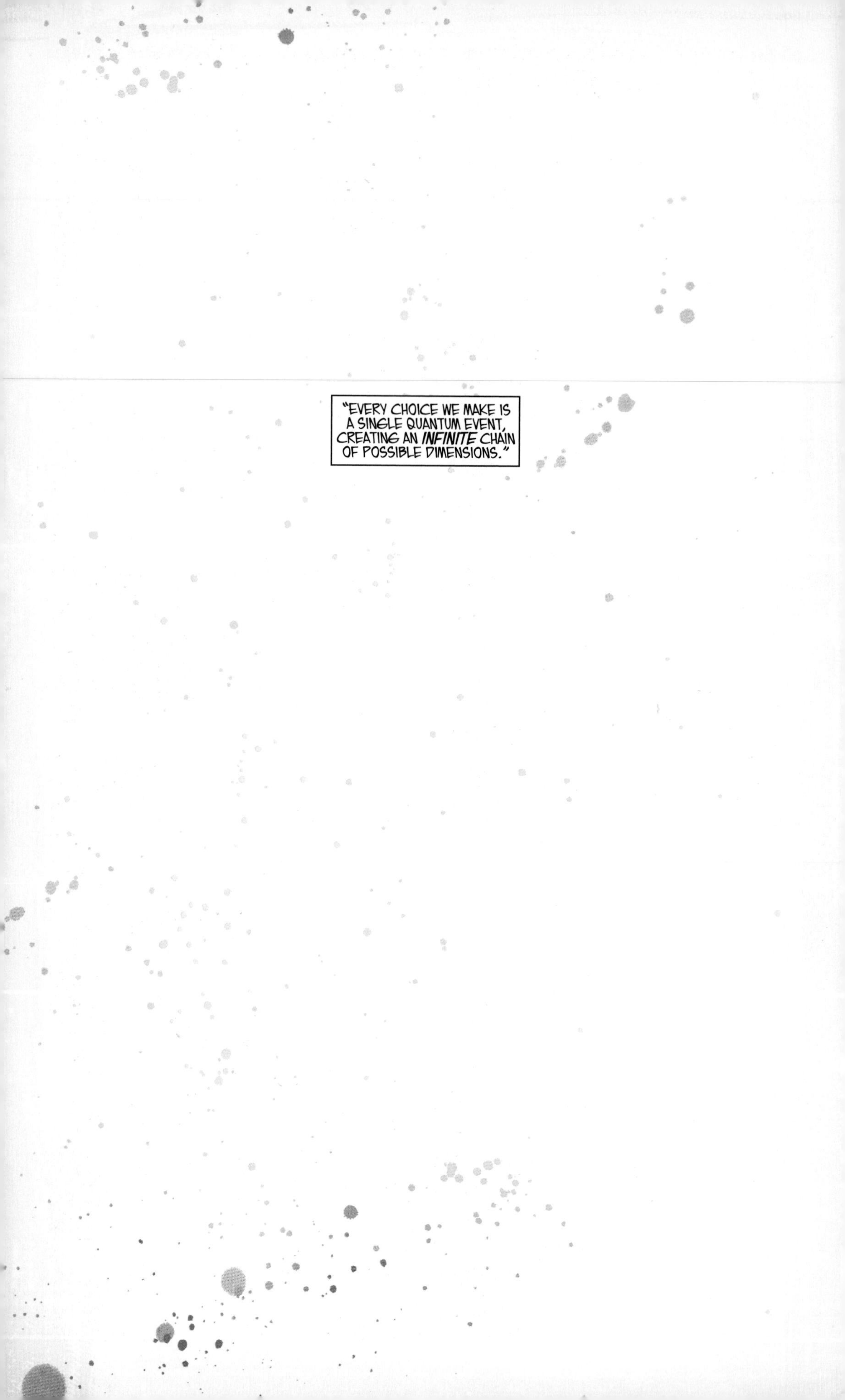
"EVERY CHOICE WE MAKE IS A SINGLE QUANTUM EVENT, CREATING AN *INFINITE* CHAIN OF POSSIBLE DIMENSIONS."

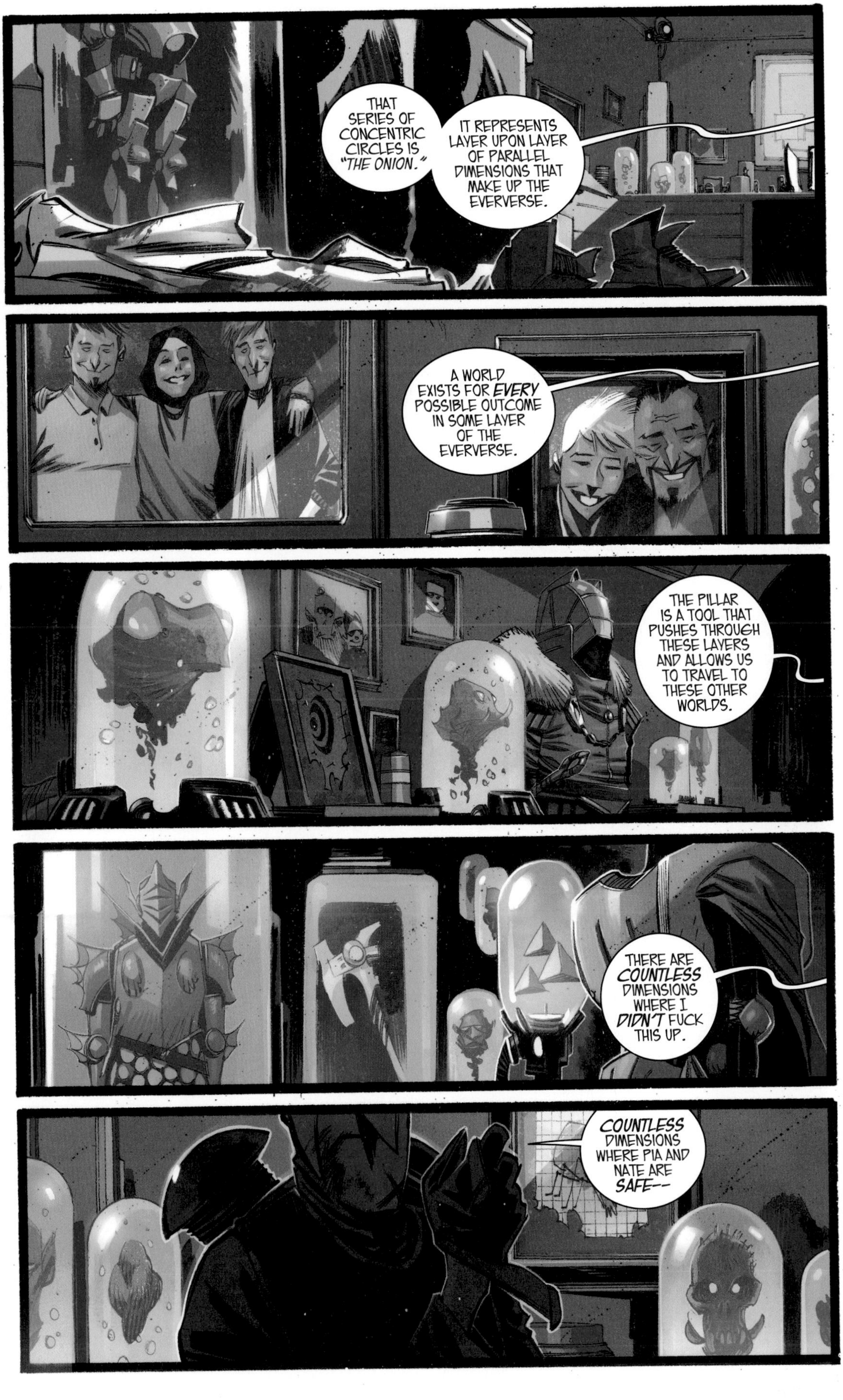

THAT SERIES OF CONCENTRIC CIRCLES IS "THE ONION."
IT REPRESENTS LAYER UPON LAYER OF PARALLEL DIMENSIONS THAT MAKE UP THE EVERVERSE.
A WORLD EXISTS FOR EVERY POSSIBLE OUTCOME IN SOME LAYER OF THE EVERVERSE.
THE PILLAR IS A TOOL THAT PUSHES THROUGH THESE LAYERS AND ALLOWS US TO TRAVEL TO THESE OTHER WORLDS.
THERE ARE COUNTLESS DIMENSIONS WHERE I DIDN'T FUCK THIS UP.
COUNTLESS DIMENSIONS WHERE PIA AND NATE ARE SAFE--

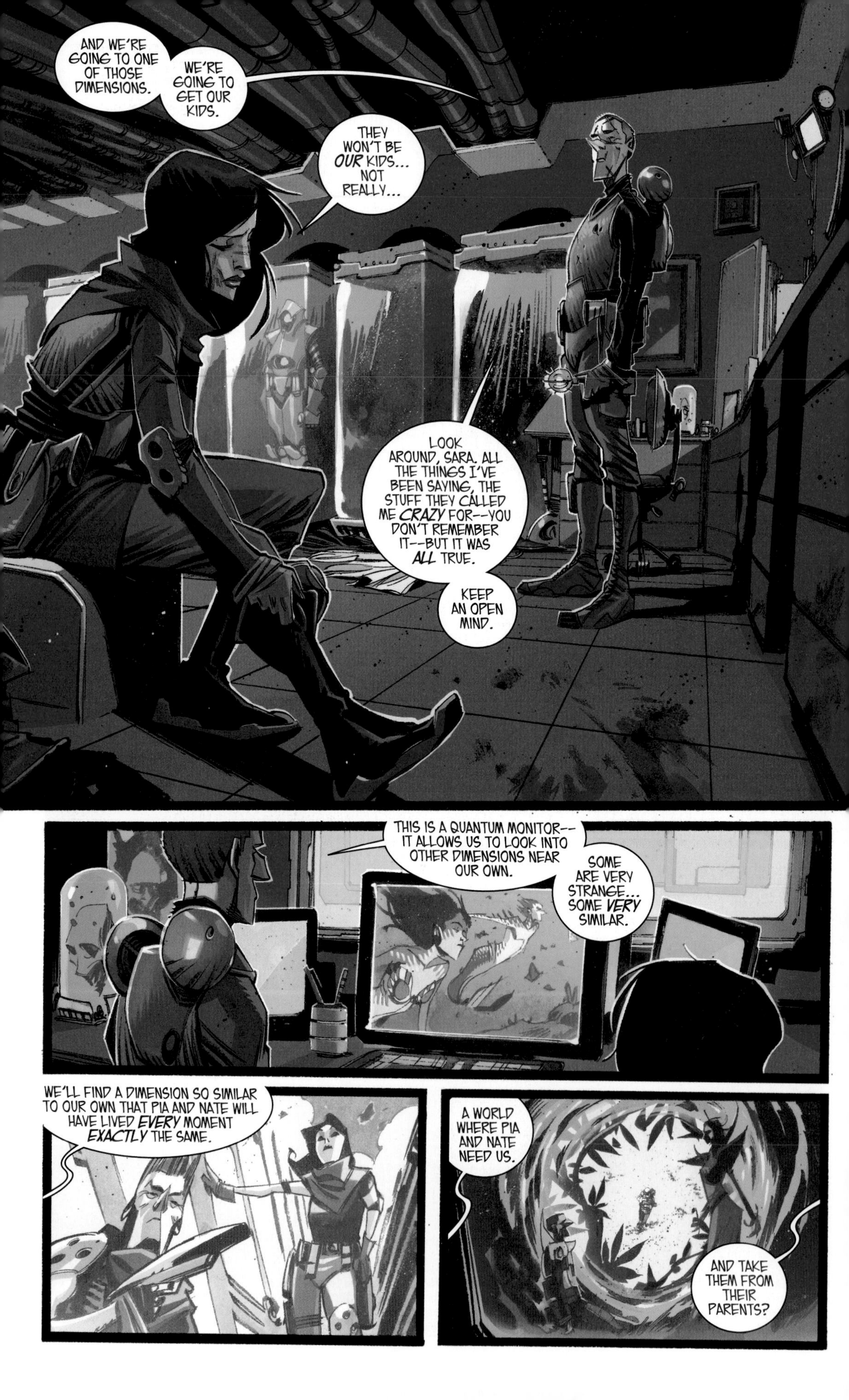
AND WE'RE GOING TO ONE OF THOSE DIMENSIONS.
WE'RE GOING TO GET OUR KIDS.
THEY WON'T BE OUR KIDS... NOT REALLY...
LOOK AROUND, SARA. ALL THE THINGS I'VE BEEN SAYING, THE STUFF THEY CALLED ME CRAZY FOR--YOU DON'T REMEMBER IT--BUT IT WAS ALL TRUE.
KEEP AN OPEN MIND.
THIS IS A QUANTUM MONITOR--IT ALLOWS US TO LOOK INTO OTHER DIMENSIONS NEAR OUR OWN.
SOME ARE VERY STRANGE... SOME VERY SIMILAR.
WE'LL FIND A DIMENSION SO SIMILAR TO OUR OWN THAT PIA AND NATE WILL HAVE LIVED EVERY MOMENT EXACTLY THE SAME.
A WORLD WHERE PIA AND NATE NEED US.
AND TAKE THEM FROM THEIR PARENTS?

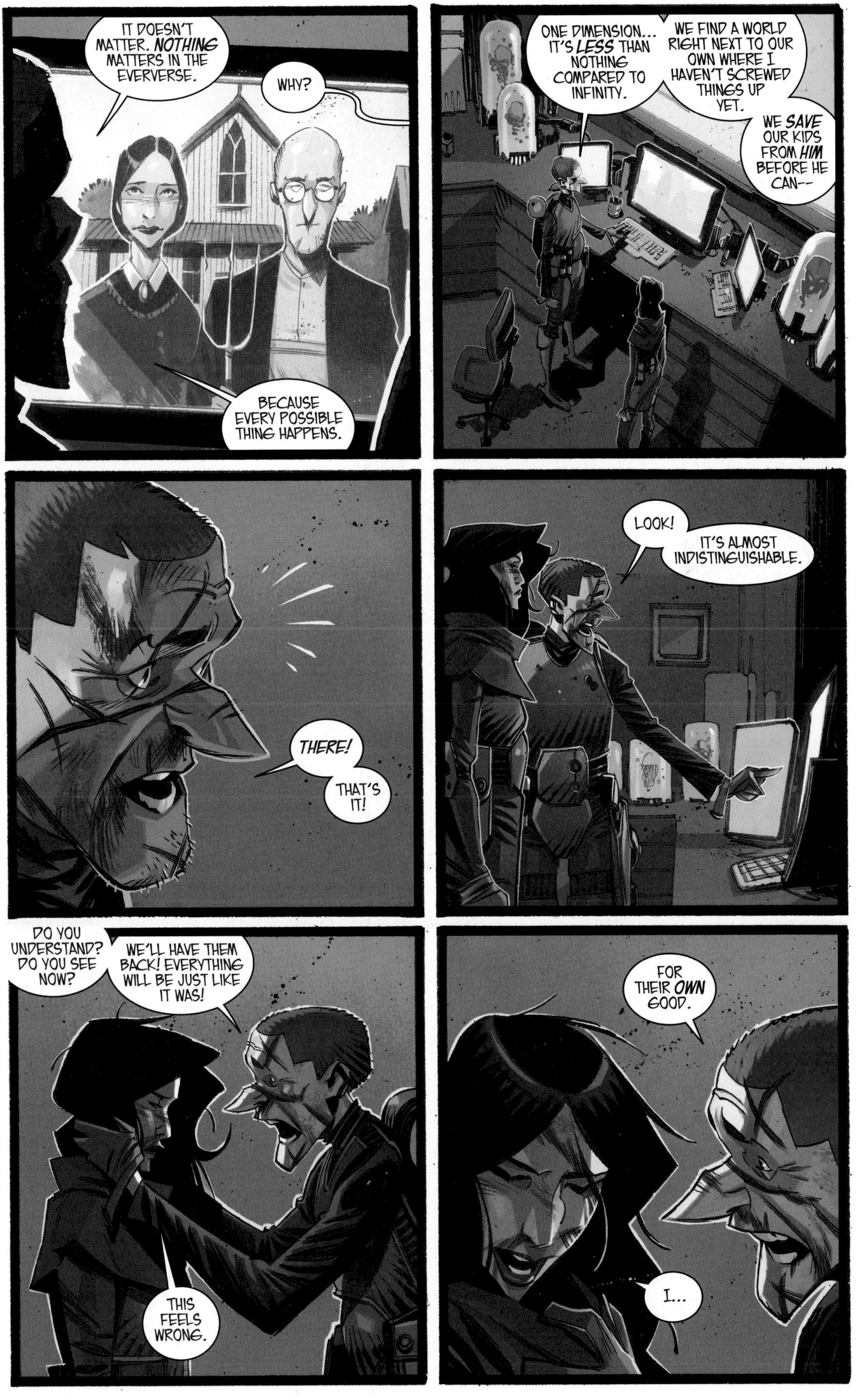
IT DOESN'T MATTER. NOTHING MATTERS IN THE EVERVERSE.
WHY?
BECAUSE EVERY POSSIBLE THING HAPPENS.
ONE DIMENSION... IT'S LESS THAN NOTHING COMPARED TO INFINITY.
WE FIND A WORLD RIGHT NEXT TO OUR OWN WHERE I HAVEN'T SCREWED THINGS UP YET.
WE SAVE OUR KIDS FROM HIM BEFORE HE CAN--
THERE!
THAT'S IT!
LOOK!
IT'S ALMOST INDISTINGUISHABLE.
DO YOU UNDERSTAND? DO YOU SEE NOW?
WE'LL HAVE THEM BACK! EVERYTHING WILL BE JUST LIKE IT WAS!
THIS FEELS WRONG.
FOR THEIR OWN GOOD.
I...

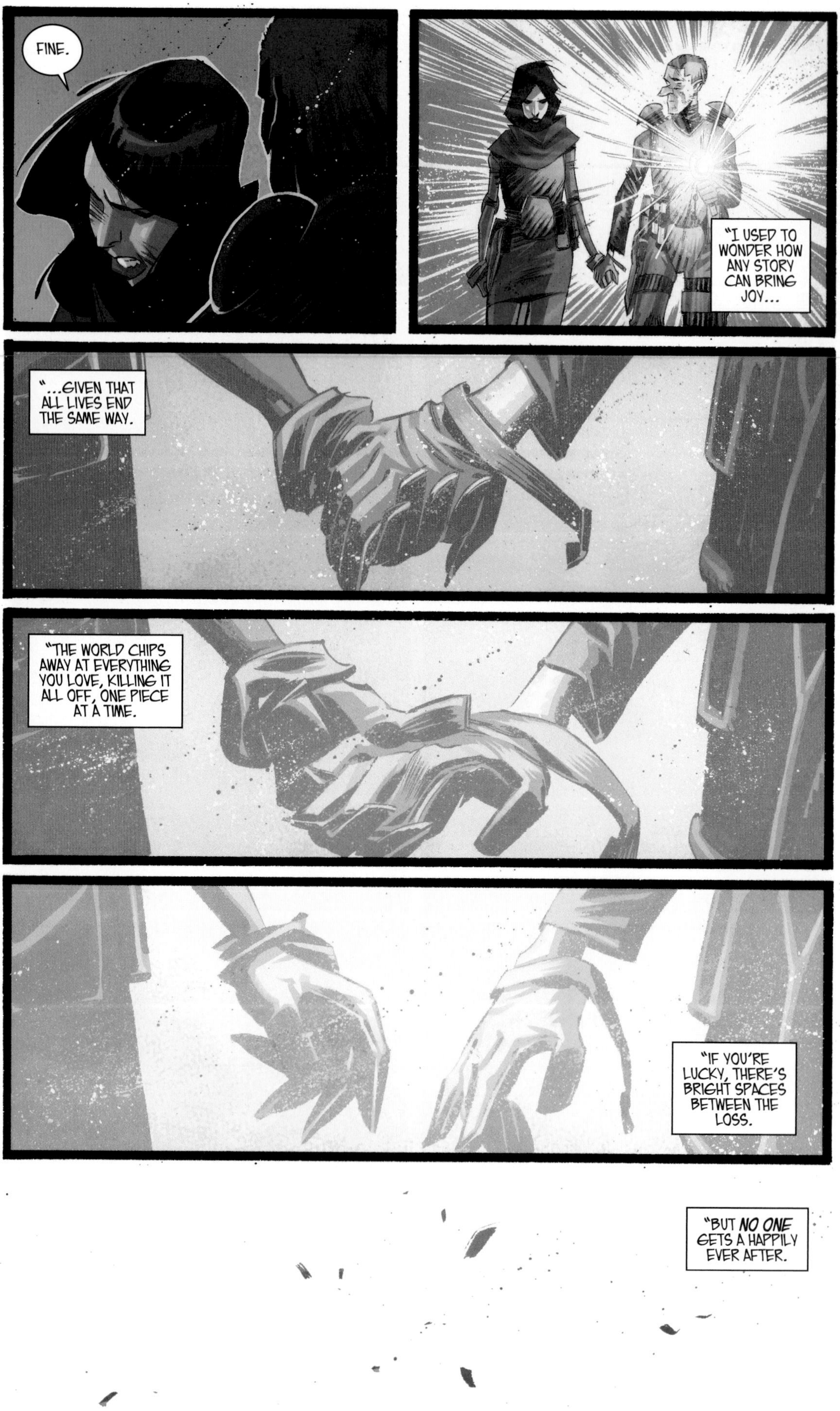
FINE.
"I USED TO WONDER HOW ANY STORY CAN BRING JOY...
"...GIVEN THAT ALL LIVES END THE SAME WAY.
"THE WORLD CHIPS AWAY AT EVERYTHING YOU LOVE, KILLING IT ALL OFF, ONE PIECE AT A TIME.
"IF YOU'RE LUCKY, THERE'S BRIGHT SPACES BETWEEN THE LOSS.
"BUT NO ONE GETS A HAPPILY EVER AFTER.

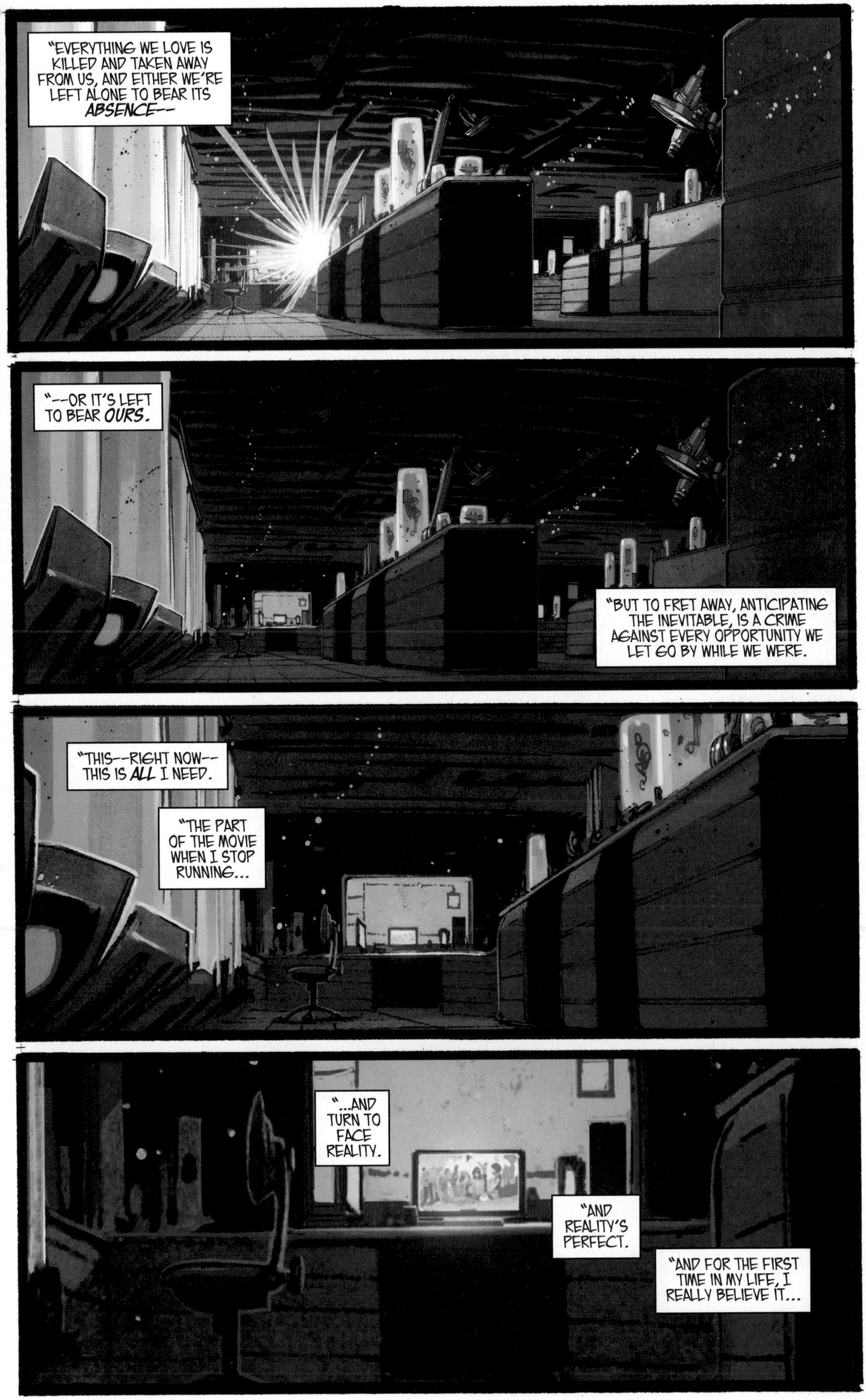
"EVERYTHING WE LOVE IS KILLED AND TAKEN AWAY FROM US, AND EITHER WE'RE LEFT ALONE TO BEAR ITS ABSENCE--
"--OR IT'S LEFT TO BEAR OURS.
"BUT TO FRET AWAY, ANTICIPATING THE INEVITABLE, IS A CRIME AGAINST EVERY OPPORTUNITY WE LET GO BY WHILE WE WERE.
"THIS--RIGHT NOW-- THIS IS ALL I NEED.
"THE PART OF THE MOVIE WHEN I STOP RUNNING...
"...AND TURN TO FACE REALITY.
"AND REALITY'S PERFECT.
"AND FOR THE FIRST TIME IN MY LIFE, I REALLY BELIEVE IT...

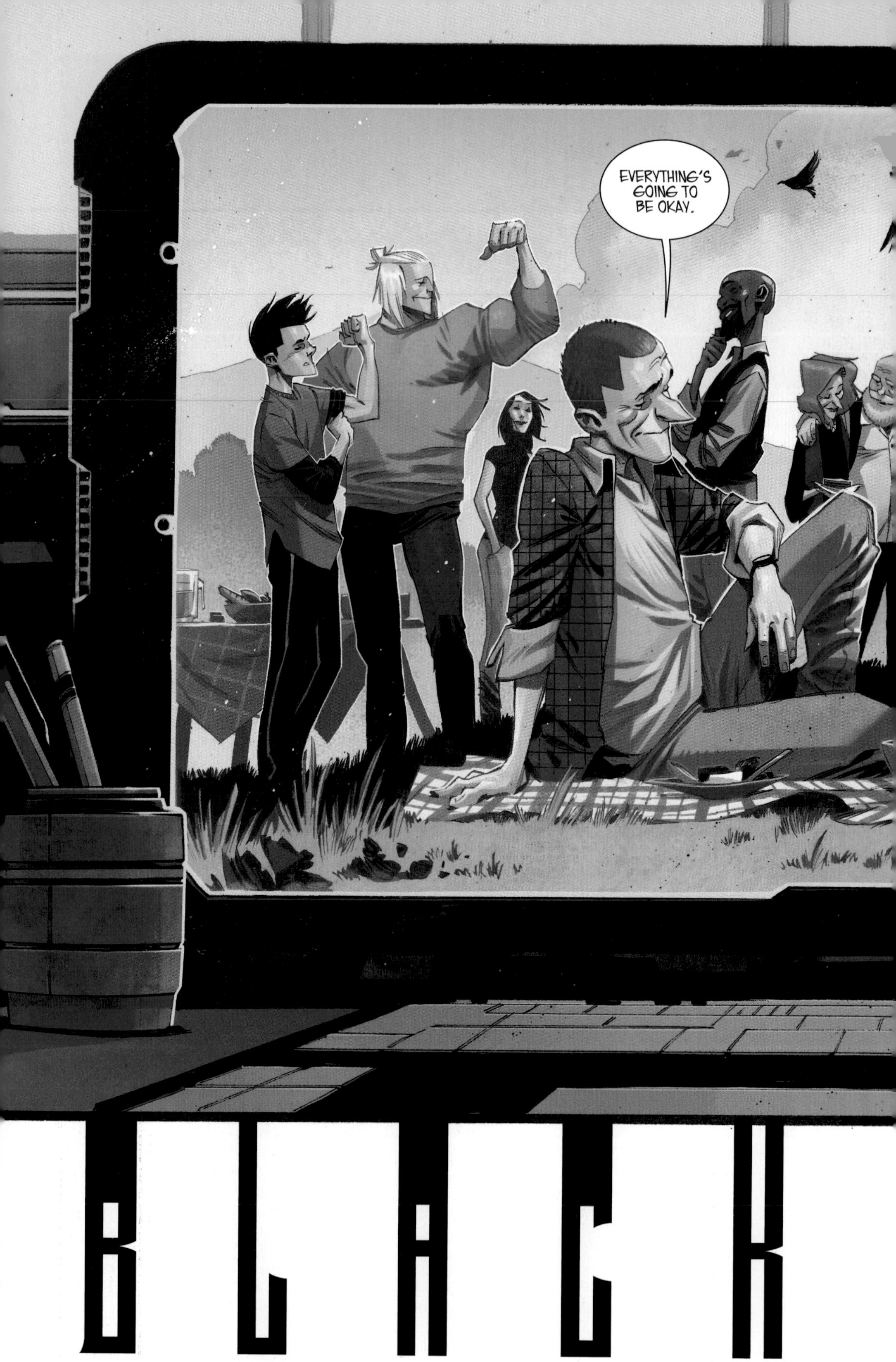
EVERYTHING'S GOING TO BE OKAY.

BLACK

RICK REMENDER
WRITER

MATTEO SCALERA
ARTIST

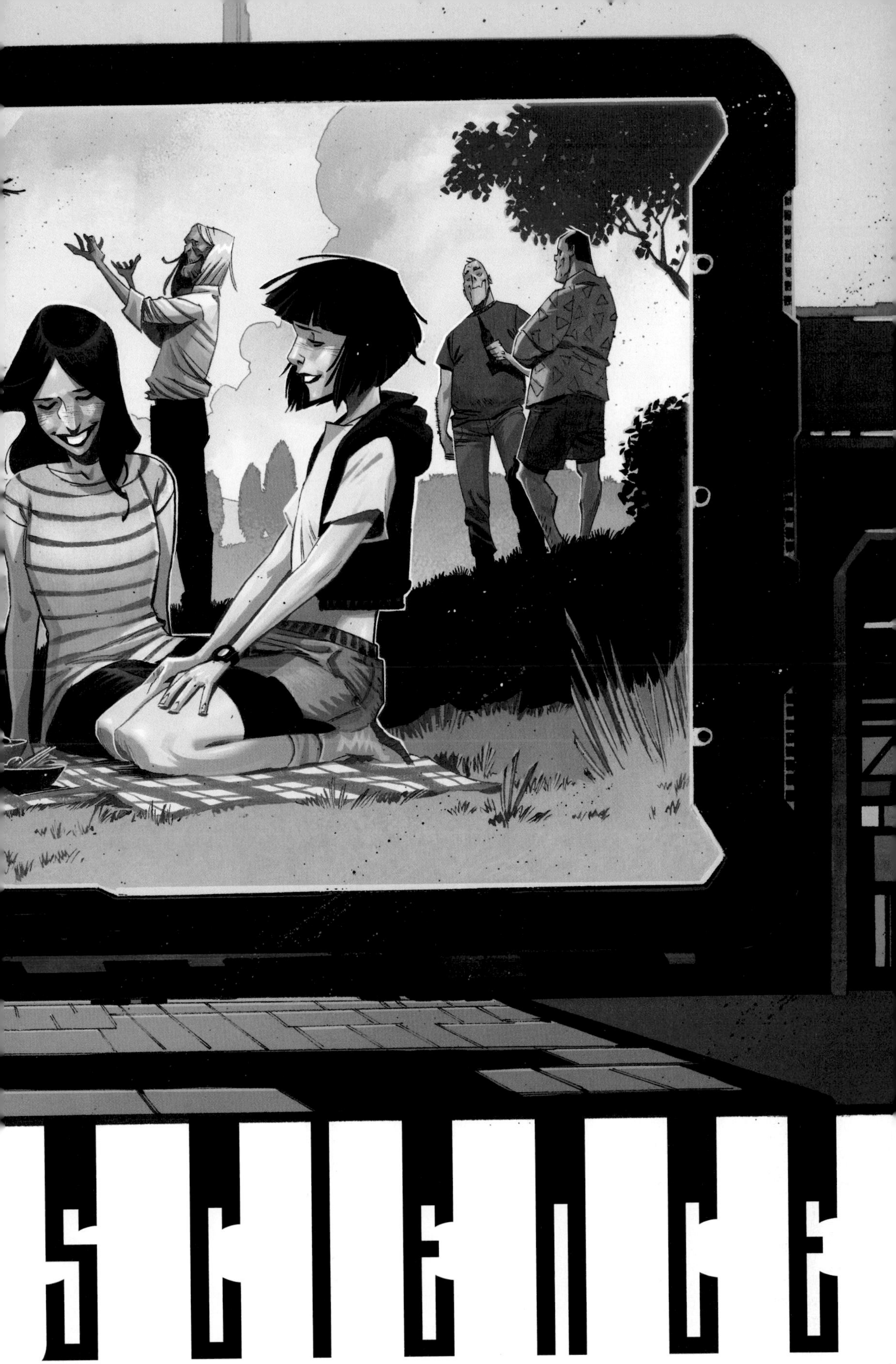

SCIENCE

MORENO DINISIO
COLORIST

RUS WOOTON
LETTERER

BRIAH SKELLY
EDITOR

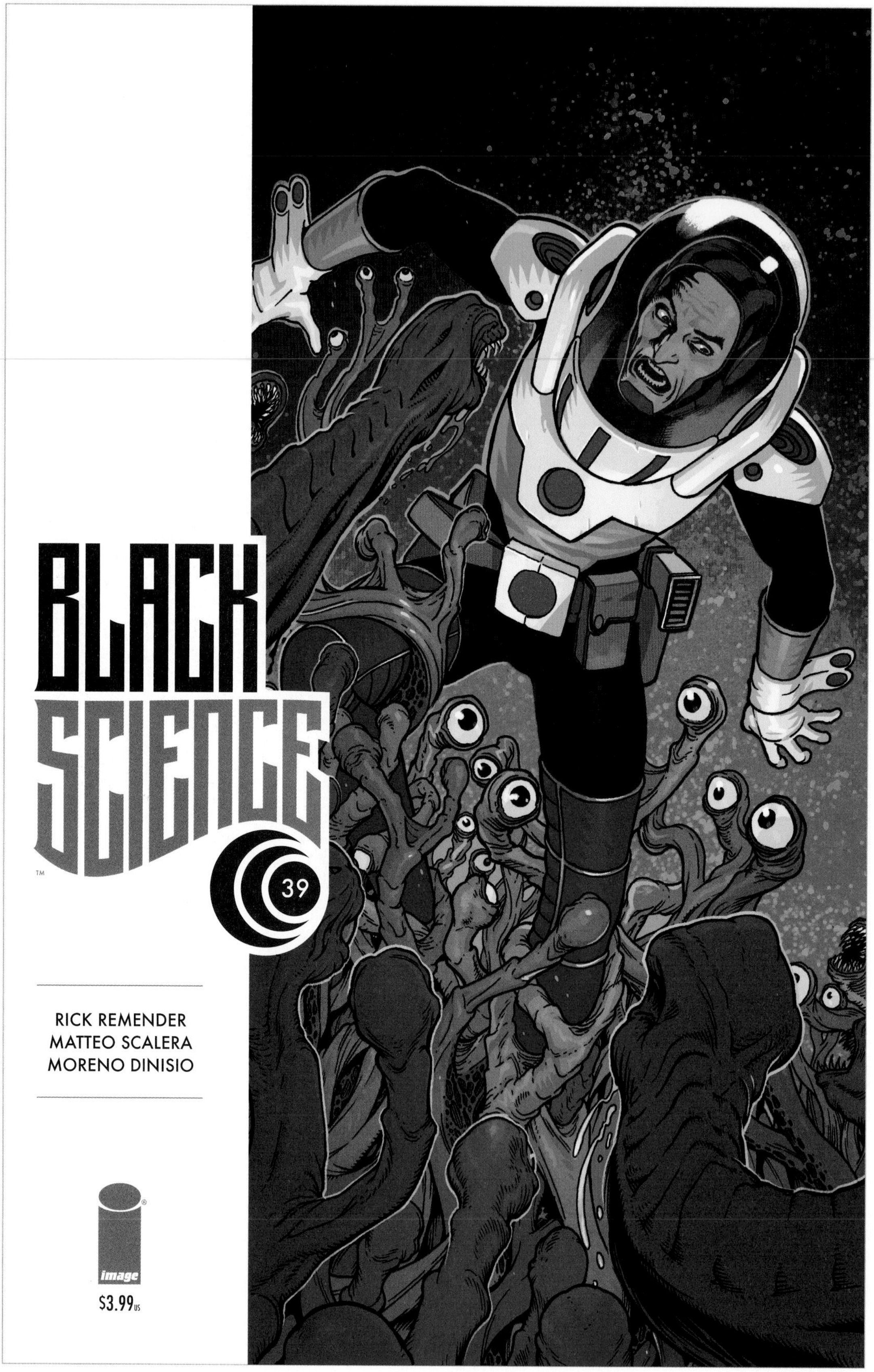
BLACK SCIENCE
TM
39
RICK REMENDER
MATTEO SCALERA
MORENO DINISIO
image
$3.99US

#39 VARIANT BY KEVIN MAGUIRE

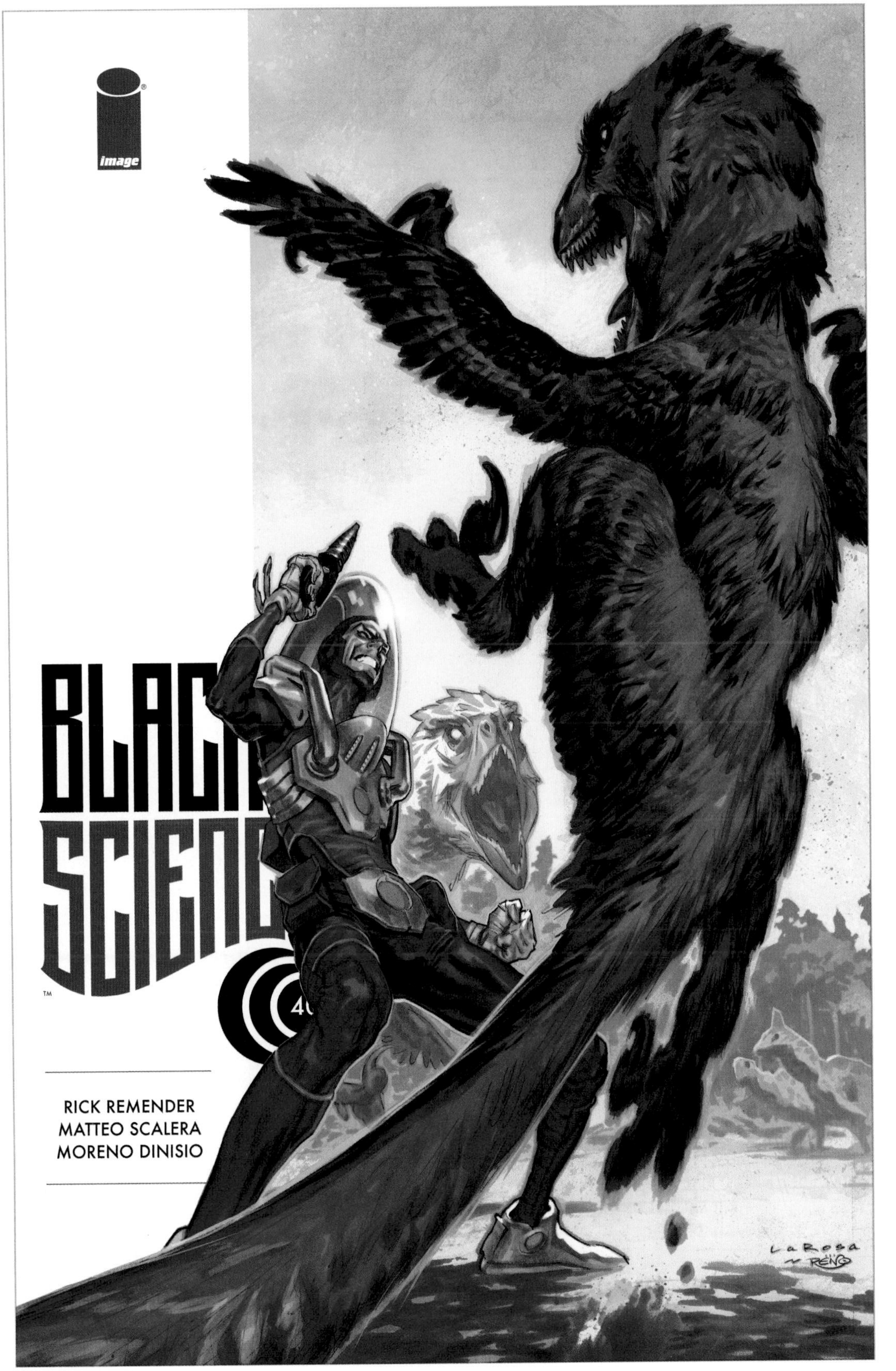
image
RICK REMENDER
MATTEO SCALERA
MORENO DINISIO

#40 VARIANT BY LEWIS LAROSA

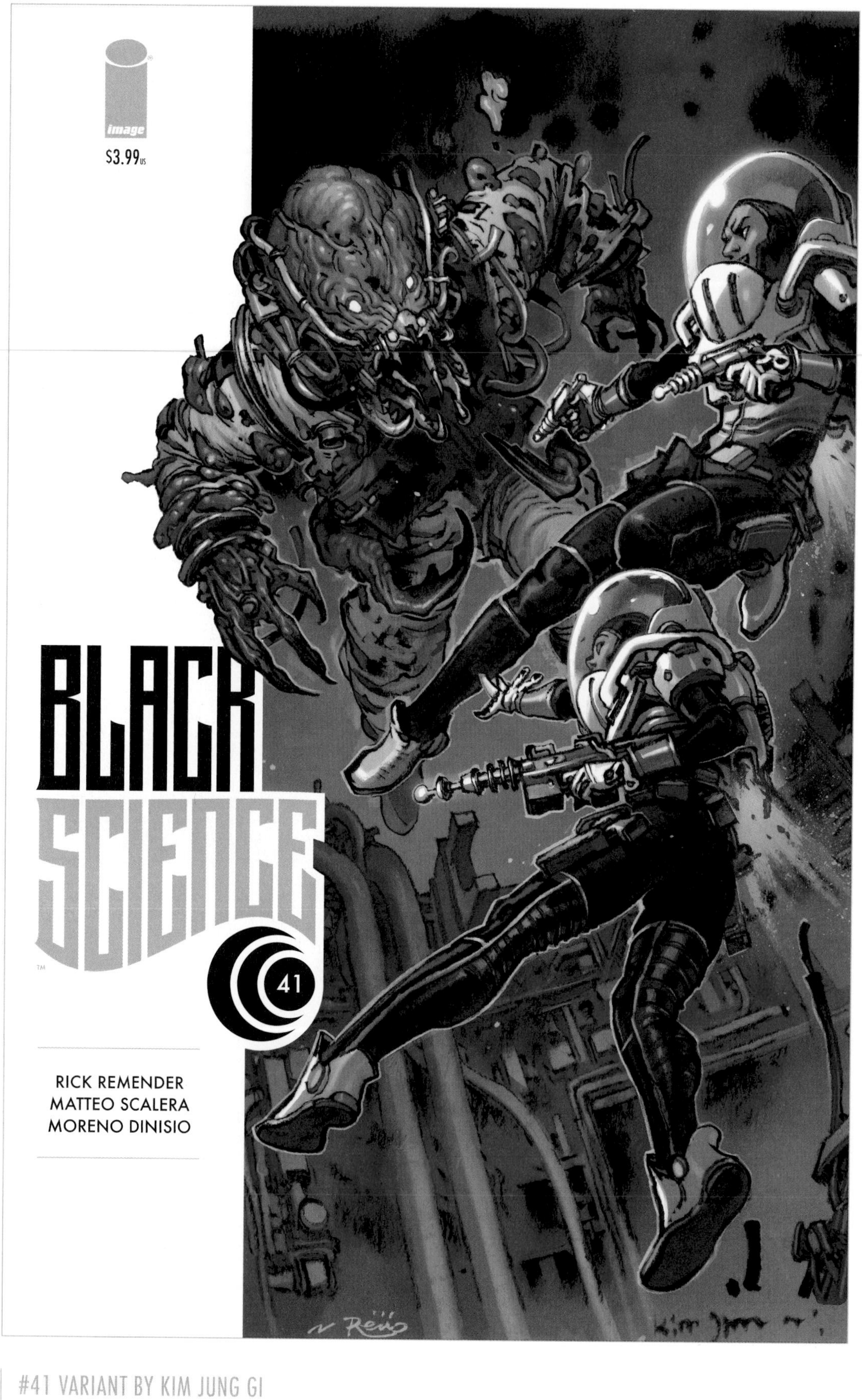
image
$3.99 US
BLACK
SCIENCE
41
RICK REMENDER
MATTEO SCALERA
MORENO DINISIO

#41 VARIANT BY KIM JUNG GI

$3.99 US

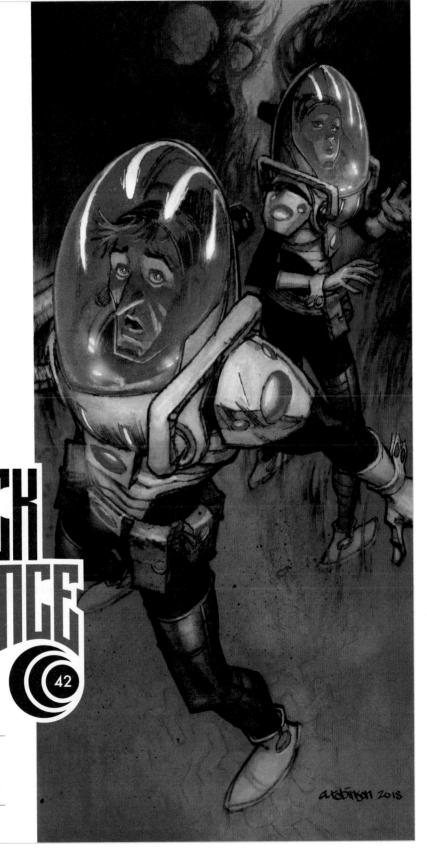

BLACK SCIENCE

42

RICK REMENDER
MATTEO SCALERA
MORENO DINISIO

#42 VARIANT BY ANDREW ROBINSON

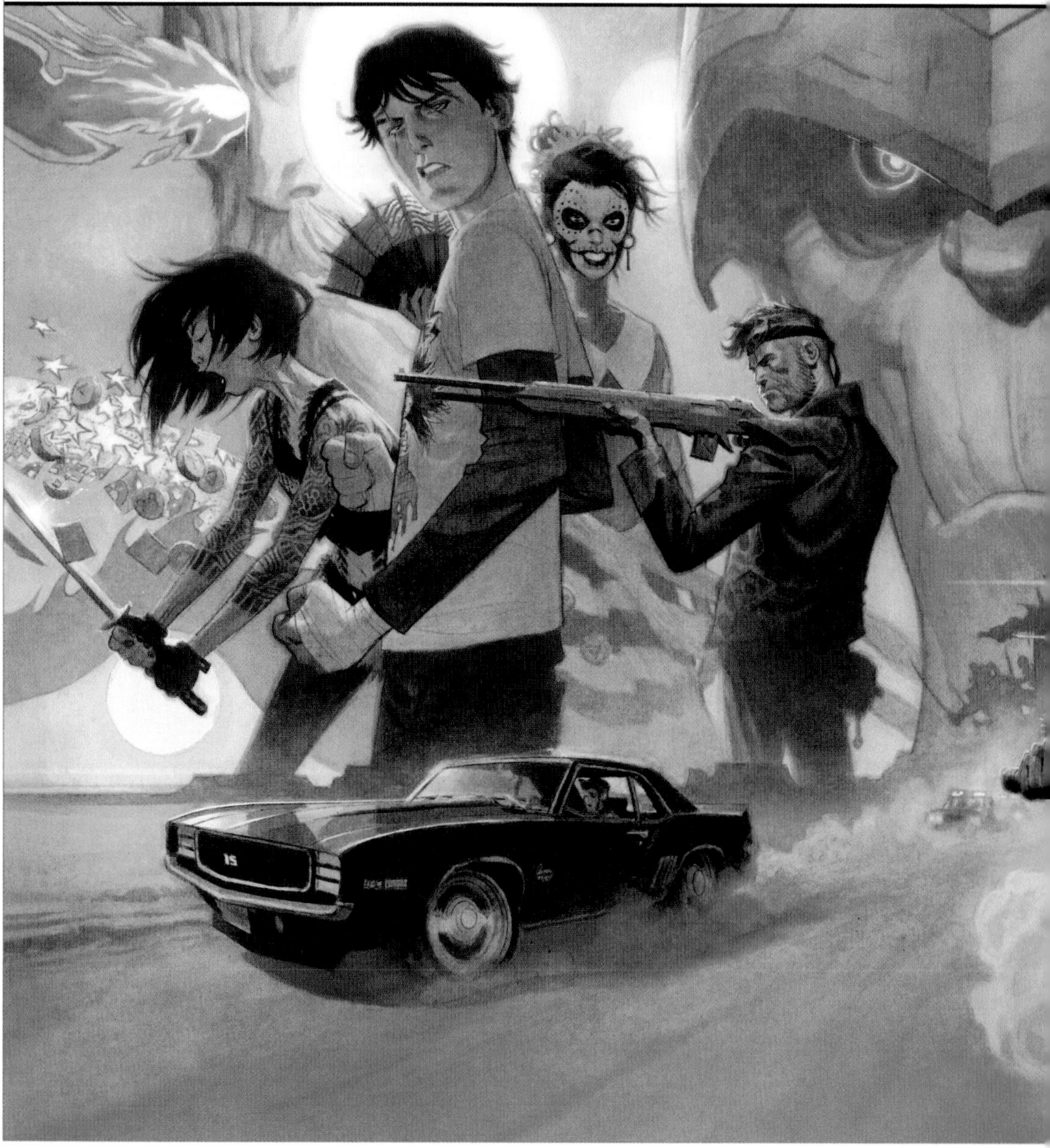

#43 VARIANT BY ANDREW ROBINSON

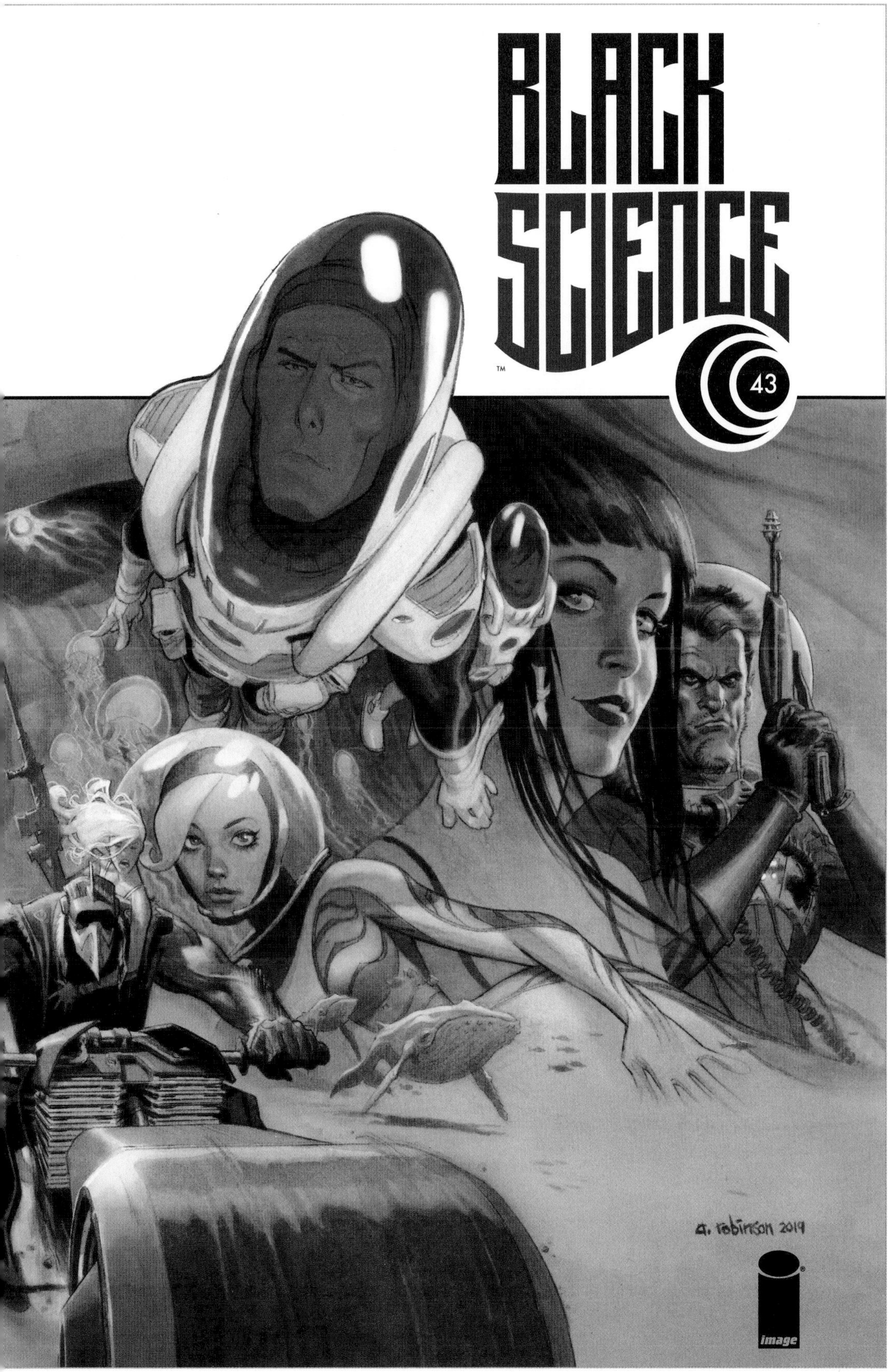
BLACK SCIENCE
™
43
a. robinson 2019
image

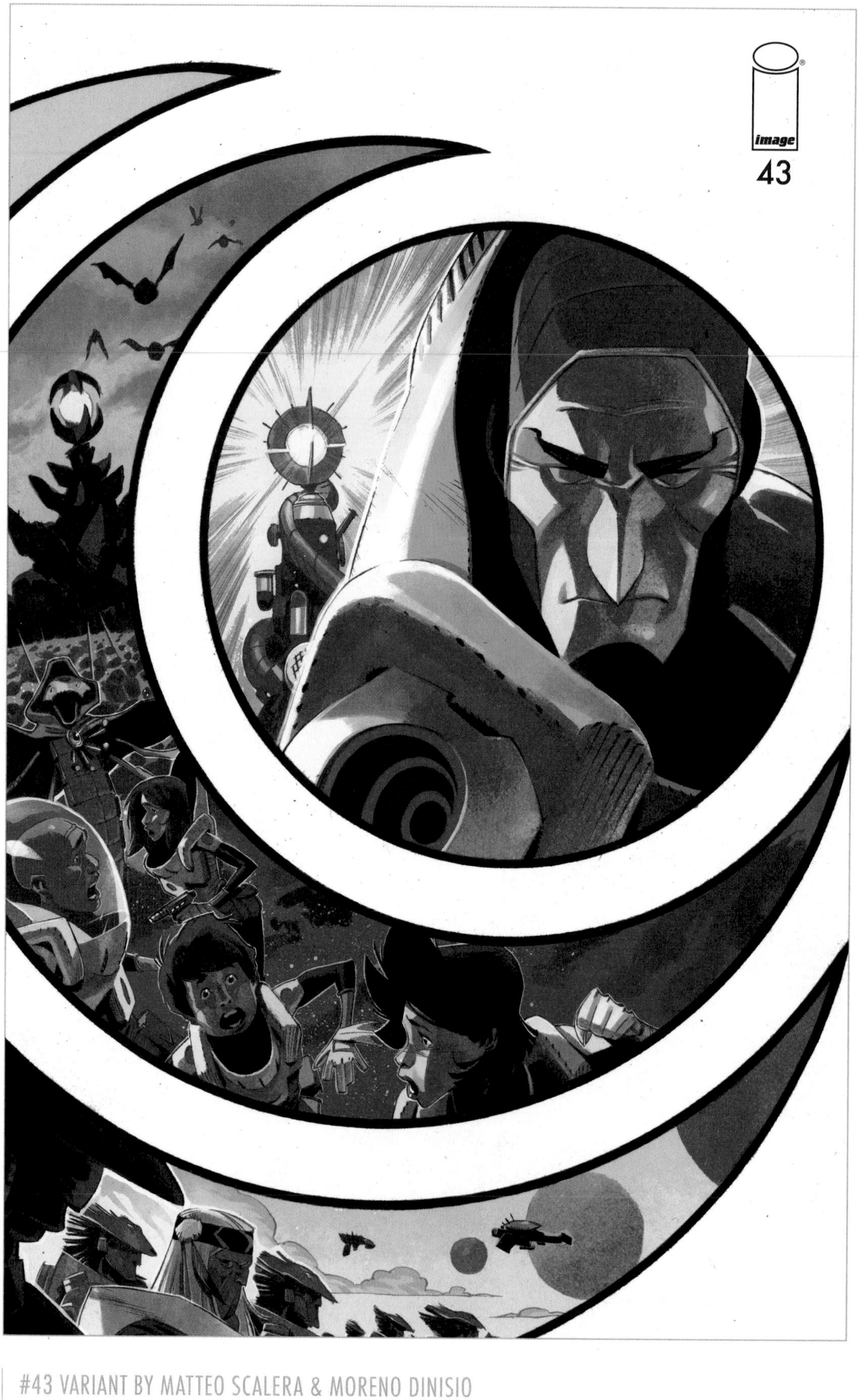
image
43

#43 VARIANT BY MATTEO SCALERA & MORENO DINISIO

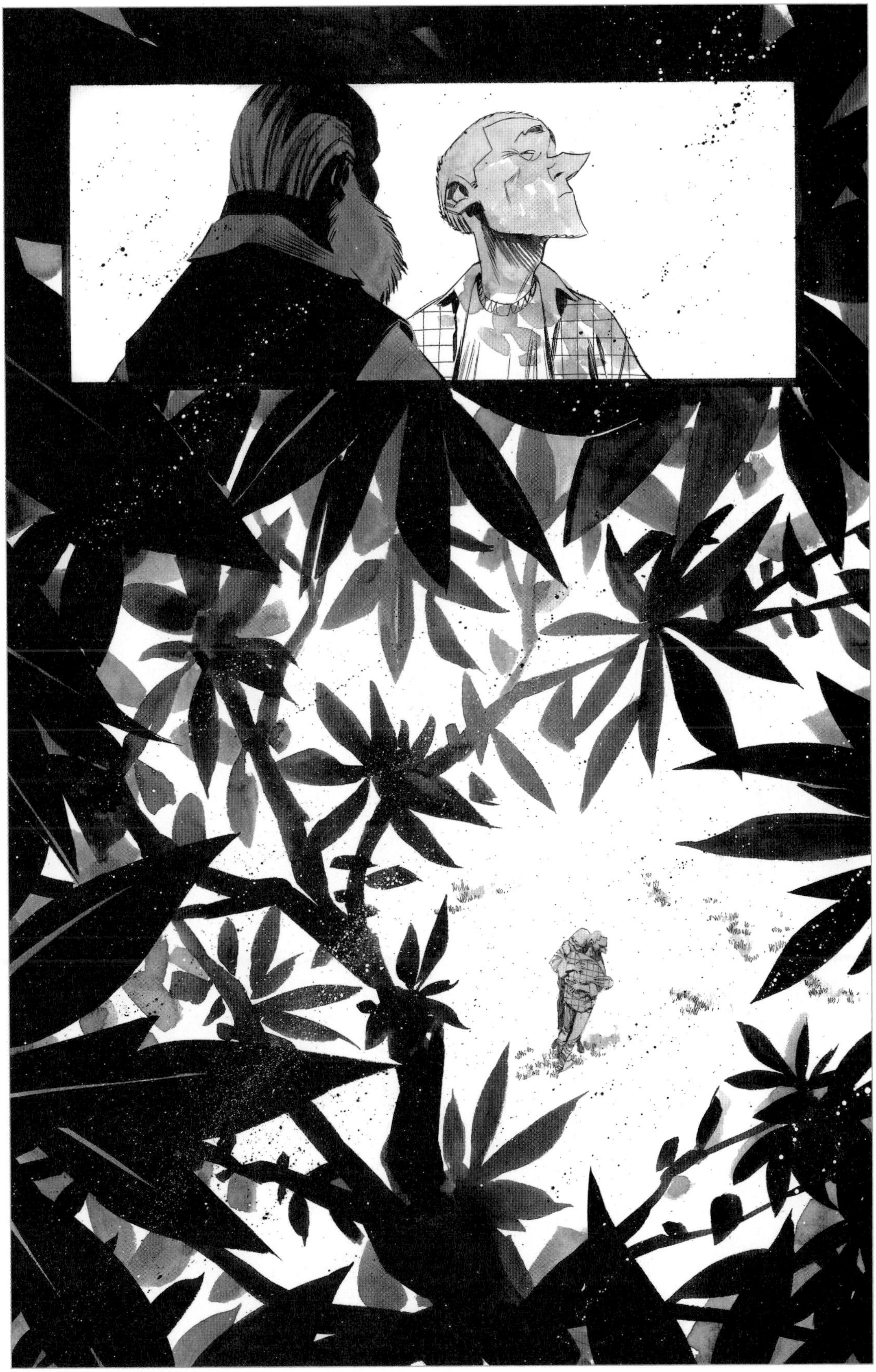

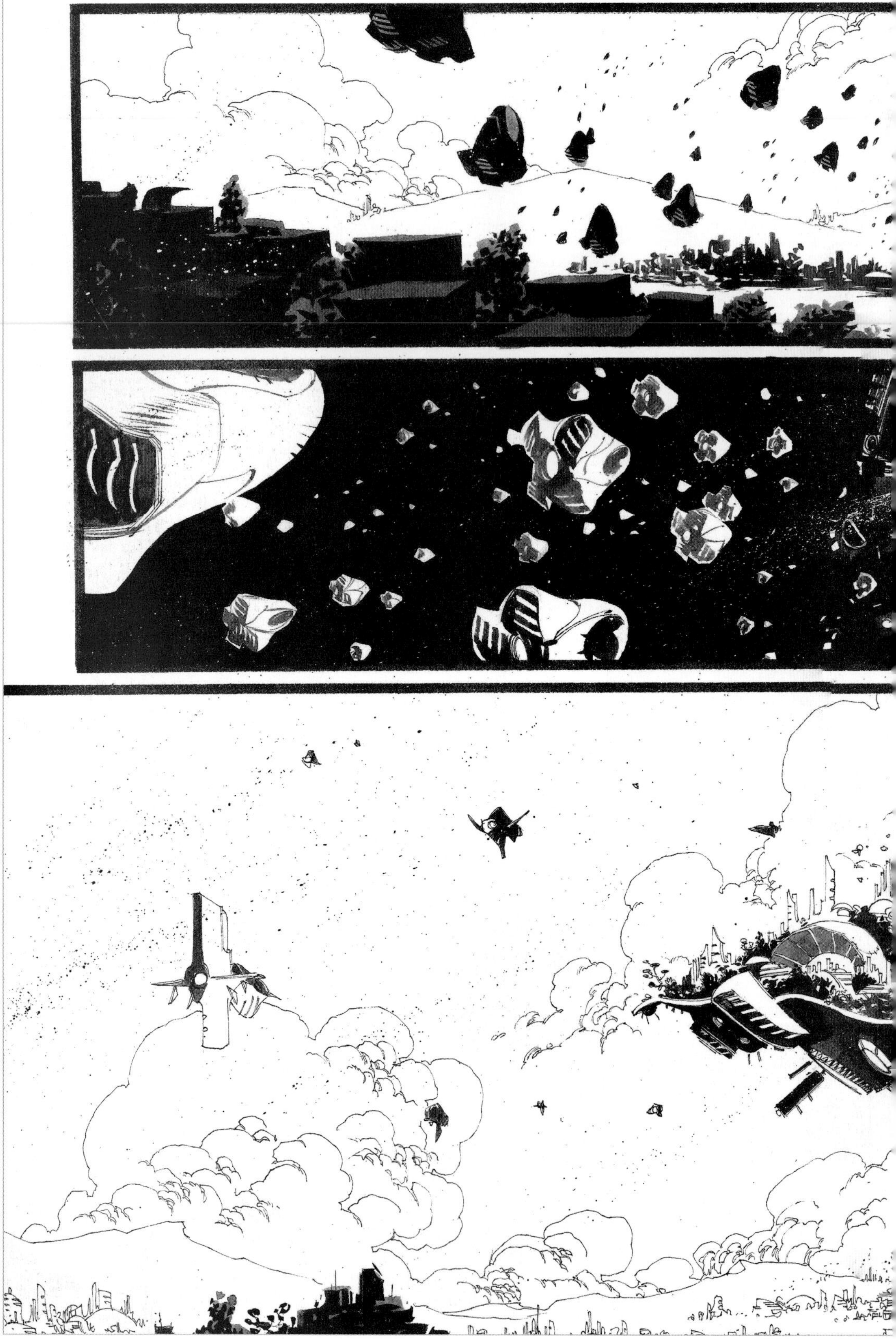

#41 PAGES 8 & 9 INKS

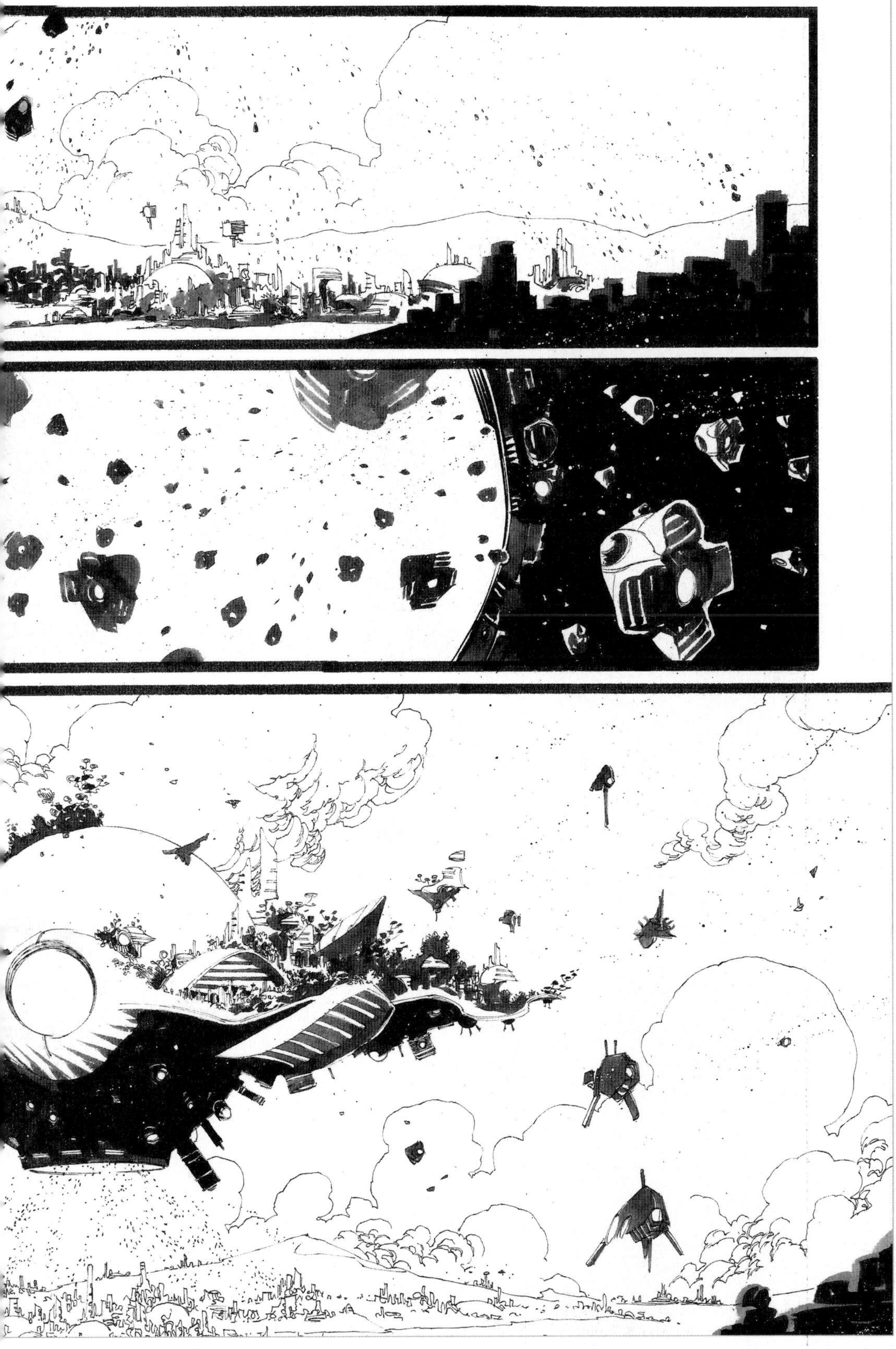

RICK REMENDER

Rick Remender is the writer/co-creator of comics such as *Black Science*, *Deadly Class*, *Fear Agent*, *Seven to Eternity*, and *Death or Glory*. During his years at Marvel, he wrote *Captain America*, *Uncanny X-Force*, and *Venom* and created *The Uncanny Avengers*. Outside of comics, he served as lead writer on EA's *Bulletstorm* game and the hit game *Dead Space*. Prior to this, he ran a satellite of Wild Brain animation, worked on films such as *The Iron Giant* and *Anastasia*, and taught sequential art and animation at San Francisco's Academy of Art University.

He currently curates his own publishing imprint, Giant Generator, at Image Comics and previously served as lead writer/co-showrunner on SyFy's adaption of his co-creation *Deadly Class*.

MATTEO SCALERA

Matteo Scalera was born in Parma, Italy, in 1982. His professional career started in 2007 with the publication of the miniseries *Hyperkinetic* for Image Comics. Over the next nine years, he has worked with all major U.S. publishers: Marvel (*Deadpool*, *Secret Avengers*, *Indestructible Hulk*), DC Comics (*Batman*), Boom! Studios (*Irredeemable*, *Valen the Outcast*, *Starborn*), and Skybound (*Dead Body Road*).

MORENO CARMINE DINISIO

Born in 1987 in southern Italy and holding a pencil since year one thanks to a painter father, Moreno grew up with the aim of becoming a professional artist. After studying comic art in Milan, he went on to work as a comic and concept artist and character designer until 2013, when he crossed into American comics, coloring *Clown Fatale* and *Resurrectionists* (Dark Horse). Moreno first collaborated with Matteo Scalera on *Dead Body Road* (Skybound). With the release of *Black Science* in December 2014, he continues their fruitful partnership.